"A delightful fashion treasure hunt involving some of my favorite Dior gowns made this book a winner for me! The present-day and 1950s narratives weave seamlessly together, the dresses dance from the pages, and Paris is resplendently depicted."

—Natasha Lester, *New York Times* bestselling author of
The Paris Secret

"After finishing Beer's latest, it was all I could do not to book the next plane to France and head straight for the House of Dior. Offering a whirlwind tour through Paris, both past and present, the novel is a rich exploration of the power of female friendships and the true meaning of family. Moving and utterly enjoyable."

—Fiona Davis, *New York Times* bestselling author of
The Lions of Fifth Avenue

"An absolute delight! *The Last Dress from Paris* is as original, elegant, and romantic as the Dior dresses the novel's mystery is woven around. Jade Beer seamlessly stitches together an illuminating story of female friendships, secrets, and a couture treasure hunt that takes the reader from postwar Paris to present-day London. The writing is a breath of fresh air, and in her leading ladies, Lucille and Alice, Beer delivers intriguing, complex characters for her readers to really care about. Magnifique!"

—Hazel Gaynor, *New York Times* bestselling author of
When We Were Young & Brave

"An unexpected trip to Paris starts this journey of discovering lost fashion treasures while uncovering a tale of forbidden love. In *The Last Dress from Paris*, Jade Beer's gorgeous prose brings Dior's fashions to life as she deftly weaves together a novel that is part homage to fashion and part romance, as well as a celebration of mothers and daughters. Readers will eat this one up!"

—Renée Rosen, *USA Today* bestselling author of
The Social Graces

"I devoured this multigenerational masterpiece! Jade Beer invites her reader on a glamorous treasure hunt through Paris, searching for exquisite Dior dresses and secrets from the past. *The Last Dress from Paris* is a stunning mix of haute couture, romance, scandal, and intrigue. With breathtaking prose and a stunning Paris backdrop, Jade Beer offers a tender, heartfelt look at love and friendship, and the sacrifices we make for both."

—Lori Nelson Spielman, *New York Times* bestselling author of
The Star-Crossed Sisters of Tuscany

"As beautifully stitched together as a couture gown, Jade Beer's book entrances with its themes of family and female friendships. I loved it."

—International bestselling author Jessica Fellowes

"An elegantly and evocatively written, thoroughly researched novel that will prove to be an absolute must-read for romantics and fashionistas. Transportive, dreamy, and aspirational, guaranteed to uplift and entertain."

—International bestselling author Adele Parks

THE
LAST DRESS
FROM
Paris

JADE BEER

BERKLEY
NEW YORK

BERKLEY
An imprint of Penguin Random House LLC
penguinrandomhouse.com

Library of Congress Cataloging-in-Publication Data

Names: Beer, Jade, author.
Title: The last dress from Paris / Jade Beer.
Description: First edition. | New York: Berkley, 2022.
Identifiers: LCCN 2021039367 (print) | LCCN 2021039368 (ebook) |
ISBN 9780593436813 (trade paperback) | ISBN 9780593436820 (ebook)
Subjects: LCSH: Family secrets—Fiction. | Grandmothers—Fiction. |
Female friendship—Fiction. | Paris (France)—Fiction. |
LCGFT: Romance fiction. | Novels.
Classification: LCC PR6102.E335 L37 2022 (print) |
LCC PR6102.E335 (ebook) | DDC 823/.92—dc23/eng/20211102
LC record available at https://lccn.loc.gov/2021039367
LC ebook record available at https://lccn.loc.gov/2021039368

First Edition: June 2022

Printed in the United States of America
2nd Printing

Book design by Kristin del Rosario

In the world today, haute couture is one of the last repositories of the marvelous, and the couturiers the last possessors of the wand of Cinderella's Fairy Godmother.

—CHRISTIAN DIOR

PROLOGUE

※

CHRISTIAN DIOR, AVENUE MONTAIGNE
SEPTEMBER 1952

Alice lowers the window an inch in the back of the Chrysler. She hopes the bite of cold air will wake her up, snap her out of herself, and make her realize just how lucky she is. She knows women compete long and hard for these invitations.

The subject of Dior's guest list has already occupied enough of the conversation in her drawing room for her to be sure of that.

"I fear you may have to walk a little way back, Madame Ainsley." Alice jolts at the mention of her new title. "Will that be okay? There are so many cars, I can't get you any closer."

"Of course, it's not a problem." Alice hops out of the chauffeur-driven Chrysler, one of the perks afforded to the wife of the British ambassador to France, and starts to pick her way back over the cobbles to the Dior town house.

In a few moments she will be surrounded by dozens of wealthy, well-connected women. She can see them now, clustered and swarming outside like tormented insects, smoking, congratulating each other, closing ranks on the tight community they want her to be a part of. But as Alice approaches, all she feels is the competitive swirl of women who want more of everything. Nothing but the best.

Alice enters through the black polished double doors and lifts her nose to the air. Fresh paint. The salon's walls must have been decorated overnight in preparation for the show today. She pauses in the lobby, smooths her hands down her navy wool jacket. There is a nervous energy pulsing around her. Much will be written about the new collection, and Alice feels those nerves seep inside her too. Why is she so anxious? She turns and looks into one of the huge spotless wall mirrors and tries to answer her own question, only to settle on another. How is it that a girl who was always happiest in old wellies and a muddy duffle coat now stands in Dior in Paris, wearing one of the designer's own pieces? She examines the neatness of her cropped dark hair. The subtle nude of her lipstick. Her classic pearls.

Alice is shown to a narrow gilt chair in the front row, feeling every pair of eyes scrutinize her, assessing, no doubt, whether she has accessorized Dior's look as she should. She can practically taste the envy poisoning the air, secreting from every woman who feels her front-row chair came too easily to Alice. What do they know? Alice takes her seat quickly, relieved that her own catwalk across the room is complete. She smiles, hoping it looks genuine. Her neighbors are yet to take their seats, so she starts to flick through the show program, raising her head every few minutes, hoping to catch a rare glimpse of the famous Dior mannequins in their white backstage overalls before they step out onto the decreasing patch of fine cream carpet in front of Alice, their stage this morning.

She wonders which of the sketches in her program will be the first to sit at her dining table. She averts her eyes from the glare of the spotlights and the chandelier overhead, the rising heat climbing up her neck with every minute that passes, and still the show doesn't start. Chairs continue to fill, and bodies pile up around the room, filling the windows where it is standing room only. Dense cigarette smoke is scratching at the back of Alice's throat, and she has to focus on the pretty clouds of ivory roses and carnations to stay calm. She pulls off her gloves, feeling the heat across her palms, and with a panic it occurs to her she can't leave now, the path to the exit is blocked by women who are still swarming through the door. Someone hands her a paper fan—which she snaps open, desperate to feel some relief across her cheeks—and a small hard fruit sweet. She will never make the mistake of arriving on time again.

"Madame Ainsley, how lovely to see you again." A tall woman expertly folds herself into the seat to Alice's left, timing her arrival much better than Alice has. "It's Delphine Lamar, we met at the welcome drinks a couple of weeks ago. Your first Dior show?" She raises an eyebrow. Clearly there is something in Alice's demeanor that makes the fact obvious.

"Yes, quite something, isn't it?" Alice is grateful for the reminder of the woman's name; there have been so many new faces these past few weeks.

"It takes a little time to get used to the circus. Worth it, of course, but in future, come about forty minutes late and you will find yourself perfectly on time." She offers a supportive smile. "Tell me, how is the search for your personal maid progressing? You were struggling, I recall, and if you are still yet to find someone, I think I can help."

"Thank you. Everyone I have seen is expertly qualified and experienced, I'm sure I could hire any one of them and not be disappointed, but I just haven't felt a particular connection with anyone yet. Maybe I am being too fussy, but . . ."

"No one could accuse you of that, not in your position."

"Perhaps." Alice returns the smile, grateful that Delphine doesn't think her foolish for wanting an emotional connection with the woman she will spend the majority of her time with inside the residence.

"Here." Delphine takes a tiny leather notepad from a handbag that isn't much bigger and writes a name and number on it, handing it to Alice. "Marianne comes very highly recommended from another senior diplomat's wife. Her husband has served his three years in Paris, and they are now being posted to the Middle East. They cannot take Marianne with them. But you will have to move very quickly. She is adored by them, and others will want her. I would snap her up myself if I had the vacancy." She bends a little closer to Alice. "I thought of you immediately. Marianne is half-British and will understand your preferences and needs without your having to overstate everything."

"Thank you." Alice gladly takes the number. "I will see her as soon as I can."

Delphine's attention is distracted by the arrival of another guest, leaving Alice to tune in to the talk around her of shopping in Milan and skiing in St. Moritz and the wardrobe essentials needed to facilitate them. Necks are being craned so women can see above the hats in front of them, people are up and down out of their seats waving to late-arriving friends, ensuring they have been seen themselves.

It is only some thirty minutes later, when the announcer calls the name and number of the first model, that silence mercifully falls, and Alice feels she can breathe normally once more.

"Marianne, thank you so much for coming, and at such short notice. I appreciate it." Alice motions for her to take the chair on the opposite side of the desk to her. "May I ask Patrice to get you a coffee?"

"Thank you. I would prefer tea, though, please, English breakfast if you have it?" She smiles, knowing that of course Alice will.

"Absolutely." Patrice nods and disappears back through the door of the library, leaving the two women alone.

"Delphine, Madame Lamar, mentioned that you are half-English?"

"Yes, my mother met my father in London when he was there on business, and they were married shortly afterward. Consequently, I have spent a lot of time on both sides of the Channel. I am the perfect blend of both cultures, I hope. Always on time, very British, and never afraid to say no, typically French." Marianne allows herself a small laugh, to let Alice know she is not taking herself too seriously. "I brought some references with me."

"You already sound like you could be a great deal of help around here." Alice takes a closer look at Marianne while she is reaching into her bag for the relevant paperwork. She is perched on the very edge of her seat, barely on it at all, in fact. Her back is perfectly straight, suggesting keenness, shoulders relaxed, perhaps not easily intimidated, and her hands are neatly clasped in her lap. She looks naturally and comfortably at ease. "What other essential advice can you offer me, Marianne, as you are years ahead of me when it comes to negotiating the peculiarities of both nationalities?"

"In my experience, the French are incapable of self-deprecation and won't understand it in you. But they do expect the British to be cold and perhaps a little distant, so it's always wonderful to surprise them by being nothing of the sort. Equally, it is probably best not to lapse into the well-trodden prejudice that the French are of questionable morality and prone to arrogance." She pauses before adding, "Although, to be honest, most are."

The door to the library swings back open.

"Ah, our tea." But it is her husband, Albert, and not Patrice who has unexpectedly joined them.

"Oh, Albert, sorry, I think I mentioned, I am just in the middle of an interview . . ."

Albert ignores Alice, strides across the room, and starts to pull books from a shelf, loudly discarding each onto a side table after a cursory glance.

"Oh, for goodness' sake," he blusters, "can someone organize this in a way that is actually useful?"

Marianne glances toward Albert, her face expressionless, then back to Alice just as quickly, expecting to continue, despite their interruption. Alice notices how Marianne's eyes fall to the contoured wool jacket she is wearing today.

"Do you have an appreciation of fashion, Marianne?"

"I think it would be impossible to live in Paris right now and not. My means are modest, but an hour with *Vogue* is a great way to feel inspired and keep up to date with all that's new. Do you have a favorite designer, Madame Ainsley?"

"Well, I've never needed one before . . ."

"Where is it!" Albert bellows at a volume that neither of them can continue to ignore.

"Can I help, Albert?" Alice tries to drown the irritation in her voice.

"The Government Art Collection anthology, I know it's here somewhere. I am being questioned out there on the contents of my own home, and it would be helpful if people would put things back where they found them."

"Third shelf from the bottom, sir. The largest of the hardbacks." Patrice has returned with the coffee and a solution to Albert's rudeness.

He locates the book, leaving all the others scattered on the table, and exits without a word of thanks, causing Alice's cheeks to warm.

"Who do you suggest, Marianne? Whom shall I make my favorite?"

"Christian Dior." Said without a moment's hesitation, and if the question were designed as a test, Marianne would surely have passed. Alice agrees, but with several designers vying for her business, she is very glad of the objective steer. "Naturally he's adored by the French, but a committed Anglophile too. You'll be in very good company. Nancy Mitford and Margot Fonteyn both wear him. And of course you'll remember Princess Margaret's twenty-first-birthday dress. So much tulle! If you can, have a look at the images from his very first show in London last year, at the Savoy Hotel. *Vogue* covered it."

"What a brilliant suggestion, Marianne." Alice looks down at the employer references still untouched on the desk in front of her. "How soon can you start?"

"Whenever is best for you." The two women instinctively stand and reach across the table to shake hands. "But please, call me Anne—all those closest to me do."

1

Lucille
THURSDAY
OCTOBER 2017, LONDON

I could resent being here. A lot of women my age would. This job, as they'd see it, would sit on their to-do list, toward the bottom, just below *order food online* and *clean bathroom*. Everything else would get a line satisfyingly struck through it, but this entry would be pushed into next week, maybe even the week after that. A fresh list would be made, and still it would be at the bottom.

But visiting my grandmother is honestly the highlight of my week, every week. I look forward to it the way other women look forward to a cocktail or an hour in the bath alone. I love her more than any other person on this planet. Granny Sylvie has outlived Concorde and Woolworths. In two hours of chitchat, we can hop from the first episode of *The Archers* to the moon landing, via the death of Elvis and the Queen's coronation.

Even now she'll surprise me. Like the time a couple of months back when she suggested we play a game of chess. I was aware of the board, tucked in the corner of her sitting room, on an elegant antique table with gently curving legs, but to my shame I'd always assumed it was my grandfather's and she couldn't bear to part with it.

It took her about twelve minutes to beat me, her mind three moves in the future, mine still warming up. So, she might look old—and I say *look* because I certainly don't think she feels it—but she's razor sharp. Unlikely as it sounds, I have to raise my game for a trip to Granny's.

I stand undetected, studying her for a few moments, wondering what scene is playing out behind her resting eyes. She sits, as usual, in her favorite wingback chair, close to the open fire, its flames dancing in the sparkle of the dragonfly brooch she never gets dressed without. I wonder if instead of staring I should be rushing to move her backward before the crocheted blanket draped across her lap catches an ember and goes up. Her slim hands, nails beautifully manicured as always, are gripping the wooden arms, but her head is relaxed backward and there is the faintest smile painted across her lips. I wonder where her subconscious has taken her today. Back to the fleeting weeks in postwar Paris when she first met my grandfather? Or perhaps to that hot midsummer afternoon when she married him in a tiny English countryside church? There is a black-and-white photograph that sits on her mantel of the two of them locked in a kiss. I used to think it was a strange choice to frame. My grandfather's back is to the camera, and he is leaning over her slightly. But he always insisted it was his favorite shot of them from the day. Her eyes are peeled wide open, full of sparkle; she is laughing through the kiss, as if she can't quite believe her luck.

I start to silently remove my wool hat and gloves, placing them on a small round trestle table near the sitting room door I've entered through. Despite my best efforts, the jangle of my keys twitches her right eyelid open. It's the only part of her that moves. She's like a poised guard dog, deciding if it needs to bare teeth. Her mouth relaxes into a smile when she sees it's me. It gets deeper, warmer, so by the time I'm at her side, it's like I'm staring into the sun.

"Lucille, my darling. Come and sit with me. Happy birthday!" She starts to pull herself up in the chair and I step forward to help. As soon as I take hold of her, I'm reminded how there is barely any flesh on her. She's all layers of warm clothes, and I feel my grip reduce as my fingers search for something solid beneath the wool. I try not to think of the one battle this incredible, strong-minded woman will never win: her spirit versus the force of time her body will one day soon succumb to.

I bend over and plant a kiss on her smooth forehead, which despite the heat from the fire feels cool beneath my lips, and I smirk at the lipstick imprint I leave there. She smells of woodsmoke and the more delicate scent of bluebells, the fragrance she has worn for as long as I can remember.

"How are you doing, Granny? Are you warm enough? Has Natasha been in again this morning?" Natasha is the local lady who comes and helps Granny. What started as a bit of cleaning has grown over the years, and Granny is reliant on her now to help her wash, dress, and prepare all her meals for the day ahead before Natasha returns in the evening to get her ready for bed. Mum picks up the bill, but I like to make sure I visit at least three times a week.

"Oh, never mind all that. How does it feel to be, gosh, thirty-two?" The words shudder out of her, her intonation rising and falling with little control. Her small hazel eyes are watering, and she reaches for a tissue to wipe them.

Despite the generous size of the room, Granny has arranged everything she needs within an easy two-meter radius of herself, effectively shrinking it to the small semicircle that surrounds the fire. Books, glasses, a small bone china plate full of telltale biscuit crumbs, the TV remote, the phone, a pad and pen.

"Well, I can't say I feel a whole lot different from yesterday, but . . ." I remove some magazines from a low square ottoman at her feet and take a seat on it, holding her hand. "Look, I brought you some birthday cake." I hold a napkin-wrapped slice aloft so she can see it.

"She got you a birthday cake?" She stiffens to attention in anticipation of my answer.

"I made it, Granny." My smile is exaggerated, hoping she'll focus on my baking efforts and not . . .

"You made your own birthday cake? Did she remember this year?" Her smile is receding now.

"She's very busy, we know that. I wasn't expecting anything. Honestly, it's fine." I'm unwrapping the cake and adding it to the biscuit plate. Mum, it has to be said, has never forgotten a hair appointment. Her balayage looks just as fresh from one week to the next. She's never *not* up to speed with the morning news. The kind of woman who has strategized her day before her feet touch down in the sheepskin slippers that she leaves carefully positioned by the side of her bed every night.

"A card?" Granny isn't giving up.

"Ummm, no."

"A call?" Oh, this doesn't look good.

"Not yet." I try to sound cheerful about it. "She will eventually, Granny, you know she will, when she gets a spare moment."

"Oh, Genevieve." An irritated sigh huffs out of her as she bows her head and diverts her gaze back to the fire, like this is somehow partially her fault. That my own mother has, in all probability, forgotten my birthday for the fifth year running.

"It really doesn't matter, you know." I sound more upbeat than I honestly feel. "She's been traveling for work again, she never quite knows what time zone she's supposed to be in, does she?"

She looks at me, her face loaded with disappointment. "You deserve so much more, Lucille."

Do I? I can't think of a single thing that marks me out as special or more deserving of love and attention than anyone else. There was a fleeting moment, right at the beginning with my last boyfriend, Billy, when I wondered if perhaps it might happen. I might feel like the center of someone's world for a while. I might wake up to a warm hand on my thigh, a freshly made cup of tea on the bedside table, a smile that said, *I want whatever you want from this life.* But the reality was so much more mundane than that, and I decided to manage my own expectations by drastically lowering them. I wouldn't hope for romantic gestures. I would stroke my own ego, something I have never been terribly good at.

Sensing the moment needs an injection of excitement, Granny claps her hands together.

"The envelope. On the mantelpiece, darling." She points to a card with my name scrawled across the front. "It's for you." Here comes the book token she knows I always appreciate.

But inside is a card, illustrated with a picture of a smart hotel, and at the bottom is printed *Hôtel Plaza Athénée.* I start to read.

Happy birthday, my darling Lucille! You are off to Paris to have an adventure. See things. Do things. Meet people. And bring home something dear to me—something I have longed to hold again for too many years.

With love always,
Your granny Sylvie

I finish reading and my eyes shoot straight back to her. She's sat there, brazenly smiling at me, like she has just outsmarted MI5.

"What does this mean, Granny?" I can't be reading it right. She can't mean actual Paris.

"I'd say it means you're going to Paris." She's actually laughing now. "Look!" She points to the side table, where there is an envelope with the word *Eurostar* printed across the front.

"But I can't, I . . ." I pick it up, snatch the ticket out, and immediately clock the departure date. Tomorrow. Friday.

For one heart-soaring moment I wonder if she intends to join me.

But of course she doesn't. She's a few weeks shy of her ninetieth birthday and rarely makes it beyond the safe triangle of her cottage on Wimbledon Common, the local church, and the village hall for film night and book club.

"I can't possibly. There's work and . . . oh no, I don't want you to have wasted your money, Granny. Did you check you can get a refund or at least change the date?"

"I have no intention of asking for a refund. Natasha booked it for me, and I doubt she stopped to wonder about that." Granny dismissively waves a hand.

She knows she's got me, that she is victorious. "So, you want me to go to Paris? On my own?" Maybe a solo trip is exactly what I need. Some time to think about what I'm doing with my life and ask myself the difficult questions I've been avoiding. Or maybe not? Maybe I just need a few days not thinking about any of it.

"That's the spirit! Yes, I do!" And with that she launches a little fist pump into the air.

I look back at the card. There are thirty-two kisses under her name, one for each of my years, which must have taken some time considering the difficulty she has holding a pen these days.

Perhaps this is all an elaborate plan on Granny's part. Get Lucille to Paris, break her out of her fug. Don't leave her to a takeaway and Netflix for another birthday (as if there could *ever* be anything wrong with that). Push her into the arms of some beautiful French boy. Unfortunately, she's overlooking the fact I'm not blessed with the same perfectly symmetrical features as her, or the wasp waist or the kind of confidence that seems to radiate from the black-and-white portraits lining her mantelpiece.

Sensing I'm not taking this terribly seriously, she suddenly tightens her bony grip on my hand.

"I *need* you to go. There is something I need you to do for me, Lucille." And whatever it is, I know I am going to say yes. I adore her. I'll do anything to make her happy in the time we have left together.

"There is a dress, the Maxim's, it was designed by Dior. I loaned it to a dear old friend many years ago, and now that she has passed away, I would so love it back. Her daughter, Veronique, has it now. I've written her address on the back of your card. Apartment 6, 10 Rue Volney 75002." When she chooses, Granny's memory can be quite impressive. "She's expecting you."

"A Dior dress? As in Christian Dior?" Granny has always been incredibly stylish, carefully sticking to a subtle palette of black, deep navy, soft creams and caramels, never overly accessorized or made-up. But it is very hard to equate a piece of valuable couture with the smart but inexpensive high street suits, dresses, and knitwear that hang in her wardrobe today, a place where something cashmere might feel like an unnecessary extravagance.

"Yes, the very one." It's not a boast, more a statement of fact, something perfectly logical.

"But how did you come to own a Dior dress? It must be worth . . ."

"An awful lot of money, yes, but let's not be crass about this, Lucille. The point is, I want to touch it one more time. It is so much more valuable to me than any price tag you could attach to it. Now, you are booked to stay for two nights, but I shan't mind in the slightest if you extend your trip—in fact, I'd be delighted if you did." She verbally draws a line through any further discussion.

And so, just like that, it seems I am going to Paris tomorrow—my smile confirms as much. How hard can it be? Collect the dress, do some minor sightseeing, get a little lost in the City of Love, make myself seem far more adventurous on social media than I actually am, return home. I start mentally tallying up all the untaken holiday I am due from work as I watch Granny lift the cake to her lips and take a satisfying large bite, her eyes sliding sideways to sneak a look at me, celebrating the calculated success she has just achieved.

One thing is for sure. There is more to this than simply returning a dress, one she can't be planning to wear again all these years later.

Jade Beer

It's just a dress, albeit a very well-made one. Couldn't this Veronique simply courier it? Granny's up to something. That much I know for sure.

AND THAT'S HOW I ENDED UP IN CARRIAGE C OF THE THREE FIF-teen Eurostar from St. Pancras to Paris on a Friday afternoon, cele-brating my recent birthday with a glass of fizz and an éclair chaser. The newspaper headlines are all a bit smug—Prince Harry's off the market, Kate and Wills have a third baby on the way—so I ease my chair back for two blissful hours alone with Marian Keyes's *Watermelon* before, thirty-six hours too late, Mum's text lands.

> Yes, this text is late, I know, but with very good reason. I
> have been giving lots of thought to what to get you this
> year. And as I can't possibly compete with Paris, I've put
> some money into your account. More than usual. Buy
> the chicest thing you can find.

Granny must have called her. I can't help noticing she still hasn't actually used the words *happy birthday*.

She'll be disappointed, but I'm not sure I will buy something chic in Paris. I am someone who dresses, for what little travel I do, with comfort firmly in mind—something Mum has never understood about me. She thinks nothing of boarding a plane in a circulation-challenging pencil skirt and seamed hosiery. For me it's joggers, loose layers, no bra, but a vest to keep things decent. I seriously doubt Mum has ever uttered the word *joggers*—the suggestion that she might ever own a pair would be deeply offensive. I recall the last time I met her outside her office after work. Naturally, she was the last to emerge, completely ignoring our agreed meeting time. When she did eventually appear, I realized she was wearing the same corporate uniform as every other woman before her, just more expensive looking, in keeping with her seniority. Everything androgynous, a sea of women stripped of their color and femininity. So much black! Even their handbags weren't allowed to look pretty. Big serious boxes with metal chains and studs or made from grotesquely dyed animal skin. More of a weapon than an accessory. I would have loved to have seen my mother emerge a butterfly among the hornets, but no. To be one of them, you have to look like them. How depressing. I couldn't help thinking how these women were supposed to represent success, wealth, and achievement, but I knew that day I didn't want any part of their conformity. Perhaps I should have felt like the oddball standing there in a billowing cream chiffon skirt that most women would save for Christmas Day. But watching them, teeming from the building like a row of identikit worker ants, I felt nothing but free.

That said, this is Paris, so I have naturally made more effort. A freshly ironed Breton shirt that isn't sure if it wants to be masculine or feminine, tucked half in and half out of the smartest jeans I own, ones that sit high above my hips. And I felt good on the train. Nothing was slicing into me or cutting me in half at the waist, but as my train pulls into the Gare du Nord and I'm swept up into a sea of smartly dressed early-evening commuters, I could kill for a pair of sunglasses. Not that anyone in Paris knows me, but I need the cloak of immediate anonymity. Just in case anyone does happen to wonder who this is trailing one battered wheelie case and two splitting WHSmith's carrier bags across the otherwise sleek concourse.

HOW CAN SOMETHING SO UNIFORMLY GRAY ALSO BE SO BEAUTIFUL? Early-evening Paris is painted in the last strokes of daylight, looking like someone turned the dimmer lights down across the whole city. Elegant apartment buildings that span the entire block have rows of identical cream-shuttered windows, the regularity broken only by imposing double-height doors in bold red, deep sage green, or glossy black. Everything seems squeezed together too tightly. Some of the stone walls I pass that are darkened from years of built-up grime and pollution neighbor the pristine fashion boutiques, their windows beckoning early Christmas shoppers in. One has giant gingerbread replicas of famous Paris landmarks—Notre-Dame, the Arc de Triomphe, and the Eiffel Tower, iced and covered in sweeties, supporting mannequins perched in party dresses.

As I search for a free taxi, the lacy iron balconies above me give a hint of the Parisian day that is drawing to a close. A push-bike, seven floors up, stands on its back wheel, until it is presumably lugged back downstairs again tomorrow for the return journey to work. A solitary man, dressed all in slim-fitting black, stands high above the city, smoking, gazing out across the fading skyline like he might be working on his latest poem. A woman in towering black ankle boots clutches a wineglass in one hand, her phone in the other, teasing her lover, I imagine.

At Granny's insistence and expense, I am staying at the hotel on the card, the Plaza Athénée, which according to her is "just across the road from Dior," not that I'm planning to spend any time there. As my taxi lumbers across the congested rush-hour city, I see the tree-lined avenues are already stripped of their foliage, bronzed leaves now carpeting the cobbles below. Tourists fight for space among stressed locals hurrying home and the endless construction that seems to be hammering a hole through the heart of the capital. Great spaces open up where shopping streets may once have flourished, diverting us blocks off route. As we're held at a set of temporary lights, I stare at the site where a building has been erased, leaving only a historic archway that seems to defiantly cling to life while everything around it is demolished. There is a patchwork of buildings swathed in temporary coverings while they are transformed beneath—like the world's largest Christmas presents waiting patiently to be unwrapped and admired.

As we pull up outside the Athénée, I remember Granny's parting words, *Look for the red window shades*, and now I see them. Every one of the windows facing onto the avenue Montaigne—and there must be at least fifty—has one, and the effect is so pretty it stops me in my tracks as I exit the taxi. Then a porter appears and says the words "Welcome to the Avenue of Fashion," and I watch with some relief as my torn and dirty carrier bags are whisked away from me.

Now I sit on the edge of my sumptuous double-canopied bed, in a room filled with red carnations, feeling like a million possibilities are flashing through the air outside my window. Like if I stepped out onto the balcony that wraps around my enormous suite, I could lift a hand high into the biting evening breeze and pluck some of that good fortune for myself. Heaven knows how Granny can afford this address. I'm high above the madness of the Parisian streets below, the honking horns, the nose-to-tail city grind, cars slowly pushing the one in front forward, up here on the edge of the stars, where every thing feels weightless. I want to venture out. I want to be *that* woman. The one who throws her case on the bed and sets forth into a foreign city with not much clue where she's going but knowing it will be thrilling.

For once, and I don't say this lightly, I need to channel a bit of Mother. She'd be down at the concierge desk right now, map splayed across the counter, not caring how big the queue might be forming behind her, demanding a bulletproof list of the best this city has to offer. Why aren't I? I want to, I really do. Maybe because I don't know how to. My own world suddenly feels surprisingly small. I feel out of my depth in this foreign city.

I might start with the easy stuff. I'll call room service, order a croque monsieur. Then I need to email Veronique, check that she's still on for meeting later tonight. Work out logistics.

As I negotiate my way through the extensive in-room dining menu, something is gnawing at the back of my mind. The look on Granny's face yesterday as she spoke about Paris. The way her eyes lit up as she talked about this hotel like she knew it so well. Why have I never bothered to delve deeper into the short time she spent here with my grandfather? I vow to ask her when I return.

2

Alice
OCTOBER 1953, PARIS
THE CYGNE NOIR

Tonight must be a success. Alice has spent the entire day ensuring it will be. Their first guests will begin arriving at the residence in two hours, which gives her just enough time to do a final check of the drawing room, to assure herself the flowers she ordered, pale nude old-fashioned roses, have arrived and been placed in the correct vases, in the correct positions. She will study the guest list one final time. Reread the notes Eloise, her social secretary, always expertly prepares for her, outlining any significant personal or professional developments pertaining to their guests. Subjects to be avoided, causes for congratulations, anything that may affect the mix of people in the room. Those to keep apart, those to maneuver together among the exciting medley of personalities who will mingle tonight beneath the giant portrait of King George and Queen Mary. Captains of industry, the minister of justice, the governor of the Bank of France, policy makers, fellow ambassadors to France, and a smattering of *social trinkets*, as Albert unflatteringly calls the more glamorous, less serious contenders—the beautiful ones that ensure the heavyweights will come to look and flirt and furnish themselves with enough interesting anecdotes to see them through the following week's parties.

The wives will arrive swathed in mink or rabbit fur, smelling expensive, looking wide-eyed and ready to judge, enjoying the fact that all the pressure to please will be on Alice tonight. She knows they'll be quietly questioning her on everything from her menu—this evening a delicately balanced selection of canapés that doesn't unreasonably favor the British or French (British partridge, French Brie)—to her weight, her clothes, how many nights a week her husband sleeps at home, where she shops, how many bags she's carrying when she leaves those shops, how much she drinks. Everything will be subject to scrutiny.

Alice makes a slow rotation of the drawing room. Has she done everything right? Will Albert be pleased? The silver is freshly polished. The whiskey and brandy selection has been restocked. She can return to her bedroom to dress with the help of Anne, who has already placed the gown they discussed Alice will wear tonight across the bed. Perhaps Albert will even join her here later, rather than spend another evening in the smaller bedroom along the corridor he seems to prefer when he is working late.

A BLACK STRAPLESS EVENING DRESS BY DIOR, A LUXURIOUS MIX OF silk satin and velvet. Alice held her breath when she registered the cost at her first fitting at the designer's town house—a sum of money that eclipsed her entire year's clothing allowance before their move to Paris. But Albert, a man who has never seemed to worry about the cost of anything, insists she must be dressed appropriately at all times, and that the bill is largely irrelevant. She was nervous at first, worried that others would see through her. A twenty-five-year-old woman, wearing a gown surely intended for a lady with far more life experience than she? Someone who could fill it with a body that had seen more and done more and was therefore more deserving of it.

But that was to totally underestimate the transformative power of this dress.

"And none of our guests tonight has seen me in this gown before, Anne?"

"Absolutely not. I have checked the record, Alice. It will be entirely new for them." Everything Alice wears is noted on cards, also referencing the relevant guest list and therefore limiting the opportunity for social blunders of the sartorial kind. Alice knows she doesn't really need to ask but can't help herself. Anne hasn't given her a moment of concern or disappointment since the day she walked through the door. Quite the opposite.

"I will help you, Alice," offers Anne, already positioned and waiting next to the enormous dark wooden bed as Alice starts to slowly remove the more practical navy wool day dress she has worn today. Anne lifts it easily over her shoulders and returns it to a wooden hanger. "The bodice first, please." The dress is in two parts. A strapless bodice that opens fully and is now facedown on the bed, revealing all the delicate inner workings that will give her the confidence she needs tonight. A run of seven slim vertical bones, held in place by fine net and supporting a lightly padded bust, negating the need for any additional underwear. As well finished inside as it is outside. The bodice is edged with a beautiful fold of rich black velvet that will sit against her skin and make the sheen of the satin glow under the soft candlelight of the drawing room.

Anne places it against Alice's naked body, being careful to avert her eyes, and sets about fastening the run of thirteen hook-and-eye catches that are perfectly spaced down the back, each one pulling Alice's body in a touch tighter. As she secures the final one into place, the bodice sits precisely as it should against Alice's skin, dipping just below her shoulder blades.

Then Alice steps into the full heavy skirt, being careful not to catch her toes in the stiff underlayer of crinoline. Only then can Anne start the process of connecting the two garments with a complex combination of more hooks and eyes and zips so that no one would ever guess the dress is two distinct pieces. That done, Anne steps back to make her final adjustments. The panels of silk satin and velvet that make up the skirt are topped at Alice's left hip by a giant bow that is padded so it holds its position, making Alice's waist look even tinier than usual. The effect is regal, and despite the fact Anne has performed this task before and she knows it is not her job to express an opinion, a broad smile breaks across her face.

"Just beautiful, Alice," she whispers.

"Thank you," Alice manages through a huge exhale of breath, a clear indicator of her nerves about tonight.

"You will be brilliant, as always." She gives Alice's hand a quick, tight squeeze before she leaves Alice to add the final touches to her makeup, to push her short, controlled curls behind each ear, and put on the pearl drop earrings she has worn every day since Albert gave them to her on their wedding day.

Alice watches her leave the room, knowing there are a hundred things she would like to seek her advice on, woman to woman. Albert briefed her early on about the need to keep her dealings with the staff purely professional, never to cross the line. And she hasn't with anyone other than Anne, being careful to use the more formal *Marianne* whenever he is within earshot.

Albert arrives back to the residence with twenty-five minutes to spare before their first guests are due, just time enough to freshen up and get into his dinner jacket.

"Is everything in order?" It isn't the warmest greeting, but Alice wasn't expecting one. He is preoccupied with the evening ahead, and perhaps he will make time to chat to her later when everyone has gone.

"Everything is just as you wanted it, Albert. I'll leave you to change, and see you downstairs. Chef has everything ready in the kitchen, and if there are any early arrivals, I will be there to greet them."

"Very good." Albert doesn't look up as she exits the room, leaving her with the feeling he prefers to be alone.

In these last precious moments of peace before the room erupts into animated conversation and loud introductions, Alice's mind drifts back to the protocol talk she attended before she and Albert were posted to Paris. Far from reassuring her, it only made her more nervous about the important task ahead and how much Albert would be relying on her. Never interrupt a flowing conversation, but always be armed with ways to start one, look out for people standing alone, respond in the language you are spoken to . . . on and on it went. She listened, took notes, saw the sense in it all, and then decided the only way she could do this was to be herself. It would be her guide, not her bible. As an only child of socially ambitious parents, Alice knows she brings valuable experience to the role too. Hours spent rotating through her parents' cocktail and dinner parties, refilling guests' champagne glasses, and absorbing the ebb and flow of good conversation. Alice watched how her mother orchestrated one conversation while deftly signaling to her husband if someone needed saving on the other side of the room. It always amazed Alice, how a woman who was often so distant in her daily life came alive in the evening when there were hearts to win, egos to placate, and personal advancement to be gained. Perhaps it was the fact their comfortable Norfolk home was in the shadow of the larger country estate it belonged to, the one her father was employed to manage, that made her parents strive for more. It certainly enticed a selection of guests who hoped such proximity to wealth might open doors for them too.

There was no greater feeling for Alice, as those guests drifted home, than if she could impart some overheard gossip or useful information she'd caught while circulating the room. Her mother would bathe her in rare praise, her father might offer a *good job, darling*, and she'd know she had pleased them. She had earned her place at the party and would head for bed, tired but happy.

One evening it was Albert, a guest of the main estate, who stepped over their threshold with an armful of fresh-cut roses for her mother and a bottle of expensive Scotch whiskey for her father, showering them and their home in compliments when it must have all seemed so modest compared to his own.

His credentials circulated the room before he did—educated at Eton and then Oxford, where he got a first in history and a reputation as an accomplished writer and uncompromising debater. There followed a swift rise through the ranks of the diplomatic service and foreign office in London and a punishing schedule of international conferences and appointments.

His appearance completely changed the dynamic of her parents' drawing room. Guests, no longer satisfied with their usual companions, would practically line up to talk to him, and he graciously obliged. The fact he was economical with any personal information beyond having a younger sister, both the offspring of wealthy Gloucestershire landowners who had tragically lost their father to tuberculosis when Albert was in his early teens, only made them warm to him more. From that moment, her parents never invited any unattached women on the nights Albert dined with them.

Alice grew up in adult company, and so a drawing room full of unfamiliar faces is not going to intimidate her tonight. But is she still capable of pleasing Albert in the way she used to? Maybe she was enough for him before they were married, when the stakes were low, the expectations of her even lower. Does he see her in their ballroom in Paris and believe she is beyond her capabilities?

"A glass of champagne, Madame Ainsley?" Patrice is floating a silver tray in front of her with a single chilled coupe at its center, knowing full well she'll take it. She might not get much chance once everyone arrives, and her spirits could do with a little kick start. Patrice replaces the tray on a sideboard, and then takes up his position in the lobby so he can announce each guest as they arrive. Terribly over-formal, Alice thinks, but quite a useful reminder of who's who when her memory faces an inevitable blank. And in the sea of sixty faces tonight, she is even more grateful for Patrice and the faultless performance she knows he will deliver.

"The secretary-general of the Élysée, Monsieur and Madame Bateaux." Patrice makes his first introduction, and with Albert nowhere to be seen yet, it is up to Alice to take charge. Thankfully the couple are already known to her. She sweeps across the drawing room in one swift movement, planting an affectionate kiss to either side of each face.

"My drawing room is already one hundred percent more elegant for having you in it, Chloe!" Alice stands holding both Chloe's arms out to the side, forming an intimate circle between them, admiring the vision before her. A full-length deep crimson gown, the color of the boudoir, scattered with delicate pearl beading so the entire dress glistens under the chandelier.

"Dior, of course!" coos Chloe. "Who else? Why haven't you invited him here yet? Oh, please do. Just a little lunch for a precious few of us. Afternoon tea in your Salon Vert? Have you met his wonderful Camila yet at avenue Montaigne? The best vendeuse in the whole of Paris, in my opinion. She can make anyone look like a lady."

"Oh, marvelous idea, so he can extract another year's wages out of me," adds the secretary before Alice has a chance to respond.

"And look at you, Alice. If I am deemed half as chic as you, then I am happy." In lieu of a compliment from Albert, it's just what Alice needs to hear.

"Come and save me from all this giddy nonsense, will you, Albert!" The secretary has spotted Albert entering through the double-height doors and is keen to capitalize on the opportunity to monopolize him.

Within half an hour, the residence drawing room is full, any artificial smiles are starting to fade as duty turns to fun, and Alice is circulating, careful to spend a few minutes with everyone before she can return to the comfortable company of Chloe. She mustn't allow herself to be distracted by the beautiful gowns. One has feathers floating over the lightest multilayer skirt; oversize blush-colored bows are cascading down the front of another; tiers of white ruffles are worn by the fiancée of one eminent diplomat. There are jackets shaped as if they have just been lifted from the most perfect female curves, and another evening gown with elaborate embroidery and expertly reimagined blooms in the prettiest colors of an English garden.

Keeping one eye on the flow of canapés so she can nod to Patrice when another service can begin, Alice moves. She's always staggered by how much is eaten at these gatherings. Three hours of constant nibbling before most guests will go on to dinner reservations elsewhere.

Alice decides to seek out one of the senior professors at the Sorbonne who is joining them this evening. Having tried and loved a taster class in modern French literature last month, she is keen to hear about next year's program of lectures, hopeful that something will spark her interest and fill some of her hours between entertaining and managing the staff.

"Dearest! Last time we met you were undecided—is it going to be the still life drawing class or the history of European art lectures?" The professor scoops his arms around her with none of the formality that so many others feel compelled to once inside the residence. "They are all filling up, you know. If you wait much longer, you'll be disappointed."

"Maybe I'll do both!" Anything has to be better, thinks Alice, than mindlessly wandering the halls of the residence seeking out ways to busy herself. Although even as she is saying it, she knows full well Albert will complain if she spends too much time away. The more official role, one not confined to entertaining, that he promised would be hers has failed to materialize despite many reminders on her part.

Alice sees then that she has managed to maneuver herself back-to-back with Albert, not that he has noticed. He's barely spoken a word to her since he arrived home. Her ears prick at the mention of her own name, and she cranes her neck, unsuccessfully trying to identify the elderly man Albert is speaking to. Patrice is not in her line of sight so is no help to her.

"And how has Madame Ainsley settled in? Enjoying Parisian diplomatic life, I hope?" It's always comforting to Alice when, having secured some of Albert's not easily afforded time, someone bothers to ask after her. Although she knows Albert will think it a wasted opportunity to be discussing matters of such little concern.

"Seamless, as expected," Albert shoots back. "Alice is made for this kind of thing, although I am under no illusions, it was obvious from day one that everyone prefers her to me." There is no jollity to Albert's tone. His words fall flat, and if he is hoping to be contradicted, he's going to be disappointed. "It is Alice they all hope to be seated next to at dinner."

"Well, then you can consider yourself a very lucky man, Albert. You have a wife who is not only beautiful and clever but adored too. Your only job is to remember to appreciate her." Whoever Albert is speaking with seems not to entirely appreciate the easy arrogance of Albert's boast, or the simmering jealousy he's barely bothering to conceal.

"I'm not sure luck has anything to do with it. I secured what I needed. She is the most efficient, least offensive person I know. No minor feat in these surroundings, wouldn't you agree?" It's said with a gentle ripple of laughter that does little to convince, and Alice hears the older gentleman say something about confirming a dinner reservation and move on.

Her cheeks warm and redden. It wasn't a discreet conversation, and she wonders if the professor has heard it too. If he has, he's being very gentlemanly and pretending otherwise, using the rotation of canapés as a handy excuse to look away, affording Alice a few moments to try to make sense of what she overheard. Theirs was never a formally arranged marriage in the traditional sense; there was still a proposal that she could choose to say yes—or no—to.

But there was also no doubt of her parents' expectations, how heartily they approved of Albert and the success he confidently owned in their company. How their hopes for a marriage were shared with friends long before it was appropriate to do so. And wouldn't her parents want the best for Alice? A husband who would honor their wedding vows? Surely Albert had been chosen for his integrity as well as his wealth and obvious ambition? If her father felt any guilt about his own shortcomings as a husband, wouldn't he ensure his only daughter was spared the same pain? She had trusted their endorsement, had no reason to doubt it.

Always the strategist, Albert laid the terms out very clearly for Alice, before and, with crushing practicality, immediately after his proposal. She would lead a privileged life, but never a purely decorative one. He knew Alice was capable of more, and he wanted her on his team, in the boardroom as well as the dining room. His delivery may have been unexpectedly functional, but it was nonetheless appealing. A chance to impress her parents, to spread her wings, to use her brain, to contribute something meaningful with the education her parents gave her.

But anyone overhearing what Alice just has would think she and Albert are in competition with each other, from the way he seemed to object to her popularity. Surely that's what he hoped for? That she would be not only accepted into this world but welcomed.

Her conversation with the professor falters while she tries to compose herself and halt the flare in her cheeks, giving him just enough time to catch the eye of another woman across the room and beckon her over.

"Madame Ainsley, please may I introduce you to Madame du

Parcq? She lectures on classic French literature at the Sorbonne. Her husband is head of asset management at the Bank of France. Both very accomplished, obviously."

"It's a great pleasure to meet you, Madame Ainsley, and thank you so very much for your kind invitation this evening. I have wanted to meet you for some time. And may I say, the roses are just perfect. Are they from the embassy gardens?"

Alice opens her mouth to respond but pauses as a young man steps into their group next to Madame du Parcq.

"Ah, please meet my son, Antoine. He is studying politics at the Sorbonne and is very keen to pursue a career in the diplomatic world, aren't you, darling?" Her hand disappears behind his back, nudging him forward, closer to Alice.

Antoine says nothing for a few seconds before nonchalantly responding, "Yes. Apparently, I am," with a subtle shift of his eyebrows that seems at his mother's expense and makes Alice pretend she missed it. Then he takes his time, letting his eyes travel over Alice, completely unrushed, not caring in the slightest that he's caused a pause in the conversation. He doesn't shake her hand, but he steps closer, so close she thinks for a wild moment he might kiss her, and it halts her breath inside her chest. Then, very slowly, he raises a finger to her lips and brushes away a rogue canapé crumb.

"Oh, thank you." Alice raises her own fingers to her mouth and notices how his eyes rest there too.

His mother breaks in, chattering on about how much she would value Alice's opinion, and might she have time to counsel Antoine a little if that isn't too much of an imposition?

"Well, I'm hardly an expert," admits Alice, "but if I can help, then of course I will."

She watches as Antoine's face slowly creeps into a small, secret smile. No one else has registered it but her. What is he trying to convey—and why is she mirroring it? It stays between the two of them. She can feel her blood pulsing in her ears—a hangover from the embarrassment caused by Albert? Or, like the tautness sitting low beneath her belly, is it more to do with the intriguing man standing in front of her? One who went to the effort of putting on a dinner jacket this evening but left the top button of his shirt undone, in defiance? His bow tie isn't quite straight; his chocolate-brown hair looks neglectfully ruffled. There is an element of swagger in the way his head is cocked to one side, his face openly admiring Alice. And why is it pitched there? A deliberate attempt to excite her? Knock her slightly off-balance? A determination not to fall into line with the social conventions of the evening? And yet he is immaculately clean-shaven. His eyebrows are as sharp as his jawline. He cares how he looks. Alice can see he has given thought to how he will be viewed tonight.

The professor and Madame du Parcq have sidetracked to timetables and student numbers, and noticing this, Antoine takes another half step toward her. She senses his body, the closeness of it to hers, his height and how he's dipping his head toward her in an act of surprise intimacy, low enough that his hair grazes her cheek and she can feel the rhythm of his breath.

"I've seen you before. At the Sorbonne. Last month."

"Yes. I was doing a short course there. But you weren't in my class." Alice arches her neck backward to create a little more space between them.

"No. I saw you from the corridor. You were engrossed. You never noticed me looking in. But I knew who you were. Like everyone else, I read about your arrival in Paris in the newspapers. But your appearance at the university was a surprise."

"Why would it surprise you?" She tries to muffle the mild offense she feels. Why should he believe her out of place there?

"You don't need to bother with—"

Alice's throat tightens as she swallows down her annoyance. She takes a slow, deep breath, breaking their gaze, and then instead of revealing her true feelings, she lets her mouth relax into a broad smile and changes her tone to mock him slightly. "And you know so much about women, do you, Antoine? Someone so young has already gained such broad experience with women like me?"

"You never let me finish." He uses his body to close the gap between them again. "You didn't need to bother with it, and yet I could see you were the only person in the room who seemed genuinely absorbed in the class. Forgive me, but I watched you for a little while, hanging off your teacher's every word. I saw something different in you, Alice. That's what kept me looking. And I remembered you because of it. The fact you were easily the most beautiful woman in the room that day, too, was barely an afterthought."

She turns her head toward him, and for a moment, Alice is completely lost in him, her face angled inward to his neck, searching out the warm freshness of him. A mix of bold citrus, undercut with something more earthy—leather or tobacco, maybe both. She would be lying if she said she wasn't very familiar with being complimented on her appearance, to being seen, even stared at. If a compliment isn't aimed specifically at her, then it is something she indirectly makes beautiful—her choice of roses in the drawing room, the way her table is laid, the smartness of her staff. But not once that Alice can remember has anyone complimented her on her intellect and any fulfillment she may crave beyond the cocktail hour. Albert paid lip service to it with the promise of a role for her here, but that all feels rather hollow now.

She feels a deep gratitude spread through her. A connection.

Perhaps some genuine common ground? He studies at the Sorbonne too. Alice feels her lips part to thank him, but the words won't come. It suddenly seems so sad to be grateful for something others so easily take for granted.

Then Madame du Parcq is back at his side, and the moment is broken. Antoine straightens and Alice snaps a look of innocence across her face before his mother drags Antoine off under the guise of more necessary introductions and Alice excuses herself to check on the arrangements, her heart knocking against her ribs, her cheeks now a deeper shade of rose.

BY ELEVEN P.M., ALICE IS BACK IN HER BEDROOM. ANNE'S FINGERS are lightly retracing her earlier routine, gradually freeing Alice from the dress she has worn this evening. Alice can feel her body gently yield as the corset is relaxed and then instinctively tighten again as Albert strides into the room. It should be him undressing me, she thinks, and wonders if that's occurring to him, too, not entirely at ease with the idea it could be. Would he like to undress his wife like he used to? To peel back the layers of silk, her feeling his increased urgency, to reveal the softness beneath, flesh that once gladly responded to him. The glacial impartiality of his face would suggest he's having no such thoughts.

"Christ, doesn't she have a home to go to!" He tosses a hand dismissively in Anne's direction. He can't even remember her name, notes Alice. She feels Anne's fingers pick up speed, and she knows the sudden urgency is for her own benefit, not Anne's. Anne will leave soon, return to the safe sanctuary of her own home, and she won't want Alice to be left to deal with an irritated Albert.

"Sorry, Monsieur Ainsley, I won't be much longer."

Albert doesn't respond, but simply kicks off his shoes, expecting Anne to put them away, and heads straight for the door again.

"Darling, I'd love to hear all about this evening." Alice loathes the mild desperation in her voice, like she's searching for the scrap of a compliment, whatever he might choose to throw her way. "Who you spoke to and what everyone had to say. It seemed a success, wouldn't you agree? Shall I ask Patrice to fix us a nightcap?"

"He can put a whiskey in the library for me. I've got at least a couple of hours' work to catch up on." The door closes and he's gone, leaving Alice and Anne alone, the latter trying very hard to look as though she isn't offended, like she wasn't really listening. But it's the slightly sympathetic dip of Anne's mouth Alice can't bear.

"I'm so sorry, Anne." Alice will do his apologizing for him again.

"You have absolutely no need to apologize to me, think nothing of it. But—"

"Will you leave tonight's guest list on the desk for me there, please?" Alice cuts her off; she's far too tired to get into the rights and wrongs of Albert's behavior now. Besides, she knows everyone who attended this evening will require a personal handwritten thank-you for doing so. "I may as well make a start on the thank-you notes now."

After she's struggled through twenty or so cards, Alice gives up. She's wide awake but lacking the inspiration to make the cards sound personal and genuine, as they need to be. Her mind repeatedly wanders back to Antoine's words from earlier this evening: *I saw something different in you.* She finds herself doodling them on one of the small brown dress cards that Anne uses.

Maybe Albert will have finished his work by now. Maybe he'll appreciate an interruption, an excuse to switch off his desk lamp and chat to her. She doesn't want to go to bed alone again tonight. She creeps along the corridor to the library. The door is shut, but she can hear her husband on the phone. It's one a.m. Who can he possibly be speaking to now? Whoever it is, his hushed, casual tone suggests it's not a business associate, and it would be a bad idea to interrupt him. She heads back to the bedroom, closing the solid wooden door. She leans against it, looking around the huge expanse of their bedroom, thinking about how few nights they have shared the same bed. Can it really only be just over a year since they would wake, tangled in each other's bodies beneath the cool white sheets of their honeymoon suite, the rhythmic lap of the waves below gently stirring them both from sleep? Since they arrived in Paris, Alice feels like her untouched body has physically hardened. With every night Albert has made his excuses not to sleep with her, her confidence has withered until there is all this space between them. Cold emptiness. In this room, in their bed, and in her heart, and absolutely nothing to fill any of it.

3

◈

Lucille
FRIDAY
PARIS

There are very long, very bare legs all over the hotel lobby this evening. Legs balanced on toothpick-thin heels. Legs draped across the arms of velvet furniture, others bending over tables loaded with flutes of champagne. Legs that are, no joke, twice the length of mine and topped with fringed sequin skirts that dance around barely covered bottoms. These legs are tan, lean; they have a sheen that speaks of the late-night parties they will be parading at later. I don't recall ever seeing limbs like these back home. Not in my local, and certainly not anywhere near the gray open-plan office where I work. Dylan, the boss at the online travel website I've worked at for the past eighteen months, was not the slightest bit impressed when I emailed last night to say I needed to take today off. I've had to promise to check emails in case anything urgent crops up. I need to make sure I am back there bright and early Monday morning. That gives me two nights in Paris, plenty of time to grab Granny's dress from Veronique's tonight and be back in London for Sunday evening.

As if to cruelly compound my own lack of glamour, I have landed in Paris at what appears to be Fashion Week, which, from what I can see, is kicking off in the hotel Granny has booked me in to. Do people actually live like this? Is it a legitimate way of life to wrap oneself up in a ribbon of pink silk, scattered with thousands of silver crystals, and posture around Paris for all to see? Yes, it is! I've never seen such beautiful women—models, presumably. They are otherworldly in their perfection, as if they have stepped off the giant billboards on the Champs-Élysées and into real life like supercharged, half-human, half-fantasy creatures, here to make love to us all. Nothing is lacking. Hair is scraped up into face-altering ponytails; skin is flawlessly luminous. Lips are full, parted, waiting to be kissed. Everyone is touching everyone else. There are no boundaries here. It's like I've stepped into a giant orgy of fashion where the cost of entry is simply to be fearlessly fabulous.

And the men. I can see at least five I could happily fall in love with right now. They're kissing necks, tracing their fingers slowly along naked thighs; they've moved in close so the space between man and woman is vacuumed shut to any would-be challengers. I watch as one man whispers something intensely into the ear of his companion, a woman who stands with her legs just wide enough apart to allow one of his between them. He's so close, his lips are touching her skin as he speaks, and he's snaking an arm around her tiny waist and up over her rib cage. Whatever he's saying is causing her to melt a little deeper into him. Then, Jesus, she lets her tongue lick briefly across his lips, into his mouth, and I can hear the rhythm of my own breath shudder with the sexiness of it.

As I step out into the cleansing evening air, I'm in need of a couple of big, heart-rate-reducing breaths. What *was* that? And will I ever in my lifetime experience a fraction of it? Dear God, *please* let it be so. You can keep the sequins and the feathers, but can I have just a little of the hotness? Not every night of the week, I couldn't cope, but maybe once or twice a month? Is that asking too much? I've only been here a few hours, and already, first chance it gets, I've allowed Paris to seduce me with its sexy sparkle. I have a word with myself and plow on to Veronique's, a bracing forty-minute walk from my hotel into the first arrondissement. I hug the river, heading east, before breaking left through some formal gardens and onto one of the quieter narrow streets just off the impressive place Vendôme.

I feel different, in the same way I imagine everyone does when they walk the streets of a foreign city. It feels good to be noticed for my unusualness. For a start, I'm not in the Parisian girl off-duty uniform of super-skinny jeans, black fine knit, cigarette. I'm in sneakers with the same jeans I traveled in, but I've switched the shirt for a ruffled blouse with gathered sleeves that puff outward at the top, giving it a slight military feel.

But it's more than that. I can't think of many times I've been seen, which makes my heart sag a little. I'm never on the list of contenders when Dylan is lining up his favorites for the best travel trips. He's always banging on about how the best pieces are the personal ones, adventures of discovery that transcend merely visiting somewhere new. Hard to achieve when he never actually sends me anywhere. But that's nothing compared to not being seen by my own mother. I know she'll feel guilty if she doesn't see me once a month, but only because she'll have failed to achieve a goal she set herself. How much does she really know about me? What keeps me awake at night (the fear I am wasting this precious life of mine)? What do I need more of (reasons to smile, an escape from the monotony) or less of (the pretense that everything is just fine when I know it's not)? I doubt she could name the company I work for. She might have to open my last email to check my job title. I'm as much a stranger to her as the woman who will bag up her next supermarket shop.

Perhaps there is little to impress her. I have no savings in the bank, no grand plan; I'm drifting through life waiting for an opportunity to find me, which doesn't bode well for my love life either. But I'm not sure I could cope with the pressure to compete with a man who needs to achieve every second of the day. One who can't exist in third gear, where I seem to spend most of my time. I remember what it did to Dad, before he finally accepted defeat and left. How the spotlight of Mum's success was too bright for him. A *diminished man*, she said, never able to keep pace with her rise through the corporate ranks and a salary that far eclipsed his. I remember the day he left, and I wondered why my mum would choose her job over my dad. I was young, I didn't know the details, but still, he stood there wanting to love her, and she chose money and business accolades. It was like the moment he questioned the way she orchestrated their lives, she no longer respected him. He became the problem. Whatever his role was, I think she assumed it would be absorbed by someone better or we would simply move on without it. We'd adapt. That's what her job did to her. It conditioned her to be ruthless. To always take emotion out of the negotiation. Mum didn't break stride. What a waste of all those years invested in each other. She cleaned him out of her life in the time it took him to remove his personal belongings. Then handed me his door key. The closeness Dad and I had built could only stretch so far. Every third weekend at his new place was too far, as it turned out.

One thing I know for sure, I'm not one of those women who thrives on pressure. I am *not* my mother. I launch a silent promise into the night sky—I need to be kinder to myself—and decide that's enough self-reflection for one night.

I ARRIVE AT THE HUGE WOODEN FRONT DOOR TO VERONIQUE'S apartment block with an unfamiliar sense of purpose. She buzzes me in, not to the foyer I'm expecting, but to an oasis of greenery, the courtyard garden that the apartment block surrounds. I walk directly across to the other side, dodging half a dozen louche-looking felines. Then I'm back into the building and facing a small metal lift with one of those caged concertina doors, just about big enough for one small adult. The ones where you get to see the solid concrete structure of the building as you pass between floors, praying you make it to the next one.

It rattles its way to the fourth floor, where Veronique is waiting to greet me. I know it must be her before she says a word, her smile is so inviting.

"Lucille, come in, come in!" Her hand is immediately at my shoulder, and she's directing me in through the door to a surprisingly vast lateral apartment, everything branching off from a central wooden corridor. I can see straight through to the other side to a balcony, topped with a green and-white-striped awning. The smell is at once of home. Not mine, but what I've always associated with the notion of happy domesticity. A mixture of soft, clean florals—there is an enormous crystal vase of white lilies on a central table—and something rich and tempting I guess has been cooking for a while.

"You will of course stay for dinner, yes?" Veronique is nudging me toward a drawing room, where I can see a bottle of red wine is opened, two large goblets waiting to be filled.

"If it's not too much trouble, I'd love to." I think Granny will be pleased if I make the effort to be sociable.

"No trouble at all, and there is lots to talk about." She's pouring us both a glass of wine the size of which certainly suggests so, although I had imagined this would be little more than some polite intros, throw the dress in the back of a cab, and off I go again.

"Let's eat, and then I will show you the dresses. You will love them."

"Dress, you mean?" Granny specifically said there was one.

"Oh, no. Just wait, you will see." Veronique's smile tells me there is a treat coming my way later, but not before we have enjoyed dinner and shared the warm headiness of a great bottle of wine together.

"I'm so sorry to hear about your mum passing away," I offer. Much as I don't want to take this conversation down an uncomfortable route for her, I can't ignore the fact Veronique has very recently lost her mother.

"Thank you. She was an old lady. She lived a wonderful life but was never quite herself after my father's death a few years ago. I miss her terribly, but I have my memories and they will have to be enough now."

I study her face for a minute. Is she just being brave?

"We were *so* close. This was her apartment, actually, although it was much smaller originally. It's been knocked through since. She always preferred the Right Bank, it put her close to the government buildings. I moved back in here with her a couple of years ago when I could see she needed more help. She was a remarkable woman. A great lover of letter writing. She always made time. For her writing, for me, for anyone she valued."

"Are you also involved in the government?" She has a hyper-efficient, organized vibe about her that could be well suited to that world.

"Oh God, no! That's not me at all. I work at the Museum of Decorative Arts. It's very close to here, near the Louvre, on rue de Rivoli. Ceramics mostly, but I also help to curate the glassware and porcelain collections. I'm just part-time now, but I've worked there forever. I never had any reason to leave."

Veronique's face is almost makeup-free. Just a touch of mascara on tired-looking eyes, the only hint of the disturbed nights her mother's passing may have caused, and a delicate shade of rose on her lips that seems to lift and illuminate her whole face. There is warmth and understanding in the creases that frame her features. As we chat, she displays none of the diversionary tactics I know I use to deflect attention. There is no wave of the hand, no dropping of eye contact. She is confident, it seems, to sit back and be read. Her hair is short, tucked behind each ear and revealing two brilliant diamond studs, an expertly chosen accessory to the crisp white shirt she is wearing tonight. Her hair is a silvery gray and has the sort of volume I think I might envy later in life. She's the definition of understated. I wonder what she would make of some of the more dubious items in my wardrobe—the multicolored ponchos, the palm tree–print shirt, the pink flares—all bought to wear to places I have yet to see. I can't help feeling the sting of her words too. It's inviting comparison with my own mother, and I worry unnecessarily that she might ask about her.

Dinner is delicious. Chicken swimming in a buttery, garlic-heavy sauce with just a fresh green salad. By the time we've finished, it's nearly ten o'clock.

"Shall I show you the dresses now?" asks Veronique, her face keen with expectation.

"Yes please!" I'm forcing the excitement for her benefit, because any dress is going to have a tough job competing with the mood-enhancing effect of good French wine and a home-cooked meal.

We both walk through to Veronique's bedroom, a high-ceilinged dove-gray space, off which is a dressing room lined on both sides with full-height closets. She must *really* love clothes.

"Here they are!" In one swift, easy move, Veronique throws back the sliding doors to reveal a lineup of dresses.

I actually take a step backward. This is no minor dress collection. Even to my totally untrained eye, the fabrics look heavy and rich. Buttons are still rigidly in place. Everything has a very ordered and deliberate symmetry. I'm guessing all the detailing has been done by hand, and one of the dresses is covered in what must be thousands of sequins and crystals. It's all from a very different world. One that

knows nothing of the fast fashion of today's high street, its clutter of
wire hangers and mass-market copies—or in other words, my
wardrobe.

I can see the love here, the care and expertise in every stitch. I can
feel the time it would have taken to conceive and then build something
so beautiful. I'm guessing weeks, maybe even months for each. There
is a lavishness that some might say borders on the wasteful. Why have
one layer to a skirt, when you can have five or six? Why hope that a
dress will hold its shape when you can structure it and pad it so its
performance is never in doubt? Granny has always been well put together, from a generation of women who care what they look like. But
this? This is not her life or her world. I can't equate what's hanging in
front of me with the wonderful woman I just left back home, wearing
a crumb-covered blanket and half watching daytime TV. Why has she
never spoken to me about these dresses? This feels instantly wrong and
confused, like some key detail or link is missing that would mean it all
made sense.

Veronique, one hand theatrically pressed to her chest, actually
looks on the verge of tears. "Have you ever seen anything like it?" she
asks, rather redundantly, I would say.

"No. No, I have not," is about all I can manage.

"It's not even the best bit. You haven't seen the notes that accompany them yet. I will show you."

SHE RETURNS FROM HER BEDROOM WITH A SMALL PEARL TRINKET
box that is lined with plush red velvet. Inside is a small bundle of eight
identical brown cards, not much bigger than a credit card and held
together with an elastic band.

"Every dress or piece has a corresponding one," she explains. "Take
a look. When Mum first showed me the dresses, she gave me the
complete bundle of cards too."

I glance down at the first one and see it is handwritten in ink that has faded over the years, but not quite enough to completely destroy its legibility.

A & A

Cygne Noir
Home
October 3, 1953

"I saw something different in you."

There is something moving about holding this note in my hand, reading words written over sixty years ago. And the quote. How intriguing.

"Cygne Noir is the name of the dress," explains Veronique. "It translates as 'Black Swan.' Instantly romantic, don't you think? My *maman* never really spoke about these dresses much, except to say that they were very special. But I did some digging through the archives at work one afternoon, and it was designed by Christian Dior, back in the late forties. It's a couture piece. It would have taken weeks to make and would have cost a significant amount of money at the time."

"Why would anyone write a note like this about the dress? What would be the need for it?"

"Yes, I asked that question, too, and it seems if you wore couture back then, if you were that sort of woman, living that sort of life, it was quite likely you would want to keep a record of when certain pieces were worn. So you could rotate them. Important people wouldn't see you wear the same thing twice. Imagine!"

"But my granny Sylvie didn't know those sorts of people. I'm confused, Veronique." It's true Granny has always been vague about the time she and my grandfather spent in Paris in her twenties, but then you can choose to be vague when you're her age, and I've never really pressed her for the details. I suppose I always assumed, without her ever correcting me, that it was her first taste of freedom away from her parents, and before they committed themselves to a more sensible married life back in England. I've seen the odd grainy picture of her from the time, and if she's beautiful now, she was mesmerizing then. But still, not this.

"I was only expecting to collect one dress for my grandmother, Veronique."

"According to my maman, all eight in the collection belong to her." I frown while Veronique tries to fill in some of the blanks.

"Maman received many letters from your grandmother Sylvie in London over the years. They always seemed to be writing to each other. I wouldn't mind betting I'll find a big bundle of them around here when I start to go through everything properly. Before she died, she told me there was a good chance Sylvie would make contact about the dresses. So, when she did, I wasn't surprised. But it was never just one dress."

"Okay, so then what or who are A and A?"

"Now, *that* is the mystery." Veronique gently opens the pearl buttons of a gray wool jacket that is hanging at the front of the rail with a densely pleated black skirt. "Can you see?"

As she lifts the designer's label positioned at the back of the neck, there are the initials again. This time stitched on the underside of the label. "I've checked, and they have been sewn into every piece, where they were clearly never intended to be seen."

"Could the dresses have been made for someone else—one half of the A and A?—and somehow my grandmother came to be given them?" It seems like the only logical explanation, although it doesn't really satisfy the clear need for my grandmother to be reunited with them.

"Yes, I have reached the same conclusion myself," adds Veronique, "but this is very intriguing, don't you think? This collection is highly valuable. We have to assume that someone who cared enough to buy and wear these clothes would not have given them away lightly. And to the same person? Why would they do that? The notes would suggest they were significant to the woman who first wore them. And yet, they were all in your grandmother's possession at one time. And then my mother's. I would love to know why, wouldn't you?"

"Yes, I would." But I'm coming up blank. Granny hasn't mentioned any of this to me, so I have no idea how much she even knows herself. "Any theories?" I can already sense from the way Veronique is excitedly shifting her weight from one foot to the other that she has more to tell me.

"Well, it was not Dior's practice to initial his pieces for customers, and while I am sure it could have been done if it was requested, look at the stitching."

I take a step toward the rail, angling my neck forward so my face is pressed up close to the delicate outline of the A&A.

"Notice anything?" Veronique's own face is trained on mine now, eyebrows angled upward.

"Nope."

"The stitching!" she announces triumphantly. "It's nowhere near the same standard as the rest of the garment. The initials were added later, I think, presumably by the A who was wearing them. It's like she was secretly marking the pieces as her own, claiming them perhaps, don't you think? Otherwise, why go to such lengths to initial the garments herself where it can't be seen? It all seems a little secretive."

Okay, now I am intrigued.

"But it's not until you see all the notes together that you get a real sense of what might have been going on—the private relationship that the notes seem to document. Look." Veronique takes all the cards out of the box and starts to lay them out on top of a glossy built-in dressing table that sits between two sections of the wardrobe doors. "Here they are in date order, starting with Black Swan. We obviously have no idea where A's home was, but it would have been somewhere very special to have warranted wearing this gown. Then, two weeks later, they see each other again, and she wears the gray jacket and black skirt."

A & A

New Look Jacket
Maison Dior
October 17, 1953

"Meet me tomorrow. I'll wait all day if I have to."

"I suppose we shouldn't assume that A and A are a man and woman, should we? Couldn't it be two women, recording something special or secrets they were both keeping?"

"It's possible, I suppose," answers Veronique, "but you might think differently when you've read all the cards. Look, the very next day we get the Maxim's dress." She points to the card that's third in her lineup.

A & A

Maxim's
Église Saint-Germain-des-Prés
October 18, 1953

"I need you as much as you need me."

"This is it! The dress my grandmother is so keen for me to return to her, this is the one." I start to imagine the furtive moment this note might have been written. Was it late at night when its owner was alone, was it rushed and immediately hidden? "Okay, then what? What happens after the church?" I'm gaining a thirst for the emerging story now.

"If the two initials represent two different people, then it seems they meet again, ten days later in the Jardin du Luxembourg, one of the prettiest parks in the whole of Paris. If you want to see a slice of true Parisian life while you are here, Lucille, spend an afternoon there. Ride on the carousel, it's one of the oldest in Paris. Look what was written next." We both let our eyes drop back to the cards.

A & A

Batignolles
Jardin du Luxembourg
October 28, 1953

"Even if you never let me touch you, this is
enough."

"It's quite a bold statement, isn't it?" I'm starting to feel like we are climbing inside A's head a little, not merely her wardrobe.

"I felt the same when I read that line!" Veronique is energized, like I've just confirmed her first thoughts may have been the right ones. "I'm not sure, but something about it just made me think there is tension bubbling beneath the surface. That maybe there were reasons to be cautious, why the cards had to be simply initialed and not fully signed." Veronique has truly come alive with this story. Her eyes are pinned wide open, her imagination running riot, sucking me right in with her. I think she notices the smirk I can't hide, because she quickly adds, "I've spent too many years living alone, Lucille, I've read a lot of romance novels, and this has all the makings of a great story! Definitely one I would read."

"You're right! But will it come to anything? What does the next one say?" We're both giggling now, like a couple of teenage girls who've never been kissed.

Veronique points to the next card and we read it aloud together.

A&A

Esther
Les Halles
November 6, 1953

"Try to love me a little, because I already love you too much."

"Then it happens!" she gushes. "Read the next one. There are no quotation marks this time, but look!"

A&A

Debussy
Musée de l'Orangerie
November 14, 1953

The kiss that saved me

"Saved her from what?" I practically yell. "My God, what was happening to her?"

"We can't possibly know, can we, but things seem to take a sinister turn for the worse next." Veronique's face is suddenly grave. She couldn't be more invested if the scene was playing out in front of her in wide screen. "Something bad happened the night she wore the next gown, the Mexico dress."

I almost don't want to look down, but how can I not? As the tiny lettering sharpens into focus, I read the words aloud.

A & A

Mexico
The garden
November 15, 1953

"I can make all this go away."

I actually feel the words catch in the back of my throat. To think of A, whoever she was, sitting alone, doing what? Quietly predicting the end of something that seemed so potent just over a month ago. What could possibly have happened? It's all so sad. I look at Veronique, willing her to deliver answers.

"Not good, is it?" She looks just as perturbed as I feel. "But then another twist comes with the final card. This one is different because it tells us so little—but perhaps will reveal a great deal. Unlike the others, there is no dress name and no location. We don't know what kind of dress it was or where it was worn. And look, the handwriting—it does not match the others."

A & A

Toile de Jouy
Off-white, puff sleeves, full length, high pleated
    collar
January 9, 1954

"I continue to hope."

"Well, that's not much use, is it?" I sulk. "It tells us nothing, then." For someone who claims to be an aspiring journalist, I realize I could probably do with being a little less defeatist.

"Well, yes, I think it might, actually. The date means it came after the others—it is the final dress in the sequence. But there is no piece to match the card. It's one of two dresses that are missing." Veronique doesn't look half as gutted as I expect she might, now that we have no way of knowing how the story will end.

"Urgh! This is so frustrating."

"I've been thinking about it, and I believe the key will be finding out more about the name of the fabric it was made from, the toile de Jouy." Veronique lifts the card closer to her face. "The description gives us a good sense of the dress, but the fabric used will define how special it was, the kind of occasion it might have been worn at. It needs more research."

I focus back on the words, written in beautifully neat writing: *I continue to hope.*

"Okay," I say slowly, more optimistically. "She had hope. Whatever it was, it wasn't over. This is not the end of the story. But hang on, you said *two* dresses were missing. What's the other one?"

"It's the Maxim's, I'm afraid. Unfortunately, Maman hit some hard times back in the fifties and was forced to sell it. I know she regretted it deeply for years and always felt awful about letting it go. She told me she cried the day she handed it over." Veronique hangs her head and sighs, and I'm not sure if it is the sad memory of her mother or the brick wall my challenge just hit that has depleted her enthusiasm. "Of course, I did tell your grandmother when she got in touch that the Maxim's is missing, but obviously she has sent you anyway to collect the other dresses, and you can take them all."

"She knew the Maxim's wasn't here with you?"

"Yes, I couldn't let her book an expensive Eurostar ticket without knowing the one dress she named is not in fact in my possession. Is something wrong?" Veronique looks nervous, like she has said the wrong thing, exposed Granny in some way, which is exactly what she has done.

"She only told me about the Maxim's yesterday, Veronique, knowing full well I wouldn't find it here. And she sent me anyway, because wherever it is, she doesn't want me to leave Paris without it." I can't help but smile at Granny's cunning.

"Okay, so now what?"

"I can't disappoint her, Veronique. I can't go back without it. I promised her I would return this dress to her, and I can't fail her— or myself."

I am suddenly overwhelmed by a need to find this dress, to hold it in my own hands, to complete the circle and try to get a sense of my grandmother's connection to it. How did she end up owning these dresses after A wore them? Why did she then give them to Veronique's mother? I feel compelled to find out. But what are the chances of locating the Maxim's after all this time?

"Who did your mother sell it to? Do you have any idea?" Veronique is my best and only chance right now. If she doesn't know, then the trail will be dead before it's even started.

"If it went to a private buyer, then no, I have no idea, and I'm not sure I could even suggest where to start. It could be anywhere in the world. But at that time in Paris, there was really only one other place it could have gone. There was a famous old dress agency called Bettina's in the Quartier du Sentier, where lots of the old fabric shops and factories were based at the time. It was very well known for stocking high-quality ready-to-wear collections. But occasionally a piece of couture would pass through its doors. Those pieces never stayed for long. The women who shopped there visited regularly, and I'm sure customers looking for specific items would have been tipped off the second they arrived."

"There's no chance it will still be there, then." How bloody disappointing. I'm surprised at how gutted I am, and Veronique senses it immediately.

"When I learned you were coming, I checked and, Lucille, the shop is still there. It's open until noon on Saturday, closed on Sunday, and reopens again at eleven Monday morning. I've no idea if it operates in the way it used to, but it's got to be worth a try, hasn't it? If it was ever there, there is a slim chance they will have a record of who bought it."

"Yes! You're right." And I don't care how hard I have to beg Dylan to let me extend my stay a little, I'm not going back to London until I have checked. And isn't this exactly the kind of story he always claims to be looking for? A journey to a new destination, exploring the hidden corners that only those deeply embedded in the place could reveal, an uncompromisingly personal piece that might start with a train journey somewhere obvious but teases with the promise of something more memorable. Isn't there a slim chance my boss might actually be impressed with the story I bring home?

I also need to speak to Granny as a matter of urgency. Obviously she knows more than she told me yesterday.

4

❦

Alice
OCTOBER 1953, PARIS
THE NEW LOOK JACKET

Alice should be examining the chic black wool day dress; it's exactly the kind of thing she might order. Instead she is thinking about the job she has done since arriving in Paris after her midsummer wedding. Has she worked hard enough? Would more hours spent perfecting everything win back the more charming, attentive Albert, who woke her with a kiss every day on their honeymoon, generously paid for by her parents, but who seems emotionally distant now that he's slipped back into his bespoke work suit? That Albert was, along with the honeymoon luggage, swiftly packed away for the seriousness of Paris and all its demands.

Is she worthy of today's front-row seat at Dior's show, where loyalty to the designer is prized more highly than wealth? Would she call herself loyal? She certainly respects commitment. That's how she is made. The lesson she was always shown. Didn't her own mother show determined commitment to a man who didn't always deserve it? Whatever her father was doing until the early hours, she knew her mother would never let mention of it enter their everyday lives, breathing life into it. It was her mother's reaction that kept the wheels turning forward. To Alice's young eyes, her mother had a resilience, an inner strength she hoped she would never have to cultivate herself.

The movement of the mannequin crossing the room, coming dangerously close to knocking over one of the pillar ashtrays that are dotted around the front row, breaks her thoughts, and that's when Alice sees him.

Everything about his slouched body language suggests Antoine has been here for some time. His dark wool suit isn't freshly pressed, the toe caps of his shoes don't gleam as other men's do, as if he is trying to communicate he doesn't want to be here. But only, perhaps, until he sees her?

Because the second their eyes connect, he mouths, "Hello," sits up a little straighter, and relaxes into a broad smile. Alice's mind empties of everything she has been worrying about this morning. Albert filters from her thoughts, like smoke weakening on the breeze. The crowded discomforts of the room fade so she is barely aware of them. Now it's a sense of anticipation she feels, and a pleasure that's making her surprisingly self-conscious. She smooths her hands down her gray wool flannel jacket, appreciating how it's molded to the perfect hourglass shape, the gently rounded collar, the pleated bust, the fine pearlized button at each pocket and cuff. Then her hands find the heavy black pleated skirt that hangs as if it were stitched to her this morning.

Neither of them is watching the show. A second mannequin cuts across Alice's line of sight, gifting her the opportunity to break the hold between them, but still she doesn't look away. Has this become a contest? A declaration of some sort? The corners of Antoine's mouth turn up naughtily, like he's seeing in her something he's feeling himself.

A warmth is spreading inside Alice. It's deliciously self-indulgent and she can't switch it off. It tugs at her belly, making her shift in her seat. Still their eyes remain connected, even though she senses his mother, seated beside him, has noticed Alice and lifts a hand to wave.

Alice returns the greeting but offers no further acknowledgment. As the show swirls on, Alice is loosely aware of movement around her, people fidgeting, a nose being powdered, a shifting of body weight in a chair beside her. Only an outburst of rapturous applause finally forces her eyes to disconnect from him. Alice diverts her attention back to the show program in her lap, grateful of the opportunity to collect herself, to take a few deep breaths. What will happen when the show ends? She knows Madame du Parcq will seek her out and she and Antoine will have to speak, to acknowledge whatever it is that has passed between them.

A regular at the shows now, she starts to circle everything she likes that she will order: more sculpted wool suits with hip-hugging pencil skirts, a white raw silk taffeta and velvet midlength cocktail dress with a daring halter neck, full-length furs, and at least three fully embroidered ball gowns. She wills her eyes to remain downward, but there are too many moments of weakness. Alice's resolve falters and her eyes move against her will in the direction of Antoine, seeking him out again and again. She doubts he has seen a single ensemble from the show. Every time, his smile deepens beyond playfulness. There is intent, even admiration. She can see it in the darkness behind his lashes and in the confidence of whatever he is trying to silently communicate, not caring that he is touching elbows with his own mother.

One hour and nearly ninety looks later, the announcer bellows, "Grand Mariage," as a multilayer wedding gown, the show's finale piece, brings everything to a close and the room erupts into chaos. Alice wants more time to appreciate this gown. The way tiny metallic threads pick out the silhouette of flower and leaf motifs, its elegant high neck and neat three-quarter-length sleeves. But it's no good. Chairs are hastily scraped backward, waiters appear with trays of champagne, and there are very loud protestations and verdicts of "dazzling," "his best yet," and "magnificent" flying from all corners of the salon. Everyone is kissing.

As Alice reaches for her bag, she is suddenly confronted by Monsieur Dior himself.

"It's a greatly controversial piece, you know, the wedding gown, Madame Ainsley." He's holding her gently in his gaze, a look so different from the other she has enjoyed this morning. This one, she is confident she can cope with.

"Surely nothing you present can be deemed anything other than an absolute success, Monsieur Dior," Alice offers, acutely aware of the number of people all jostling around them, ready to pounce and interrupt the second their conversation presents the slightest opening.

"It is not so much in the finished ensemble, but in the making of it, you see. The girls who work on the dress sew a lock of their own hair into the hem in order to find a husband during the coming year."

"What a truly romantic notion." And a wonderful definition of hope, thinks Alice. That a woman would trust the universe—and not her parents or society's will—to deliver the most wonderful husband to her.

"Yes, but the mannequins pretend that it is unlucky to wear the dress. They say that the girl who shows it will never be a bride in real life. Anyway, I am so glad that you came, and I look forward to dressing you more this season." He cradles her hand in both of his for a few moments, then releases her.

Before Alice can even offer her thanks, Monsieur Dior is engulfed in kisses and handshakes and all manner of frankly quite undignified behavior. It is Alice's cue to leave. She starts to make her way across the salon, toward the door and her waiting driver, but is intercepted by Antoine and his mother, as she predicted she would be.

"Oh my goodness, have you ever seen anything quite like it?" gushes Madame du Parcq. "How are any of us supposed to decide? I would wear nothing but Dior if I had the resources. Oh, what will you select, Madame Ainsley? The beautiful strapless sheath evening gown?

It would be perfect to show off some of your exquisite jewelry and with one of your fur stoles."

"You know, I never decide on the day." Alice forces her eyes to remain with Antoine's mother. "Far too much pressure. I will go home, have a glass of champagne, and spend a glorious hour with my program and my notes. Then Marianne and I will return when the decisions are made." Alice can already see she has lost Madame du Parcq's attention to Monsieur Dior. She's watching him circulate the room, trying to quickly assess if he is likely to pass her way or if she needs to adjust her own position to stand the best possible chance of an introduction.

But Antoine's focus is entirely on her.

"Apart from this one," he offers with a nod toward the program she is still holding. It is open at the page that features a quite spectacular sequin-covered gown, one that is belted at the waist with the neatest blue tulle ribbon before it feathers gloriously at the top of the bodice, mimicking a bird's luxurious plumage. Alice's pencil had hovered over it, a special piece from the Dior archives and not the new collection, one that had caused a collective intake of breath from the audience. It was only the inevitably high cost of such a gown that had prevented her from allowing her own excitement to overcome sense. She settled for a question mark instead of a tick.

"I think you should order it." Antoine holds her eye contact. "There can't be many women in the room worthy of it. The layers, the intricacy, its complicated construction. And yet it's so easy to read, its beauty immediately translatable. I think it will suit you perfectly."

Alice feels him press something hard into the palm of her right hand. A tightly folded piece of paper. As her fingers close around it, she looks to his face to see him gently place a finger to his lips, silencing her, before his mother's attention is back with them.

"Well, I must be on my way," says Alice, stepping out of the group.

"I think I've kept my poor driver waiting quite long enough." She kisses Madame du Parcq, offers her best wishes to Antoine, the absolute most she feels she can do while his mother's eyes are on her, and makes her swift escape.

As she reclines back heavily into the rear passenger seat, Alice slowly unfurls the paper and reads his scrawl. *Meet me tomorrow, the Church of Saint-Germain-des-Prés, noon. I'll wait all day if I have to.*

A flicker of something ripples up through Alice's entire body. Nerves, fear, horror . . . excitement? She can't define it. She knows the church. It's one of the oldest in Paris, across the Seine on the Left Bank, and somewhere she has planned to visit. As her driver begins the journey back to the residence, she tries to rationalize a decision. Of course she shouldn't go. It's one thing to exchange a few furtive looks across a crowded room, quite another to meet independently and alone. Isn't it a little juvenile to squirrel a secret note to someone in her position? Disrespectful even? He knows very well that she is married. But then . . . For now, she squeezes the note back into the slim internal pocket of her purse, somewhere it won't be seen, somewhere there is no chance of it falling from.

5

❧❦❧

Lucille
SATURDAY TO MONDAY
PARIS

By the time Veronique and I finished indulging our romantic fantasies last night, it was far too late to call Granny Sylvie. But she is top of my list this morning. I need to find out how much she knows about the identity of A&A. Why she sent me here, knowing full well the gown she asked me to return is lost. I need her to tell me how she came to own those incredible dresses and then why she gave them to Veronique's mother, because I've slept on it, and none of it makes any more sense this morning.

I dial Granny's number and wait an age for her to answer, running through a few horror scenarios in my head (fallen into the fire, starved to death) before the line connects. No one speaks, and I picture Granny trying to talk into the wrong end of the handset, mouthpiece pressed to her ear.

"Granny, it's Lucille!" I bellow.

"Lucille! Is that you?" All those miles away and I can still detect the excitement in her voice.

"Yes! I'm calling from Paris." I deliberately quicken the speed of my speech so as not to sound patronizing, which I know infuriates her.

"Wonderful! How is everything? How is the Athénée? Still beautiful after all these years, is it?" She sounds all wistful and daydreamy.

"Everything is just perfect, Granny. I am having a wonderful time. I had dinner with Veronique last night—"

"Oh my goodness . . . did you really?" she splutters into the phone.

"Yes, she's great."

"Did the two of you get on well? Was it a lovely evening?" Her voice is clearer, stronger for a moment.

"It really was. She's quite beautiful. Petite, glamorous in that understated French way. Loves a bit of romance. But more than that, Granny, she's kind. I like her a lot and I'm sure you would too. She cooked me dinner and we chatted for hours about her job at the museum—and the dresses." I try to nudge the conversation the way I need it to go.

I want to get her onto the subject of the dresses. I know from experience that conversations with Granny on the phone can be very taxing, for both of us. With no face in front of her to read for conversational clues, she often gets annoyed with herself and loses focus. "She showed me *all* the dresses, Granny."

There is a pause long enough for me to consider repeating myself before she adds, "Oh, that sounds wonderful."

I expected her to be more excited about the dresses, but she sounds distracted, and I sense she's going to end the call.

"The thing is, Granny, she has more of your dresses, not just one. Did you know that?"

"Does she still have the Debussy?" Now she's getting excited.

"Sorry, the what?" I'm trying to remember the roll call of dress names that we ran through last night, but it's hard. That bottle of red we polished off isn't helping my powers of recall.

Granny has no such problem. "Sequins, feathers, blue. *Exquisite.*" She's gone all breathy.

"She does!" Yes, that one I do remember.

Granny lets out the strangest sound.

"Are you okay, Granny?"

"Such a special dress."

"But the Maxim's is missing—although you know that, don't you?" I allow a hint of good humor to lace my voice. I'm not cross with her, how could I be? Just baffled by the whole thing.

"Oh, I know. But finding it will be the fun part."

"That's why I'm here, isn't it? For the dresses? But there are eight of them, Granny, not just one. And actually, two of them are missing. And do you know about the cards that accompany each dress? And what about the initials, A and A? How is this all connected to you, Granny?" I blurt it all out, feeling certain she'll be as confused as I am, but her response comes with clarity.

"Which dress are you going to start with, Lucille?"

"Start with?"

"It will be easier if you start at the beginning. It will make more sense that way. Don't be tempted to jump around. Stick to the dates."

My God, none of this is a surprise to her at all. She knew exactly what I was going to find at Veronique's apartment last night, as well as what would be missing. Which only makes me wonder what else she isn't telling me. What other surprises are in store?

"You know all about this, don't you?" I suddenly feel incredibly tense.

"Well, more than I let on, that's true. Follow the dresses, Lucille, let them show you the story. Then bring it all back to me."

"But why, what does any of this have to do with you? I don't understand."

"Neither do I, my darling, not all of it. But I hope by the time you return that I will. I have lived with not knowing for quite long enough."

I hear her take a deep inhalation of breath to steady herself and gather her thoughts.

"I am a very old lady, and it is no longer in my power to find the answers. But you can, Lucille, you can do this for me, and for yourself. You can retrace the story and finish it, once and for all. It will be worth it in the end, I'm sure. Good luck, my darling."

And then I think she actually hangs up on me, because the line clears, and I can't ask her a single other thing.

I SPEND THE NEXT HOUR LOST IN A SWIRL OF MY OWN THOUGHTS. None of which make sense. I head to the hotel pool and commit myself to fifty lengths. But I'm so distracted I keep losing count and give up, my lungs screaming from the surprise exertion. I try to force myself to relax in the steam room, but then listen to the sound of my own breath getting increasingly panicked as the fog thickens around me. I can't bear it for more than a few minutes before I force the door open and suck in mouthfuls of cool, clear air.

I keep coming back to Granny's words. *Stick to the dates*, she said. Well, I can't visit the location of dress number one, the Cygne Noir, because that was "home." Whose home, and where it is, remains unanswered, but what about number two? The New Look jacket and skirt that A wore to Dior, a boutique I can see from the window of my hotel room. I've no idea if it was *this* Dior boutique that A would have visited, but it seems lazy not to go and have a look, so I dry off and think about the least offensively casual thing I have packed to wear before I head over there.

THE BOUTIQUE, ALL SIX FLOORS OF IT, GREEDILY CLAIMS THE block, bending around the corner onto rue François, and is swathed in a temporary covering that seems to glow blue and gold. It has a fairy-tale quality, as if suspended in time, untouched by pollution or architectural modernism. Which is all very well and good, but according to the sign it's also closed for renovations and won't open again until next year. And I could actually cry. I stand there gazing up at it, feeling like I've fallen at the first hurdle, when a smart lady in a neat suit emerges from within.

"Just glorious, isn't it? The trompe l'oeil facade evoking all the magic of another era, the colors, Dior's favorites, of course. It's like being transported back in time to 1946 when he opened, when this was his very first boutique."

"Really? This was the original building?" If I can't get inside, perhaps I can at least glean a little information from her. "My grandmother was living in Paris in the early fifties. I was really hoping to get inside for a sense of what life might have been like here then."

"Not possible, I'm afraid, not for some time." She's starting to walk away. "We do have the temporary boutique on the Champs-Élysées though. You could head there. There's a courtesy bus to take you." She points to the minibus parked a few feet away and overflowing with excited Japanese tourists.

"Thank you, but I'm not sure it would be the same. It has to be this one. I was hoping to chat with someone who knew about the dresses, who might be able to bring them to life for me." This is what Granny wants, after all, me to work it all out for myself. The way my face has collapsed seems to spark a little sympathy, because she stops, glances back toward my hotel, and adds, "Then head to the Plaza Athénée. There's a little bookshop on the second floor, run by a lady called Nancy. She was one of Dior's favorite mannequins back in the day. She knows more than most."

And with that, she's gone, heels clacking over the cobbles away from me. I glance back toward the hotel, knowing if I head there now it will only be to seek comfort in the room service menu. I glance at my watch, and it's one hour until Bettina's closes. It's going to require a very sweaty speed walk, but this day needs a positive result, so off I set. Nancy will have to wait.

I STAND OUTSIDE THE SIMPLY TITLED BETTINA ON RUE MONT-orgueil, thinking this simply can't be it. It's tiny and sandwiched between a busy café on the right and a greengrocer on its left, like it's occupying a narrow alleyway that never should have been built on. It reminds me instantly of one of those dated out-of-town hair salons back home. The sort Granny's friends willingly spend half the day in. Somewhere I wouldn't dare set foot in, even if my roots were three months overdue and I had a job interview that afternoon. The window is stuffed full of what looks like a load of old jumble to me. There are posters taped all over the glass advertising various local events, and in between them I can make out the clutter that is spilling forth inside. If I had an expensive piece of couture that I was aiming to resell, would I bring it here? I don't think so. This has got nonstarter written all over it.

But it's my strongest lead, and with ten minutes until the shop's closing time, I clatter through the door, sounding a bell that will immediately alert the owner to my arrival. The shop is indeed no wider than the exterior. It's little more than one slim corridor that runs through to a curtained changing room, a counter with an ancient-looking till on top—not that I imagine it's used much—and one high stool. The air is musty and stale, and my breath shallows as I attempt not to inhale any more than I have to. There are rails running down either side of the shop, with probably three times the number of clothes wedged on them than there should be. I can see pulling anything out will take some muscle and probably dislodge several other items. Above the rails is shelving that is piled high with folded pieces, mostly knitwear. Granny's dress is never going to be among this lot.

If the clothes say nothing of the world of couture, then the man working here also conveys nothing of an appreciation for high fashion.

Or my arrival so near to closing time. I watch as his shoulders slump the second he sees me. He actually lets out an audible sigh, tilting his head sideways as if to question why anyone would be inconsiderate enough to arrive at this moment.

"I'm about to close," he says in perfect English, immediately identifying me as a non-native. He picks up a set of keys and turns off a light in the back room.

"Sorry, I thought you closed at noon?" I offer, trying to smile through such an unfriendly welcome.

"We do. You have six minutes, and it will take me that long to close up."

He's much younger than I'm expecting and looks almost as out of place here as I do, in his low-slung jeans and a Rolling Stones T-shirt, a camera swinging from his neck like some sort of style statement, me looking like Annie Hall in wide-leg cream trousers and an oversize Dad blazer that should have taken me to California or New York City, not this forgotten, dusty corner of Paris.

"This is a real long shot, but I am looking for a particular dress."

He's got his back to me now, bending down behind the counter to reach his backpack. He doesn't respond, so I plow on.

"It's not for me. It's a dress that used to belong to my grandmother, and I think it may have been brought here some time ago."

"How long ago?"

"I think back in the fifties."

He looks at his watch, huffs, slides his bag off his shoulder, and dumps it onto the counter.

"My grandfather, who owns this shop, was a meticulously organized man. If it came in, he would have recorded it. Whether it is still here now is a different matter, but . . . what's your grandmother's name, and can you be more specific about the date?"

"It's Sylvie Lord, and I think it would have been early fifties, but I can't be sure."

"I'm definitely going to need more details if I can help you. Otherwise we'll be here all year, and . . ." He glances at his watch again. "You're out of time today. Was it definitely your grandmother who brought the dress in?"

"Oh, no, it wasn't! It was a friend of hers." Only now am I realizing I don't actually know Veronique's mother's name. "Her daughter is Veronique . . ." I'm waving a hand around, trying to insinuate the mother's name will come to me at any moment, when I know full well it won't.

"But it wasn't the daughter who brought the dress in?"

"No."

"So, we don't have a date and we don't have a name?" His eyes are over my shoulder on the door of the shop, clearly desperate to be heading out if it.

I place my hands on the counter, keeping my eyes fixed on him.

"Please, I'm not in Paris for long and I have to find this dress. It means so much to my grandmother and I promised her I would bring it back. It's a Dior dress, if that helps?"

"Dior?"

"Yes. It had a name, hang on . . ." I rest my forehead in the palm of my hand and close my eyes, willing my brain to reach back inside itself and extract this one vital piece of information that might convince him to be helpful. That's all I will ask of it today; come on, think, think. "The Maxim's, that was it!" I triumphantly fling my arms in the air, as if to prove I haven't made this whole thing up.

"Never heard of it, and I have to go. I'm late. We're open again on Monday morning. Come back with some information that might actually help us trace it, and maybe we can have another go."

I can see from the dismissive look on his face that he doesn't expect to ever see me again.

"I'm not sure I'll even still be here on Monday, but please, here's my number." I scrawl it on an old receipt pulled from the depths of my bag and place it on the counter, where it stays, because he's already at the door. "Just in case you remember anything that might help." Then I'm back on the pavement, and I watch as he throws a leg over his moped, yanks on his helmet, and speeds off without even the briefest look back at me.

What would Granny think if she could see me now? Incapable of holding a man's attention long enough to convince him to help me. Not in possession of even the basic information to piece all this together. An hour's painful walk back to the hotel ahead of me and pinning all my hopes on an old lady who once modeled for Dior and, with my luck, probably won't remember the first thing about those days or how they might be relevant to this increasingly wild goose chase.

NANCY, UNLIKE MR. FRIENDLY AT BETTINA, HAS GOT ALL THE time in the world for me. I find her sat at a shiny wooden table in the bookshop, sipping a cappuccino. But as soon as I explain myself, she is up, out of her chair at a speed that belies her age, pulling books from the shelves and turning straight to the pages that feature her younger self—one gliding down stone steps as her long black woolen skirt flares out around her and another with her hips pushed forward, a white-gloved hand resting on the glossy black belt at her waist. Then she talks me through the couture dressmaking process in the richest detail, enlightening and confusing me in equal measure.

"Every piece of a new collection was made as a toile with a plain white cotton to gauge the cut, the line, and the shape. The seamstresses would pin the fabric to a dummy first to make sure the engineering was right." She's illustrating all this by pointing to the relevant photographs in the books, completely ignoring the queue of customers that have started to fill the room.

"They might make sixty toiles before they started eliminating the

ones they weren't happy with. Only once they were satisfied did I have
to walk back and forth in the toiles, so Dior himself could check the
movement and if the proportions were right. I can still do the walk."
She's up again, hands wedged to her hips, snaking across the carpeted
floor with an elegance and confidence I don't think anyone in her audience today is expecting.

"Then different fabrics would be draped across me. I saw Dior ask
for thirty different samples of black wool once before he settled on the
best one. And all the while I had to stand absolutely still, which is an
awful lot harder than it sounds. The following day, he might change
his mind and we'd start all over again."

I'm enthralled. All this, to make one dress.

"People thought we mannequins had a glamorous life." She slides
back into her seat, folding her legs at the ankle. "But it was incredibly
hard work. In the weeks leading up to a show, we'd start at ten a.m.
and rarely finish before eight p.m., sometimes as late as midnight.
We'd eat, sleep, and smoke all squashed up together in the *cabine*, the
dressing room, gossiping and writing our love letters. But not one of
us ever complained, we were the ambassadresses of fashion, and my
goodness, did we know it!" No one, least of all me, is about to contradict her.

"Did you ever model a New Look jacket, Nancy?" I ask.

She closes her eyes. It's the first time she has fallen silent since I sat
down with her.

"I certainly did. A truly unforgettable piece of magic. Was your
grandmother lucky enough to wear one?"

"She owned one, yes."

"My goodness. If it comes your way, look after it well. It will be
imprinted with memories and secrets that have remained silent for
decades—I hope you are intuitive enough to hear them."

I feel my skin prickle as I thank Nancy for her time.

. . .

I KILL A FEW HOURS ON THE HOTEL'S PRETTY ENCLOSED SUN TER-
race with my book, sipping strong French coffee and listening to Camila Cabello's "Havana"—why does everything have to be a reminder
of all the places I haven't been to? My thoughts turn to Mum. How
much I would love a hug right now. Some words of encouragement. I
decide to call her, something I should really do more often but don't
for fear of trespassing on her precious time. But I decide it's worth a
try on the off chance she is between meetings and might have a few
minutes to spare.

Her assistant answers the phone, and I have to give my full name
before she realizes it's her boss's daughter calling.

"Oh, right. I'll see if she's free."

I imagine Mum then, visible to her assistant through her glass office wall, shaking her head or wagging her finger, silently signaling not
to connect my call.

"She's quite busy, Lucille. She has asked if it is something specific,
or can it wait?"

How many seconds of the day would it cost her to just take the call
and ask me if I'm okay?

"I'll hold if I need to, but I would like to speak to her, please." I flick
the handset to speakerphone, predicting this won't be a short wait.

Twelve minutes she keeps me listening to the nauseating hold music
before finally she's there.

"Yes, Lucille? It's a manic day, I'm afraid. You've picked a bad one.
We aren't all lucky enough to get our weekends off."

"Is there any such thing as a good one?"

"Probably not. How can I help?" I can hear the stress in her voice.
How tight she sounds from not breathing deeply. I imagine the half-
eaten sushi on her desk, abandoned to impending deadlines. I hear other

voices, people filing into her office and pulling up chairs. Whatever meeting is about to start, she has chosen not to delay it to take my call.

"Are you joining us, Genevieve?" The question isn't intended to be one, I can tell that even from where I am.

"I'm going to have to go. Sorry."

"Before you do, Mum, I just want to say, you have worked for that company for a long time. You're very senior and you deserve some respect, and if your daughter calls in the middle of the day, it's probably for good reason. You should be able to spare her five minutes without judgments being made about your professionalism."

"You're right," she says sadly. "Unfortunately, it doesn't work like that."

"Genevieve?" More irritated now, the speaker may as well just order her to hang up.

"I'll try to call you later," she sighs in a quiet voice, clearly not wanting her private life to intrude into the corporate world, "but I'll be here way past nine p.m. Bye."

I FINISH MY COFFEE AND THINK ABOUT WHETHER THERE WAS EVER a moment for Mum—maybe after I was born or when her marriage was falling apart or as the promotions rolled in and the workload swelled—when she questioned if her life choices were the right ones. Maybe the first time it was made clear her family life and how happy she was in it were of no interest to her bosses. A fleeting moment of opportunity when she could have altered the course of her life and our relationship. Said no. Or just no more.

I wonder why a woman so outwardly strong seems so incapable of using that word at work. Why there was never a breaking point that didn't need to mean the end of professional ambition, just a reimagining of it to make room in her life for love. For me.

I pick up my phone and text Veronique.

If I'm to solve this mystery, I need your help, Veronique.
Are you in?

She responds immediately with a line of thumbs-up emojis.

Yes I am, Lucille! I'm here for you, whatever you need!

I think I love her already.

I MUST BE THE ONLY PERSON IN THE WHOLE OF PARIS WHO WASTES my Sunday chained to a laptop in my hotel room. Perhaps I'm more like Mum than I care to admit. Obviously, news of my late arrival back to London goes down spectacularly badly with Dylan, who shows precisely no interest in my emerging story idea. He's not concerned about my deadlines as such, just his next freebie trip. This time it's him; his wife, Serena; their two kids, Ben, nine, and Holly, six; and of course the nanny, so they can off-load all the childcare. I've organized so many of these trips for him now that I know every one of their passport numbers by heart. I can tell you exactly what their springer spaniel will need at the kennel in the time they are away. I can probably recite the brief to the cleaner without calling it up on-screen, I've delivered it so many times.

In three days, they all depart for five nights of skiing in Courchevel—and I'm the wet lettuce who has to liaise with the hotel public relations team to ensure everything is organized, minute by minute, with zero room for error. Return flights, private limo transfers up and down the mountain, massive supply of anti-sickness pills on hand, lift passes, ski and boot hire, Serena's spa bookings, the kids' ski school sessions, all restaurant reservations, one husky excursion, a group ice-skating outing, and God help me if any of it isn't micromanaged and little Holly doesn't get her *chocolat chaud* on time. Last time they went skiing, Dylan actually messaged me from the resort to report how disappointing it was that there was "no boot-warming service" and moaned that it made getting the kids to the slopes each morning "a living hell." All I could think was where I'd like to shove his ski pole.

I thought when I took this job and became a travel writer on travelsmart.com I might actually get to do some travel. That was the carrot that was dangled to me at the interview, anyway. But no, it seems I just organize it all for the boss. I'm a glorified PA who gets tossed all the minor writing assignments no one else wants, usually with an unspeakably tight deadline. But might that change, if I deliver a piece at the end of this trip that shows him what I am really capable of? Maybe then I will be assigned a bigger piece. I'm craving a complicated itinerary to somewhere no one's heard of, multiple stops, visa applications, tightly timed internal flight connections. I'd like to see my name sitting proudly at the top of the site for once, not a small *extra reporting by* credit at the bottom, where no one can see it.

Anyway, it may have taken most of the day, but the bookings are done and I am now ready to attack this city first thing tomorrow morning.

I decide to treat myself to something astronomically expensive from the minibar and climb into bed with it just as a text lands from a number I don't recognize.

> You have to come back to the shop. I've spoken to my grandfather, he knows the Maxim's. I'm so sorry I didn't help you yesterday. Come tomorrow. We open at 11 a.m. It's important. Leon

The thought of seeing that rude guy again does not fill me with any joy whatsoever—but the idea of some much-needed progress to report to Granny does. I take a few undignified gulps of peppery red wine and let its warmth and this good news lull me into a wonderfully sound sleep.

COME MONDAY MORNING, I PAY MUCH MORE ATTENTION AT BETtina the second time. It's impossible not to when the place is so chockfull of things most of us would have decluttered from our homes without a moment's hesitation. There is a break in each of the clothes rails that run on either side of the shop where two large dressing tables, minus their stools, sit. They are overflowing with all sorts of curiosities. What look like original designer's sketches with fabric measurements annotated up the side are stuck to the wall next to cards filled with postage-stamp-size swatches of brightly colored materials. There is a run of names added to the former, and I wonder if they are the models who wore the gowns, or the women who made them. There is a framed black-and-white photograph of a model in a tweed jacket circulating a small room of immaculately dressed men and women, every pair of eyes focused intently on her. I glance past it to original invitations to Dior's new season collection shows dated 1952 and a stack of old French *Vogue*s from around the same time. A box of weathered paper dress patterns spills onto one table that is strewn with old mismatched buttons, what I think are enamel jewels, and an aerial shot of Paris that is doubling as a tablecloth. It's impossible to tell if this is a deliberate display or the result of years of neglect.

"Thank goodness you came back" is the greeting I get this time. Leon, as I now know he's called, comes striding out from behind the counter and ushers me onto a stool on the opposite side of it. This better be worth the blisters that are now covering both my feet.

"I need to explain a little about my grandfather so that what I have to tell you makes sense." He's keen, nothing like the man I encountered on Saturday.

"I'm all ears." I allow a little cockiness to enter my voice now that my presence seems important to him.

"My family has owned this shop for more than eighty years. It might not look like it now, but back in the fifties, it was a thriving business. My grandfather's contacts book was unrivaled. His knowledge of the different couture houses even more so. Every well-dressed woman in Paris—and those aspiring to be—knew of him and his shop. Trust me, I've listened to his stories over and over again since I was a little boy—I'm not exaggerating." He remains standing, studying my face to check I am paying attention.

"But what does this have to do specifically with the Maxim's? You said he knew it."

"Since he had to step back from the business and I agreed to help him out temporarily, he has occasionally talked about a specific dress, although I'm sorry to say I never paid too much attention. Everyone in the family has heard the story." He pulls a second stool in close and sits facing me, creating a level of intimacy he seems to think matches the importance of his tale.

"One afternoon, back in the midfifties, a young woman entered the shop sobbing and clutching a gown. She was distraught at having to part with the dress, and vowed she would be back for it as soon as she could afford to buy it back from him." This must be Veronique's mother, just as she told me. I nod, encouraging him to go on.

"She assumed, naturally, that he would sell it to the first person who made him a decent offer. And according to him, he could have sold it ten times over in the first week alone. It was Dior's time, he said—postwar Paris, and women's clothes were feminine again. The demand for his work was huge, according to my grandfather. His popularity in America was really taking off." He leans forward, his eye line directly matching mine, and smiles broadly like he knows good news is coming.

"But what I didn't know, until I spoke to him yesterday, was that my grandfather was so moved by the woman that the dress was never put into the shop. He was determined it should never be sold and that one day she would return for it."

I immediately feel my back straighten. "Are you saying he's kept it for all these years? Really! My goodness, what an incredibly kind thing for him to do. It's still here? And I can see it?" I'm firing questions at him now, mirroring his smile because this could be it, a genuine breakthrough.

"Yes. Although I never knew it. He told me it's locked in a wardrobe in the back room, one I assumed must have contained old accounts and paperwork that he wanted to keep safe. When I saw him on Saturday night, he said I looked stressed. I was explaining that I'd left the shop a little late and it had set me back for the day. When I told him why I was late leaving—that was you, I'm afraid—he started to put two and two together. It wasn't until he mentioned the name of the dress—the Maxim's—that I realized you had used the very same name." I suppose it is reassuring that he was at least partially listening to what I was saying that day. "He has insisted that I help you. Practically ordered me to, in fact."

And he doesn't look unhappy about it. *This* is more like it, and I can't help but lift a knowing eyebrow at Leon.

"Quite something, isn't it? But, listen, there was never just one Maxim's dress made. It was couture, and so each dress was specifically tailored to precisely fit the woman buying it, but lots would have been made. How can we possibly know for sure this was *your* grandmother's dress? There is a chance this is all just some strange coincidence, isn't there?" I can see in his face, the way his eyes are widening, that the slight downturn of his mouth is preparing for disappointment, but that just as much as I do, he wants this story to end well, the way it should. He wants to give his grandfather the news he has waited so long for.

"If you'll let me see the dress, I will be able to tell you if it's the one." I think about my call with Granny. Her duplicitous plan in sending me here, knowing I couldn't simply collect what I had been sent to—and why on earth she felt the need to be so secretive. I think about Veronique, who said if the dress isn't here, we are looking at a dead end, or at least a *much* bigger research job with the near-impossible task of identifying a starting point. And I think about how much I want a win, something to go my way so I can tell Granny I did it, even if I'm not entirely sure what the bigger *it* is yet. Please just let this be the dress. I can see from Leon's wide eyes that he's hoping it is too.

"Come on." He leads me through to the back of the shop, where there is even less space to move. We are surrounded on all sides by floor-to-ceiling box files, and I can see the daunting task we would have faced had the name of the dress remained a mystery too. On the back wall, facing us, is a small whitewashed wooden armoire.

"It's in there. I've unlocked it for you." He looks like he doesn't want to be the one to open the door, so I step forward and do it myself.

And there it is. One dress, hanging all on its own, its exterior loosely swathed in brown paper. I can feel the expectation of the moment climb up the back of my throat. All this time. In a nondescript corner of Paris, in this tiny unassuming shop, where there is barely room to move and this precious dress has been given its own wardrobe. How much longer might it have hung here if Granny had never bought my Eurostar ticket?

"I need to touch it," I say as I look back over my shoulder to where Leon is standing respectfully back where we entered the room.

"Be my guest." He nods his approval.

I let my fingers gently crawl up under the paper, acutely aware that I'm the first person to touch it in decades, lifting the paper away from the shoulders of the gown. The jet-black velvet under my fingers is butter soft, and I immediately sense the thrill of having something so lavish next to my skin. It's incredibly glamorous and yet sublimely understated all at once.

"Did your grandfather tell you anything else about this dress? How it was made? What it might have been worn for?"

"He did, actually. It would have been owned by someone of significant wealth. Because of the way it's constructed, it's impossible to get it on yourself. Something about separate pieces and lots of zippers? Basically, you need someone to help you get in and out of it. The square neckline would have been quite daring at the time, he said. It's cut very low, and it's only the velvet bow that is keeping it modest."

If there was any doubt, now I know for sure this dress was never made for my Granny Sylvie.

"It was named after a fashionable Parisian café of the time."

I lift the wool skirt of the dress, feeling its weight, knowing exactly what I am looking for, and start to feel my way around the silk petticoat underneath until my fingers settle on a label. I turn it over and there they are, the embroidered initials I am hoping to find: A&A.

"It's the dress," I declare. "It's initialed, just like the others in her collection."

I hear him sigh loudly behind me, but it's one of relief and not irritation this time.

"So, there are *more* dresses?"

"Yes, this is number three. There are eight that belonged to my grandmother that she has asked me to return to her, but one other is also missing." Even as I'm saying it, I know I'm going to have to find that one too. "It seems there might be more to my trip to Paris than I originally thought. My grandmother sent me to collect the Maxim's, knowing it was not where she told me it would be."

"Okay, well, my grandfather never mentioned any initials or any other dresses that were brought in by the same woman, but I could ask him, just in case he knows anything more—although I'm pretty sure he would have mentioned it."

"Any help would be wonderful, thank you." I do a bit of a dramatic eye to the skies, but only because I hope it will make him take pity on me, see the difficulty of my task, and maybe offer to help. "My mum is so busy with work and, to be honest, the two of them are not particularly close, so a lot of what my grandmother needs falls to me—although her requests are not usually as elaborate as this one!"

He smiles like he completely understands my predicament. That while I never asked to be sent on this mission, I can't refuse it. I can't let Granny down.

"I get it. There isn't much I wouldn't do for my grandfather either. I may not always understand his motives, but as long as he needs my help, then he'll get it. Do you have any idea what you're looking for?" I sense the slightest hint of an offer of assistance coming my way and seize on it.

"Not really. But every dress has a handwritten note. The one for the Maxim's said 'I need you as much as you need me.' Whoever owned the dress at the time wore it to meet someone in the church in Saint-Germain-des-Prés."

It works. His eyes light up, just as I know mine did at Veronique's on Friday night.

"Wow. You can sense the longing in every word." I can't help being a little impressed that he's happy to admit that to me.

"I know. And things only get more intense from there. So, that's where I'm heading next, the church. I'm starting at the beginning. The plan is to visit each of the locations, in date order, and hopefully all of this will start to make some sense. I'm hoping a story will emerge that I can take back to my grandmother."

He looks seriously intrigued now. "Look, it's a very famous church but a fair way from here, the other side of the river. Do you know where you are going?"

I do, but I'm not going to tell him that. This is what I was hoping for. A local, and quite a handsome one at that, to take all the hassle out of the logistics for me.

"No, not really." I poke around in my handbag as if looking for a map or guidebook I know isn't there, while he peers back out into the shop, perhaps reminding himself that the doorbell hasn't rung once since I entered.

"I'm sort of heading that way. Well, I was going to drop into the Pompidou, that's where my real job is. I work as a photographer there." Okay, that explains the oversize necklace. "But I could take you to the church first, if you like, just to make sure you find it okay? My grandfather did insist I help you. If he was in the shop today, he would have accompanied you himself, so I feel a little obliged. Besides, it will be a great story to tell him."

"Yes please!" I'm not even trying to sound surprised or cool about it.

He's already pulling his coat on as I glance back nervously at the Maxim's, wondering how much it might cost today and how on earth I'm going to pay for it.

"He'll insist that you take it."

"Sorry?"

"My grandfather. He will want you to have the dress, in case you're worried about the cost. He's always refused to sell it. And besides, his business days are long behind him now. The old romantic in him has taken over."

"Wow, I mean, that is so incredibly generous. I'm not sure I can just . . ." But Leon isn't going to tolerate any more faffing around from me.

"Come on, it will be perfectly safe here for now. But if we're going to do this, I should at least know your name."

"Sorry, it's Lucille." I hit him with the biggest smile I've got, hoping it will go some way to conveying how grateful I am.

"Come on then, Lucille. Let's do this."

6

Alice
OCTOBER 1953, PARIS
THE MAXIM'S

Fifty steps. She counts every one that propels her from the church entrance under the bell tower, through the nave, and toward the altar. Her nerves deepen with each slow, steady stride. And yet she doesn't turn back. She doesn't even look back to the entrance to assess how quick a retreat she could make if she changes her mind. Glancing up at the vast vaulted ceiling above, Alice feels a great sense of insignificance in this reflective place of principled contemplation. Why did she come? She doesn't want to answer that, not yet. But now that she is here, surrounded by all these people she imagines are trying to better themselves, can she honestly say her intentions are all good?

Six minutes to noon. She's early. Force of habit. The church is reassuringly busy. Tourists, school groups, locals who have come to pray, study, and think, weave in and out of the pews and into the side aisles, disappearing out of sight behind towering columns and through supportive stone archways that stretch and open wide to keep this magnificent building anchored. She avoids eye contact with every one of them, terrified if she looks, they'll see on her face what she is barely able to admit to herself yet. She wants a pleasure that is not hers to seek.

She's too tense to sit, so as she reaches the top of the nave, Alice turns left and diverts her course through a heavy iron gate and into the smaller series of chapels that sit in a semicircle behind the choir pews. Despite the watchful faces of saints on the stained glass windows above, the space back here is deeply shadowed, more private. She walks past several wooden confessional boxes, allowing her mind to drift to the many secrets they hold, wondering how long it might be before she returns to take a seat herself, before she stands in front of a marble statue of the Virgin holding an infant Jesus. She can't draw her eyes away from the purity of it. The stark simplicity of mother and child. It's not the religious significance that holds Alice in place, it's the way the sculptor has captured the duality of a mother's delicate touch with her determination to protect. Golden angels rest at the Virgin's feet, and she is flanked by tall candelabras stacked with slim, tapered white candles, their smoke adding a ghostliness to the darkness. She considers taking a step onto the black-and-white-tiled floor inside the chapel, but just as her body starts to tilt forward, she is stopped by a gentle hand on her shoulder.

"I'm so glad you came," he whispers. In the glow of the candlelight, Antoine's face looks flawless, like he has been carved from marble. But then he smiles, and every one of his features loosens and warms. He looks relieved to see her. He ruffles a hand back through his hair like he's trying to distract himself from something he really wants to do. To kiss her? Alice feels the tension stretch between them, and then she moves to defuse it.

"Antoine, it's so lovely to see you again." She extends a hand to be shaken and watches as he stares at it, making no attempt to take it. Her forced attempt at formality is all wrong and she knows it. He smiles more deeply, more reassuring than mocking, loops an arm through hers, and turns her right so they can complete the semicircular walk together. The implication is clear. He's not going to pretend for anyone's benefit that this is some sort of business meeting. Alice allows herself to be turned, then unhooks their arms, refusing to make eye contact but continuing to walk slowly beside him.

Why did she come? What good can possibly come from it?

Every movement she makes feels performed and studied. The way she is holding her gloved hands in front of her skirt, the upright angle of her chin, the deliberate movement of her feet, suddenly so unable to function naturally. But despite the awkwardness she feels and the doubt that is multiplying inside of her, the magnificence of the building is impossible to ignore. Her eyes dart from pillar to window, flash to the painted artworks above and the tombs set below their feet.

"I knew you would love it." Antoine beams. "My brother loved it here too." He is paying no attention to the flow of people walking in the opposite direction toward them. His neck is angled left so he can watch her and how she responds to everything, forcing everyone to alter their path to bend around them. "I fell in love the first time I set foot in here too." Only now do his eyes leave Alice's face. "So many of the great Parisian artists have been inspired in this church. The way the light falls and refracts, the balance of light and shade, the dependence of the stronger colors above us on the earthy, darker tones below. Just being here is a reminder of the power of creativity—and of our own insignificance in the world."

She can't disagree. Alice feels the tension seep a little from her shoulders. Antoine has articulated so well the sense of harmony that radiates from every windowpane and carefully carved stone archway. She feels more peaceful, here, in his company. She takes a deep breath, grateful for the Maxim's dress that Anne helped her into this morning. With every snap she fastened on the bodice and its camisole, the gentle rise of the zip up her back and the one from her collar to her waist, nipping her inward, Alice hoped she wouldn't ask about her appointment today.

When Anne inquired if she would be needing her gloves, all Alice could manage was a curt "yes," concerned that anything else might lead to further questions and a direct lie on her part. But the finished look is perfect. The Maxim's might not be one of Dior's newer pieces, but Alice has the confidence to order what she knows looks best on her, never succumbing to the pressure to order what's new over what's right. And this is a dress that speaks outwardly of substance and respectability.

"Thank you for inviting me." The conversation pauses, Alice a little lost for anything more to say. "Did your mother enjoy the Dior show?" It's a convenient question to break the intimacy he is trying to create.

"I guess so. She never buys much, but it seems very important to her to be seen at those things. Such a needless waste of her time, and mine. I get dragged along because she can't bear to go alone." He sighs deeply. "I wonder at what age one can stop feeling controlled by or indebted to one's parents?"

It's not how Alice would have expressed it, but she perfectly understands the sentiment. The schools she attended, the subjects she studied, the friends she made, how she dressed, whom she sat next to at dinner parties—wasn't it all closely governed by her own parents? There aren't many things in life she's considered doing without first wondering how they might react.

"Whatever the age, I'm not sure I'm there yet," sighs Alice. "Anyway, your mother is very welcome to come with me next time, if she'd like to?"

Antoine arches an eyebrow like he knows that will never happen. That he wouldn't want it to and that, very soon, neither will Alice.

THEY COMPLETE THEIR JOURNEY AROUND THE CHAPELS, ANTOINE allowing his fingers to brush against her gloved hand. More than anything, she wants her fingers to link with his, to feel the tension in his grip, but she holds back, caught between the role she has to play and the one she'd like to. They take a few steps back down into the main church, making their way along the opposite-side aisle now.

"Do you live nearby, Antoine?" Alice can't bear the quiet that's settled between them, giving her the room to question again what she is doing here.

"Yes, I'm very close. The rue des Beaux-Arts, right here in Saint-Germain. The Right Bank is not for me. Too formal, too official, so cold. I prefer the narrow back alleys and the hidden courtyards of this neighborhood. There is an energy, a creativity here that doesn't exist in the broad boulevards on the other side of the river."

"Where I live, you mean?" Alice allows herself a wry smile.

"Yes, I'm afraid so," he deadpans.

"Well, maybe you have a point." They stop in front of a statue and Alice reads the inscription. Our Lady of Consolation. She can't make her eyes read any further because she can feel Antoine's face set on hers again, studying her, drawing closer than is probably appropriate, making every muscle in her slender neck tighten. She can feel herself weaken.

"Do you know what makes me so sad about this church?" he whispers.

"Tell me." His admission of sadness softens Alice. It's an emotion Albert would never confess to, whether he felt it or not.

"How forcibly muted everything is. Perhaps because of the position it holds, the job it has to do, and the people it has to serve. I'd like to strip it back to its original best because, beautiful and impressive as it is, I can't help thinking it's been neglected and taken for granted—and that shouldn't be allowed to happen."

Alice can't speak. It's such a beautifully observant thing to say, and she feels herself involuntarily drawn toward him, this man who is so perceptive—and unafraid to show it. Maybe she's reading too much into it, but it doesn't feel as if his comments are purely aimed at the stone surrounding them. Is there a comparison he is trying to convey?

She wants to have this conversation, to know if Antoine can see in her what she hasn't yet voiced herself. If in their three brief but powerful encounters, he has already understood her veneer, the doubts, the building uneasiness, and the questions she has started to ask herself with alarming frequency. Yes, she wants to have this conversation, but she's frightened of where it might lead. The conclusions that might be drawn, the actions they'll lead to. But her silence only makes his questions more direct.

"Do you honestly enjoy living in that building?" He steps around to the front of her so it's impossible to avoid looking at him. His face is full of concern, and it tugs at something deep inside her that he has considered her happiness.

She wants to be honest with him, to reward his interest with some frankness of her own, but she's too well practiced at the official line. "The Hôtel de Charost? It's a great honor, Antoine. A position of privilege. We are playing our part in the history books. There is value in that, don't you think?" Instead she just sounds pompous.

"That's not what I asked you." He inches forward, searching for another response, allowing his hand to settle on her shoulder, then brush down the length of her arm. "Talk to me like a human being, Alice, not one of your official visitors. Can the rue du Faubourg ever feel like home? *Your* home? Do you have any freedom there to be the woman you are?"

He knows; he's read her perfectly and with such speed. Alice feels as if she is barely one more question away from tears, but she rallies, forcing the emotion back down.

"Well, I'm here now, aren't I? No one stopped me coming to meet you." What she can't say is that's because she never told anyone where she was going or whom she was meeting. Albert will be at his office and won't think about her day and what or who might be filling it.

Alice turns on her heel and starts to retrace her steps back the way they just walked. She thinks about her home. The imposing gray stone blocks of its exterior. The barred lower windows that look onto the Faubourg. The waist-high black stone pillars that line the pavement outside, each one linked by thick black metal chains. The armed guards' green century boxes. The official flags. The enormous black lacquered door that she has never seen open. If she was describing the building to a stranger, they might easily think she was speaking about a prison. There are the beautiful gardens on the other side, but they are surrounded by high stone walls, railings topped with spikes and the tallest trees preventing a view in. She stands at her bedroom window on the first floor sometimes and looks out onto the small green park beyond, where local people walk their miniature dogs and elderly men congregate to chat on a Sunday afternoon. Beyond that is the Champs-Élysées with its never-ending stream of tourists, explorers, lovers. People having unscheduled, spontaneous fun. The vision makes her long to see where Antoine lives, knowing it couldn't be more different.

By the time they reach the top of the aisle, her eyes are full of tears. One slow blink is all it will take to send one sliding down her cheek. Antoine sees her emotion and sighs heavily, then directs her into a row of pews that are facing inward toward the nave in front of two beautiful statues of angels. Then, with no warning, he takes hold of her arm and slides a finger under the cuff of her sleeve.

She visibly jumps.

"Your snap. It's come undone." He indicates the small fastening that tapers the sleeve, now hanging open.

"Oh, thank you." The warmth of his fingers on the delicate skin of her wrist, tracing across her veins, makes her entire body loosen. His touch is so gentle, so intimate, as he keeps his fingers there a second or two longer than necessary before reclining onto the cold wood of the pew. She realizes with an ache in her heart that she's been so deprived of this tenderness. That she craves it. And here he is, so willing to offer it to her, if only she could let him.

"How old is he?" Antoine angles his body toward her, his elbows propped on his knees so he can lean in closer.

"Forty-eight."

"Nearly double your age?"

"Twenty-three years older." Alice tries to keep her face as impassive as possible, knowing full well the point he is making. Then, when he refuses to respond, she asks, "Why are you asking me this?" The attention is wonderful; Alice can't deny it. But she can't tell if this is all a bit of fun for Antoine, some macho game playing, while her emotions get tossed around, before he moves on to his next challenge.

"Why do you think?"

"I thought you asked me here today because you wanted some advice about your career. That you were keen to get to know Albert perhaps, thinking that he might be useful to you." It's an absolute lie and she hates herself for telling it.

"No, you didn't." He's patient with her, not cross or irritated that she can't say what she means.

"Antoine. Please, I can't just sit here and . . ."

"Yes, you can. There are many things I could envy about your husband, Alice. I've seen the way he is. How ambitious men want his ear. How beautiful women want his company. The power and influence he has. Those qualities are attractive to many people, I understand that. And, of course, he has you. But please don't confuse my mother's ambitions for me with my own."

"And what *do* you want, Antoine? What is it that you seem unable to find in my world, that you want for yourself? What's in your future?" She wonders if he's even considered it.

"I want to feel things, Alice, to experience the real world in the way people beyond the government walls seem to." He has swung his legs toward her now, his hands clasped between them, almost resting on her lap. "Not because it's considered cultured, not because it's something that will make me look intelligent and informed at the next dinner party. Not from a book. We're living in Paris at one of the most expressive times in this city's history, Alice, and what are we doing with our time? Entertaining pompous foreign dignitaries, pretending to care about people we would never have genuine friendships with? Not being cared for ourselves? Do you want another twenty or thirty years of that?"

She can see the passion in Antoine's face and wishes so much she could match it with her own. The intensity of his confession. Like she's the first person he's ever been able to say this to. She wants to return the favor, to make him pleased that he chose her to share it with. But she's going to disappoint him. Her marriage means she's from the very world he seems to despise. The image of her wedding day intrudes on the conversation. The uneasiness Alice had felt in her mother-in-law's company, when it should have been nothing but joyous. She deliberately shifts the conversation.

"Surely you can convince your parents of the validity of another career if politics is not for you. There are plenty of things you could do, things that might not be so disappointing to them. You mentioned your brother. Is his relationship with your parents difficult too?"

His eyes drop to his lap.

"He died three years ago."

"Oh, Antoine, I'm so sorry."

"Thank you. I still miss him very much."

Alice watches as he clenches his fingers tightly together, using the discomfort to distract himself from the sorrow of losing a sibling.

He gazes up toward the domed ceiling.

"Thomas was the one who first brought me here. He knew I'd love the colors, that I'd find it inspiring. But in answer to your question, no, his relationship with my parents was very different from mine. He was training to be a doctor, and about halfway through his studies he left the girl he loved behind and volunteered to join the war effort. Within a few weeks he was one of the medics with the troops in eastern France. He was just twenty-two. I was sixteen. I cried when he left."

"But he made it back? He survived the war?"

"Yes, although I sometimes wonder if it might have been easier if . . ." Antoine's words are lost to the acoustics. "If he was the golden son before he left, he was awarded a hero's status on his return. It was as if him coming back to us symbolized an end to everyone's suffering and restored a sense of hope. Our parents believed all the bad days were behind us."

"And what about you? Did you share their optimism?"

"My parents idolized Thomas for all his academic achievements and his bravery . . . but to me he was simply the very best older brother. He encouraged me to sketch, even when he could see how much it irritated my parents. He secretly paid for me to have private lessons with an art scholar he knew through school. He'd buy me new materials and reference books, accompany me to places he knew would inspire my work . . ."

"But?" Alice delicately nudges the conversation forward, wanting to know all there is to know about Antoine and his background.

"I ruined it all, and I've been paying for my mistake ever since, trying to live the life my parents want me to lead. Trying so hard not to disappoint them. I've begged them to let me pursue my love of art, to enroll at art school. They've seen my sketches, they know they're good. But as a career? There's no way. They see no value in it. It's whimsical. Unrealistic. Not what a young man like me should be doing with his time. I'm as trapped as you are."

She wants to question him further, to understand why he feels responsible for the breakdown of his relationship with his parents, but he has shifted upward in his seat, visibly breaking off from the subject.

Alice feels her own body stiffen at the conclusion he's drawn about her own life. Is that what she is? Is that what he—and others—see? A woman who is trapped? She allows herself the smallest cursory look left and right. Is anyone overhearing their conversation? A small group of students and their guide have gathered behind the pews the two of them are sitting on and in front of the winged statues.

"I understand why you will want to leave now, and of course I won't stop you. But please, meet me again. It doesn't have to be anything more than a walk, Alice. That's all I ask. A chance to talk, to get to know each other."

He reaches for her hand, and their fingers briefly lace together, hers equally searching out his this time, squeezing together in secret agreement.

"I think I need you as much as you need me."

He is interrupted by the voice of the guide behind them. "They are the symbols of piety and fidelity," he announces, explaining the significance of the statues to his students.

Alice and Antoine's eyes momentarily meet before she stands and walks briskly toward the exit with no goodbye and no direct answer to his request.

It isn't Antoine's face she sees as she leaves the church, it's Albert's, on their wedding day, the slight strain of panic across it when he saw her deep in conversation with his mother, Greta, and younger sister, Rebecca. She remembers the emotion that poured from his mother that day, the endless tears, the delicate white handkerchief that seemed permanently pressed to her eyes.

"She feared this day would never come," explained Rebecca. "She is so proud that Albert has not allowed the sadness in our family to define the man he became."

Alice immediately understood. "Losing your father to such a cruel disease so young must have been terribly hard for all of you."

She visibly shuddered as the conversation sheared off abruptly with Rebecca's response. "That's not true! Our father wasn't ill."

Then it was Albert's firm hand on Alice's arm, steering her away, but not before his mother quietly added, "It is up to Albert to correct any inaccuracies, Rebecca. Today is not the day."

Alice withheld all her questions, hoping Albert would offer his own explanation, until the final day of their honeymoon, not wanting to burst the bubble of happiness they had both enjoyed.

"Never ask me about him again," he had barked. And the subject was closed, the bond of their easy togetherness broken.

Alice looks for her driver. Her eyes have started to pool with tears again, but there is a glimmer of something else inside. A curiosity for the world Antoine has described and the woman she might be in it.

❧

7

Lucille
MONDAY
PARIS

I have never seen a church quite like it—not that I exactly make a habit of hanging out in churches. But the colors! From the moment Leon and I step inside, it's a total assault on the senses, which is so unexpected. I'm prepared for quiet, meaningful good thoughts. No smiles. Definitely no chatter. But this is, well, a celebration. A happy place that has been stripped of all the dirt and grime that must have built up in the hundreds of years it's been standing. This place is alive, singing to the sound of the giant organ that sits high above the entrance. There are no pews, but rows and rows of wooden chairs that seem much friendlier.

I worry it's just me having a moment of awe, but then I look at Leon, who has already made it halfway up the aisle and paused, hands on hips, head thrown backward, shoulders tilting the same way to allow him to gaze at the ceiling above.

"Whoa!" he half shouts back at me. And he's right to. The ceiling, arched way above us, is painted royal blue and speckled with hundreds of gold stars. It's flanked by walls that are covered at the top with the most vivid painted scenes from the Bible, which look perfect enough to be photographs. There are bloodred and bright turquoise columns, and gold detailing everywhere. Even the tiny candle votives you can buy and light in memory of a loved one are a cheerful mix of green, red, orange, and blue.

"Why have I never been here before?" marvels Leon as the two of us start to track a circular route around the perimeter. "It's just mind-blowing."

"Isn't it!" Why have I never been *anywhere* before, is what I'm wondering.

"It's not exactly an obvious date location, but isn't it fascinating to think that A and A met here all those years ago? That we might be walking in the same tentative first footsteps of some undiscovered love affair?" I realize as soon as I unleash the words that he'll probably think I'm a slushy romantic, but if he does, his face doesn't give him away. He's too busy gawping at everything around him, touching the paintwork, sniffing the air, snapping away with his big camera. He's quite hilarious to watch.

"I'll have to bring my grandfather here so he can see where the Maxim's was worn. He would absolutely love that. It would kind of bring the story alive for him."

We pass into a darker part of the church, and I quicken my pace and pull my wool coat tighter across my chest. It's cold, dank, and feels very different, even gloomy, compared to the main body of the church.

"Do you think it would have looked much different back in the fifties?" I ask Leon as we return to the lighter space near the altar, in the spotlight beaming from three stained glass windows above us.

"According to this"—he's reading a small pink leaflet that he's picked up somewhere along the way—"there's been a major restoration project underway since 2015, so I'd say so, yes. For a start, this wouldn't have been here. It was discovered in 1999." We've both come to a stop in front of an unfinished statue of the Virgin Mary and child. It's the oddest thing. Her face looks distorted, not having felt the refining final touches of her creator's hand. Her bended arm is without a hand, and the baby she is holding is nothing more than a crude, barely human outline of what remained locked in someone else's imagination. From the torso down she is nothing; she disappears as the stone is bluntly sheared off. It's the saddest thing, this object of beauty that was never allowed to reach its glorious conclusion. A story that will stay forever unfinished. I can't help wondering what stopped the sculptor in his tracks. To have got so far and then felt he couldn't or shouldn't go on. I'm distracted by the sound of Leon rubbing his hands together for warmth, and I realize the tips of my own fingers and the end of my nose are icy cold.

"We need hot chocolate," offers Leon with a smile. "I know the perfect place. Come on."

WE DART ACROSS THE SMOOTH GREEN-AND-CREAM FLOOR TILES and take the last free table at the back of Brasserie Lipp, which is just across the square on the boulevard Saint-Germain. The waiters, all older men, are dressed in the smartest penguin suits, thick white aprons knotted tightly around waists, the short cut of their black jackets emphasizing bellies that were left to their own devices years ago. We're seated in a corner where the brown leather banquette that runs the entire left-hand side of the restaurant curves around under the stairs. The perfect spot for planning and plotting. Perhaps A&A came here too? It looks like it's been here forever. The painterly ceiling with its heavy black iron chandeliers and the pretty floral tiles that line the walls around giant mirrors all seem to talk of a different time. I can almost hear the dark wooden paneling creak under the strain of all those memories—all the glamorous parties it must have witnessed. Who might have danced on these café tables, draped themselves over the smooth curving banister, or sunk deep below the restaurant to the cloakrooms to steal a kiss from someone they shouldn't? The crease-free white tablecloths only serve to make it feel more special, and I pick up a menu printed entirely in French apart from five words at the top: "No salad as a meal."

Sometimes the French get it so right.

Leon orders the hot chocolate, and I'm suddenly aware that I'm sitting in a chic café in Paris with a man I barely know. Granny would be proud! I am determined not to start getting all awkward about this, especially as he has the relaxed demeanor of someone who just rolled out of bed.

"I feel bad I've taken up so much of your time today, Leon. Are you sure you're not being missed at the shop?"

"What do you think?" His broad smile is back, so I'm reassured he's not just being polite. Sitting as close as we are, side by side, it's my first real chance to take a proper look at him. His hair is a dirty blond, pushed back off his face and streaked with the memory of last summer's sun. I wonder how he spent it. In whose arms he spent it. His skin has none of that English paleness that borders on gray at this time of year. He's dappled with freckles across his nose, and lightly tanned, enough to make his green eyes sparkle a little under the soft lighting. He also has just enough facial hair to make him look intriguing but not unclean.

"I'm just sorry today didn't really throw up any real clues or developments for me to share with my grandfather. Or for you, of course." He curls the side of his mouth downward in sympathy.

"Well, I suppose all the answers were never going to fall conveniently into my lap, were they? But I think the location of their date, if we can call it that, tells us something about A and A, don't you?"

"That they shouldn't have been meeting? Or else why the church? It's a great foil if they had been seen by someone they knew. Much easier to explain away than getting caught, just the two of them, hunched over a cozy restaurant table together."

Given that we are doing exactly that ourselves, Leon does make me briefly think of my own lack of boyfriend. But the arrival of our hot chocolate is all it takes for that flicker of sadness to evaporate.

Our waiter is back with a small white china jug that is full of steaming chocolate the thickness of soup. No frills. No marshmallows, definitely none of that synthetic squirty cream I normally drown mine in at home. Leon pours us a cup each and then nods for me to take the first taste. And of course, it's heaven. Silky smooth, filling my mouth and coating my tongue; the sweetness and the heat swim luxuriously down my throat, and all I can think is how much more I want. And not just of this but of Paris too.

Of just a little more adventure.

I notice the look of recognition on Leon's face, like he's remembering the first time he ordered hot chocolate at Brasserie Lipp, and as he raises his own cup to his full pink lips, my eyes linger there longer than is probably decent.

"Thank you," I say when he lowers the cup and licks his top lip unselfconsciously.

"For what?"

"For your time, for closing the shop and coming with me. You were only supposed to be dropping me off, not coming on the full tour," I remind him.

"No thanks necessary, I did it for my grandfather, really. He'll be hanging on my every word when I relay all this to him later. And I suppose you've done me a favor. They always say you never see the beautiful places in your own city, and today, thanks to you, I managed to tick one off. My arrangement with the Pompidou is quite casual, I'll text them and let them know I'll make up the hours another day."

"And I'm not keeping you from any*one* else?" I'm fiddling with the spoon, trying to make the inquiry sound super casual. It just seems that someone as obviously handsome as Leon would have a partner, and I don't want to get excited about stealing some more of his time if it's out of the question.

"Ha! No, no furious girlfriend about to burst in here and demand to know who you are, don't worry."

"Okay, good to know." I am willing myself not to blush at this point.

"What about you? Anyone waiting for you back in England?"

I don't know why I falter over my response. It should be a straight, easy no, I don't have a boyfriend, but somehow it comes out as "Well, no, not exactly. There is someone who is lingering, and shouldn't be, but that's my fault as much as his" before I drain the last of my hot chocolate, more to give my mouth something to do beyond blathering on, I think.

"You are funny!" chuckles Leon for some reason. "Let me just send that text before I forget."

While he taps away, I notice a woman sitting on her own on the opposite side of the restaurant. She's a little older than me but not much, wearing a smart black skirt and jacket. She's eating a crème brûlée, one that's not far off the size of your average dinner plate. She's enjoying every spoonful she raises to her mouth. She's not flicking through her phone, reading a newspaper, or fiddling with her handbag. She's focusing on nothing more than eating her dessert, just sitting with herself. There is nothing self-conscious about her at all. She seems very at ease with her own company. She reminds me of why I always longed to travel. To gain that window, however small, into a foreign life that isn't yours but that you understand and maybe aspire to. Perhaps to realize people aren't so different.

She also makes me cast my mind back to the Christmases after Dad left, when Mum and I would go away for the holidays, just the two of us. It was nothing like this. It was never the authentic experience I now realize I craved. The house was always the best in whatever town or village she chose. But every year my heart would sink when on day one the chef she'd hired would arrive and I knew this was yet another place we'd never get to explore where the locals ate. A driver meant we never got lost in the backstreets, never discovered a hidden beach or a tourist-free patch of sun that might be just ours for the afternoon. I wanted adventure and realness. Mum wanted ease and convenience, a different view from the window while she worked, as she always did, missing everything that was new and interesting—missing another chance to get to know me because deadlines couldn't be missed and targets had to be hit.

At first it made me angry. What was the point of going away together if we weren't going to be together? Then, as I got older, I realized how sad her situation was. Earning all that money, but never having the freedom to enjoy it. What pleasure could there be seeing it accumulate in a bank account, knowing whatever she spent it on came with a second price tag that could never be fully repaid to bosses who would never be satisfied? I think she saw spending the money as a way to alleviate her guilt. If I couldn't have *her*, then I could at least go on a better holiday than anyone else in my class because of her.

There's something about this woman's confidence in particular that makes me want to stay right here in Paris, now that I realize, unlike back then with Mum, that I can. I can do it my way until I've followed the path of all of the dresses and maybe worked out how A&A's story ends, just as Granny asked me to do. I cast my eyes back toward Leon. Could it be *our* story now? Mine and Leon's? Might he want to share the journey with me and really throw some light on why Veronique's mother got so upset about a dress—why his grandfather was right never to sell it? He certainly seems interested enough so far.

"So, aside from the one dress that's still missing, and the Maxim's you've found—there are six more, is that right?" He's tossed his phone back on the table and his attention has returned to me.

"Yes, six more, all in my hotel room now, with their accompanying notes. Some of the locations the dresses were worn to I recognize, like a visit to the Orangerie Museum, but others don't mean anything to me, like Les Halles. But it's what else the notes say that's so intriguing. On one she has simply written, 'The kiss that saved me.'"

He sits for a moment, taking it all in, maybe feeling the futility of trying to solve the mystery with relatively so little to go on. If only Granny had sent me here while Veronique's mother was still alive. She could have given us so much more detail and information, facts that Granny is holding back for me to discover myself.

"Oh, who are they, Leon? How am I ever going to find out and connect this to my grandmother?" Please let him say he'll help a little more. I know I have Veronique, but together the three of us can do this, I just know it.

"You're going to need a guide. And you're going to need more time in Paris. I can fix the first one for you, you'll need to sort the other."

"What?"

"Where is the next location? What dress comes next after the Maxim's, and where did A wear it?"

"It's dress number four, and if I remember rightly, it's called the Batignolles. She wore it to the Jardin du Luxembourg."

He looks at his watch, throws some euros onto the table, and then slides his arms back into his jacket. "Okay, I've got some catching up on work to do today, but how about I meet you there tomorrow, late morning?"

"Really? You would do that? You've got time?" Bloody hell, this is amazing.

"To be honest, no, I don't really have time, but I've been meaning to shoot parts of the city for months, and this will force me to get it done." Then he pauses before adding, "And something's telling me there is more to this, and the only way I'm going to find out if I'm right is to join you on your mad romantic chase across Paris, Lucille." There's the megawatt smile again.

And I have to be honest, I'm not sure in this moment what I am most happy about. That I'm staying in Paris, or that—even if he's only doing it for the story—he's staying with me.

8

Alice
OCTOBER 1953, PARIS
THE BATIGNOLLES

Albert's side of the bed is empty again when Alice wakes this morning. The sheets are smooth and unwrinkled, obviously undisturbed by his body while she slept. She has no idea if he spent another night working in his office . . . or in someone else's bed. Her chest rises and then falls deeply with the weariness of thinking about the answer to that.

She lets her mind wash back over the months since they arrived in Paris. She knew the move here would be hard. That Albert's job would present challenges—new people to impress, making a mark for herself where others were poised to see failure. She just never imagined she would be doing it alone. Does the fault lie in her own naivety, or a cruel manipulation on Albert's part? In the days when he was not yet sure he'd won her, he painted a picture of a partnership, the two of them masterminding a successful future together. She saw in those months a softer Albert, one whose eyes studied her, whose relief she could feel when she walked into a room to take up her place at his side. He visibly relaxed in her presence. But now, in Paris, it's as if his ego has ordered that version of himself to stay hidden. Like he's ashamed of the Albert who once let his fingers frivolously trace across her sun-warmed belly as they laughed together about the chubby babies they'd love one day soon.

The small clock on her bedside table reads eight fifteen a.m. It won't be long until Anne arrives with Alice's breakfast. Then, when she's dressed, she'll meet Albert downstairs. He has asked to run through the details of several upcoming social events they'll be hosting, not least of which are the Queen's birthday celebrations in April next year. With a guest list nudging three hundred, plus Christmas just a couple of months away, there is little time to waste. Once the decisions have been made, it will be Alice's job to mobilize the staff and make sure the entire thing is hosted to perfection.

She hears Anne knock softly at the door before she steps into the room carrying a small silver tray with Alice's plate of bacon and eggs and a china pot of English breakfast tea.

"Good morning, Madame Ainsley," she half whispers, probably imagining Alice is barely awake yet. The room is still in semidarkness, so she places the tray at the end of the bed and then walks toward the double-height windows and pulls back the heavy drapes, casting a cold light into the room. Alice notices how Anne's eyes flick to Albert's vacant side of the bed. And then how she deliberately pretends not to notice it. She wonders whether Anne knows things that Alice doesn't. Does she see and hear things when she is moving around the residence late at night? Would a few quick questions now, in the privacy of her bedroom and with Albert occupied elsewhere, answer whether her husband is a faithful man or not? It's the uncertainty that feels more unsettling than the answers themselves.

Alice tried to broach the subject with her own mother once. She wasn't seeking her view on Albert specifically, but more on Alice's role as a high-ranking diplomatic wife. Is it guileless of her to expect his loyalty? Should she gently question and confront him on where he is and what he's doing? She can't bear feeling so unsure—of herself, of her marriage, of the man she loved enough to marry. Didn't she? Doesn't she still? Is it that her feelings for him have receded, or is she pulling back to protect herself because she feels rejected, squashed under the weight of his all-consuming ambition? She misses what they had, however fleetingly they had it. When he would bother to ask how she was and be interested in her answer; when he would absentmindedly reach for her across the breakfast table, look at her like she was everything he ever wanted. Why did it all stop almost as soon as they unpacked their lives together in Paris? Did she do something wrong? Whatever the truth of it, her self-doubt feels like it's breeding inside of her, growing stronger by the day.

Her mother spoke of *the burden a woman must bear* and how *we do what we do for the love of our husbands*. It was foolish of Alice to ask, she reasoned afterward. She'd seen the sacrifices her mother had made to ensure her own marriage was unbreakable. Why would she advise a more outspoken approach for Alice now? She had learned the art of obedience early. Hers was not a childhood filled with hugs and kisses. She was rewarded for her compliance and her ability to amuse herself with the gift of another prim doll with piercing eyes and a shiny face, or with a trip to the beach with her nanny for another ice cream she didn't particularly want.

As Alice watches Anne prepare for the day ahead, she remembers how much she and Albert laughed in Italy. It still makes her smile. The slightest thing seemed to set them off. A foolish mispronunciation at the food market that led to great confusion. An overly officious waiter. They had fun. *He* had fun. How did that man become the one who knocks on his own front door so the staff can let him in? It feels like something has switched off inside of Albert. Like he ticked romance off his to-do list on the honeymoon, and now there are better, more important things to focus on that don't involve her. Now they have been swallowed up, into the big bureaucratic beast that is the British government overseas. The alternative is almost too shocking to contemplate—that it was his behavior in the run-up to his proposal and on their honeymoon that was the act, and the real Albert is the man she now finds herself married to.

But why show her that man if he never intended to remain that way? She thought at first the Albert she saw in Paris was the impostor. A newcomer who was keen to stamp his authority on his new position, responding to his seniors who made clear the need for a strict hierarchy between his personal and professional life. Now she has to wonder, was his acting performed in Italy, the first scenes unfolding in her parents' drawing room when he needed her to believe he could be kind, loyal, and passionate? The awkward exchange on their wedding day with his mother and sister remains unexplained. Was his final act the promise of the babies he knows she longs for, delivered when her heart was full of excitement, her head swimming from the flow of Bellinis magically arriving at their honeymoon table? Much like the role Albert vowed to find for her, the promise of children has slipped away, relegated by Albert to something the future may hold when the important business of the day has been dealt with.

Anne lifts and plumps the pillows behind Alice's head and helps her sit up before placing the tray across her lap.

"Is there anything specific you need me to do for you today, Alice?" Anne perches on the edge of the bed, awaiting instructions, her usual small lined notepad and pencil in her hands.

"I just need the driver later to run me over to the Jardin du Luxembourg at three p.m., please. No need to bother Albert with this. He has a lunch from one p.m., so that's the last we'll see of him until this evening."

"Of course, Alice. And do you know what you would like to wear today, or can I suggest something?"

"The Batignolles, please, with my fox fur gloves and a hat. Perhaps you can pick which one you think looks best?"

Anne visibly lights up at the opportunity to show off her styling skills, relishing the trust Alice is showing in her. And it only makes Alice want to do more to please her.

"Why don't you choose something for yourself, too, while you're there?" She smiles, nodding her head, trying to convey it's a serious suggestion.

"Sorry?" Anne glances back over her shoulder, confused. "What did you say, Alice?"

"Why don't you borrow something? Whatever you like, I don't mind. Surprise Sébastien and wear something special for dinner tonight. We're not far off the same size, there's plenty in there that will fit you. Really, whatever you like. And I'm in no hurry for it back."

"I couldn't, Alice, it wouldn't be right. It's very kind of you, but honestly . . ."

"If you don't choose something, I will, so go on, help yourself."

And it's like Alice has fired a starting pistol. Anne launches herself at the dressing room, then stands there, looking from one end of the rails to the next, hands held in front of herself, not knowing what to touch first.

"Go on!" encourages Alice. "Don't disappoint me, Anne!"

When she does eventually start to move apart a run of tweed jackets in various shades of black, she does so with immense care, her eyes studying every button and appliquéd detail, delivering a range of appreciative noises that make Alice laugh quietly to herself. She would have made the suggestion much sooner if she'd realized how much joy it would bring her friend.

"Is this okay?" Anne is holding aloft a petite silk black-and-white-spotted neck scarf.

"Oh, for goodness' sake, Anne." Alice is howling with laughter now. "An entire room full of the most exquisite couture Paris has to offer and you choose that?" She's exaggerating, of course. The scarf in question is from Chanel, an unnecessarily extravagant gift from a political wife hoping to win favor.

"Sorry." Anne is laughing, too, now. "I didn't want to be too presumptuous."

"Well, your punishment for choosing so badly is that you must keep the scarf, I never want to see it again, but you must also take the lavender-green tweed suit I sometimes wear it with." Alice starts to hunt for it along the rail as Anne shakes her head. "Don't even think of arguing me out of the decision." She knows full well how much Anne adores the suit. Last time Alice wore it, Anne actually sat down to admire her in it, despite their both knowing Albert was waiting downstairs. "I hope Sébastien loves it as much as you and I do.

"Oh." Alice stops abruptly. "The Maxim's is back already . . ." She catches herself too late.

"Yes, I had it cleaned. I hope that's okay?"

"Of course, yes, sorry, I just wasn't expecting to see it back so quickly." Alice isn't making any sense. Anne always has her items cleaned immediately, never giving Alice cause to question the timing.

"I should update the cards . . ." Anne pauses as Alice turns and walks away from her, back into the main bedroom.

"Yes, I would like you to update the card, please." Alice can hear the slight nervousness in her own voice. She has wanted to confide in Anne on the subject of Antoine since he first attended their drinks party, and now that they have met alone it feels more . . . legitimate, like there is more to say on the subject. Telling her will make it real, incontrovertible, and that feels right after everything that was said in the church. There are also the practicalities to consider. If she intends to see Antoine again, she will need Anne's help, and the one thing she cannot do is lie to her friend, even if it is merely bending the details about her whereabouts.

Anne follows her, heading for the desk and the small black box where the cards are kept. "I'll just grab the relevant one. So the date would have been . . . ?"

"It's not the date that's important this time, Anne, but who I was with. Please come and sit next to me." There is no one more qualified for the job of understanding confidant. Alice just hopes her judgment is right, and Anne won't think any less of her. She'll be incapable of hiding her true feelings if she does.

"I met Antoine du Parcq there. You may remember he was invited to the embassy for drinks earlier this month, with his parents? The night I last wore the Cygne Noir."

"Yes, I remember." Already Anne looks concerned, unsure of what this conversation is about to reveal.

"Well, we talked only briefly that night. But I was captivated by him. I think he felt the same too." She is speaking slowly, trying to choose her words carefully. "He said he saw something different in me, Anne. Do you know how wonderful it felt to hear that?" Alice's eyes shift toward the box of cards. "Then quite unexpectedly we bumped into each other at the Dior show. That's when he asked me to meet him again. Just the two of us. He suggested the church at Saint-Germain and said he would wait all day if he had to." Alice's face has lit up with the memory of it. "And so I went. That's where I wore the Maxim's."

"And what happened?" The two women are seated next to each other on the small chaise at the end of the bed, Alice the only one smiling.

"He said a lot of things I needed to hear. He was painfully honest, not caring if he offended me at all. But he wasn't judging me, Anne . . . 'I need you as much as you need me.' That's how he put it. I can't stop thinking about it."

"Alice . . ."

"He seems to understand a lot of what I'm feeling without my ever having shared it with him, with anyone, even you, Anne. And more than that, he trusts me with his own feelings too."

"I haven't been blind to it, but I can't pry. You didn't need to tell me. If the subject ever arose, it had to come from you first, I hope you understand that?"

Alice nods, noticing how Anne holds eye contact, encouraging her to continue.

Alice takes a deep breath.

"To use Antoine's word, because it is precisely the right one, I feel . . . trapped. Deceived."

She is too far into her confession to stop now. "Albert isn't the man I thought I was marrying. I *wouldn't* have married this Albert. He doesn't care about me at all—and there is very little I can do about it."

Anne smiles gently, like this is no surprise at all, like she has spent the past year privately questioning the choices Alice has made.

"And you've tried to talk to him? To explain how you feel?"

Alice lets the question hang between the two of them for a few moments. "You've seen enough of Albert, I think, to understand the futility of that approach. But yes, I have tried, many times."

She feels Anne's hand tighten around hers.

"I have to ask, Alice—do you think this is wise? Shouldn't you try to solve your problems with Albert before you complicate the situation by allowing someone else to get close to you?" Alice feels the warning in Anne's eyes, but not strongly enough.

"I've spent the past days telling myself the very same thing. But it's been over a year, Anne. Do you honestly think it will get better? That he will become a better husband? If I'm ever going to be happy again, something has to change. He won't and I can't, not in this life. I doubt in this marriage. I would never have chosen this, but when I left the church that day, I felt differently, more understood than I have in so long." She pauses, wondering whether to go on. "I'm seeing Antoine today, this afternoon."

Alice watches Anne close her eyes, as if she wants to be supportive, to give Alice her approval to enjoy this glimmer of lightness. But she's always been practical, her Anne, and is duty bound to remind her of the dangers too.

"I will do everything I can to help you, but I must caution you to be very careful, Alice. What is it you want from this? And if you get it, will you know what to do with it? Will it, in fact, cause you a much bigger problem than the one you already have?"

"Maybe I just need the supportive friendship of another man more my age? Or maybe it's more than that, I don't know. It might sound weak, but he makes me feel more like the woman I want to be. He makes me want to put myself before anything else."

"That isn't weak, Alice, but it is the exact opposite of the life you came here for, whether you realized it or not. You need to be very sure he is worth the risk."

She can't be sure. Of Antoine or Albert or even herself right now. Alice is back on her feet, no longer listening, drawing a line through their conversation. Anne stands, too, but is forced to direct her comments to Alice's back.

"I am speaking to you purely as a friend, Alice. And what sort of friend would I be if I told you not to put your own happiness first? I do want you to be happy, but please, take it very slowly. You've only seen what Antoine has chosen to share with you so far, and nothing else. How much can anyone truly know in a few short meetings?"

"Perhaps you are right." Alice turns to face Anne again. "But every minute I spend with Antoine brilliantly highlights what little happiness there was before him."

"Okay, so he can maybe help you decide what is *missing* from your private life, but whether he is the man to provide that for you? That is an entirely different question. One that surely takes much longer to be convinced of."

The two women stand, looking at each other, Anne's face pleading for caution, Alice's impassive to the warning. Anne makes one final attempt.

"Enjoy his company, if you think you can do it unnoticed. Be happy, Alice. Remember how he makes you feel, create some wonderful memories and use them to inform your decisions, but . . ."

Alice hears the permission and elects to gloss over the caveat that is implied.

"Can you also please call Dior and order me the Debussy dress from the last show?"

"Yes." Anne reaches for her notepad, slipping seamlessly back into her professional role.

"But when you do, please warn them that I need it very soon. I don't want to go through all the usual fittings. They have all my latest measurements. I'd like them to do it quickly." Alice pauses as Anne finishes scribbling, and then tries to justify the urgency. "We have lots of big events coming up and, well, I just think it could be perfect for one of them."

"I'll update the cards too."

Anne smiles. It is perhaps impossible not to when, for the first time since Anne arrived at the residence a year ago, Alice seems to have a genuine reason to smile.

ASKING HER DRIVER TO DELIVER A HANDWRITTEN NOTE TO ANtoine's home on the rue des Beaux-Arts after she cut their meeting short in the church was reckless, stupid, and quite possibly futile. She has no idea if he's read it or if, as he suggested, he'd still like to join her for a walk in the Jardin du Luxembourg today. But she's calculated the risk is worth it, because standing next to him in total silence she would feel more appreciated than she does sat at Albert's lavish dining table, dripping in jewels. The way Antoine is with her feels thrilling and terrifying, and either way she knows she wants more of it—of him. The way he makes every part of her body switch on.

Antoine's been present in her thoughts practically every day. They've done nothing wrong, so far, and it can stay that way. But she wants to be out of the residence, in the fresh air, to feel seen and be heard by someone who isn't interested in anything other than her. Is that so wrong when it feels so needed, when she has been so starved of it by the man who promised to put her first? And maybe she does want to dive a little deeper too. To hear more of what he has to say about her life.

How it could be different.

Besides, meeting a man for a walk through a public park may well be mild compared to what Albert would consider acceptable for himself.

THE MEETING WITH HER HUSBAND GOES EXACTLY AS ALICE MIGHT have predicted. Just like she imagines most of Albert's business meetings might be conducted. It's short, to the point, an efficient exchange of needs and preferences, and then she is effectively dismissed with a hefty to-do list to carve up among the staff. He has a lunch date with *associates* at Chez Georges in the second arrondissement and doesn't want to be late. There is a mild moment of panic toward the end of their meeting when she thinks he is going to request the driver she has already booked, before he confirms he is being collected. She stands back at her bedroom window when he leaves half an hour later, looking onto the courtyard when a sleek black Jaguar pulls in. It's not a car she recognizes, but clearly it is known to the guards, who would never have let it enter otherwise. The driver is obviously well known to Albert, too, since he chooses to sit in the front passenger seat. The last thing Alice sees is the long blond hair of the driver drape over the shoulder of her husband as the two of them embrace before the car pulls back out onto the rue du Faubourg.

Perhaps it's telling that her first thought, her very first feeling, is one of utter stupidity. How could he, yes, but how could *she* not have fully understood his capability? His brazenness? Tears fill Alice's eyes. She feels their heat on her cheeks, fueled by anger more than sorrow.

All those hours questioning her own behavior, when he clearly applies no such self-assessment. Perhaps the despair will come later in the quiet of another night alone when she will look again at the splendor of her bedroom and know she could live with much less, with a man who truly loved her. For now, it's more a boiling frustration. Of course, a man prepared to lie about his immediate hope of becoming a father, to flatter her desires, ones he only ever claimed to share, will think nothing of giving himself to another woman.

Alice wonders what lies he's telling *her*, even as the wheels of their car are moving across the congested Paris streets. Perhaps he's telling her the truth, he's not sleeping with his own wife and hasn't been for months. Alice won't torment herself any further. She forces her breath to slow and closes her eyes, turning everything black until she feels a stillness, a resolve, the smallest release to think about her own needs. Is this how her own mother felt the first time she knew—before she decided to commit herself to a life of being second best?

Alice doubts she has the strength to be that dutiful.

ALICE ASKS HER DRIVER TO TAKE THE FASTEST ROUTE FROM THE embassy, cutting between the Grand and Petit Palais, over the Pont Alexandre, and face-to-face with one of her favorite views in Paris— the Hôtel des Invalides, its central golden dome towering above the low city skyline. From there they speed down the wide boulevards that border Montparnasse before bending back north to enter the park on the west side.

"Collect me from here in two hours, please." She confirms her return journey with the driver before making the short five-minute walk south across the park to the children's carousel, where her note suggested they meet.

She can hear the laughter and screams of the ride's passengers long before it comes into view. As she gets closer, she notices how its horses have seen better days. There are deep cracks in their legs, chunks missing from their wooden flanks, and paint peeling from their multicolored manes. But not one of the red-cheeked children astride them, enjoying their magical gallop, could care less. Alice smiles.

The noise takes her back for a moment to the seafront at Holkham Bay, the coastline closest to the family house in Norfolk, and how she envied the gaggles of children who always seemed to have someone to play with. She remembers the house always feeling so cold, not just the drafty corridors that were never heated, but the lack of laughter, no siblings to cause trouble with. She looks at the children flying round on the ride, bundled up to keep warm. She feels like she spent her entire childhood in a winter coat thanks to a nanny who felt fresh air was a cure for everything—illness, boredom, disobedience. The children today lean their bodies away from the horses, playing *jeu de bagues*, swinging a wand in their hands, attempting to hook iron rings as they pass around while an elderly man manually cranks the ride into action.

"You want a go?" comes a voice from over her shoulder.

Yes, she does, actually, despite knowing she won't get one.

"Antoine, hello. I wasn't sure you would . . ."

"Why wouldn't I?" He steps closer, immediately shrinking the space between them, sending her heart up into her mouth. "I have been hoping to see you again." He is wrapped up warm in a long black wool coat, his collar turned upward to frame his face beneath a homburg. It's a beautiful blue-sky day, but the cold bite is lurking in the background. She imagines what it might feel like if he opened his coat, pulled her into his chest, and closed it around the two of them. She's so absorbed by the image she can't speak, and they stand, looking at each other, wondering where the possibilities might take them in the next couple of hours.

"Shall we walk?" Antoine tilts his head away from the ride as Alice realizes she would probably say yes to anything he suggested right now.

She doesn't walk anywhere anymore. Nothing about the impracticality of the clothes she wears or her weekly schedule of commitments allows her to. There are people to do everything. To collect things, buy things, return things, to respond to any errand that may need doing. Antoine instinctively reaches for her hand, then changes his mind, looping his arm through hers in a gesture that could easily mean mere friendship.

Despite its relative bareness at this time of year, the park still looks beautiful. They pass apple and pear orchards, still bearing fruit in late October, and beehives dotted among the bushes, before they reach the orderly ranks of chestnut trees that file toward the view of the central fountain and the Senate buildings beyond. Alice is trying to soak in the views, but it's hard when he is so close to her and she can hear his breath moving in and out of his chest.

Most people have chosen to sit facing the building, but Antoine walks on farther. He takes her beyond the lake that's circled with children launching their tiny sailboats into its cold water and guides them both to a bench, where they sit with their backs to the Senate.

"May I buy you some tea?" he asks, looking around to see how far off the nearest seller might be.

"I would love one, but please let me get it."

"Okay." He's smiling like he understands what a novelty this is for her, and she's grateful he isn't about to make a chivalrous attempt to stop her from enjoying it. There is a small café to the right of the Senate building, so that's where she heads, leaving him watching her from the bench. She disappears inside for a few minutes, and when she steps back out into the park, he has procured a small sketch pad and is studying her. She slows her pace, allowing him as much time as possible to capture her. As she rejoins him on the bench, placing two metal cups of hot tea at their feet, she can see he has marked the outline of her navy dress perfectly.

"It's very good, Antoine. The shape is entirely in proportion. You only had a couple of minutes to do that." And it is. He's captured the way the collar sits high up on her slender neck and the two front pleats are angled over her breasts, defining her shape. The sharpness of his pencil has cut the bracelet-length sleeves off at just the right spot before her gloves begin. From her refined waist, two deep pleats drop down the front of the skirt in perfect symmetry. It's one of the most complicated day dresses Dior has created, according to the vendeuse at avenue Montaigne, with one single piece of cloth performing the near-impossible task of forming the front of the garment, and another the back. And yet, Antoine has reproduced it in mere moments.

But what of the woman wearing it?

There is no smile on her face. Her eyes are cast off the page, looking lost, as if they belong to someone else. How can she look so polished and yet so detached, so soulless? The way he has drawn her lips, tight and determined, is more severe than she imagined, and she immediately parts her lips to relax her mouth. Her hands, she notices, are stiff, her fingers outstretched, not as fluid as they should be. He sees someone who is coping, not living.

"Thank you. I have a very good memory. But I try to look deeper, to see the person underneath the clothes that hide them." He says it so nonchalantly, like he expects the words to have little impact. But for Alice, they are causing a deep swell of longing.

There has never been a moment like this in her life. Not even right back at the beginning with Albert when he was trying his best to impress her. It was never uncontrollable, as if her desire were moving beyond her. She enjoyed Albert's attention, she was flattered. He made her feel grown-up, like she was progressing with her life, no longer the superfluous third person in the house. But did he ever make her breath catch in the back of her throat? She doesn't remember it. She answered his questions at those dinner parties with a cool detachment, never believing they would lead anywhere. Not really understanding then that he wanted them to. Or that her parents did. What were her interests? Did she like travel? What foreign languages could she speak? Not once did her stomach flip, but the pleasure his attention seemed to bring her parents kept her just engaged enough. It was an opportunity to gain their approval.

The fun they had together on honeymoon, away from all the interested observers, when he loosened up wonderfully, seemed to suggest she'd got it right. But was there an undeniable moment of passion that convinced her they simply *had* to be together? Wasn't that what more frivolous women looked for, those not serious about their future? It was more a slow, informed understanding that everything about her and Albert was beneficial and a sensibly good choice, undercut by frequent reminders from her parents that she couldn't hope to do better. What else was there for her to consider? It wasn't like she needed to be sure he would support her career ambitions. In hindsight, it was more about his assuring himself that she was up to the task of being a future ambassador's wife.

"Do you speak to other women like this, Antoine?" Saying his name out loud, so close to him, feels wonderfully personal and intimate. "Are there other women that you sketch and try to convince to fall in love with you?"

He lowers the sketch pad into his lap and allows a deep frown to form across his forehead. "You shouldn't undervalue yourself like that. I can't think why I would need to." He catches her eye and holds it.

"Even if you never let me touch you, Alice, this is enough. To be in your company. At least that's what I tell myself. I want to see you smile more often. I hope to be the one to make you smile."

And like a fool, she does smile, then tries to halt it, and the two of them laugh together.

"Can you turn around so I can see the back of your dress again, please?"

Alice angles her legs to her right, away from him.

"I need you to stand."

She does as he asks, and for the first time since she stepped into the park this afternoon, she is aware of everyone around them. Faces that could be watching them, faces that might be known to her. She is about to sit straight back down when she feels Antoine's hands slide around her waist and meet in front of her. It's an intimacy she didn't grant, but it makes the skin beneath her dress instantly warm, and she imagines his hands dipping lower, the pleasure it would give her if they did.

"I want to feel how the fabric fits you." He runs his fingers gently backward to her hips, then lets them ease down over the folds of her skirt, lowering his head toward her neck. She can hear how uneven his breath has become.

Alice closes her eyes, seeing the imprint of the flowers that border the lake, lemon and orange chrysanthemums. She smiles again, more deeply and just for herself this time. She wants to remember this moment of unguarded abandon. She wishes she could allow herself to be held for longer by him, to feel his arms fold in around her, pull her down onto the bench, where they would stay wrapped up together, drinking tea and kissing for the afternoon, their faces hidden under the brim of his hat. She knows she's projecting a fantasy onto this moment that is dangerous to nurture, one that can only end in disappointment. But there are other feelings rising up within her that are stronger: desire and an overwhelming need to be touched.

"When can I show you the finished sketch?" Antoine asks as she sits back down, closer to him this time.

"Your parents are coming to the embassy drinks next week, aren't they? I will make sure you are added to the guest list. You can show me then—if the correct moment presents itself."

"You're really going to keep me waiting that long?" Antoine looks toward her, unsmiling, tilting his head sideways, like he might dip forward to kiss her at any moment. Would she stop him if he did? He's so close she can see the smooth, unblemished contours of his skin, the softness of his lips, the frustration in his jaw.

"I think I'll have to." She wants to tell him the wait will be every bit as hard for her, that she can think of nothing better than spending the rest of the day with him, but how can she? So Alice stands and gives Antoine one last smile.

"Wait. I wanted you to have this. I bought it before you arrived." He hands her a beautiful postcard of the carousel. "A memento of our time together."

Alice turns the card over to see one solitary kiss marked in pencil on the back. "I'm glad of one thing," she whispers.

"Of what?" Antoine takes a step closer to her so there is barely room for the breeze to pass between them.

"I'm glad you don't say those things to anyone else." Then she retraces her steps back to the west entrance, where she knows her driver will be waiting.

9

⤜❦⤛

Lucille
TUESDAY
PARIS

"I don't want to sound unreasonable here"—Dylan's voice is loaded with sarcasm—"but I'm struggling to understand why it's Tuesday morning and you're still in Paris when we had a nine a.m. meeting scheduled in my office. And now you're telling me you're not coming back today, and in fact you're not even sure when you'll be back?"

"Yes, Dylan. Sorry, it's a long story. Family stuff that I need to sort. It really can't be helped. I've never taken time off at such short notice like this before. I hope you know I wouldn't unless I really had to." Leon is standing in front of me, watching me squirm through the call. I need to hang up quickly before Dylan senses the mock seriousness in my voice.

"Well, I'm going skiing tomorrow, and you know how important this trip is. You've read my email about all the additional luggage needs, I assume, and that Serena's mum is joining us now?"

"Yes, of course." No, I haven't, but I will, *I will*. "It's all under control, please don't worry."

"I'm not going to worry, Lucille. Because that's *your* job. It's what *you* get paid for."

"Yes, absolutely, yes, it is, and I'm telling you everything will be perfect."

"Good, because the last thing I want is to find myself locked in a three-way of stress with my wife and mother-in-law."

"Quite. No three-ways with the mother-in-law." At this point Leon snorts so loudly I have to place my hand over the phone. "Leave it to me. I will run through all the arrangements again when I get back to my laptop later."

I'm not even sure if he hears that last bit, as the line goes dead and I realize as I jab the off button on my phone that I don't much care. A couple of weeks ago I would have cared a lot. The knot in my stomach would have sent me racing straight back to the office. Maybe it's finally having some physical distance from it that's making me realize quite how much Dylan's moods affect my own. How long does a means-to-an-end job have to last? Because even the thought of returning to the toxic low-level fear that Dylan encourages to breed among the team is making my stomach tighten. And this, what I am doing here with Leon and for Granny, feels way more important than whether Dylan's kids graduate to the green runs this season.

Obviously, I will make the booking changes, though, the second I am back to the hotel. I do not have a death wish.

Just as my phone is powering down, I see alerts for three missed calls from Mum, which is practically unheard of. Three calls in one hour is more than I typically get in a month. She'll have a list of things she wants me to bring back from Paris for her, no doubt. Well, she can wait. We're on a mission here.

"Let's go!" shouts Leon as he removes his scarf and knots it around my neck, tucking his camera under his coat. "It's freezing, have this." And it's like he's there, curling himself under my coat collar. The smell of his scarf is soft and fruity and indescribably foreign, and I, slightly embarrassingly, think of his bedsheets. "You are going to love this park."

OH, AND I DO. AS SOON AS WE ENTER ON THE WEST SIDE, I CAN see the vast orangerie building, and we head left toward it. We pass under a protected gazebo area before we reach it with small groups of people gathered around iron tables. They've slung moped helmets onto the floor and tied dogs that look cheated out of walks to the table legs. Everyone is wrapped up in heavy coats, scarves, and woolly hats, bent over in concentrated effort, and it isn't until we get closer that I can make out what they're doing.

"Chess!" I'm darting ahead of Leon now, looking for a space at one of the tables. One man is just rising from his seat and I slide into it, assuming his last partner will vacate, too, and let Leon sit down, but he doesn't. He sits there looking at me quizzically.

Leon has yet to catch up, so I offer a rather pathetic "Yes? We play?" motioning toward the board in front of us. He laughs but starts to rearrange the pieces, which I take to mean we are on. Then, yes, he lifts a pawn, and it's quick, each one of us taking turns to shuffle our pieces across the board before bringing our hands down hard on the timer that sits in between us. I am perched on the very edge of my seat, hyperalert to every move he makes. This guy is good.

But I am better.

Soon the intervals between his moves are stretching longer and longer, his face getting more and more pained as his recorded time creeps higher, way beyond mine, and he realizes he is beaten and knocks his king over. He slumps back in his cold metal chair and nods a respectful approval. Then he's up and the next guy takes his place. This is fun! Once I've beaten him, another one is there in front of me, and I'm looking around for Leon.

I see him, leaning casually against one of the gazebo posts, his camera held high as he clicks away, although I can see he's having trouble holding it steady because he's laughing so hard. What's tickled him? He's mouthing something to me and gesturing over the crowd that has gathered around what I would have to consider *my* table now. And then I get it. *Hommes.* They are all men. There is not a single woman aside from me involved in any of this, not playing or watching. I hadn't even stopped to think I was infiltrating some closed social group. I just plowed in and, well, they all seem pretty pleased that I did. Next time I glance up, Leon is holding aloft two steaming cups of coffee, and I have to reluctantly bow out, causing a flurry of disappointed cries from the men, old and young, who have yet to take me on. Leon approaches, hands me a cup, and says, "They are all asking if you will come back tomorrow." He laughs.

"What? And risk losing my unbeaten crown, I don't think so. Sorry, gentlemen, but that is it. I have to leave you now." I ham it up with a little bow.

Leon translates and they all erupt into a spontaneous round of applause. It is the single most joyous moment, and I want to capture this feeling and haul it back to London with me.

"You are brilliant, Lucille. Full of surprises!" says Leon as we edge away from the group. "Where did you learn to play like that?"

"Hours with my granny Sylvie and some of her friends who fancy their chances. She likes me to read to her mainly, or play chess, so she is to thank for that little performance. Come on, let's see where A and A had their lovely walk, shall we?"

We continue on our path, past the orangerie, its windows stuffed with enormous palm leaves and ferns, and beyond a café, where women sit at a table covered in pastel-colored chalks, casually sketching unsuspecting passersby. I notice a group of people spread out in a clearing among the trees, all bending and lunging in unison, practicing some sort of martial arts. Everything about their slow, methodical movements radiates calm.

We pause at the lake that sits in front of the impressive Senate building, and I take a big sweeping look around me. There is something familiar about this place that I am a million miles from putting my finger on, but it's here, trying to make itself seen, gently pulsing at the back of my mind. But the more I try to free it, the fainter it becomes.

"Don't kill yourself trying to work it out, Lucille." Leon is studying my face as perhaps only a photographer can. "It will come, if it's meant to. Something will click into place."

It's such a sensitive thing to say. He's so perceptive to how I'm feeling that I ask the question before I even realize I'm going to.

"Do you really not have a girlfriend, Leon?" I expect him to laugh, but he looks shocked at my nosiness, then sad and depleted, like this is the last thing on earth he wants to talk to me about. "Sorry, that's really personal, isn't it? You don't have to answer." But I'm too late, the awkwardness is already there between us.

"I don't think I will, if that's okay with you."

And I hate myself in this moment. I need to remember Leon is here for his grandfather's sake—not mine—and that I need his help. He's hardly going to volunteer his time to someone who clumsily crashes into his private life. To make matters worse, I start blathering on about Billy, just to fill the silence I've caused.

"Billy wasn't the most inspiring, romantic, or even the most thoughtful boyfriend on earth, but at least he never hurt me, so . . ." So, what? I have no idea where I am going with this, the point I'm trying to make.

Leon looks at me closely as we continue to walk.

"Anyone you share your life with should make you feel happy. Every single day. You should feel important to them and loved. Anything less just isn't enough."

I wasn't expecting an appraisal of my failed relationship with Billy, but then I started it, taking us down a route I really wish I hadn't now. And neither do I want to confront Leon's view, because I'm not sure

Billy or I ever lived up to his expectations, and perhaps my silence, my inability to respond, tells Leon all he needs to know.

"I think there are many ways to have your heart broken, Lucille. A slow, steady decline into not caring or valuing someone is just as wasteful and sad as something more dramatic."

I can't disagree, so I shut up after that.

WE CONTINUE TO WALK THROUGH THE PARK, PAST AN ARCH OF smooth gray statues that border the lake. One in particular catches my eye. A woman, perfect plaits running down either side of her face, her eyes closed to the beauty of everything surrounding her. I reach out a hand and she is icy cold to my touch. The plaque tells me it's sainte Genevieve, patron of Paris. It reminds me, I must call Mum.

We turn away from the Senate building now, curving right past an avenue of tall trees, on a loop back toward the entrance where we came in. Leon seems happy, snapping away, taking pictures of everything and occasionally of me, which I am surprisingly okay with. I don't pose, and he doesn't ask me to, he just seems to want to capture our visit to the park today. Then I see it. Ahead of us is the vintage carousel Veronique mentioned. It's nothing like the Disney versions you see, all artificial lights and neon colors. It's not double height or pumping out loud music, but it is so pretty, and I know instantly that I have seen it before. It's the first time I have been to this park, the first time I have visited this city, but I know for sure I have seen this carousel before. The way the trees frame and partially obscure it, its green triangular fabric top, and the metal benches that run in a perfect circle around it for all those excited children to wait their turn.

"What is it?" Leon is wondering why I've stopped.

"I've seen this." I point at the carousel. "I just can't work out where . . ." I can feel the deep frown creasing across my forehead.

"It's pretty famous. Most people have come across a snap of it online or in a travel guide. Maybe through your work?"

It's a good suggestion, but no, that's not it. Think, Lucille, think. It's a memory from long back that won't fully present itself, buried deep where it hasn't been thought about or needed for decades.

Could my grandfather have mentioned it? From their time in Paris, before London? Could this have something to do with them? Did they spend time in this park? Did the carousel star in one of his trips down memory lane that punctuated my childhood?

I have to get on it, and when I do, slightly worried that the old and brittle body of the horse will shatter beneath me, I close my eyes as it gathers speed. As the wind lifts my hair off my shoulders, I'm desperately trying to open my mind to the story I know lies within it. But it won't come, and when I get off, I can't hide my disappointment. I'm sulking, embarrassingly close to tears, from pure frustration more than anything else.

"You said you're staying at the Hôtel Athénée, yes?" Leon is trying to cheer me up.

I manage a nod.

"I bet you haven't tried the almond and hazelnut financiers yet, have you?"

"Nope, but if you're offering me cake, the answer will always be yes."

WE DECIDE ON THE TAXI RIDE BACK TO THE HOTEL THAT LEON should definitely see the rest of the dresses, and I call Veronique to see if she'd like to join us too. There must be more that she knows that I never thought to ask over dinner at her apartment. By the time we pull up outside on the avenue Montaigne, it's getting dark and all of the tiny fairy lights that dot the perimeter hedges are glowing like trapped fireflies. I decide not to bother with the formality of sitting in the hotel's lobby restaurant, and we shoot straight up to my suite on the second floor together.

By the time Veronique arrives an hour later, we've eaten three of the heavenly financiers each and ordered a round of burgers and fries from room service. We're also halfway through a second bottle of Petit Chablis that I deliberately didn't check the cost of before I brazenly ordered it like I'm made of money.

Veronique is wearing the sort of leopard-print coat that would look cheap on anyone else, but the way she has styled it with cropped black cigarette pants and a high roll-neck navy sweater effortlessly elevates it to superchic. She and Leon fall into an easy chat about each other's jobs, and I am slightly shamed to realize she is asking him all the polite questions that I haven't bothered to in nearly two full days in his company. They seem to know a lot of the same people from the Paris art scene, and Leon fills her in on the Maxim's and how his grandfather preserved it for all these years.

"This is turning into quite the treasure hunt, isn't it?" She smiles. "You must give me a job, Lucille! Perhaps the task of trying to trace the other missing dress? The one we have a card for but no gown?"

"Fantastic idea!" Especially as I have precisely no idea where to start with that one. "But you know it's going to be the most challenging one, Veronique? We might have the card, but no location. And the message, 'I continue to hope,'" I remind her.

"I've done some initial research on the fabric, the toile de Jouy. It's a term that originated in France in the late eighteenth century, far predating the time we are talking about here. It refers to the repeat pattern of a fabric, I believe. The literal translation is 'cloth from Jouy-en-Josas,' which is a town in the southwest suburbs of the city. Fashion is not my area of expertise at all, but we have staged many visiting designer exhibitions at the museum. Someone will know something that can help us. I'm sure of it." She's on the scent, and I can see from the determination in her eyes that she won't let this go until she has exhausted all our options. "Of all the dresses, it sounds like this one was intended to be the most special and possibly the most expensive. So what could it have been ordered for?"

Our eyes shift back and forth across the room between each other, hoping to see a flicker of understanding, but there is none.

"Let me take the card and I will do my best," she says. I have every confidence in her.

"So, what is the plan for tomorrow?" asks Leon. "Which dress is next, and where was it worn?"

"It's dress number five, the Esther, worn to somewhere called Les Halles. What is that?" I look to Veronique.

"So, Esther. That's the deep red velvet one. It's covered in thousands of silver beads."

"Yes, here she is!" I pull the dress from the rail in the vast walk-in wardrobe that is way too large for the half a dozen items of my own hanging in there. Items that I am having to repeatedly wash through the hotel's horrifically expensive laundry service until I can find a moment to buy some more.

"You can't mean Forum des Halles, as in the Westfield shopping center?" adds Leon, obviously confused.

"Yes, I think so," confirms Veronique, "but remember, it would have looked very different back in the fifties. Today it's a monument to modern-day capitalism with its fast fashion and food chains. But back then it was a huge fresh food market—the filthy, chaotic, beating heart of the city. I remember my maman going there for fresh pears, insisting on the best ones from the South of France for her tarte tatin. She wouldn't make it otherwise. Certainly not the sort of place that required you to wear a couture Dior gown, that's for sure."

"I'm afraid you're on your own tomorrow, Lucille." Leon slumps back in his chair, looking a little disappointed, I think. "I have to be back at the shop, or it won't open. There is no one else scheduled to help out on Wednesday."

"Don't worry, you've already given me so much of your time." I'm trying to look cheerful and grateful about this, but really, I haven't forgiven myself for the clanger I dropped earlier today, almost ruining it for both of us. I want to apologize again to Leon, but there hasn't seemed to be the right moment yet.

"I can come," offers Veronique. "I'm not working tomorrow and there's nothing else in my diary. I'd love to, if you don't mind?"

"Okay, great, thank you!"

The three of us all dig into the remaining food and manage to see the bottom of a third bottle of wine. This results in Veronique trying on the Esther dress, which fits her perfectly. She parades back and forth across the room while Leon and I sit on the end of the bed as if watching a model in a fashion show. She pulls it off quite beautifully. By then it's getting late and we've all had a bit too much to drink. While Leon is getting his coat, Veronique plonks herself down next to me on the sofa.

"Maman kept all her letters from your granny Sylvie. They're all tied up together somewhere in among her belongings. I haven't sorted through much of it yet, but . . . I'm wondering whether to read the letters when I find them. Do you think I should?" she asks.

"Most people probably would read them, I think. Theirs was obviously a very close relationship, and I can see it will be a wonderful opportunity to connect to your mum again. Did she ever share any of them with you when she was alive?"

"No. Not once. I often saw them arrive with their London postmark and thought how much I'd love to read them, but she never left them lying around, not that I would have dared to read them without her permission. But I can't ask her for that now, can I." It's the first time since we met that I see her mood really dip, and I'm reminded of how recently she lost her mother.

"I think it has to be your decision. I'm not sure I would, but I completely understand why you would want to."

"I'm worried about how I might feel when I've read them all. Because that will truly be the end then, won't it? I'll know as much as there is to know about her, all the tiny nuances that never got communicated between us. There will never be anything new . . . and the process of forgetting her might begin. As long as those letters remain unread, there are still parts of her to discover," I notice her eyes have glassed over at the precise moment she does too. "Oh, ignore me, Lucille, it's the wine." I give her hand a squeeze, and a brisk shake of her head tells me she's okay.

I see them both to the door of my suite, and we all say our goodbyes before Leon asks if we can catch up later tomorrow, when he's finished at the shop, so I can update him on any developments.

"I've got to visit the Pompidou late afternoon to edit some work. It's very close to where you'll be. If you're still there, call me. You've got my number."

"Okay, I will, thanks, Leon." Perhaps I'll get my chance to apologize properly tomorrow.

THE ROOM FEELS TOO BIG AND LONELY ONCE THEY'VE BOTH GONE, so I get into my pj's and climb into bed to scroll through my messages. Then I remember I haven't listened to Mum's voicemail yet. Perhaps it's a little selfish, but I decide it can wait until the morning. I want to hold on to this happy feeling just a little longer.

10

✦

Alice
NOVEMBER 1953, PARIS
THE ESTHER

Does it make her a bad person to admit that she loves the way the dress feels next to her skin? The softness of the expensive silk lining as it gently lifts and rotates with the movement of her hips is exquisite— at least twenty skilled artisans will have worked on the piece she is wearing this evening. For the previous week, every woman in this room will have been guessing what she would wear tonight. Some will have gone to the effort of placing a perfectly timed phone call to their own contact at the house of Dior—Alice's well-documented designer of choice—or to Anne under the ruse of checking timings, to try to elicit an answer that would then guide their own choice. How to shine, without outshining your hostess? Alice knows the wives gossip about her perceived disloyalty of favoring a French designer over a British one. But she will not waver. Anne's recommendation was the right one. These dresses are Alice's armor, her enhanced reality, placing her outside time and far beyond the reach of the society gossips.

Alice is pondering all this as she circulates the salon, a coupe of fine French champagne in hand. She's angling her pretty face left and then right, avoiding the bores while also acknowledging as many of their guests as she can in one well-plotted route to the door Antoine has just entered through—flanked, as always, by his mother. Alice's is a practiced expression. One that says, *I am delighted you are here*, but that also gently warns, *Not now, I am needed elsewhere and delays will not be appreciated*. She deliberately does not make Antoine her first focus when she reaches him.

"Madame du Parcq, how wonderful to see you again." Alice forces her eyes to remain fixed on Antoine's mother, despite the grin she knows will be creeping across Antoine's lips and how his own eyes will have no interest beyond her.

"The feeling is entirely mutual. You do give the absolute best parties. Well, of course you do, everyone knows that." Madame du Parcq is allowing her gaze to be drawn beyond Alice's right shoulder, to the woman behind her. Alice can tell without looking from the smooth velvet tones filling the air with confident predictions about the success of the new collection that it is Adrienne from Dior, the woman whose job it is to decide who attends the shows and, crucially, where they sit.

"Dearest Adrienne." Alice signals with a small wave of her hand. "The lovely Madame du Parcq is here . . ." It is all that needs to be said. The rules of engagement are clear. Alice is confident that Adrienne will pick up the conversation like she and Madame du Parcq are old friends as Alice gently guides the two women into the center of the room together, leaving her and Antoine pushed a little farther to the outskirts. An act that seems to make Madame du Parcq's evening, if her breathlessness is anything to go by. Adrienne will lose her soon enough, when she has sufficiently satisfied the favor needed.

"Alice." Antoine bends his head low, allowing their faces to almost touch, breathing her name into her ear as soon as his mother is safely embedded in her new conversation. And maybe it's the champagne or the fact she feels invincible in the Esther. Maybe Alice just feels protected by the sheer number of bodies pushed up against each other in the salon tonight, but she isn't the slightest bit inclined to dissuade him. Quite the opposite. She allows their bodies to come together, she feels her hips connect with him, and the effect of it pulses through her entire body.

"I'm hoping you've brought a present for me this evening, Antoine?" The urge to take his hand is almost overwhelming.

"I have. When can I give it to you? I want us to be alone when you see it." His hand hovers above his heart, and Alice doesn't want to wait the hours stretching out ahead of her to see his finished sketch. Perhaps it's pure vanity or the thrill of their little secret, but she needs to see it as soon as possible.

"In thirty minutes from now, I'm going to step out of the room and walk across the hall to the bottom of the staircase. There's a small curtained alcove on the left-hand side with a window seat. Meet me there. But we will have to be very quick or my absence will be noticed. Don't speak to me again until I see you there."

Alice doesn't wait for a response but immediately steps away from him and joins a group of wives who have gathered around the mantelpiece, all trying to outdo each other with their lavish Christmas plans. Why do they crave this rarefied world? she wonders. Probably because they don't truly understand it, not the way Alice does from her elevated position. She knows invitations from her and Albert are highly prized and there is fierce resentment from those who don't make the guest list. But do they understand the fragility of it all? How immense popularity, troubled by one quick reshuffle of cabinet or a falling out of favor, might see them pushed to the sidelines and forced to jealously gaze inward from the cold?

Despite his position, Alice is more natural at all of this than Albert. *I can't entertain without Alice*, she heard him tell a colleague one evening, just after they arrived in Paris. His tone seemed appreciative of her contribution then, not barbed and full of resentment at her popularity. She looks at him now, across the room and cornered by one of the more junior French diplomats. He's dressed the part in a perfectly tailored dinner jacket that seems to emphasize his size—his broad shoulders, his solid chest, his imposing height. But the mental commitment—the one thing no one else can do for him—is sadly lacking. She recognizes the inattentive blankness on his face; he's directed it at her enough times. When his companion eventually stops talking, he won't have a thing to say in response and will be forced to fall back on excusing himself or making a rushed and inappropriate introduction to someone nearby. The man is of little use to Albert, so he won't waste his energy on him.

Alice is pleased she's not close enough to be able to help him this time. She absolutely would have once, but not tonight, when she can't risk getting stuck herself. She knows if the two of them happen to make eye contact now, Albert will signal for help. His eyes will flare, and there will be the smallest toss of his head backward to summon her. He stated the rule that the two of them should never talk once a party is underway. That by dividing their efforts they can achieve more.

Well, now he will have to rely on his own wits to save himself.

THE HALLWAY IS CLEAR. SHE HAS DISPATCHED PATRICE TO THE kitchen to check on the rotation of canapés and asked him to prepare the library for later, knowing full well Albert and some of his favorites will retreat there for whiskey and cigars. At least she's hoping they do. Despite the noise from the salon, she can hear the frantic click-clack of her heels on the polished tiled floor, the speed of her steps beating out her excitement. This is madness. She'll wait just two minutes and then she'll have to go back in.

When Antoine appears, he seems to do so with no sense of urgency at all, casually striding across the hall like the night is theirs alone. As he walks, he starts to pull a small piece of rolled paper from his jacket pocket, maintaining eye contact with her as he does. He gently unfurls it and holds it against his chest, the soft pencil lines facing her. Alice is so desperate to see what he has created, how he has fully interpreted her, that she ignores the very slight movement in the background far behind him. Her eyes are too busy greedily searching out her image.

She's expecting to see the fully formed Batignolles dress she wore to the Jardin du Luxembourg that day, the gentle curve of her own body and the angled dip of her waist. But it is her own face that her eyes settle on first, and the vision is shocking, just as Antoine's mother comes into sharp, unwelcome focus a mere ten steps behind him.

Knowing that she mustn't let her face give them away, Alice smiles broadly but demands, "Put it away," just as Madame du Parcq draws level with her son.

"Oh my goodness, please tell me you are not boring Madame Ainsley with your doodles, Antoine." Her lips are pursed with irritation.

Antoine stuffs the sketch back into his pocket before his mother sees it, for once looking unsure of what to say next.

"It's no problem at all, Madame du Parcq, really. I enjoyed the brief moment of calm, and I suspect Antoine may have been too shy to show me in front of all our guests." Alice's words seem to remind her of the numerous opportunities she is missing out on while she stands in the hallway scolding Antoine.

"Well, I for one am going back to the party, and I suggest you join me, Antoine. I'm sure Madame Ainsley has much more pressing things to attend to." She turns on her heel and heads at speed back toward the salon.

"I will wait for you outside tonight," Antoine whispers, "beyond the garden. Come to me when the party is finished." There is such longing in his face, Alice can't refuse him.

"It could be a very long wait."

"I don't care. I want to be with you." Alice smiles, just as Madame du Parcq flings her head back over her shoulders toward them, checking Antoine is following, and registering the covert nature of Alice's look. Antoine sighs deeply and leaves Alice wondering how on earth she will get through the next four hours.

AS THE PARTY FINALLY DRAWS TO A CLOSE, IT IS FOUR A.M. AND the last determined guests make their way out to the courtyard and their drivers. Alice is sure Antoine can't possibly be waiting for her at this hour. As the hands crawled around the carriage clock in the salon this evening, she felt her excitement slowly ebb, her emotions plummeting from fevered expectation to a rising panic at what little time was left. Now, in the early hours of the morning, she feels the only place she should be heading is upstairs, for another night alone in that huge bed, until Albert finally drags himself away from the whiskey bottle. And even if Antoine is still outside, which seems entirely unlikely, can she really go through with their arrangement? Perhaps the lateness of the hour has done her an enormous favor, saved her from something she would surely regret. Because . . . what if he is still waiting?

If she meets Antoine tonight as promised, something will happen. She feels sure of it. They would be alone. It's late; Albert will be occupied for hours. She can't look at that sketch, see the way he has given such detailed, studied thought to how he views her, and promise herself she will return to the residence the same woman who stands here now. In a crowded room full of people, under the spotlight of Antoine's attention, she was weakened. What will he do to her when they are alone? Has she already crossed a line? Most of the women who drank her champagne this evening would happily sit in judgment, confirming she has.

As she is saying goodbye to the Greek ambassador and his diminutive wife, she realizes Albert is nowhere to be seen and wonders if he has already made his way to the library.

"Ah, Patrice, did Albert get everything he needed in the library this evening?" Her brilliant butler has appeared to remove the last of the glassware and check for any discarded or forgotten items that will need to be returned to their owners later today.

"Oh, sorry, madame, I thought you knew." Alice can see the faintest flicker of awkwardness on Patrice's usually professional poker face.

"Knew what?"

"He said he had an engagement, madame. I believe he also mentioned it to Eloise, but perhaps she never got a moment to share the information with you?"

Alice pauses and considers apologizing to Patrice that he should be forced to impart this grubby detail to her. It's glaringly obvious to both of them what a four a.m. engagement really is. But something about the way Patrice refuses to look sorry for Alice, to brand her as the victim, makes her rally.

Please let Antoine still be there is all Alice can think now. *Please let him be waiting for me.*

"Thank you, Patrice. May I ask one more thing of you before you finish this evening, please?"

"Anything, madame. I am in no hurry to be anywhere." And this is why she loves Patrice so dearly. Because of course he wants to get home. He must be shattered, but nothing in his body language or his words would ever lead an observer to believe so.

"My full fur, my gloves, and my wool scarf. And my clutch, which is on the dressing table. Would you mind?"

"An excellent idea! I'll be as quick as I can." She watches as he disappears up the grand staircase, determined now that she must at least satisfy her curiosity. Did Antoine really wait all those hours for her?

SHE RECOGNIZES THE OUTLINE OF HIS SILHOUETTE IMMEDIATELY. He is sitting on a bench, reading a book by the light of a streetlamp, his head dipped well below the collar of his coat. It's eerily quiet, the

traffic and crowds of the nearby Champs-Élysées all gone. As soon as
he hears her footsteps, he stands.

"You waited? This entire time?" She's so happy he kept his promise,
but she feels obliged now to give him the option of returning home.
"You must be so tired and cold, Antoine. Why don't you go home? We
can meet another time."

"There is somewhere I'd like to show you." It's only then she sees
the taxi waiting a little farther up the road, its lights dimmed, the low
hum of its engine the only noise at this hour.

They climb into the back, and Alice allows her body to collapse
heavily against his, aware of the tiredness washing over her, all the
stress and irritation from the evening seeping out of her. He drapes an
arm around her, pulling her closer, smiling as the sparkle of her beautiful dress falls across his legs, covering them both like a glamorous
blanket.

"Where are we going?" Alice's voice is heavy with exhaustion. But
she trusts him, whatever their destination. She has a feeling it will be
different and interesting and somewhere only he would think to
take her.

"The heart of the city. I want you to see *real* Paris, Alice." His arm
closes in tighter around her, and she wants nothing more in this moment than to bury herself in him, to feel treasured and protected and
wanted while the driver speeds them through the vast deserted streets,
the Eiffel Tower looming behind them to the west.

THE NOISE WHEN THEY EXIT THE CAR SHAKES ANY LAST THOUGHTS
of sleep from Alice; the blazing beam from the spotlights yanks her
back into the loud, messy, stench-filled present. There must be two
hundred people here and it's not yet five a.m. Not one of them registers
their arrival.

"Welcome to Le Ventre de Paris!" Antoine beams, sweeping an

arm over the tower of produce that spreads out before them. "This is about as real as it gets."

While her guests are sleeping off the excesses of last night's party, curled up under the finest sheets, this part of Paris, the one that stands in the shadow of Saint-Eustache, is carving out its living. There is an energy pumping through the market. Antoine takes her hand, and they venture deeper into the makeshift alleyways that have grown out of towering wooden boxes of pears, swollen squash, spring onions, flour-covered loaves, and peaches the size of a strongman's fist. Mud-covered pumpkins as big as car wheels mark their route. The floor is wet, blanketed with sodden straw. Angry dogs fight over scraps tossed to them by the sellers. Robust women twice the size of Alice, with filthy aprons pulled tight across their hips, make themselves heard above the crowd. Cauliflowers are thrown across the cobbled paths from one seller to another to be examined by the earliest buyers.

"It's the restaurant owners who come first," Antoine tells her. "The professional chefs and the hotel kitchen staff. They drive the hardest bargain because they buy in the biggest quantities. Later, when the sun is just rising, it will be the housewives and mothers with big families to feed, then the lovers to buy pastries and flowers."

"I've never seen anything like it." It's astonishing, the sheer size of it. "Like a whole other secret city within a city." Alice recalls with some relief that there is no formal dinner planned at the residence tonight and therefore no need for her own chef to be here competing for the best deals.

Antoine laces his fingers through hers, and they continue their route farther in, past a man who stands holding a dirty blade at his side, a pig's head pinned with the other hand to a wet butcher's block in front of him, a lit cigarette expertly balanced between his lips. Another man pushes a huge two-wheeled cart piled high with rubbish through the crowd, singing as he goes. Alice pulls her fur in closer to her body. It's cold, but everyone around her is wearing much less to protect them against the chill of this November morning. No one seems to notice the temperature at all. Most are smiling, helping each other, united in their common cause. The tang of human exertion carries through the air, mixed with a meatiness and smokiness. While the odor is without doubt unpleasant, Alice finds herself freely inhaling it, lifting her nose to it, not avoiding it.

"You've obviously been here before?" Alice asks. Antoine has stopped and perched on a stack of empty wooden boxes, clearly enjoying the sight of her dressed so finely, ankle deep in vegetable offcuts and discarded potato sacks.

"Many times since Thomas first told me about it. I like to sketch people, but you get the best results when your subject doesn't know it's being watched. Where better than here? No one cares about us, they are all too busy looking after their own. I've spent hours here, feeling completely unnoticed, slipping between the stalls as if I were invisible."

"Do you still have my sketch?" Alice feels a little vain for asking, but she has waited long enough.

"Yes. Let's have a coffee and I'll show you. I think we both need one."

They dart into the nearest bistro, open early like everything else bordering the market to service the men and women whose working day started hours ago. They sit at one of the small round tables just big enough for two and order two black coffees. A man still wearing his bloodstained white butcher's coat sits at the next table, hunched over a bowl of steaming stew, tiredness pulling at his eyelids. Three more are standing at the bar, sharing one newspaper and a carafe of red wine before they return to the market to finish their shift. Alice moves her chair beside Antoine, wanting more privacy.

"What do you think?"

He unrolls the sketch again for her, close enough for Alice to see every movement his pencil has made, every mark where he has corrected himself and reimagined her. This time, her arms have fallen open at her sides, her head elevated, her face composed and gently smiling, looking toward the sky, as if it is the last remaining place to appeal for strength and inspiration. If before she looked defeated and lost, now she looks more capable, almost content.

It is the most moving and intensely personal thing she has ever seen. For a second or two she is completely lost for words.

"I'm crying," she whispers. Despite the smile, her eyes in the sketch are closed and there is a single swollen tear balanced on her otherwise smooth cheek, on the very cusp of falling. She feels those same tears press at her eyelids now.

"Do you think it's accurate?" There is barely any space between their faces now. He is giving her no chance to avoid the question.

"It's not what I expected. This level of scrutiny."

"But do you recognize yourself?"

"Yes. It's . . . alarming in its accuracy."

"For me, it's the honesty of the image that makes it so beautiful. You are human, Alice, you are allowed to feel things. I didn't seek to erase your emotions. It's how I see you. You have spirit. When will you allow yourself to use it?"

Alice swallows hard. "I don't know what to say to you, Antoine. I can't answer your question. Your sketch is beautiful. In one sense, it's the most beautiful anyone has ever made me look, made me feel. But I'm married. You know I am. Just meeting you here is a huge risk for me. This won't be an easy thing to explain." She needs him to understand the significance of what they're doing, the impact it could have on her.

"Do you have to explain yourself? Does Albert explain himself to you?" There is an indignant edge to his voice that makes her recoil slightly.

"That's not how it works, is it? You know that as well as I do. I don't have the choices or freedoms open to me that he does. He doesn't stop to consider the rights or wrongs of meeting another woman. But I must."

"And yet you *are* here?" His boldness gives way to hope.

"Yes, I am. Please don't make me feel like I shouldn't be."

Antoine finishes his coffee in serious silence while Alice worries she has said the wrong thing again. That he'll realize it *is* a mistake to bring her here and suggest they go their separate ways home. She braces herself for the disappointment. He slowly replaces his cup onto its saucer.

"I want you to sit for me, Alice. I want to see all of you. I want to know all of you. And I want to capture it." If it were merely a question of him saying the right thing, Alice knows she would already be in his bed. He has understood perfectly what she needs, what's lacking in her life: the freedom to be completely herself, to drop her guard, to say precisely what she thinks and feels with no sense of right or wrong, to be equal in every sense. For a man to put her pleasure before his own. But as strongly as she feels it, she can't say any of it.

"How, Antoine? How can I say yes to any of these things without risking everything that I have?"

"Would you really consider it such a very great risk? Is it so much to lose?"

Her mouth instinctively moves to say yes, but she stops herself, not wanting to give a predictable, expected answer rather than a truthful one.

Antoine releases a huge sigh and looks toward the café door.

"The car is waiting where it dropped us off. I think I should get you home. It will be getting light soon, and I don't want you to get into trouble."

She feels she has let him down. That he waited all those hours in the cold and all he wants in return is some sign that she is brave enough to perhaps just try. To open her mind to what might be. To a happiness that might exist beyond the fickle glamour and privilege of embassy life and its cliché cast of characters—and a husband who has probably not even paused to wonder where Alice might be at this hour, whether she is sleeping soundly in their bed or not.

Antoine sees her into the car, then closes the rear passenger door behind her, remaining on the pavement as she lowers the window.

"I'll walk," he tells her. "It won't help if anyone sees me when you get dropped off." He leans in through the open window and cradles her chin in his hand, angling her face toward him so he can place the softest of kisses on her cheek. It's fleeting, gone before Alice has time to turn and offer him her lips instead.

"Try to love me a little, Alice," he whispers, "because I think I already love you too much."

Then he bangs on the side of the car, signaling the driver to pull away—an act it takes all of Alice's strength not to stop.

11

Lucille

I wake late with a parched mouth and the sort of headache I know will take a fistful of painkillers to shift. In hindsight, that third bottle of wine last night was probably not the smartest move. Where's my phone? I grope around for it, knowing it will be buried in the plume of duvet somewhere. Wednesday morning. I should be sniffing out the last slice of mold-free bread to toast for breakfast. Or standing in a piping hot shower, giving myself the usual midweek pep talk about remaining positive and how everyone has to do a job they hate to get where they want to be. My time will come, et cetera.

I've got about an hour until I need to leave the hotel and head over to the Les Halles shopping center to meet Veronique. I'm annoyed with myself, because I had planned to walk there after Veronique suggested I cut through the pretty Jardin des Tuileries, which hugs the river. But there won't be enough time now. I call room service, order the pastry basket that's big enough for two (so what?), an orange juice, and a coffee, and then I hit the shower so I can be washed and dressed by the time the doorbell to my suite rings. This motivates me.

No one wants to answer the door to a handsome French bellboy while wearing a towel that barely covers their backside, prickly pale legs poking out the bottom.

I pull on the same pair of jeans I've been wearing since I arrived and a blouse bursting with red roses. I bought it with Florence in mind. I thought it might like to introduce me to Botticelli and da Vinci in the Uffizi Gallery, that I might wander the busy backstreets, gelato in hand, before disappearing into the nearby vine-covered hills of Chianti. Until now, it hasn't made it any farther than the back of my wardrobe, but this morning I tuck it into my jeans, making a vague attempt to look a little smarter for Veronique. As breakfast appears, I hit play on Mum's voicemail, switching to speakerphone so I can eat and listen at the same time. And I have to hand it to her, she's good. If you're the sort of person who is impressed by a little gentle manipulation.

Please call me, Lucille. I need to talk to you, darling.

Darling? Mum's voice is slightly breathy and tinged with vulnerability.

In my thirty-two years, I have never, not once, heard my mother cry.

Not when Dad left, not in one of the very rare moments I unloaded seemingly world-ending teenage angst on her, not when it became clear that Granny Sylvie couldn't cope on her own anymore and Natasha was hired. So my first thought is that the emotion might be deliberately constructed for my benefit. If it was anything to do with Granny, she would surely have called the hotel direct. It's been twenty-four hours since she left the message; any news that was desperately urgent would have reached me by now. Although, I admit, I feel the faintest tremor of nerves—something obviously isn't right. This probably wasn't the best morning to wake with a thunderous hangover.

I dial her number. On a weekday morning at this time, she will be at her office just off Shaftesbury Avenue. She will have been there for some time, a slave to the presenteeism that rules her working world, feeling there is some sort of badge of honor to be gained from arriving much earlier than the newbies who are half her age. She certainly wouldn't ordinarily be answering calls from me, but her mobile connects on the second ring.

"Lucille?" She sounds just as shaky as her message.

"Yes, Mum, it's me. Are you okay?"

"I'm trying to be, darling." I hear her sigh and notice how ragged her breath is.

"What is it, Mum, has something happened?"

"I shouldn't have bothered you, darling. Sorry. You're on your trip and the last thing you need is me getting in the way of your fun. I just needed someone to talk to."

Now I am worried. Neediness is not something I would ever associate with my mother. And not something she would ever willingly confess to. I glance at my watch. I've got a little time before I need to leave to meet Veronique.

"Go on, Mum, I've got time. What is it?"

"Perhaps we can talk about it in person. When are you coming back?"

"Not yet. Things have developed a little here. I won't go into it all now, but I'll be here a bit longer than I thought."

"Oh." She pauses, hoping I might change my mind, I think, and then when I don't, she adds, "Well, I suppose collecting a dress for Granny is more important."

"It's not more important, Mum, but . . ."

"It's just, I don't have anyone to talk to." A firmness has returned to her voice, and I sense she is trying to back me into a corner, so I change tack.

"How is Granny? Have you been to check on her since I left?"

"Natasha is there twice a day." This is typical of Mum. She hasn't made the personal time investment herself, she has paid someone else to, and I'm torn between being cross with her and deeply sad that she is wedded to a job that allows her no personal life.

"I know she is, but I think Granny would really appreciate seeing . . ."

"I've lost my job, Lucille." She blurts it out, trying, I think, to move us away from her failures with her own elderly mother. "Thirty-five years of my life, all gone with the utter of two words, *rationalization* and *consolidation*."

And thirty-two of mine, I'm tempted to add, but don't. She must hear the relieved sigh I let go, because her more usual abrupt coping mechanism kicks in.

"I've helped shape it, build it, I've brought in fresh talent. Well, foolish me, because those very people are the ones they now feel can take the reins. It's so insulting, Lucille."

"Listen, Mum, you're nudging sixty. You can't have thought you were going to work at the same pace indefinitely, can you? You can't have seriously wanted to?"

"That job is everything to me." Perhaps she's momentarily forgotten who she's talking to. "I care about it more than anything. I was consumed by it. I gave it every bit of energy I had. All of me. I should be the one who decides when it's over. Not them. And do you know how they did it?" She doesn't wait for my response. "They couriered a standard letter to me. I didn't even warrant a meeting! What am I supposed to do now?"

And she really has no idea. No idea how hurtful what she's saying is. How empty and worthless it makes me, her only daughter, feel. That she doesn't consider for one moment the upside of having more time on her hands. That we might finally get to spend some of it together. That she might bring some joy into her own mother's final years on this earth. We are both so far from her thoughts, and I can't even excuse it as the result of the first punch of her rejection. She's had twenty-four hours to absorb the news.

I'm also surprised there isn't a part of her that saw this coming. Maybe she saw it too late and that's why she's angry. Weren't the warning signs there every weekend she was required to work with no apology or time off later? If they truly valued her and wanted her to stay, wouldn't they have treated her better? Has that realization finally dawned, too late to be useful?

"Mum, you've been a brilliant, hugely accomplished management consultant for thirty-five years, you've dealt with far bigger problems than this. You can work it out. When I get back, we can sit down, and you can tell me all about it and what plans you've made." Because I can guarantee there will be a strategy document in the house somewhere that she's already working on.

Now she gives me the silent treatment.

"I'm not coming back home yet, I can't. Not until I have finished what Granny has asked me to do here."

I SAY GOODBYE AND RELUCTANTLY END THE CALL. I KNOW SHE'S hurting, but I also know she has to accept some personal responsibility for the position she finds herself in. I'm confident she is strong enough to get through this. As I hang up, I see a text message, written entirely in capitals, and impossible to ignore.

> AT THE AIRPORT. NO SEAT BOOKED FOR MY MOTHER-
> IN-LAW. THE WRONG LUGGAGE ALLOWANCE.
> IMAGINE THE JOY. GET IT SORTED!

I think the phrase *blood runs cold* was probably invented for moments like this, because I feel my body drain of all its heat and vitality.

All I can see is a furious Dylan, arguing at the check-in desk, convinced initially it's the airline's fault and not mine. The excruciating moment witnessed by his mother-in-law when he realized otherwise. He only reminded me about the booking changes yesterday.

It's not until I am exiting the hotel that Dylan's name pops up again, and I barely have the courage to look. He's still using caps.

I'VE SORTED IT. NO THANKS TO YOU. DO YOU EVEN
CARE ABOUT YOUR JOB?

It's a good question. I decide for the sake of both our stress levels not to answer him.

GIVEN THE CHOICE, WHY WOULD ANYONE COME HERE TO SHOP, I wonder as I approach the sprawling mall where Veronique and I have arranged to meet. It's the least Parisian thing Paris has shown me so far. I know from the bit of background reading I managed on my phone on the way here that back in the fifties it was central to city life. Famous for its personality, its life force. The very place that fed and sustained its people, bringing them all the culinary delicacies they longed for after years of enforced wartime deprivation and rationing. But the original buildings were torn down in the seventies, and now the high street conglomerates have taken over. All its uniqueness has gone. Today you can buy the same nylon knickers in Victoria's Secret here as you can anywhere else in the world. Trying to reimagine the working market I've seen in images online, A wearing the Esther dress here among the sweat and dirt, is impossible.

Try to love me a little, because I already love you too much.

What an incredible thing to have said to you. As I look skyward, back up to the neighboring Saint-Eustache church in all its Gothic glory, I think about everything this beautiful building might have witnessed back then. How the same stained-glass angels may have watched over A and her lover, seen something I am trying so hard to piece together now. Did they know why she wore such a dress to the market? Having touched the dress and studied the market, it's still a mystery to me. Did she know she was coming? Perhaps not. One thing is for sure, that dress does not belong naturally in this location—then or now.

I'm still standing there with my mouth hanging open when Veronique's hand gently takes my elbow.

"Sorry I'm late. Oh, you look like you need a glass of wine. Am I right?"

"You may never have been *more* right, Veronique. Just not here? It's a bit soulless, isn't it? I reckon I've had enough of that for one day."

"Have you eaten? I know the perfect place if you haven't."

"Lead on!"

WE ORDER TWO GLASSES OF ICE-COLD WHITE WINE AND A PLATE of different cheeses and cold meats that come with (what I would call stale) bread and no butter. But somehow, it's exactly what I need. Veronique's company is, too, and I don't wait for an invitation to off-load the morning's events.

"The thing is, Veronique, Mum and I have just never been close." I don't want to sound mean or uncaring—it hurts every single time I acknowledge the fact, privately or aloud. It feels shameful. How can a mother and daughter not be close? By mere definition, shouldn't there be some unbreakable bond between us, one that can outlast any personality clash, generational difference, or teenage drama?

Veronique sits back in her chair a little, seeming to signal that she is happy for me to go on.

"I've got used to it over the years and explained it away to myself as just the way she is. I thought as I got older, I might need her less, but . . . the opposite seems to be true." Veronique nods her head slowly, and I'm reassured she doesn't mind me dumping all this on her. I am painfully aware that her sense of loss is far fresher than mine.

"Was there ever a time when it was different? Did something happen to make her withdraw?" she asks.

"It's an awful thing to say, but she has never been much of a mother to me." I lower my head, knowing how judgmental this sounds—but also knowing it is true. "I never interested her. I have often asked myself why she bothered to have me at all. She never wanted to spend time with me. I've never felt that she was on my side, ready to jump in with advice or a protective arm if I needed it." I take another large gulp of wine. Now that I've started, I want to say it all, to really unburden myself in a way that feels necessary but won't hurt Mum at all. "I grew up knowing I *couldn't* rely on her. And with Dad gone . . ." I pause again and take a breath, trying to suck the emotion back down deep inside of me. "There have been a lot of lonely times."

"Oh, Lucille, I am so sorry." Her hand reaches across the table now and rubs my arm. "I can only think she has her reasons. What is her relationship like with her own maman, your granny Sylvie?" Veronique is only doing what most kind people would. Searching for some reasoning where I'm sure none can be found beyond the fact my mother always put her career first.

"Functional. Practical. Mum pays her bills and makes sure someone else is there to do the caring bit. I'd like to say I hope that will change now that she has more time, but I can't believe it will. Granny is the loveliest, sweetest woman; she deserves so much more. It breaks my heart, if I'm honest." It's the mention of Granny that finally sends my warm tears spilling down my face and onto the table in front of us, and I can't even be bothered to be embarrassed. Crying in public is really the least of my worries right now. Veronique reaches into her neat little handbag and passes me a tissue, then rests her hand on top of mine.

"You can confide in me anytime, Lucille. You have my number and email now, and we can spend as much time as you like together while you are here."

"I would like that, thank you." Veronique is very good at this, and it occurs to me that maybe she is a little lonely too. There has been no mention of a husband or partner, and I wonder who she has to lean on, especially now that her mother has gone.

"I know you are cross with your maman and, probably quite rightly, feel hurt by her actions, but I think she sounds like she needs your kindness."

I raise my eyes from the tissue back up to meet Veronique's. "I know. It's just very hard to give it when I feel so rejected."

"I understand why she might need it, that's all. I feel what she is feeling a little, too, Lucille. But I have had more time to feel less hurt by it. I am older now. I have worked at the museum for many years, but never for fewer hours than I do now. And so naturally I am less important. They value my knowledge, I know they do, but they need me less." Which makes me wonder again why Mum wants to feel so vital at work but doesn't recognize that I need her too.

"Big decisions that I would definitely have been consulted on before, I don't even get to hear about until they have been made," continues Veronique. "People forget to tell me things. Some of the younger staff question the decisions I do make. Privately I wonder if they question my relevance to the business at all. I feel the loss of my importance, of my essentialness to the day." Put this way by Veronique, I understand it. I really do. But would it be so very hard for Mum to talk to me, to share these worries, if this is what she is feeling too? Maybe there are things she needed to hear from me. That I'm proud of all she's achieved and how hard she works, even if that work ethic has driven an unbearable wedge between us.

"I expect one day, when the budgets are tightened, I might be on the receiving end of the same treatment as your maman. And yet, they are hiring new, younger people all the time. People who bring fresh ideas, who love travel. Storytellers who care about the personal journeys behind the precious items we show. Every exhibition has to work so much harder now, on so many different levels, to attract its audience. They are advertising many positions."

I make a conscious effort not to look excited about this information, but I think I fail, because Veronique adds, "They're the kind of jobs I would have killed for back at the beginning. They need people to travel to and liaise with all our partner locations, mostly. To help promote our traveling exhibitions and to come up with the best ways to market those ideas. They would pay for an intensive language course, too, so anyone landing the job would be fluent within a year." She raises her eyebrows across the table at me, like she's trying to seduce me with the idea.

We both take a pause and sip our wine, watching Parisian life unfolding around us. Early lunch breakers coming in. Rushed customers who venture no farther than the bar, order an espresso, drink it in two large gulps, and are gone again seconds later. The owner, a tall, slender man who makes a point of acknowledging everyone, circulates the café, refilling bread baskets, recommending wine, and generally presenting himself as the perfect advert for a stress-free life. He's unrushed and quietly, happily going about his business. Without realizing it, he's making me question every life choice I ever made—and those of everyone in here, I suspect.

I turn my focus back to Veronique, who is delicately hoovering up all the salami. "But you must have such great knowledge and expertise in your area, just like Mum?"

"So do lots of other people. Younger people who don't cost as much as we do. I own Maman's place now and so I can afford to slow down a little. Your mum sounds like she has never known another life and, trust me, I think she could be a little frightened by that, despite her success."

"Really?" It's hard to imagine Mum being frightened of anything.

"Give her the time, now that she has it, to realize the impact her actions have had on you. But remember, something will have made her the way she is, and until you know what that is, it's unwise to judge."

Veronique is probably the most reasonable person I have ever met, and it's hard to imagine someone hasn't fallen deeply in love with her. And since we're sharing so much, I decide to ask the question.

"Did you never marry, Veronique?" I have to assume she has not, or surely it would have come up in conversation. There was no evidence of a husband or wife at her apartment on Friday night, no ring on her finger.

"No, I never desired it, to be honest. I still don't. Although I'm glad to say there have been offers!"

"How many offers?"

"Four or five."

"Bloody hell!" Not that I should be surprised. She's beautiful and clever and great company, but I laugh and say, "Bit greedy, isn't it?"

"Very! But I was never inclined to accept any of them. Not even close." She's leaned in a little over the table to emphasize the juiciness of her confession.

"But you never got lonely when everyone else was pairing off and settling down?"

"Not for a second. My life has always been very full. I spent most of my twenties traveling around Europe when my friends were getting serious about their boyfriends, and my thirties were all about building my career. Now, while they're celebrating milestone wedding anniversaries, I'm dating three different men. They're all interesting, in their own ways. They all have their stories to tell. It's the variety that I love, Lucille, not the monogamy."

Okay, I was not expecting that. And it's a bit of a wake-up call. She's well into her sixties and having way more fun than I am, it seems.

"I've always loved to wander. The travel ignited a free spirit in me that tipped into my romantic life too. I never wanted to be tethered, in any sense. Even when I eventually returned to Paris, I explored every inch of the city, I was always moving to a different apartment in a new district."

It is now blindingly obvious that Veronique saw more of the world by her midtwenties than I probably ever will.

"And the best bit is that I've found all sorts of reminders while I've been looking through Maman's things. Souvenirs and collectibles, items I sent home from my travels that I can't believe she kept all these years."

"What kinds of things?" My own mother used to bin the childish birthday cards I drew for her on the same day I handed them over, optimistically standing there waiting for praise.

"So many things. A faded menu from a restaurant I worked at in Ravello, still stained with red wine rings. A program from an open-air opera festival in Verona. Oh, I remember that night so well. The evening I met the only man I ever truly loved, who never loved me back. That's Italians for you, Lucille. Never date one." She wags a finger at me by way of a warning.

"Okay, noted!" Although the mere thought seems so unlikely.

"There was a handmade fan I sent her from Madrid, still perfectly concertinaed in its original box. She had a trio of small unused ceramic bowls I'd completely forgotten I sent back from Porto. It was so wonderful to be taken back there, Lucille, to those ancient, cobbled backstreets I would wander alone hour after hour with only myself to please. The city that inspired a career that would fulfill me for decades. It has been the most joyous meander back through my twenties, and I wish I could thank her now for holding on to all those memories. It's made me feel young again—but also incredibly grateful that I had that time. I have those stories to tell."

"Will you stay in Paris? Is this your forever home?"

"For now, yes, but I imagine there is a little farmhouse for me in the south, with crumbling stone walls and white wooden shutters. Somewhere I can see the sunflowers. Not because I'm stopping, Lucille, but because soon it will be time to meet new people, seek fresh adventures."

We order another couple of glasses of wine, and then she moves the conversation back to our task.

"I've read the first letter your granny wrote to my maman." She studies my face, hoping I think that she's made the right decision.

"And . . ."

"It was written in September 1954 and Sylvie had just moved to London. I think it was a very unsettled time for her, because she talks about losing contact with her parents, something she seemed to regret, but she doesn't explain why. My maman presumably already knew the reason."

"How did they know each other?"

"I'm not sure exactly, but it struck me as odd that she signed the letter off as 'your new friend Sylvie.'"

"Why?"

"My maman met your grandmother about two years *before* this letter was written. They weren't new friends at this point, so why describe herself as such?"

There's no obvious explanation that I can think of beyond Veronique being wrong about the dates, or a friendly in-joke between the two women that we can't hope to understand now.

"I'm going to keep reading the letters, Lucille. I know they are written by Sylvie, not by my maman, but I can almost hear her thoughts and feelings. There are so many of them."

"Of course." Because, really, what harm can it do? In fact, these letters may be our best source for clues.

Before we can theorize any further, a text pops up on my phone from Leon.

I've finished work. Still fancy that catch-up?

I ask Veronique if she'd like to join us, but she politely declines. Presumably she has a date lined up for later, and is it so wrong that I am pleased about that? Maybe I'm still basking in the glow of Veronique's love affair with Europe, but I find myself wanting to wander this foreign city with only Leon tonight.

12

❧

Alice
NOVEMBER 1953, PARIS
THE DEBUSSY

The embassy buildings are still cloaked in darkness when Alice arrives home just before seven a.m. She asks the taxi driver to pull up at the back of the building so she can walk through the gardens and enter at the less-public-facing entrance at the rear. She scans the building, searching for clues. Which lights are already on, who might be occupied where. Some of the staff will have arrived by now. Patrice certainly. Anne probably. Eloise within the hour. Plus, there will be a good number of cleaning staff already working their way through the salons on the ground floor. And she is still wearing last night's dress. She knows she has no option if she encounters someone but to act as if this is all perfectly normal. What she doesn't know is whether Albert is home and, if he is, where he is.

As soon as she is inside, she removes her shoes, only adding to her sense of guilty retreat, and scoots toward the staircase as quickly as seems appropriate. Just as her stockinged right foot makes contact with the very first step, she hears his voice.

"Alice?"

She holds her breath, instinctively drops her shoes, and pushes her feet back into them. She can tell from the faintness of his call that he is not close. It was a question; he can't yet see her. She checks the clasp on her bag, where Antoine's sketch is hidden, and prepares herself for whatever confrontation may be coming her way.

"Alice!" Albert's voice is louder now. "I'm in the billiards room." In which case, he can't possibly know for sure that it is Alice who has just entered the building. There is no clear line of sight from there to the staircase. She could still make a break for it and dart up the stairs. She seriously considers it. But what would be the point? He clearly already knows she has been out. He's obviously expecting this to be her.

Alice walks into the billiards room, where it is dark, illuminated only by the glow from a fire that Albert has had lit. It's burned down to a deep orange, suggesting he may have been sitting here for some time. There is an empty whiskey glass on the table next to him and the stub of a cigar squashed into a heavy glass ashtray. He makes no attempt to stand as she enters the room, but sits with his hands clasped in his lap, staring at her, waiting for her explanation. Even in the near darkness, she can tell from the controlled rise and fall of his chest that he is holding something in. Annoyance, anger, disappointment? Something he wants to let out.

"Patrice told me you were heading out late last night. Where were you? Did you have fun?" The forced jolliness in her voice makes her cringe. She's fooling no one, least of all Albert, she suspects.

"I was about to ask you the same thing." His voice is flat, controlled. Too controlled. Alice watches as his arms shift, folding across his chest, his left foot lifting onto his right knee, spreading his legs in a move that seems deliberately masculine and confrontational, almost daring her to be honest.

"Sorry, darling, I would have stayed home if I'd thought you were too. Did your plans change?" She says it like it's the most normal thing in the world for a married woman like her to disappear in the early hours of the morning with no explanation.

Albert stands, and she knows whatever he says next is going to determine everything. The mood of the day. Her opinion of herself. Where he sleeps tonight. Whether she'll be able to see Antoine again. She can barely breathe. She feels a sharpness in her fingertips from the strength with which she is gripping her clutch.

He steps slowly toward her, then stops at her side, shifting his head sideways so, while the direction of his body continues to confirm his exit route, his face is angled to her. Then she watches as his eyes slowly run up and down the length of her body in a way that carries none of the pleasure that Antoine's gaze does.

"Be very careful, Alice. He's young and probably quite foolish—don't allow yourself to be played. I can tolerate many things, but I won't be made a fool of."

Albert continues past her and out of the door, not waiting for or expecting a response. His verdict has been delivered. Alice feels the nerves trigger through her body, instantly drying her throat. And she's mortified.

As she stands there, not daring to move an inch, the question of how he could possibly have known is immediately replaced by the realization that of course he knows. He knows everything. He has eyes all over the building, all over Paris probably, and how stupid of her to ever imagine it might be otherwise. And now that he knows, it will be impossible for her to ever snatch another moment alone with Antoine. Every look from this point on will have to be guarded and assessed. Albert will be alert to the slightest hint that anyone else may be questioning his wife's actions or motivations. And she realizes she's crushed by the thought—far more so than when she saw the long blond hair that confirmed Albert's duplicity draped across her husband's shoulders.

As she approaches their bedroom door, she has no idea if Albert will be there on the other side, intending to carry on as if their exchange in the billiards room never happened. She pushes the door open, bracing herself for more of his cold judgment, but, to her great relief, it is Anne she sees, already busy with the day's jobs.

"Good morning, Alice. I can be out of your way in a few moments. Have you had any breakfast? Is there something I can ask Chef to make for you?" Anne turns to see Alice crumple onto the bed, sobbing into the smooth coolness of the covers, the overwhelming tiredness of a missed night's sleep weighing so heavily on her now.

Anne takes a seat next to her, placing a hand on Alice's arm.

"What can I do, Alice?" There is no panic in Anne's voice at all. "How can I help to make things better?" It's as if she knows exactly why Alice is crying, like this is the only logical conclusion to the warning she wishes Alice had listened to.

"There's nothing anyone can do, Anne." Alice's voice is loaded with defeat. "It is all my own fault and only I can make things better, although Lord knows how." Alice lifts her head from the bed, wiping the tears away with the soft pads of her fingertips. Anne raises a hand and gently pushes a lock of wet hair off Alice's face.

"You know you can trust me. If there are things you need to say, Alice, if it helps to say them, it will never go beyond the two of us." Anne's smile is so understanding, almost begging Alice to share her most guarded thoughts.

Alice looks at her devoted maid, so grateful not to be alone in this moment. Why does she feel so full of shame when she knows what she has done is certainly far less than Albert has himself? Is it because she knows she wants more, to cross that imaginary line that will change everything?

"I can see how terribly lonely you are, Alice." Anne is trying her best to coax a few words out of her, and it doesn't take much effort.

"I am. I'm surrounded by people practically every night of the week, but none of it is real, is it? I just wanted some genuine company, Anne, I wasn't expecting it to . . ." Her words tail off. She doesn't want to insult Anne by saying what she knows isn't true.

"I understand. Everyone needs to feel loved and valued—you are no different. What else matters, really?"

Alice takes a moment to really look at Anne. The natural kindness in her face, the delicate creases around her eyes from the long hours she works. The modest but always immaculately pressed navy cotton day dress she wears when she is on duty.

"Tell me about Sébastien, Anne. Is he well?" At the mere mention of her husband's name, Anne's face lifts, all the concern she is feeling for Alice replaced by a love that sits so comfortably in her features.

"He is, but working so hard at the Banque Transatlantique. He'll be fully qualified soon."

"And how many years have you been married now?"

"Seven. We met at school, so it feels much longer in one sense, but our years of marriage have flown by quicker than any others." Alice can see Anne is being careful not to elaborate. She won't sit here and crow about the joys of her own marriage when she understands how unhappy Alice is in hers.

"You've never mentioned children. Will they come soon?" Alice can't help but let a little sadness taint her words, knowing the gift of babies does not lie in her own immediate future.

"Well, I'm not sure we . . ." Anne is suddenly struggling to find the words.

"Don't worry, I'm not asking as your employer. I would miss you terribly, but that's not why I ask."

Alice watches as Anne shifts position on the edge of the bed, no longer comfortable in this conversation.

"I know, it's not that, it's just that . . ."

Alice gives her the space to elaborate, and she can see Anne is trying to work out how to phrase something she is not used to speaking about.

"We would both dearly love a family, more than anything. As soon as we were married, we prayed we would be lucky enough. A boy first, that's what we hoped." She sweeps her hands up over her face, tracing her fingers under her eyes, trying to rub away the hurt. "Then a girl. Even more if we could. We agreed four would be the ideal number, which just seems horribly greedy and foolish now."

Anne's eyes have filled with tears, and Alice can feel a bubble of pain expanding in her own chest. "It wasn't to be. And so far, there hasn't been a doctor in the whole of Paris who can tell us why."

"Oh, Anne, I am so sorry. I had no idea. I would never have mentioned it if I had known." Alice reaches out to take Anne's hand in hers.

"No, I'm glad you did. It's hard for me to talk about it, but sometimes I feel I have to, or the sadness is too much to bear. I am growing to accept it, I have no choice, but the feeling of loss never leaves me, or Sébastien. Something will always be missing for us."

"You're still very young. Isn't it worth continuing to try? You often hear about couples who get lucky eventually."

"Perhaps. It's just so hard to cope with the constant disappointment every month. To allow myself to dream. To think all those positive thoughts and to completely convince myself that this time it could happen, and our little family will be off and running. Only to be knocked sideways again. It's very hard for Sébastien to see me so sad so often too. We wonder if it might be easier to let go. To accept it's not something we have been chosen for. I am very grateful to have a man who loves me as passionately as he does. Maybe I should accept he has to be enough."

Alice wonders if it would be enough for her too.

She pulls Anne into an unreserved hug, holds her there long enough to convey how deep Alice's love for her runs. When their eyes meet again, there is an understanding between them. Both women, denied the one thing they so dearly want. Alice because of her manipulative husband, Anne despite the enduring love of hers.

"He never asked me why."

"Albert?" Anne looks relieved to have the focus shift away from her.

"Yes. Nothing has happened really, not . . ." Alice searches for the appropriate word. "Physically. But maybe I wanted it to. And Albert doesn't question why. Can you imagine it, Anne? A husband who doesn't care about his own wife's feelings? He doesn't want to make me happy. All he cares about is what other people, relative strangers, think. He just wants his life to remain uninterrupted by scandal or inconvenience." Alice's tears well in her eyes as the realization hits her. All those empty years stretching out ahead of her. She thinks about the tender moments Anne and Sébastien have shared, the difficult conversations they have supported each other through, compared to the brutal rewriting of their future Albert has done.

"It must seem so cold to you," she whispers.

"Most things can be changed," says Anne. "Not without pain or sacrifice. But most things are within our power to alter. You just need to work out what you really want—and what you're prepared to give up to get it."

"Look what he did for me." Alice stands, retrieves her clutch from the bedside table, and hands over Antoine's sketch. "This is how he sees me."

Anne holds it in both her hands, studying it for a minute. "It really is you." And Alice can tell from the appreciative look on Anne's face that she, too, is seeing the skill that Antoine has brought to the sketch. But more than that, the longing and desire barely hidden beneath his strokes.

"I don't want to be sad anymore, Anne. Is that really so selfish?" She needs to hear she is not being unreasonable in wanting to be desired and loved and truer to herself.

"No, it's not. But there is a lot at stake. Are you really ready to make those choices?"

"I don't know."

There is a long pause while both women imagine the torturous scenarios that could be witnessed within the residence if Alice isn't very careful.

"If and when you decide you need my help, I will be here, whatever you need from me. Never be afraid to ask."

And in that moment Alice's love for Anne swells and soars. She understands she is not merely offering her the supportive hand of friendship, there is risk too. She is placing herself in direct conflict with Albert, who will act swiftly and severely if he thinks he has been crossed.

"Every day I see how sad you are. I don't want you to feel like you don't deserve to be loved, because you do, and there are people who will love you. There is always another way."

Alice pulls her into a deep hug. "Thank you, Anne. I'm not sure how I would cope without you, my dearest friend."

THE DEBUSSY DRESS IS DELIVERED TO THE EMBASSY RESIDENCE, A little over two weeks after Anne ordered it. Alice's deadline was impossibly tight, even for the talented team at Dior, so they insisted she be gifted the very dress Antoine had admired at the show, after it was altered to precisely fit her measurements—a mark of how much the designer values her business. But looking at it now, Alice can't bear to revisit the memory of that day when Antoine said how much it would suit her, then handed her the note asking if they could meet alone. It was the only reason she frivolously requested the gown. Now here it is in front of her, ready to be worn to a private drinks reception at the Monet *Water Lilies* exhibition at the Musée de l'Orangerie tonight.

In the long, lonely days and nights since she last saw him, Alice has wrestled with her conscience relentlessly, until she feels giddy from the indecision. Antoine has plagued her thoughts, testing her self-control, forcing her to punish herself with the idea that she must remain loyal to her wedding vows. She must not contact Antoine.

But he is so very hard to let go.

It's like he opened her up, filled her with an optimism she never had before. Dared her to believe she can direct her own future, not merely pass through life as someone who is admired and envied from afar. At nearly half his age, he is ten times the man that Albert is.

He may not be powerful or connected or rich himself, but he's passionate, and she wants to mirror him, to sit with him talking late into the night, knowing he would reveal every part of himself to her. Since he's ignited a part of her that Albert has never found, let alone nurtured, she's not sure she has the strength or the resolve to put it out again. To live the responsible, obedient life that is Madame Ainsley's.

But she also knows she has to try. To see if she can force this man from her mind and her dreams. If she can, it will be best for everyone in the long run. She will only have her own disappointment to contend with. Her heart is broken anyway. Albert has seen to that.

The arrangement was that she and Albert would attend together tonight as guests of the museum board, a thank you for all their fundraising efforts this year. But this morning over a silent breakfast, as Albert studied his newspaper and ignored her, he coldly announced otherwise.

"I won't make this evening. Something has come up." Then he wiped his mouth on the pristine white napkin, tossed it onto his plate, and left the room. His unscheduled visit to the barber's later this afternoon confirmed, in Alice's mind at least, that it is female company he will be enjoying tonight. It just won't be hers.

Now she is looking at the dress, thinking only of what could have been. The reaction it might have caused if Antoine had ever got to see her wear it. What would he have said to her? Something that might reverse her agonizing decision not to respond to any of his messages? Not seeing Antoine is the only way, she has reasoned, to completely trust herself not to do something that will cause the kind of hurtful exposure that none of them might recover from. She has deliberately removed his name and that of his parents from future guest lists, knowing Albert won't question her on it. How, quite the opposite, he will appreciate that his point has been listened to.

Alice is putting as much space as possible between herself and temptation. She is determined to erase the memory, to take herself back to those days, two months ago, before Antoine walked into the Salon Bleu and threw a metaphorical grenade into her marriage. And how she made little attempt to stop him. Because as much as her feelings for Albert have shifted from dutiful tolerance through indifference to something that closer resembles loathing, she is still his wife. She can't ignore the many obligations that places on her. And regardless of how he chooses to behave, shouldn't she come out of this able to respect herself?

But the dress. Only now that she is wearing the gown for the very first time can she truly appreciate the complete cleverness of Dior in creating a piece of clothing that is statuesque, womanly, modest, and sensual all at once. Alice stands in front of her full-length mirror and angles her body to the left, checking her side and rear view. The strapless bodice drops away low under her arms, showing off her beautifully toned décolletage and the glow of her freshly moisturized skin. The dress nips immediately inward at the waist, accentuating the shape of her bust before it flares into a hand-sewn bead-and-sequin-scattered train. It is nothing short of total perfection. That the one person this dress is intended for won't see her in it is something she must push to one side.

She has invited Anne to join her this evening, and the pleasure of wearing the Debussy has been eclipsed only by the joy of their earlier role reversal. It was Anne who stood statue still while Alice dressed her in a gown of her own choosing this time, a respectfully understated navy silk coatdress. Alice knots and bows it at the front, retying it several times until she is happy it makes the very most of Anne's figure. Then she adds enough jewels to absorb Anne in her own reflection in the mirror, her eyes widening appreciatively while Alice steps back to admire her work. She watches as Anne moves from side to side, not quite believing she will step out into the Paris evening looking every inch Alice's equal.

THE TRAFFIC IS SO BAD THEY'RE LATE TO ARRIVE, RACING INSIDE past a bank of photographers all snapping away. They are handed a glass of champagne each and slip into the first of two rooms where Monet's groundbreaking work is displayed. They are just in time to catch the tail end of the curator's talk.

"So please take your time this evening to enjoy this *great decoration*, as Monet himself described it. It was some thirty years in the making and inspired by the water garden he built at his Normandy estate. There are eight panels, all practically seamless, one hundred linear meters of the finest impressionist art you will see." There is a soft ripple of applause, and Alice and Anne start to move through the room, making their way closer to the panels. Alice recognizes several faces in the crowd tonight but blissfully feels none of the usual obligation to offer anything other than the briefest acknowledgment. She wants to enjoy her evening with Anne, who she knows would never ordinarily have the time or connections to secure such an invitation.

The vast artwork seems to bend around the walls of the egg-shaped rooms, enveloping them within it. Alice feels she could stand and stare for hours at the way the colors and textures expertly capture the movement and varied depth of the water, the lilies floating on it, the reflections of the clouds on its surface, the bending willow branches breaking the stillness. It's captivating, and she is completely lost in the sheer size of it.

She follows the path of the painting around the room, faintly aware that Anne is tracing her footsteps. They pass in and out of the arches that link the two rooms, enjoying the increasing feeling of space as people are gradually leaving, benefiting from the snatched pieces of information they overhear on their way. Monet wanted to create the illusion of an endless whole, of a wave with no horizon and no shore, a refuge of peaceful meditation. He even dictated the shape of the rooms the paintings are hung in, creating a double ellipse, the mathematical symbol of infinity.

And Alice feels it. She feels for the first time in weeks that there is a sense of peace descending upon her, that her lungs are opening, and she can breathe easily. Being in the presence of something so magnificent has taken her above and beyond the agony of her own reality. She breathes it in and enjoys the briefest feeling of pure calm until the sound of a shattering champagne flute on the stone floor jolts her out of herself. She hears her name being repeated by Anne and realizes to her horror that it is her glass that has fallen from her hand. She can't look down to assess the damage or mess because her eyes are fixed on him, at the far end of the room, now making his way slowly toward her. Antoine has found her, and she knows before he reaches her that she will not be able to resist him tonight.

She is not in control of whatever happens next.

13

Lucille
WEDNESDAY
PARIS

I've arranged to meet Leon in front of the Louvre so we can walk through the Jardin des Tuileries together. The Musée de l'Orangerie is at the far west end, and it's where we know the next dress in the sequence was worn. Dress number six, the Debussy. The dress Granny breathlessly told me was *exquisite*.

I'm waiting under the arch in the place du Carrousel, looking back toward the giant glass-and-metal triangles of the Louvre, thinking how completely incongruous they look, seemingly floating on the water. One of the world's most photographed architectural monuments, but it still looks so out of place surrounded by the ornate buildings that came all those decades before it. A little like me in this city? I might have said that six days ago when I first arrived and I was pathetically reluctant to leave the hotel room. But here I am, about to meet a beautiful French boy. Better than that, one who has asked to meet me.

I should feel nervous, but I don't. The old me would be debating whether to leg it before he appears, to save myself the embarrassment of trying to be interesting and intriguing for him. But I can't wait for him to arrive, camera swinging from his neck, that relaxed smile of his penetrating right through me. And I realize there was no old me.

This *is* me.

No one changes as much as I feel I have in six days. Maybe this confidence was always buried inside me, trapped beneath the surface, and I just needed Paris and Veronique and Leon to tease it out. Did Granny Sylvie know this too?

I'm early, and while I stand watching couples walk hand in hand into the gardens and open-top tourist buses glide past, their passengers hanging dangerously over the side of the top deck in pursuit of the perfect picture, my thoughts turn to Mum and what I'm going to do about her wanting me to return home. I wonder why she has never been able to just gently cruise through life as some people can. Be more accepting of and grateful for what naturally comes her way. Why does everything have to be organized and dictated with no room to simply relax into life, to let it take her where it will? She's probably the most selfish person I know. Most focused, she'd say. But why? Veronique seems to think there must be a reason. Mum's certainly not close to Granny, and I always assumed that was Mum's fault. Is it me who's been unfair? Have I missed something? Is Mum actually the product of her own unhappy childhood?

I'm chewing all this over and getting nowhere when Leon bounds up to me, energy levels brilliantly high. He grabs me by both shoulders.

"So, it was the Debussy next, wasn't it? Worn to the Monet exhibition. Am I right?" I can't fault his enthusiasm, or that he obviously paid attention and remembered the details from last night's wine-fueled summit with Veronique and me.

"You are spot on. But is there any point in going now?" I glance at my watch. "It's five thirty p.m. We've missed the last entry time and it will be closing."

"Yes, it will. But not to us. Come on. I do have one or two connections in this city, you know." He winks at me, and all I can think is how much I would like time to slow down tonight. For every hour to count as three so I can explore the parts of him he has yet to show me. To see if together we can tease out a little more of the real Lucille from inside.

We circle past the broad central fountain and down through the park's wide pedestrian boulevard, our faces brought to life by the neon glare of the giant Ferris wheel and funfair rides to our right. Even by the time we reach the bottom, we can still hear the laughter and screams floating up into the night sky from children ecstatic about being out after dark. The park is like a giant pause button in the middle of this crowded, hectic city. I'm aware of the buildings looming over us on either side. But no towering concrete trespasses onto the footprint of the park, planted as it is onto the city for everyone to enjoy.

"You are very quiet tonight, Lucille." I realize we have walked most of the way to the museum in silence, something that might have been horribly awkward with anyone else, but not Leon. I don't feel the need to hide the reason why, so I tell him.

"My mum wants me to go home. She called today." I may have told her I'm not returning yet, but I know I'll have to. My conscience will get the better of me in the end.

"But your mission." He stops and turns to face me. "We're not finished yet." And I love that he has anchored himself to this story, too, even if not directly for my benefit.

"I know. But, well, she's lost her job and she's very upset about it. She says she needs me." My insides are flipping between a boiling rage that Mum is going to cut this trip short for me and a tender joy that Leon doesn't want it to end either.

"Just a couple more days? That might be all we need to complete the trail. I think I made a little breakthrough today. Let's get inside in the warmth and I will tell you."

I feel my mood instantly level out. As we approach the doors, which are clearly locked, a security guard greets Leon, and the two exchange a few whispered words before he stands aside and lets us in.

"Seriously, how did you manage this?" I am mightily impressed. We are going to have the entire exhibition to ourselves.

"My boss at the Pompidou knows the boss here. I said I needed a big favor, that there is a girl I need to help. But we haven't got long." He holds my gaze for a second or two longer than necessary, and I wonder if he can feel the static between us like I can.

Then we are shown into the first of two bright oval-shaped rooms where a series of giant Monet water lily paintings wrap around the walls in one continuous colorful curve.

Leon's camera is clicking away, snapping me as much as the paintings, as we instinctively separate, him circling right, me left. The temptation to reach out and touch the canvas, this piece of history brought to life in front of me, is almost overwhelming. There is nothing to stop me, other than a trust that I won't. Nothing dominates the image. There is no great central water lily, as you might expect. Some parts of the painting require me to stand back and take in the broader view of the water and its lightness and shade. Other sections demand closer inspection, and I bring my face toward the paint strokes that shift from deep to bright blue, through light green, muddy orange, pale pink, and the clouded white of the flower's distinctively shaped petals.

"I'd never have seen this if it weren't for you," I tell Leon as we are reunited at the top of the room. "It's just incredible. The patience and devotion. It must have taken years to complete!" With no warning, he lifts his camera and snaps me while I'm mid-gush.

"Hey! Why did you do that?" I mock complain, because I am actually quite flattered that he wants to. He's taken so many of me these past few days.

"Because you look so happy, and I don't want to forget how special your smile is." He moves the camera away from his eye and looks at me for real. I mean, *really* looks at me.

"I wonder if our secret lovers felt the same way when they stood in here. Were they as moved by it as I am? Either way, I bet they didn't get the entire place to themselves, did they? Thank you." That Leon cares enough to organize tonight with everything else he's juggling is more than a little heart melting.

"You are very welcome. Listen, I spoke to my grandfather today and he remembers the Debussy dress very well." Leon has stepped closer to me.

"Really? All these years later? Although, you've seen it, it would be a very difficult dress to forget."

"It's more than that. He was invited to a private exhibition held here in the early fifties. He told me this afternoon how Monet's paintings had hung in this museum for years, since the midtwenties in fact, but public interest in them just wasn't there. People cared so little that the museum used to cover the panels with the work of other painters. Can you imagine? That all changed after the Second World War, when the Americans started to appreciate the impressionists and private buyers started seeking out Monet's work. That's when the exhibition was held. A sort of relaunch, I suppose."

"Okay, go on. I'm not quite sure how this helps us."

"He specifically remembers a woman wearing the dress. There was some sort of scene apparently, glasses were dropped, a bit of a commotion—and an almighty fuss between a young man and a beautiful woman in the Debussy. They kissed. It's got to be her, Lucille, the woman we have been following all over Paris. We know from the card that she was at the Orangerie and wearing that dress. I can't think of another explanation, can you?"

I feel everything inside me tighten and still. "You told me yourself, she wouldn't be the only woman to buy any one of these dresses . . . but what are the chances that more than one woman bought it and then both wore it to the same exhibition? It has to be her." My heart is thumping against my ribs. This is definitely progress!

"It gets better." Leon can't contain his excitement either. He's gripping my arms now. "There were photographers here that night. It was a special evening, and my grandfather is sure there is a picture of the lady in the Debussy somewhere in the shop, in Bettina. It's exactly the sort of thing he collected over the years. He was going to have a look for it himself, but he might not get back there for days. I say we go there now—I have the keys—and see if we can find it for ourselves. What d'you think?"

I can't quite believe it. "If we find it, we will be looking at A. It will be her, won't it? Perhaps then I will understand why my grandmother was so keen for me to come to Paris and follow this trail." I feel excited and edgy and fearful, but also cautious about getting my hopes up.

"Yes!"

I throw my arms around him. "You are amazing, Leon. I would be nowhere with this without you." And then, in a moment of utter abandon, I kiss him. I aim for his cheek, but he turns his head and our lips meet each other. There is the slightest pause when I think neither of us is quite sure if this is what the other one intended, and then, without breaking our connection, Leon pushes his camera over his left shoulder and pulls me in tighter to him. Our bodies are touching and his hands slide from either side of my face and up into the back of my hair. Then, in a moment worthy of the finest Hollywood producer, every light in the place goes out. I jolt slightly, but he refuses to let me pull away, and in the total darkness of the museum, with only Monet as our witness, the kiss goes on and on.

I text Veronique from the taxi to Bettina.

I think she will want to be there for this. It seems wrong to exclude her when we might be about to have a major breakthrough. She's going to meet us there and claims to have more information to share herself too. It's all starting to come together! Then, just when everything seems pretty bloody perfect—I'm curled up on the back seat of the taxi, speeding across Paris, with Leon's hand in mine—my phone rings and it's Mum. I consider bumping the call, but then I think about the number of times she's bumped mine and how it made me feel. I answer it.

"Yes, Mum?" She senses the exasperation in my voice, which is what I am hoping for.

"Oh. I'm interrupting, aren't I? I was just wondering about your plans, darling. Whether you know when you'll be back exactly?" She never believed my determination to stay in Paris either then.

"Not really, no. I'm making real progress here and I think I just need a few more days, then we'll have all the time you need to chat about you." I can feel Leon's eyes turn to me at the mention of my return home.

"Okay, I was just going to offer to book your return ticket for you if you're pushed for time? That way you can get a refund on the ticket you don't use, and you'll be up, seeing as you didn't pay for it in the first place. Perhaps I can send a car to pick you up at the airport?" And that bit is appealing, if it means I can avoid the claustrophobic crush of the Piccadilly line. Another time I might have wavered, but she can't see the man I'm sitting next to.

"Thanks, Mum, but I'm not ready to leave just yet."

"I'm not sure I understand"—by which she means she hasn't been paying attention to much of what I've said since I got here. "Why is this trip so important?" Her steely edge is always simmering just beneath the surface.

"Because it's important to Granny, that's why."

There is a very long silence that I'm reluctant to fill, until finally she adds, "I'm pleased you and Granny are so close, Lucille, you have such a different relationship with her to the one I had growing up. I just wish you and I, well, that we were . . . closer too." And, I have to say, the admission floors me. Why now? Why does she have to pick this moment, when I am curled into Leon, to start a conversation that needs more than the two minutes I can currently give it?

"Oh, Mum, we need to talk about this properly, when I'm back, not now when it's all so rushed. What I'm doing here is important, but I'm also having fun, doing something for me for once, and to be honest, I'm not ready for that to end yet." As soon as I say it, I feel bad. It's just not in my nature to be as ruthless with her as she has been with me over the years. "Look, I'm sorry." I'm backtracking already. "I'm just on my way to sort something out now, and then I'll make plans to come home. I promise." That satisfies her, and I end the call.

"I really hope that photograph is in the shop, Leon, because my time in Paris is running out." The thought of returning home to unpick everything with Mum and face the dressing-down Dylan will be readying for me is coming very close to ruining this magical evening altogether.

"Only if you let it," says Leon. "And for what it's worth, I'd love for you to stay. And not just for a few days. Longer." Then he kisses me again, letting his hands wander over me and under my coat this time, and I want to redirect this taxi back to his place and forget everything else in the world.

IT FEELS LIKE SO MUCH HAS HAPPENED SINCE I LAST STOOD IN Bettina two days ago. Veronique has beaten us here, so now all three of us are on the hunt, searching carefully through every cluttered surface in the shop. Veronique, who has already allowed herself to be totally sidetracked by what she tells me is a sample of the finest French hand-sewn guipure lace, says her news can wait. Finding the photograph, if it is here, has to come first.

We plan to divide and conquer. Leon disappears onto his knees behind the till to tackle the massive disorganized clutter of paperwork that sits beneath it. Veronique takes the left-hand side of the shop, I take the right. If this throws up no results, we agree we will have to move into the back room and go through every one of the box files.

Please, God, no.

We work in silence, sifting through everything that is stuffed within this Aladdin's cave. I check the wall behind a hanger of silk scarves, and painstakingly pick through a box of hundreds of vintage postcards in case our photograph is nestled within them. I open a small heart-shaped jewelry box, its lid embroidered with a bunch of garden roses. I examine the inside of every handbag in the place. I run a hand through a display of leather belts and rearrange a glass cabinet of old cologne bottles. Nothing. I get down on my hands and knees and effectively crawl under the hanging clothes, feeling the dust re-settle on me as I go. I debate whether I need to push apart every item of clothing on my rail in case the picture has somehow got wedged between two items that haven't been touched for years. And I do, a completely fruitless task that wastes another forty minutes.

We've all been in the shop for well over an hour now, and our enthusiasm is definitely starting to wane. Leon disappears out the back, returning moments later with three ice-cold beers that we all sip from the bottles. He's leaning over the counter drinking his while Veronique offers to share her news, to revive our spirits a little.

"I did some digging around at work on the fabric of the missing dress—the Toile de Jouy—and it was used by Dior around the same time as the other dresses we've been following. Perhaps it is safe to assume, given that all the other gowns have been by Dior, that this one is too. Interestingly, it is also very similar to the pattern of fabric that he chose to decorate some parts of his first boutique. From what I found, it is not a fabric he used in a general collection, so I think we can assume this dress was a special commission."

"Do you have any idea where it might be now? A dress that important must be documented somewhere, mustn't it?" Leon is looking for the much-needed good news that he knows will cheer me up in the absence of any photograph.

"I know exactly where it is." Veronique beams. "You are right, a dress that important *has* been documented, and somewhere much closer to your own home, Lucille."

"What? Where?!"

"It's being held in the archives of the Victoria and Albert Museum in London. They wouldn't tell me much over the phone, but we are right about one thing. Whoever had the dress made, at great expense by Dior, later donated it. But with one strict caveat."

"Really? What is it?" Blimey, this is getting really intriguing now.

"That their name must never be published or listed anywhere in connection with the dress." Veronique's eyes are blazing with excitement.

I'm trying to piece all this together in my head. I deliver my thoughts slowly out loud, hoping they will make more sense that way. "So, we know the owner was A, the card tells us that. But we still don't know who A is. How are we going to . . ." I trail off, realizing I am no further along with knowing the answers.

"They can pull it from the archive for you, Lucille. You can go and view it. I went ahead and made an appointment for you on Sunday. I hope that's okay? I felt sure you would want to see it."

"Yes, I do, I absolutely do." I look back toward Leon, who is still hunched over the desk, listening closely to everything that is being said. I wonder if he might like to come with me to London. My eyes shift off to the noticeboard on the wall behind Leon's head.

"Did you check the noticeboard yet?" I ask, motioning behind him.

"No, let me do that." He starts to carefully remove every piece of paper pushed under the crisscross of once-white ribbon that's holding everything in place. My eyes are fixed on a small black-and-white image at the very bottom right-hand corner, buried so only a very small corner of it is visible.

The beautiful hem of an evening gown.

I wait patiently while Leon continues around the board until, finally, he has removed nearly everything. There is one last postcard to lift away before the image is fully revealed, but I think I already know what I can't bring myself to say out loud. Not until I am 100 percent sure. Leon has his back to us, and as he lifts the postcard, I see his shoulder blades tense together. He can see it too. He spins to face us both, holding it aloft.

"Here she is!" he shouts, far louder than necessary in this tiny shop, and Veronique and I both lunge forward toward him. He places the photograph on the counter in front of the three of us, and I honestly think my heart stops beating. There she is. The woman we have been looking for, wearing the beautiful Debussy that is currently hanging in my hotel wardrobe. And while the years have been stripped away, her skin blended back to its youthful best, her features are unmistakable to me.

It's my grandmother.

14

✧✦✧

Alice
NOVEMBER 1953, PARIS
THE DEBUSSY

The kiss is intense.

Not the kind of kiss that should be seen by others.

A kiss that is never going to stay just a kiss.

It's leading somewhere it shouldn't, and Alice can't stop it. Antoine doesn't say a word before he places his lips on hers, but she can feel his passion flowing into her mouth and in the strength of his hands at the small of her back. It's like everything else in the room is falling away. Nothing else matters. Alice doesn't think about Albert, or Anne. She doesn't think about anyone else in the room and how they might retell this story. *Whom* they might retell it to. She doesn't even think about the photographers still circulating and whether this kiss is being captured. Every cell in her body is tuned perfectly to Antoine. His familiar smell, the low moan he makes as the kiss moves deeper and deeper into her.

It is Anne who interrupts them.

"Alice, *please*. This is not a good idea. We need to leave." Her words are whispered but urgent enough to break the two of them apart.

All three of them move swiftly toward the exit. Just as they are about to make it to the relative safety of the darkness outside, they come face-to-face with Antoine's mother, one hand wedged at her hip. There is no way to exit the building without dealing with her first.

"This really has got to stop, don't you think, Madame Ainsley? I mean, *really*. Is it your ambition to be the subject of every gossip in Paris?" There is no deference being shown to Alice now. They are a long way from the social hierarchy of the residence salon. "What on earth will Monsieur Ainsley say when he finds out? It's not just your reputation you're ruining, you know. It's my son's."

Before she can say a word, Antoine jumps to Alice's defense. "No. It isn't going to stop, Maman. Not unless Alice wants it to."

"Your father is going to have a great deal to say about this, you realize. Why can't you just be more like your brother?" Her words are thrown at Antoine with an air of malice that makes Alice stiffen by his side and provokes a level of anger in Antoine that she has not seen before.

"You're never going to forgive me, are you? I'll never live up to your impossible expectations!" he hisses, brushing past her, Alice and Anne trailing with him, out toward Alice's waiting driver.

Having had no success with her son, Madame du Parcq turns on Alice. "I'm warning you, Madame Ainsley, this will not end well for you. *Please*, stop it now." She delivers the words with a studied shake of her head. "What might seem like fun certainly won't be in the weeks to come. He won't be able to cope with it."

Alice isn't sure whether she means Antoine or Albert, but there is no time to ponder it further.

"You take the car back to the residence, Anne. I'll make sure Alice is safe," says Antoine.

"Is that what you want, Alice?" Poor Anne looks close to tears. At least one of them understands the severity of what has happened tonight.

Alice just looks shell-shocked, mentally detached from everything that is going on around her, and it's Antoine who has to take charge. This was supposed to be a lovely evening for her and Anne. She had not anticipated for one moment it might end this way. She's being jostled by the crowds now exiting the building behind them, and in the absence of any other plan, she nods her head, signaling that Anne can go, wondering if she will make it back to the residence first or whether news of the evening's events will beat her to it. And then what?

"Let's take the boat back to my apartment," offers Antoine.

THEY BOARD THE RIVER TAXI AT PORT DES CHAMPS-ÉLYSÉES AND take shelter under the glass canopy inside, right at the back, where two Italian tourists only have eyes for Paris.

All the color has drained from Alice's face, and she feels a little dizzy.

"How did you know I would be there, Antoine?"

"That was easy enough. I knew how desperately my mother was hoping for an invitation. Hers came very late. She was clearly the second tier, meaning you of course would be the first. My father had no interest in attending, so I took the risk that your husband would feel the same way. And I'm so glad I did. Why didn't you return any of my messages?" He's searching her face, desperate to understand where he went wrong.

"He knows about us."

Alice is expecting this to silence Antoine, to scare him into some level of contrition at least. But it has the reverse effect—it emboldens him.

"Good. If nothing else, that will take the wind out of Maman's sails. She can hardly hang the threat of our exposure to him over us now, can she?"

"He confronted me the night I came back from Les Halles. He was waiting for me. He warned me, Antoine, that it has to stop. That he won't be made a fool of—and we've just kissed in front of a room full of, what, two hundred people? There were photographers there."

Antoine buries his face into the soft warmth of Alice's neck, allowing his lips to move beneath the softness of her fur coat and delicately trace along her collarbone.

"I love you, Alice. I've tried very hard not to, but I do—I'm not going to lose you."

She has never felt so desired.

"Take off your earrings."

Alice lifts her fingers to the expensive drop pearls, the ones she has worn every day since her wedding, feeling that to discard them would be equivalent to removing her wedding ring—and is she really contemplating doing that?

"Why?"

"He bought them for you, didn't he?"

"Yes."

"I don't want him to have any part of tonight."

In the year she has been in Paris, Alice has never ridden on a water taxi. She's never needed to. Darkness has engulfed the city, and she can feel the unfamiliar yet protective cocoon of the architecture on either side of them, flanking the river that's sunken low beyond the basements of the buildings. How many eyes might be watching them now? The gray of the rooftops above blends into the night sky, blurring the edges, giving the whole evening a fairy-tale quality.

They pass under bridges so dense that, for a few tantalizing moments, they are plunged into complete darkness. Every time it happens, she feels Antoine absorb a little more into her. She senses his impatience to get her home in the tautness of his body, exaggerated by the surprising speed of the boat. The city's famous landmarks appear alongside them and then just as quickly are gone, like an ever-changing movie set, telling a story that is just for them tonight.

"Let's go outside," she suggests. She knows it will be cold, but she doesn't want the glass windows of the boat to dilute an experience she may never repeat. The air is laced with the tang of fuel and the laughter of friends dining together on the many stationary restaurant boats they pass. How she envies the ease of their happy evening.

Now that they are standing at the back of the boat, Alice is revived somewhat by the wind whipping across her face and a sense they are speeding away from everything. Smaller boats appear to chase them. What if Albert were in one of them, pursuing her, trying to put a stop to all this before it really is too late? Would she want him to reach her in time? One look at Antoine smiling, his whole face alive with anticipation and intent, is all the encouragement she needs to stay on the boat. She wishes she could lean over the back and cut loose the French flag that is flying from its stern, a sorry reminder of the role she should be playing in Paris and her many obligations. She would like to see it falter, collapse, and slowly sink into the dark waters beneath them. Is that where her marriage is heading too?

As the Seine gently bends, the boat slows, taking up its position alongside many others in front of the illuminated Eiffel Tower, standing proud over Paris, confident of its ability to impress. Every face on every boat is looking at this one bold landmark, watching as its elevators slowly rise through the heart of the metal structure like mechanical bugs chewing their way to the top. Antoine doesn't look at the tower, he looks at Alice. Taking advantage of everyone's gaze being directed elsewhere, he kisses her deeply, and she can feel all the hurt and doubt of the lost time since they were last together melt into relief now that he has her in his arms again.

The boat turns and starts to retrace its journey back past the Hôtel des Invalides, on their right now, and the huge twin clock towers of the Musée d'Orsay before it docks at Quai Malaquais and Antoine takes her hand to disembark. Within ten minutes they are turning right onto the narrow, gallery-lined rue des Beaux-Arts, Alice feeling a long way from the wealthier boulevards of the Right Bank.

"I know, it's everything my mother despises, isn't it?" suggests Antoine, trying to read her thoughts. "It's partly why I live here and not in the cosseted mausoleum they want me in, north of the river."

"Would she really despise it?" It seems like an odd thing for Madame du Parcq to direct her anger at.

"Yes. The place is crawling with actors, writers, singers, musicians, poets. Everyone she would deem frivolous, those of us with no desire to be doctors, lawyers, or politicians. Where other people see creativity and diversity, she smells wastefulness and procrastination. She will never understand people who work from a café table during the day and from the dark cellar of a jazz bar at night. This is not her world, Alice. It's mine. She hasn't once visited me here, preferring to rely on tales from her equally ill-informed friends rather than experiencing it for herself."

"And you'll never go back?"

"I doubt they'd want me back. Not the real me anyway, only the version they hoped would continue where Thomas couldn't." As they continue down the quiet, cobbled road, he gestures back over their shoulders to the beautiful building, its black railings barely visible behind the student bicycles attached there. "I live in the shadow of the art school for a reason. To remind myself. Maybe one day I'll get there."

They turn into a small covered alleyway that opens onto a secluded courtyard at the end, completely enclosed by the residential buildings surrounding it for several floors up. She notices all the windows of the ground-floor apartments are barred, and the tiny gated garden off to the left, encircled by black railings, is overgrown. The garden has one small metal table just big enough for two, and two rusty chairs that no one would trust to sit on. They're hard to pick out in the darkness. Broken bulbs in the lantern lamps haven't been replaced, and there are tangles of neglected shrubs running wild. Someone went to the effort of planting several stone pots, then ignored them all, their now un-identifiable contents left to brown and shrivel.

"Follow me." Antoine unlocks the garden gate. He takes her in-side, up two small flights of stairs, and into one big room that seems to be his entire living space. There is a large, low bed pushed against one wall that remains unmade from last night, its white sheets and blankets thrown open and left. A battered old chaise, its fabric fraying around the legs, sits closer to the window, providing a view onto the courtyard below. There is nothing covering the wooden floor, and Al-ice can feel the coldness creeping through the wide cracks between the exposed boards. Overstuffed bookshelves line one entire wall on either side of an open fireplace that's overflowing with ashes. Another wall is covered in Antoine's own sketches—people, mostly, going about their everyday lives, unframed and carelessly tacked to the paintwork. Otherwise there is a small desk positioned between the two windows, a wooden wardrobe, and a cluttered side table piled high with more books and a half-finished bottle of red wine on one side of the bed. It's all the furniture Antoine appears to own. Another door leads to what she assumes must be his bathroom.

"Is that him? Thomas?" she asks, pointing to a sketch of a smiling young man with striking features whose face appears several times across the wall.

"Yes, that's him. It's how I like to remember him."

"What happened to him, Antoine?" She wants to hear more and senses, after the earlier confrontation with his mother, now might be the chance for him to open up.

Antoine is preparing a fire, throwing a few last remaining logs into the grate before he slowly stands.

"His death was my fault, at least they see it that way." He takes a few steps toward her. "He was back with us, his part in the war was done. We were all walking home from a café where we'd had dinner."

Antoine's eyes lose focus, like he's deep within his memories. "Thomas had told us he was going to propose to his girlfriend, Estelle. He'd even shown us the ring. My mother had burst into tears at the table, my father offered his firmest handshake. They were so happy. When we were saying our goodbyes at the roadside before Thomas diverted back to his apartment, I was messing around—making fun of him for being so in love. For being . . . so happy."

He pauses for a few seconds, hesitating, questioning whether he can finish the story.

"As he crossed the road, I shouted good luck for his proposal, and he glanced back at me for a couple of seconds." His voice grows so soft, Alice can barely hear it. "I remember his smile was so wide I couldn't see his eyes. He didn't even register the bicycle taxi swinging onto the path he was taking."

Alice feels her breath still.

"I knew he was dead the second he hit the ground. It was going so fast. It was like I watched the life be knocked out of him. My perfect brother who had conquered so much was lying lifeless in the road, an impossible tangle of limbs."

He leans an elbow against the mantelpiece, needing the support.

"He looked so pale, Alice, and so still . . . but he was still smiling."

Alice raises a hand to Antoine's chest and lets it sit there. After a moment, he places his hand over hers and holds it to his heart.

"When he returned from the war, he never spoke of the things he'd seen, other than to say he had no regrets about going, that he felt he had done his duty and learned skills he never would have in the classroom. He planned to go straight back to school, to graduate and specialize in surgery. He wanted to help people. He was going to get married."

"It was a horrible accident, Antoine, how can you possibly believe it was your fault?" More than anything, Alice wants to make him see it wasn't.

"I'll never forget the look on my father's face that night. The sense of irony that the one son who might have been some use in this situation was the one lying broken on the ground. In the seconds that counted most, I cried over his body. I didn't know what else to do. I'm not sure my father ever recovered from telling Estelle. To this day I have no idea if he told her that Thomas had planned to propose. But honestly, all I cared about was that I had lost my brother, my champion. In a split second his life was gone. It was only later I realized that with it, I'd lost any chance I stood of my parents ever being content with the son they still had. It's why I finally agreed to enroll in the politics course."

"How did that help?"

"It hasn't, but at the time it was the one sacrifice I could make that I thought might bring them some comfort. It was the only form of an apology I could think of. That I would try every day to be the son they wanted, even though it went against all my own wishes. Now it just feels like an insult to them—and Thomas—to pretend I ever could. Being reminded of my failure to make them proud, in every look, every sigh, every slump of their shoulders, feels like an eternal grief I'll never overcome."

"Have you told them any of this, Antoine?"

"No, I've never discussed it with anyone, until you." He places a light kiss on the palm of Alice's hand. "I feel closer to him every time I pick up a pencil. Your reaction to my sketches is the only thing that has come close to the way he encouraged me."

"I think you are very brave, far more than you give yourself credit for. I hope one day your parents will see that too. Thank you for trusting me."

"Thank you for understanding." He seems visibly lighter now after talking about Thomas. "Let's have a glass of wine."

He grabs the bottle from the bedside table and a couple of glasses from the windowsill by his desk. Then he is standing in front of her, handing her the glass, and she can see the urgency there in his face again. Isn't this exactly what she wanted? To be taken out of her world?

"I want to undress you."

Alice feels her heart rate immediately spike. The nerves shudder up her legs, and she instinctively raises the glass to her lips, saying nothing.

He allows her to take two large mouthfuls of the red wine before he takes the glass from her hand and places both of them on the mantelpiece. Then he pushes the fur from her shoulders and allows it to drop to the floor. Turning her so she is facing the fire, he traces his fingers across her smooth skin, sweeping across her collarbone, and allowing his fingers to dip just beneath the bodice. Her back is to him, but their bodies are so close they feel joined. He unties the stiff navy ribbon that is fixed at her waist, and Alice can feel the dress give a little next to her skin. She knows the number of buttons and hooks that run down the back of this dress and how far he will get before it falls from her body. She knows how naked she is underneath, just a pair of blush silk knickers edged in soft satin that sit low beneath her hip bones, and her Dior heels. Nothing else. With every unfastening that his fingers expertly make, she allows her head to collapse backward onto him, a feeling of total surrender swimming through her.

"My God. You are even more beautiful than I believed."

And it's as if every touch, every kiss from this point on is designed to right that fault. She can feel how much he wants to please her. How important it is. As he lays her gently down onto her fur, there isn't an inch of her body that he doesn't explore. And every second he's connected to her scorches every doubt she ever had. Alice doesn't care what he does to her or what the consequences might be; she couldn't stop him now even if she wanted to.

She's lost.

15

Lucille
THURSDAY
PARIS

It came to me on the journey back to the hotel from Bettina last night, where I had seen the carousel from the Jardin du Luxembourg before.

It's an image that accompanied a thousand of my bedtime stories at Granny's house. The first and last thing I saw as a child when she lifted the storybook from her bedside table and replaced it back there twenty minutes later as my eyelids were heavy and closing. The dog-eared and weathered postcard, its glossy image detaching from the paper behind it, that she used as a bookmark. It was always the same, whatever book she was reading to me. Some nights Granddad would join us, sit on the end of the bed while she read. I don't think it mattered to him that it was the Famous Five or *The Wind in the Willows*, it was just another opportunity to be in her company. He'd gently prod her if she nodded off, exhausted from running around after an eight-year-old all weekend while Mum worked again. He knew she'd insist on finishing the story. I bet if I look through the pile of books that sit on her ottoman at home by the fire, that bookmark will be there somewhere. All these years later.

It feels like we are long overdue for a chat. I want to hear her confirm what I already know. That she is the woman in the photograph at Bettina. That she lived this whole other life beyond everything I thought I knew about her—a life I'm not even sure her own daughter is aware of. Because when I think of her and my granddad, I remember two people so comfortable in their companionship, their relationship spectacular in its simplicity. On frosty mornings he was always the one to brave the cold. He would sit in the car at the end of their garden path, rubbing his hands together until the heater made it warm enough for my grandmother to join him. He always carved a Sunday roast and, later, he washed while she dried the dishes, always together. I never recall seeing them hold hands. They preferred the proximity of being arm in arm. Sometimes, when I was staying the night, I was allowed to join them for dinner at a friend's house, staying up way past my bedtime. On the walk home later, Granddad would keep me awake by getting me to chase my own shadow. I never got bored of the games he invented. There was never a limitation on the attention he would give me. It makes me shudder to think two people so suited to each other so nearly never got together. I like to think the stars aligned in some otherworldly way to ensure their paths crossed the day they first met in Paris, when they so easily might not have.

It's all a long time and a great distance from this beautiful suite where my stay is nearing its end. As I lie in splendor, there is a long and highly unappealing list of jobs clouding my thoughts. Ones I must do, each one making me more anxious than the last.

Number one: Call the front desk of this hotel and find out what on earth my room bill is. That one is truly terrifying. I know Granny is supposed to be paying for this trip, but there are limits to anyone's generosity, and I'm not sure she expected me to be here quite this long, or to live quite so lavishly.

Number two: Say goodbye to Leon. This is the one I want to do least of all.

Number three: Go home to Mum and try to fully understand the complexities of her life and the decisions she has made, a job I feel woefully underqualified to do.

Number four: Face the music at work—assuming I still actually have a job at all.

Perhaps this is the most surprising present to me from Paris. Nothing can compete with Granny's story for drama and intrigue, that's for sure. But I can see now how I have allowed myself to drift—into a job I don't want; through a relationship that didn't make me feel *anything*, that was coasting when it should have been soaring; moving in silent circles with my own mother, never once having the courage to tell her how she makes me feel, to make the necessary effort to understand how she feels.

Even with Granny. All those hours spent in front of the fire with her playing chess and chatting, and I never really knew her, not all of her. The things we *could* have been talking about and sharing. The stories she could have told me that might have inspired me. And now there is so little time left together.

So, I'm going home tomorrow, carefully packing up these gowns and taking them back to the woman they belong to and confronting everything else. What a week that's going to be. Veronique has offered to join me, so we'll visit the Victoria and Albert archive together. I can't think of a more fitting end than her helping me put the final piece of this jigsaw in place. Dress number seven, the Mexico, was worn in "the garden," which isn't specific enough to be able to locate, so we'll finish with dress number eight. Then I can sit down with Granny, hear her retell the whole story, and know that I did what she asked me to do.

But first I need to hear her say it. I need to hear her say that she is the woman who owned these dresses, that this is *her* great love story. I want her to tell me I am right, she is A, that I haven't somehow misunderstood the whole thing—and how it ended. I pick up my phone by the side of my bed and dial her number. But it isn't Granny's voice I hear when the line connects.

"Natasha?"

"Oh, hello, Lucille, yes, it's me," she whispers. "I'm afraid your grandmother is still asleep. Can I help with anything?"

"But it's . . ." I glance at the clock on the bedside table. "It's very late for her to still be in bed." Granny has always been an early riser, and I know that any other day she would be up, dressed, and finishing her breakfast by now.

"Yes, it is. She was sound asleep when I arrived this morning and it took some time to rouse her. I don't think it's anything to worry about, but she does seem to be a little low on energy this week. I've left a couple of messages for your mum, but I haven't been able to chat with her yet."

I feel a shot of anger at that and try my best not to react. More than anything, I just desperately want to talk to Granny, to see her again.

"Okay, please will you call me, rather than Mum, if anything changes, and I'll be there myself as soon as I can."

"I know you will, Lucille, thank you. I'll let her know you phoned. I'm sure she'll want to talk to you."

LEON TEXTS AFTER I'VE HUNG UP WITH NATASHA TO SAY THERE'S something he should have told me. I'm too worried about Granny to spend much time thinking about what that might be, and quickly arrange to meet him in the hotel lobby in an hour.

Having him in my room feels like it might be asking for trouble. The memory of his kiss is still fresh on my lips. I don't need any more temptation, not when I feel this mentally weak. Then I call Veronique and make sure she is still okay to meet at the Gare du Nord tomorrow afternoon to catch the five p.m. Eurostar back to London. She's booked a hotel nearby for a few nights. We'll see the dress together and she'll have a couple of days hanging out with some old friends in London before heading back to Paris.

"Yes, the arrangements are all ready," confirms Veronique. "I have the Eurostar tickets and all the paperwork. You just need to remember your passport and all those dresses. Leave nothing behind!"

I EXIT THE LIFT INTO THE HOTEL LOBBY AND HEAD FOR THE RE-ception desk. I may as well take a look at my room bill now and get one horrendous job out of the way. The flawless creature behind the desk prints it out for me, and I am presented with confirmation of every itemized luxury I have enjoyed since I arrived seven days ago. Four hundred euros of laundry charges! I never did get around to buy-ing that *something chic* Mum told me to. And did I really eat seven croque monsieurs in that time? Apparently so.

As I scan down the list of items, I see that a payment has been made. The night Veronique, Leon, and I sat cross-legged on the floor of my suite, drank all that wine, and ate the best burgers in Paris has a card payment registered beneath it. It was covered by a Mr. Manivet.

Leon.

He must have paid the bill on his way out that night. Wow. It would have been the easiest thing in the world to skip through recep-tion without giving the cost a second thought. But he didn't. He didn't just do the decent thing, he did the totally unexpected thing, and I just love him for it. The comparison is cruel, but Billy never bought me dinner. I honestly can't remember it happening.

I'm pretending to still be examining my bill, panic-thinking about my payment options. To make matters worse, an older man in a sharp suit has appeared, whispering to his immaculate colleague while checking my details on the computer screen. Clearly, *obviously*, they don't think I can pay this bill. They're right. I could ask Mum to cover it, but I know she'll use it as leverage to extract a favor (or ten) before I can pay her back. Or, I can hope my credit card, which I only ever use in extreme emergencies, won't be declined. It has to be that. I hand it over and watch as it sits on the counter, ignored.

"There is nothing to pay, mademoiselle," offers the man in the suit, who looks a lot less intimidating now that he's smiling.

My first thought is to thank him and run before they realize their mistake, but my damned conscience has other ideas.

"The first two nights are covered, I know, but the rest I do need to settle." I can't have Granny being charged for all this. Frankly, I wouldn't want her to even *see* these laundry charges.

"No, no. *Everything* is covered. Apologies, mademoiselle, we assumed you had been told. We have a very small number of lifetime VIPs associated with the hotel, and your reservation was made by one of them. Therefore, no charge!" He says it with a triumphant flourish of his fingers. When I don't move, because I am waiting for the penny to drop and him to realize it must be the guest in the room next to mine they're thinking of, he adds, "I can assure you, mademoiselle, senior management checks these details *very* carefully. It is decided at their total discretion. There is no mistake. The reservation was made by your grandmother, correct? She must have been a great supporter of the hotel."

"Yes, but . . ." I glance over my shoulder and scan around the lobby. Leon's sitting, looking completely at home, sipping a cappuccino and getting stuck into more of those posh financiers he introduced me to. Something else I'm going to miss about Paris. I don't want to keep him waiting, but this isn't right. How long will I have to stand here before they understand that? The queue behind me is not small, so I insist they take my credit card details—for when the blunder becomes apparent, as it surely will—and head Leon's way.

"I saved you one," he offers as I approach his table.

"I'm honored." I reject the chair opposite and take a seat next to him, and I can't help it, it's corny as all hell, but I plant a kiss on his cheek. "Thank you for dinner."

"Am I buying you dinner?" He looks elated at the thought that he might be.

"Not tonight." And possibly not any other night, I realize with a sad sigh. "The burgers and wine from Tuesday? I just checked my bill and saw you covered it. That was incredibly generous, thank you."

He bats the words away with the back of his hand. "It's nothing, don't even mention it. So, now what? What does the day hold?"

"Mostly me packing. I'm going home tomorrow." I'm genuinely sad to be leaving him—but there are things I need to face, and I try to focus on that. And how I probably wouldn't be facing any of them if Granny hadn't sent me here in the first place. "But your text said there was something you needed to tell me?"

His face dips, and I'm suddenly wishing I hadn't reminded him.

"Oh, yes." This is not going to be good, I can feel it. I consider telling him not to bother, whatever it is can stay a secret, I might rather not know. But I'm too late.

"The other day, you asked me if I have a girlfriend—and I should have been honest with you."

Oh no, please don't let this end the predictable way I fear it might now. Don't let this be my postscript from Paris. It will ruin everything. I know we've only kissed, once, and we're not about to skip up the aisle together, but there has been a closeness we've both felt. I can't bear to think he was holding my hand in the back of a taxi and then frantically texting another woman explaining why he would be late. Not Leon, please.

"Her name is Emma. She's English too."

I feel the lump in my throat swell, and for one awful moment I think I'm going to cry.

"She's also the reason I've tried to stay away from women for a while. But it's been much harder with you." His face is searching mine, trying to read my thoughts.

"I don't understand." I don't want to say any more because the tears are threatening to fall, and I'm having to blink furiously to stop them.

"We were together for two years. She was studying here at the Sorbonne when we were introduced by a good friend of mine. We connected straightaway, and about a month later we were living together." He scans my face for a reaction, and I work hard to hide the fact that it hurts to know he could fall for someone else that quickly.

"I couldn't see how anything would ever break us apart." I don't know how he can say all this with such ease. Maybe, if he's not emotional about it, I don't need to be either? I stamp down on that thought.

"About six months ago, I came home early from a job one afternoon and caught her in bed with the same friend who had introduced us. I just stood there like an idiot, staring at them. Not believing what I was seeing." It's reassuring that he hasn't lowered his voice to tell me any of this.

"Turns out, she had been seeing him since the very beginning. All that time and I never realized. So, I lost what I thought was my soul mate and a good friend the same day." I feel myself let out the breath I had been holding in.

"Blimey. Leon, I'm so sorry." But then I can't help but smile because, despite his initial reticence, he didn't hide this from me. He was open and honest.

He smiles back. "Well, it's taken a while, but I am beyond it now. The first few months weren't fun, but I have some great friends, genuine ones, who have pulled me through. It was the deception more than anything. Once I realized all the lies it had taken for her to do that, well, that's the bit that really knocked a hole in me."

"I'm glad you told me."

"I'm sorry I didn't tell you when you asked, but I didn't want you to think I make a habit of collecting English women." He leans in closer, like he's thinking of kissing me.

"Well then, I'm even more glad I met you now and not six months ago when you might not have wanted to spend time together," I gently tease.

"You're different, Lucille. I can see that. I doubt you could hide your true feelings from anyone for long."

I wonder if he's thinking what I'm thinking. There is a beautiful hotel suite upstairs, one I apparently don't even have to pay for, with a minibar and an unopened bottle of champagne in it. We could, if we wanted to, head up there now and spend the next six hours or so doing what I've been imagining us doing for too long since I arrived here, with no need to feel embarrassed, because he's just not like that—and I might not be, either, now. I hope he is thinking it. I hope he is imagining me that way. Although the fact he doesn't suggest it could be a very good thing. I think he knows I'm worth more than a fumbled quickie before he trots off to work and I crack on with my travel admin. And, more importantly, so do I.

"I wish we had more time together, Lucille." He takes my hand under the table. "I wish I was going with you back to London."

"So do I." The suite is still there.

"Will you call me and let me know how it all ends? I mean it, Lucille, I really do want to know."

"I . . . I'll tell you. In person. I don't want this to be the last time I see you." There, I said it.

His smile is blinding as he says, "Well then, it won't be. Goodbyes are awful, so I'm going to leave now. But it was truly wonderful to meet you, lovely Lucille. Thank you for letting me show you Paris." He places some euros on the table, gathers his things, and stands. "Please keep your promise. Come back and see me, won't you?"

"I will." And then I kiss him, not caring in the slightest that we're in the middle of a bustling hotel lobby. It doesn't matter that our teeth clash a bit and our lips are not quite aligned as they should be. It's not a perfect kiss, but it's our kiss. And I happen to think it's better than any those models shared in this same lobby on my first night.

Our kiss is real.

16

Alice
NOVEMBER 1953, PARIS
THE MEXICO

Daylight is creeping through the thin, partially drawn drapes at the window before sleep finally begins to cradle her. Completely exhausted by Antoine and the unavoidable truth that she is past the point of no return, Alice can't fight the fatigue any longer. As she is drifting further from the tangible world around her—the one where her dress and fur still lie crumpled on the floor and the candles on either side of the fire have burned down to almost nothing—and deeper into a dreamy detachment from reality, she wonders when the moment of fear will come. When she wakes? When she sees Albert? Will it come at all? It's hard to imagine, when she is still warm from Antoine's body.

Her eyes feel as though they have barely closed, her cheek just softening into the safety of Antoine's chest, when she is startled by someone hammering on the door downstairs that leads directly into the apartment. She can't move and is happy to ignore it. Antoine isn't.

"Who is that? It's not even eight a.m. yet!" Still the hammering continues. Antoine slides from the bed naked, pulls back the voile, and looks down into the courtyard below. He says nothing, but stares for a few moments as if trying to be sure of what he is seeing. Then Alice sees him shake his head and turn slowly toward her.

"I don't believe it. He has sent someone for you."

"What?"

Alice forces her tired, unwilling body up, wrapping it roughly in one of the bedsheets, and moves toward the window. Antoine holds an arm out, preventing her from being seen, but she is close enough to recognize the man waiting for her below. Patrice.

"How could he?" Her eyes immediately fill with tears. She's far too tired to think straight, but she knows this is a callous and deliberate move by Albert. To send a close member of staff, one she has to face every day of the week.

"You don't have to go. I can easily go down there and tell him he's had a wasted journey."

"And then what? Albert turns up here?" She can feel the rising panic start to throb in her chest.

"He wouldn't dare."

He wouldn't be bothered, she thinks. "Or worse. He sends your mother."

Alice can see that possibility has far more impact as Antoine's face twists and recoils at the mere thought.

"He wouldn't."

"Yes, I think he would, and she would probably jump at the chance to ingratiate herself. How else do you think he knows where I am this morning?"

Antoine drops one hand to his hip and places the other on his forehead, trying to think this through. Neither of them is well equipped enough this morning to come up with the best course of action.

"I'll help you back into your dress."

If only she had something else to wear this morning. The thought of returning to the embassy residence in last night's dress, heavy with the memory of all that happened in it, is excruciating.

"No. You go downstairs and tell him I'll be ten minutes."

As Antoine somewhat reluctantly pulls on a robe and disappears downstairs, Alice goes into the bathroom to freshen up. She splashes cold water onto her face, then uses her wet fingers to tame her hair back behind her ears. She attempts to remove the more obvious traces of last night's smudged makeup with some damp tissue and uses some of Antoine's cologne. She only manages to secure some of the fastenings at the back of her dress, but it's enough to keep it up, and her fur will hide the rest.

"When will I see you again?" Antoine holds the bedroom door open for her.

"Soon, I hope. I'll think of something." All she wants to do is collapse back into the bed behind her, pulling Antoine in with her.

"I love you. Please don't keep me waiting too long—I'll worry."

They kiss, but it's more tense this time, all the freedom of last night's passion deserting them now, replaced by the prospect of consequences. Alice is acutely aware that in about twenty minutes she will be face-to-face with Albert again, and she is hardly dressed or mentally sharp enough for a showdown. She steps out into the sobering morning sunlight to see the reassuring smile of Patrice. Something in it suggests that, if not necessarily on her side, he at least understands the malice at play in Albert's decision to send him here this morning.

"Good morning, madame." Patrice's professionalism is never unappreciated. "The car is parked just out on the main road. Can we stop to get you anything on the way back?"

"Thank you, Patrice, but that won't be necessary." Alice pulls the fur in tighter across her body and buries her hands deep in its pockets, where the fingers of her right hand connect with something small and smooth. One of her pearl earrings—but not the pair. Oh goodness.

She can't go back inside now, so she makes a mental note to retrieve it later. Then she settles into the warmth of the back seat, wondering how Albert intended her to feel at this point—like a disgraced adolescent summoned home after missing her curfew, but knowing her punishment is likely to be considerably more severe? And yes, she fears his anger . . . but not enough to regret her decision to spend the night with Antoine.

As they enter the residence, Alice can hear Albert's loud voice echoing around the main ground-floor hallway. What is he doing? As she steps in through the garden doors, Patrice a few paces behind her, she sees he has gathered several of the household staff and appears to be briefing them on plans for a forthcoming dinner. They all look just as confused as she is. This is not Albert's domain.

"Ah, there you are, darling. I was expecting you much sooner. Where have you been?"

And then she understands. He wants her to have an audience. To have to stand there, her dress balancing precariously under the fur, feeling the awkwardness of every member of staff forced to witness her return home.

She can feel Patrice pause behind her, perhaps for once not knowing how to react. Should he save Alice and cause a diversion, only to scupper Albert's plan and risk angering him? A few unfilled seconds hang between them all. Then she sees Anne's pained face at the back of the crowd, about to break ranks. Alice must speak now, or it will be Anne whom Albert is cross with.

"Oh, you know very well where I have been. I will give you all the juicy details later. But for now, do excuse me, everyone, I need a bath and a sleep." Then, with her head held high, she makes for the staircase, Anne following closely behind.

THE BATH AND THE SLEEP, MUCH AS THEY ARE NEEDED, ONLY DELAY the inevitable.

Albert won't let her get away with the mild embarrassment she suffered in front of the staff. It's past six p.m. when she finally wakes, feeling completely out of sync. Her post-sleep mind is telling her it must be morning. But the total darkness of the room suggests evening. The bedside clock confirms it. She slips on a simple shift dress, feeling immensely grateful there are no plans in the diary for this evening, and heads for the staircase. On the landing, she passes Patrice, who tells her Albert is waiting for her in the library.

"Thank you, Patrice. Can you ask Chef to fix me something to eat, please? Some soup and a sandwich would be lovely."

"I certainly will. I'll bring it to the library for you." He looks uneasy, as if he knows the version of Albert waiting for her there. As though he knows she won't feel like eating when Albert has finished with her.

Albert is standing, whiskey in hand, when she enters the room, and wastes no time in getting straight to the point. He's had hours to prepare himself while she is trying to hastily shrug off the disorientating fug of a daytime sleep.

"So, you chose to ignore my advice, Alice, and in doing so have opened both of us up to ridicule. You know that, don't you?" He isn't angry, not yet, more enjoying the feeling of total superiority this moment is delivering for him.

She walks across the room, feeling the need to be occupied, and pours herself a gin and tonic from the selection of decanters on the sideboard.

"You're the one who made it public by inviting half the staff to welcome me home."

She's not going to let him see the fear she can feel slowly building inside her. She can see it in the unsteadiness of her own hand on the glass, so aware of his looming behind her. He knows how to use his size and authority to dominate a room, in a way that requires him to say very little. He'll let his body language impose his thoughts on the room, on her. She's never given him any reason to go further. Perhaps until now.

She feels his eyes trained on the back of her head, waiting for her to turn so he can say whatever he's been planning.

"Where are your earrings?" His voice is cold and inquiring, and the question catches her off guard.

"Oh, um. I'm not sure." Her hand instinctively rises to her right ear, the source of her guilt, where she lets it hang, unsure what to do or say next.

"So careless, Alice," he says through a pointed little laugh. "Are you really sure you're cut out for all this? It all seems very amateurish to me. Kissing in public, allowing yourself to be photographed, not covering your tracks, being reckless with your personal belongings." As he delivers her roll call of offenses, she can see his anger building, his teeth clenched together so he has to force the words through them. It's also clear that if not Madame du Parcq, someone who attended the Monet exhibition last night has shared the evening's events with him.

Patrice enters the room carrying a tray with her supper, and Alice knows Albert won't be considerate enough to pause their conversation until he has cleared the room again.

"What I'd like to know," he demands, "is why none of this"—he circles his hand in front of him, as if to show off the room's contents—"is enough for you? Why you feel you have to look elsewhere and to a man who can provide you with nothing more than basic carnal pleasures."

Alice wants to tell him it was very far from basic, that Antoine made her entire body sing, hour after hour, all through the night until neither of them had the strength to keep going. But also that what Albert believes he provides for her falls woefully short of what she truly needs. She doesn't live for possessions and demonstrable wealth. She needs affection, to know that she is loved and respected, that she is more important to her husband than anything else ever could be.

But she won't answer in front of Patrice, who is working as quickly as he can to set her supper things on a small console table beside her. He must have sensed her eyes on him, because he moves, angling his body so that his back is to Albert, and then gives her another support-ive smile.

"Well? Don't you have an answer?" She can feel Albert's irritation rising, but still Alice won't respond until Patrice leaves the room, for his sake as much as hers.

"You can happily stay out all night with a man you barely know, but you can't say why—what is it that's so lacking in your life, Alice, that you feel you have to humiliate me like this?" He slams his whiskey glass down hard on the table beside him, making Alice jump. Patrice, who is outside the room now, falters in his tracks, then busies himself straightening newspapers on a table. Waiting to see if he's needed.

"You have everything you need. A vibrant social life, enough staff to ensure you don't have to lift a finger, and a clothing allowance that most women can only dream of. You don't want for anything." He's bellowing now, loud enough for anyone on the first floor to hear them, his face puce with rage.

"So why, *why* are you so bloody ungrateful!"

She's scared. Of how much further Albert's anger will escalate, what he might be capable of.

But also of everything she wants to say. The words that are teeter-ing on the very edge of her tongue, wanting to be released into the room. She decides it's safer to move away from the bowl of scalding hot soup in front of her and stands instead by the fireplace, a safe distance from Albert but still visible to Patrice, who continues to linger outside.

"Do you think it's fair that it's so different for you?" She sounds so much weaker than she wants to. She tries again, firmer this time. "Do you think I don't know about the late-night phone calls or your glamorous blond friend who collects you some evenings?"

His hands clench into fists. His chest swells beneath his shirt.

"That's all okay, is it? I'm supposed to just accept it's one rule for you and one rule for me?" She knows she should stop, just accept his telling off and then he'll leave her alone, but she refuses to be the only one to blame.

"You stupid woman." She watches as his lips curl back over his teeth, like he despises the very sight of her. "It's just sex, Alice, that's all. Meaningless. No one's falling in love or planning some ludicrous elopement. Do you think I'm the only husband in Paris to need that release? There isn't a married man at our table on any given night who isn't doing exactly the same thing. The difference is, most of *their* wives sensibly turn a blind eye and accept they are onto a very good thing."

"We've barely been married a year." She immediately regrets saying it, knowing it makes her sound naive and wounded by his actions.

"I'm not about to change just because we got married." He says it like it's the most obvious thing in the world. Like he's speaking to a child who is struggling to understand the most basic instructions. "Is this because I don't want children yet? Are you punishing me for expecting your full support and not to have you distracted and reduced by the impact a baby would have on your life?" He's desperate to find some way to make this all Alice's fault.

Hearing him say the words aloud still hurts—knowing there were days filled with the hopes and dreams of a more trusting woman from a different time, one who believed in him and the two of them together.

Alice looks at Albert now and wonders how she could ever have let those huge hands of his work across her body in the clumsy way they have, grabbing at her, never caressing or appreciating her. How she could ever have lain beneath him trying to keep pace with his predictable rhythm.

"You're supposed to be my wife. I made it very clear, the role you would play here. I ask so little of you. Did you imagine I would let you ruin everything? All those years of hard work, grafting my way up while the rewards came so easily to others. Do you have any idea what it was like, Alice, to play a part that was palatable to everyone, while I had to worry about money every second of the day?" He stops, looks shocked at his own outburst, like he has said far too much.

Alice is confused. "But, your family? They supported you. There was plenty of money, you said. You were well looked after, just like I was."

"Did I? Or is that what you all wanted to believe? Think about it." His voice has softened slightly. "No one was interested in the truth. You wouldn't be here now if they were. Your parents would never have allowed it." He has slumped backward in the chair, drained by his confession.

Alice looks at him, feeling something approaching pity, her mind thrown back again to their wedding day and her conversation with his mother and sister, how Albert deliberately cut it short. What secrets has he been carrying all this time that she has yet to discover? Do they explain why he has so little idea of what she needs to make her happy?

She pauses, gathering in a deep, calming breath.

"It's not the lifestyle, Albert," she sighs. "I don't measure my happiness against how many dresses I own or how many parties I'm hosting this month. I don't judge my worth according to the size of my staff."

"Well, then you are alone. Because the world around you does. You really have no fucking idea how lucky you are, do you? To have it all land in your lap." He's all out of patience.

Alice refuses to be cowed by him. She turns toward the door. Why should she stay here and listen to any more of this from a man who won't judge himself by the same standards he expects her to live by?

"Don't you dare turn your back on me," he growls.

The volume of his words forces her to turn to face him. He's sitting forward in his chair now, legs aggressively stamped open.

"It ends. Now!" Alice hears the rasp in the back of his throat, senses the pain his bellow must be causing, and she can hold her tears back no longer. They cough out of her in one uncontrolled heave.

"But I . . ."

"Antoine will be collected from his grubby little apartment in one hour from now. He will be driven here, and you will end it with him. You will meet him in the garden and tell him it's over. I don't want that boy in my house."

Alice feels her mouth drop open, her bottom lip quivering so violently she can hear her teeth clash together.

"You see, I'm not entirely unkind, am I? I am giving you the chance to say your goodbyes, which is a damn sight more than either of you deserves. Make sure he understands just how serious you are." He watches her very closely for a sign of capitulation, enjoying the reaction he has caused, reveling in the tears that are now streaming down her face. He stands and takes two steps closer to her. "I warned you. I can and will destroy your reputation, what's left of it, and any credibility his family connections may still be affording him. It will be easy, just the matter of a few well-placed phone calls. I'm sure you don't want to see that happen to him, and I know his mother will do everything she can to ensure it doesn't."

Alice isn't sure what to be most horrified by. The fact that Albert thinks he can exert control over her like she's an unruly pet, the startling level of planning that has gone into today's ultimatum, or the speed with which he has responded to last night's events.

"I am working on something . . . something bigger, Alice, that will change our lives. Something that will help put this horrible mess behind you. You'll hear more about that, when I'm ready." He stands, drains the rest of his drink, and hitches his trousers up by the belt, seemingly satisfied with his performance today.

"One hour, Alice. Go and make yourself presentable. You look a mess."

ANNE HELPS ALICE INTO HER GOWN, BEING CAREFUL TO CAPTURE every one of the fastenings that secure the internal corsetry. It takes several minutes for her to work her way through the layers of the boned bra, the bodice, the silk overlay, and the lower band of mesh that will pull everything together as it sits undetected below the skirt's waistline. The two women negotiate each other in companionable silence, a sense of gnawing dread growing inside Alice with every tightening of the fabric around her. Anne sweeps a hand under the skirt's silk organza tiers, ensuring they float up and settle exactly as they should, before she straightens the blousy red silk flower that sits on the waistband.

Of all the dresses Alice owns, this is the one that makes her feel the most womanly. Not sexy, exactly, but the heavier, hidden layer of crinoline that is structured outward from her waist to her thighs gives the illusion of rolling, curvaceous hips. The second-skin fit of the corset has been designed to make the absolute most of her décolletage, and the neckline has been cut daringly open so the prim cap sleeves seem to almost defy gravity, clinging unsupported to her shoulders. In any other fabric it might be too much, but Dior's choice of translucent silk in cream and black with delicate scalloped edging will hold Alice, giving her the confidence to say the words she knows she has to.

"I will be here waiting when you return," says Anne. "And I will stay for as long as you need me. You will get through this, Alice, we will find a way, together."

AS SHE STEPS OUT INTO THE GARDEN, ANTOINE IS ALREADY WAITing for her, presumably as instructed. He looks nervous and confused; clearly whoever collected him did not enlighten him on the exact nature of his visit.

"What's going on?" He throws his arms wide and pulls Alice into the warmth of his coat, burying his face in the softness of her exposed neck. She has deliberately chosen not to wear one herself, despite the temperature. She wants their exchange to be as brief as possible. She knows Albert will be watching from the shadows behind an upstairs window, and she won't give him a second more pleasure than absolutely necessary.

"Albert knows everything. He has demanded that it ends, that we must never see each other again or he will do everything in his power to destroy both of us." The facts have had time to settle on her. She can deliver them with much less emotion than she felt an hour ago.

"Do you think I care what he wants? Leave him, Alice. Take away his power. You can come with me now and all this will be over. He doesn't own you, no one does." He's pulling her toward the back gates he entered through, just as she knew he would.

"I can't, Antoine." She shakes her head, determined. "I need to think this through. It's not that easy. There is so much to consider."

"Come with me and I can make all this go away. You never need to be bullied by him again." He's taken hold of both her arms now and is walking them both to the gates, to the exit from her marriage and everything she despises about Albert and their life together. She can see the tears filling Antoine's eyes, the distress in every one of his sweet features, and hopes Albert can too.

"Kiss me."

"What?"

"I want you to kiss me like it is the last time you ever will. Then turn and walk through those gates and don't look back."

"I can't. Please, Alice, please do not ask me to do that. I've already lost the person I loved most once—I can't lose you too." His tone is more desperate now. The two of them tussle as he tries to pull her closer again, to physically remind her that he's stronger than he might look, that he can protect her from all of this.

"You don't have a choice. Do it. Please, trust me."

Their lips connect, and she is immediately swallowed by the intensity of his longing. Shocked by how gentle and yet how passionate his mouth feels against hers. As the two of them blend into one another, their bodies connected at every possible point, she can hear the repetitive click of a camera lens somewhere back over her shoulder toward the house. Albert clearly felt it was important to record the moment.

"Go!" She pushes him, forcing some distance between them, then turns and marches back to the house, glancing briefly upward to see her reward, Albert's smug smile framed in the first-floor windows. She looks backward just once, to see Antoine finally disappear through the metal gates, his shoulders rounded, his face buried in his own hands.

Alice waits until she has dismissed Anne and closed the bedroom door behind her before she allows the tears to fall hot and fast down her face. Then she takes last night's Debussy dress from its hanger in the dressing room and sits at her desk, and slowly, carefully, lovingly begins to sew her and Antoine's initials into the deepest layer of the gown.

Where they will never be seen.

17

Lucille
FRIDAY
PARIS

It's really not the time to be stuck in traffic. And especially not in the back of a taxi that reeks of stale cigarettes and sweat. I only left the hotel ten minutes ago, cut across the Champs-Élysées, made a right, and then ground to a halt.

"*Excusez-moi, monsieur.*" I don't know why I bother to start the conversation in French, because I certainly can't finish it that way. "Can you see what the problem is? I've got a train to catch."

"Pardon?" The driver is frowning at me in his rearview mirror with a look of such utter confusion that I don't bother to repeat myself. I've got an hour and a half to do a journey the concierge promised me would take no longer than an hour, so I decide to just chill and hope for the best. Worst case, I'm on the Eurostar after the one Veronique's on, which will be annoying but not a disaster.

I wind the window down, keen to smell something that isn't ingrained nicotine or some stranger's armpit, and look across the road at the building we've stopped in front of. There are black metal bars at the ground-floor windows and humorless-looking guards marching between green wooden century boxes with large guns strapped to their waists. I have another stab at making myself understood with the driver, this time jabbing a finger in the direction of the guards.

"*Qu'est-ce que c'est, s'il vous plaît?*" I'm glad Leon isn't here to hear my crude attempt at a French accent.

Silence.

In the absence of anything else to do, I lift my phone and start googling it. I'm sure Veronique will know what it is. A prison, by the looks of it. It's very serious, with huge black lacquered doors that look completely impractical, like they'd be impossible to open. There is no sign of life from within.

The next thing I know, the stern face of one of those armed guards is suddenly filling the car window and shouting at me.

"*Arrêtez Pas de photos!*" This is followed by something equally cross to the taxi driver that I don't quite catch, but the horrified look on his face as his head spins toward me basically says it all. The man with the gun is very cross with me.

"No pictures, mademoiselle. You have to delete them. It's a British embassy building, no pictures are allowed."

Now he speaks perfect English! I consider pointing out that, as I am indeed British, I really don't see what the problem is, but instead turn my screen toward him so he can see it's Google and not my camera that I've been using. The guard remains bent through the window, pointing at my phone, until I access my pictures to prove none of the building have been taken. Only then does he slap the taxi roof hard enough to dent it, and we're off, the driver muttering what I assume are uncomplimentary things about me all the way to the Gare du Nord.

I FEEL VIOLENTLY NAUSEATED BY THE TIME I GET OUT AT THE STAtion from all the unnecessarily aggressive driving, but for some reason I still hand the driver an overly generous tip. Not even that gets a smile. I think he's just desperate to be rid of me. But frankly, who cares, because there is Veronique, hanging out of the still-open train door, waving and beckoning me to join her. But my phone is buzzing in my pocket and I can't ignore it. I pause on the platform and see that it's Granny. I raise an index finger to Veronique to let her know I'll be as quick as I can and watch her eyes flick to the giant digital clock that warns our train departs in eight minutes.

Granny sounds exhausted when I answer.

"Hello, Granny. How are you feeling?"

"Not my best, darling. I'm a bit all over the place today. Thank goodness for Natasha. She stayed much longer than usual and made sure I have everything I need."

I hate that I'm not there with her. She sounds like she needs a hug. I can hear the vulnerability and loneliness in her voice, the lack of energy. Why isn't Mum putting her time to better use instead of calling me? It hits me that Granny will never spring out of bed again ready to tackle the day with full force. I try not to think about how scared she must feel about that on mornings like these.

"Tell me, Lucille, how are you getting on?" Her usual enthusiasm just isn't there today. Perhaps she senses my great adventure, and hers, is coming to an end.

"I've done it, Granny. I followed the notes, far enough to work it all out. I've visited the places across Paris that A and A did. I've walked in their footsteps. I've walked in *your* footsteps, Granny."

She's silent and I give her time, listening to how her breath is trying to hold on to a sob, feeling the sting as it brings tears to my own eyes. I picture her hand moving to cover her mouth.

"It's okay, Granny," I say as I grip the phone to my ear, my eyes flicking back to the clock and an increasingly stressed-looking Veronique.

"What eventually led you to me?" She delivers the confirmation I am looking for.

"It was the night at Musée de l'Orangerie, the Monet exhibition, when you wore the Debussy."

"Oh, that evening. The undoing and the making of me in so many ways." She sighs, and I can feel all the pent-up emotion tumbling out of her.

Then I feel the fabric and foundations of my own life start to splinter and shift. If my grandmother isn't the woman I thought she was, then who am I?

How do I fit into all of this? Everything around me seems to still and quieten.

I think of my family—small, broken, disappointing. But there was always Granny Sylvie, who delivered strength and kindness and truth; at least, I thought she did. Do I still believe that when there is so much I don't know about her and the life she led, this wide expanse of secrecy revealed so late?

"I really hadn't guessed at all until then," I say. "But we found a photograph that was taken on that very night. A photo of you."

What was she even doing in Paris? What was her life like here? How does my grandfather fit into all of this? How much does Mum know? Why did she return to London?

Was she happy?

"Ah, so many people. So many cameras clicking. I was never going to come away unscathed. But it was worth it. I have many deep, deep regrets, Lucille, but that night is not one of them."

There is so much we need to discuss, but it's five minutes until the train doors will close and Veronique will be forced to leave without me. I hear announcements over the platform loudspeaker and watch Veronique wildly gesticulating for me to get on the train.

Granny's fragility and the seconds passing too quickly stop me from firing all these questions at her, and I resign myself to having them answered in person, when I am back in London.

"What do the A and A stand for, Granny? That's the bit I still don't understand." I have no choice now but to clamp the phone between my ear and shoulder and start to run, dragging the rest of my belongings behind me.

Again, she falls silent. I try not to rush her, but my heart is starting to bang in my chest.

"Alice."

"And . . . ?"

"Alice and . . . Antoine."

I hear her small, quiet, controlled sobs, and more than anything, I want to be by her side, holding her hand and telling her that whatever happened, it's okay. I love her just as much as I ever did.

What could have happened to her that, all these years later, still reduces her to tears? The possibilities are frightening. "I don't think I've said his name out loud since I left Paris all those years ago."

"I'm so sorry this is upsetting for you." I try my best to soothe her. "But has this at least helped, Granny? Will the dresses bring you some sort of closure?" I really hope so, for her sake.

She's stopped crying, and there is purpose in her voice. I'm at the train door and Veronique is heaving my case from me, pulling it into the carriage and disappearing to dump it on the luggage rack. I can't help but turn back for one last glimpse of Paris before I head home.

"Oh, this is only just the beginning, darling."

"What do you mean?" I freeze, one leg on the train step, one still on the platform.

"It was never really about the dresses at all. I'm sure you know that deep down, Lucille. There is so much more to this. Only your grandfather knew the full story, and he took every word of it to his grave."

"I don't understand. What more is there?" A guard is marching up the platform toward me, but I'm frozen to the spot, straining not to miss a word Granny says in the chaos surrounding me.

"It's what the dresses helped to create that's important, the bigger secret that lies within them that really matters." As she speaks, I can hear the smile in her voice as she drops this revelation on me, like it should be blindingly obvious, like I am mere seconds from it all finally making perfect sense.

"The reason I had to let Alice go and become Sylvie. That's what I need you to find."

I thought I was done, finished. That I had completed my task and she'd be pleased with me. I was looking forward to seeing the smile on her face when I visited with the dresses in a couple of days. Now I wonder if I should be staying in Paris.

"Mademoiselle!" The guard is level with me now.

"I'm coming home. The last dress from Paris—the one made from the special toile de Jouy fabric. It's at the V and A. I'm going to see it." I spit the words out as fast as I can as I wave at the guard.

Her voice is very calm and measured then. "I haven't spoken about any of this for over sixty years, Lucille. I couldn't, not without hurting the one person who had remained loyal to me for a lifetime. I have no right to ask, but I am asking it of you anyway. Please, finish the story. Finish my story for me. I am running out of time."

Veronique's hand is on my arm, and she pulls me onto the train as the guard slams the door behind me. I realize as metal hits metal that there will be no ending unless I can complete her story.

"The final dress at the V and A will help you. It's different. Everything you need to know is in that dress, Lucille." And then she's gone and I am at a complete loss, feeling for the first time in my life like my connection to Granny, someone I have loved so dearly for so long, is somehow no longer strong or solid.

MERCIFULLY, WE HAVE AN ENTIRELY EMPTY CARRIAGE BACK TO London all to ourselves. No irritating fellow travelers loudly crunching crisps, prattling on to a loved one on their mobile about whether there's enough cheese in the fridge to make a decent omelet tonight.

It's just me, Veronique, some trashy mags, a vast array of snacks (including liberated financiers), and a half bottle of fizz between us. I decide not to ruin the experience by moping for the next two hours, but it's not easy, and I feel lost from my conversation with Granny.

"Are you okay, Lucille? You look very pale." Veronique is staring at me from across the table. "I know that was a little tight, but you made the train, you can relax now."

"I'm not sure I can. That was Granny on the phone. She just told me that she *was* one half of A and A. That when she lived in Paris, she was known as Alice. But why did she change her name to Sylvie?"

Veronique's eyes widen. "Maybe this will help explain that." She delves into her bag, pulls out an unopened letter, and holds it aloft. "There were lots of letters written from your Granny to my maman, but this one is different."

"How?"

"For one thing, the handwriting is different, it's not one I recognize. And it's addressed to an Alice."

"Is there a postmark on it? Is it dated?"

"Yes, February 13, 1956. I suppose whoever sent it must have hoped Maman would get it to your grandmother. I wonder why she never forwarded it to her? There seems to be something inside it, something small and hard. Should we open it?" I can tell from her voice that she wants to.

"No. No, we shouldn't, Veronique. Whatever is written in that letter, whoever it is from, I think Granny needs to read it first, don't you?"

"Yes, of course. You're right," she sighs.

Veronique gives me some time to reflect. She rests her chin in the palm of her hand and stares intently out of the window, like she's not seeing the view at all but perhaps my family tree, rewriting itself on the windowpane.

She waits until the grayness of Paris gives way to the surrounding countryside and she's listened to me exhale at least four big sighs before she pulls her laptop out of her expensive-looking leather rucksack. Does she have any items of clothing or accessories that linger shame-faced at the back of the wardrobe? I wonder.

"Seriously, you're not actually working, are you?" I sound like a whining toddler, but *really*? This is my last chance to enjoy her company before I disembark from this train in London, and reality hits me hard from all angles.

"No, I am not!" I shouldn't have doubted her. "But I am wondering . . ." She trails off.

I watch as she opens the laptop and logs on to reveal a beautiful photo of her, arm in arm with a woman I assume must be her mum. Their faces are both raised to the sky as if soaking up the warmth of a sunny day, their smiles stretching freely and easily outward. They've allowed their heads to recline together, and the intimacy between them is so easily expressed, it tugs at my heart a little. You could search my mother's home from now until eternity and not find anything to equal the natural warmth displayed in this one snatched shot. "Is that . . ."

"Yes, it's Maman. Isn't she beautiful?" Obviously, everyone thinks their mother is beautiful, but in this case Veronique's verdict is entirely justified. Her mum's features are strong and reassuring, blemish-free, her hair solid and coarse-looking, like it needs a lot of taming. Veronique's face is more delicate, there's a suppleness to her, her hair more fluid, easily sculpted—although unfortunately for her, Veronique is cursed with the same splash of freckles across her nose that I have always hated on myself. But as a pair, they complemented each other wonderfully. There is something almost magical about their bond that I can't help but envy. The happiness enveloping them in the second this picture was taken seems to radiate out through the screen in a way that no one could ever doubt.

"God, I miss her." There is so much sadness weighing on Veronique's words, I'm reminded again that despite all the help she has given me this past week, she is still grieving.

"I know it's an odd thing to say, but more than anything, I miss the years after my father died, when I nursed her through a broken heart. For the first time, our roles reversed, and she really needed me. She was such a strong, capable woman. She'd worked hard all her life, and there I was having to wash and dress her some mornings, when she couldn't find a good enough reason to do it herself. When she lacked the motivation to even lift her head from the pillow. Watching her struggle like that very nearly broke me too. It was painfully sad at the time, and there were moments I wondered if she'd ever recover. But it showed me that the love she felt for my father was light-years beyond anything I had experienced with a man myself. It gave me an opportunity to show her how much I loved her."

I give her hand a squeeze, and it seems to do the trick. She blinks back from the screen and half smiles at me. Then she logs on to Google, and I watch as she enters the words *Alice, British embassy,* and *Paris* into the search bar.

What I see next completely floors me. Image after image of my grandmother is floating up in front of me. I can't take it all in. I grab the laptop and angle it sharply toward me, almost knocking my glass across the table. There she is, surrounded by men in smart dinner jackets, escorting dignitaries across a glossy black-and-white-checkered floor, lining up for what look like press photo ops, shaking hands with an endless number of people, some official, some the general public. In one she is emerging through heavy deep red velvet curtains, wearing a light blue, full-length evening gown that has pale flowers the color of the Mediterranean climbing up it. Then she is descending a large sweeping stone staircase wearing another incredible gown or seated with dozens of equally finely dressed guests at a long banquet table for dinner or within a small but crowded room, her legs neatly crossed in front of her, watching models circulate the space.

"How did you . . ."

"Well, I didn't know at all, until just a few moments ago when you shared the name your grandmother used to go by. We now know that she was Alice and not Sylvie when she lived in Paris. She was very close to my maman, who, at that time, worked at the British embassy, so I just put those two pieces of information together, and here we are."

We both lean over the computer screen, and my eyes flicker across every image, back and forth, unable to comprehend quite how beautiful, how refined she looks, the setting so wildly different from the one she inhabits today. Veronique leans closer, studying the screen more intently.

"Why are there so many images of her?" I ask, overjoyed that there are, that technology has allowed me to step back into a life that has eluded me until now.

Veronique sits back in her chair, silent just long enough for me to feel a prickle of concern.

"Perhaps because she was married to someone very important at the time."

"Sorry?" I really need to stop drinking in the middle of the day—it is seriously hampering my ability to grasp plot twists that seem so clear to Veronique.

"Look at some of the picture captions. Alice Ainsley, and according to this, the wife to the British ambassador to France, Albert Ainsley."

My mouth drops open, my brain refusing to accept what I am hearing. "She couldn't have been." I pull the laptop closer to me and scan the words Veronique has read for myself. "It must be wrong. The internet is full of inaccuracies. What site are we even on?"

"They all say the same, Lucille. Look. A lot of these images are from official government sites, both British and French. I don't think it's wrong."

"Are you telling me my grandmother was some sort of diplomat? That she was married to another man before my grandfather?" While I'm saying that aloud, I look back at the screen, running the cursor up and down, allowing my eyes to skate back across every image again, still not quite believing what I am seeing. One man is present throughout.

A man who is decidedly not the grandfather I grew up with.

"I guess this is Albert?" I point to a giant of a man with noticeably large hands and who, despite the regularity of his appearance, does not seem to fit with my granny at all. If you didn't know they were married, you would never guess it. They are the opposite of the image of Veronique and her mother. They don't work together. There is no intimacy. I'm struggling, in fact, to find a shared smile. He dwarfs rather than complements her, and in some of the images, he rudely angles his back to her, cutting her out of an introduction or conversation.

"Yes, it looks like it. In her position, she would have lived at the official residence—the Hôtel de Charost on rue du Faubourg Saint-Honoré—just around the corner from where you have been staying in Paris, in fact." She points to an image of the building on her screen. "It was right under our noses all along."

I slump back into the seat and help myself to another mouthful of fizz. "I saw that building, Veronique! The taxi to the station took me past the embassy buildings. I saw where she lived; that must be the location of dresses number one and seven, the Cygne Noir she wore at home and the Mexico she wore in the garden. It must have been there, at the embassy residence. What was it the later note said?"

Veronique beats me to it: "'I can make all this go away.'"

My mind is racing. Granny was also having a love affair with a man I now know was called Antoine. Her marriage to Albert obviously didn't last, it couldn't have, because she married my grandfather—a man who feels a very, very long way from this story. The fact she married him is indisputable, but my belief that he is my grandfather . . .

I feel the moisture inside my mouth evaporate. "We've tracked them all. What happened behind those giant black doors I saw this morning?"

"I don't know, but it doesn't feel good." She's still scanning through pages, pulling information off the sites.

"You'll have to take some time to read through it all, Lucille, but from what I can see, the story goes frustratingly cold in the winter of 1953, which is when I assume she must have left the embassy. Look, her departure seems to coincide with Albert being posted to America in the new year, and I suppose that would have been the focus of all the interest at the time. Not what happened to Alice. Why would it? She was only his wife, which probably didn't count for a great deal in the fifties."

I'm not sure either of us knows quite how to feel. Elated that there are solid answers, finally? Or slightly rocked by the significance of Granny's former life and what it might mean?

I pause for a moment to take it all in, allowing the view outside the window to flash past while my own mind skids back over the lost years, searching for clues. Has Granny ever mentioned the embassy in Paris or an Albert? I don't think so. She said my grandfather was the only person she confided in, and he took it all to the grave with him. My own thoughts are frustratingly muddled by the realization that it has once again taken Veronique's intervention to piece this story together. I've hardly been the roving reporter, too distracted by Leon to allow myself the headspace to move these nuggets of information into position so I can see them all from above—the connection of nearly all the dots that are starting to shape Granny's story for me.

"Could it be simply that Albert is the other A?" asks Veronique. "We have been looking for a secret love affair, but perhaps she wore the dresses with her husband. Alice and Albert. A and A?"

"He isn't the other A," I say with some relief. I don't want this hulk of a man to be the one Granny was passionate about. "Granny told me the A stands for Antoine." As I say his name, we both shift our eyes back to the screen, scanning the images once more, wondering if he might be here somewhere before our very eyes. Are we looking at him?

Even if we are, we have no way of knowing it. But one image suddenly stands out. It's grainy and slightly out of focus, but it's definitely my grandmother, and she is in a passionate embrace with someone who is definitely not Albert. And she's wearing the Mexico dress—I can just make out the black-and-white pattern and its scalloped edges. We missed it before because it wasn't posed like the others. In fact, it looks snatched, like neither of them knew it was being taken.

"I'd say that's our man, wouldn't you?" asks Veronique, pointing at the image.

"Yes," I add quietly, because something seems off. There is something unpleasant about this picture that I can't quite put my finger on. Something not entirely happy about the way they are clinging to each other.

"I'll ask Leon to do some digging for me while we're in London," I say, "to see if he can find out anything more about Antoine." But Veronique isn't listening to me.

"You haven't spotted her yet, have you?" she asks.

"Who?" Oh, for goodness' sake, *now* what am I missing?

"Maman."

"What? She's here too?"

"Yes, look."

Veronique points to a group shot, taken in what looks like one of the grand embassy reception rooms. Albert is holding court at the center of the shot, an array of important-looking people fanning out around him. Granny has chosen to position herself toward the back, or been pushed there, and is somewhat swallowed by the volume of people. But I can just make her out, and the woman next to her, who is giving her a look of total support.

There is something in the tautness of Veronique's mother's shoulders and the determined fix of her smile that says, *We will get through this together.* Then I see as I search a little deeper into the image that the two of them are holding hands, and it's so moving that my eyes completely glass over.

Whatever else was going on, however unpleasant it might have got for Granny, it looks like she had someone to share her problems with, someone she could call a friend.

We shut the laptop after that. It's all a bit draining, and we need a switch-off. A few gulps of fizz, some artificially flavored, breath-destroying crisps, and half an hour of silence to reflect. When I do finally pipe up again, I am surprised at what comes out of my own mouth.

"I'm going to resign when I get back to the office."

"Good!" It's not what I was expecting to hear from Veronique.

"Really? Is it a good thing?" I love the show of support, but I'm surprised that she's so emphatic about it.

"Yes, it's good! You don't like the job. You don't respect your boss, entirely reasonably, and you are far too young to be wasting your years doing something you don't want to do. It's not like you have three children to support, is it? Make the changes now, while you can." She slaps the table as she finishes speaking, like the subject shouldn't even be up for debate.

"There is still the small matter of rent to pay and bills to cover." I want to leave, but I don't want to romanticize the problems it will cause.

"I'm sure your mum will help you out in the short term. Or take in a lodger? Or better yet, apply for the job I mentioned at the Museum of Decorative Arts!" Her eyebrows shoot skyward, tempting me to love the idea.

"The Museum of Decorative Arts *in Paris*, you mean? Because as determined as I am to escape Dylan, that is one beast of a commute by anyone's standards." I drain the last of the fizz and pinch open my second packet of crisps.

"Obviously you could stay with me, at least until you got yourself sorted. It's an amazing job, Lucille, and you are qualified for it, even if you don't think you are. You'd get to travel, which I know you really want to do. The museum has many partner locations across the world, and yes, it would be a lot of admin at first while they train you, but they will cover the cost of the extra studies, and then you will be qualified to do something really interesting, something you would look forward to every day." She has clearly given this plenty of thought. "What's the worst that can happen?"

"Oh, I don't know, I'm absolutely useless at it and it reflects really badly on you for ever recommending me?"

"I'm not going to recommend you." She shakes her head.

"Oh." That's slightly awkward. "Well, then I stand little chance of getting it."

"We're going to keep me right out of this so that I can tell you everything you need to put on the application form to ensure you at least get an interview. And when you do, it's up to you. But, Lucille, the worst that can happen is that you come to Paris, give it a year, get qualified, and then return home. Doesn't sound so bad to me." She reaches into her rucksack and pulls out a tiny mirror, which she flips open and uses to touch up her rosy lips. I see her sneak a sideways glance at me, smirking, knowing she is right.

And with that, the laptop is flipped back open and the online application form hastily loaded in front of us. What I don't say, but am most definitely thinking, is that if I do handily manage to land this job—and yes, it's a massive if—it would conveniently solve one more problem. How to see a whole lot more of Leon.

18

Alice

"Are you sure all the arrangements are in place? He suspects nothing?" Alice whispers. It's a force of habit now. She's pacing back and forth across the bedroom floor, every muscle flexed and strained, a swirl of nervous energy making her feel queasy.

Anne absorbs her stress, knowing very well the potential consequences of what the two of them have planned for today.

"Everything is in place." A huge sigh heaves from deep within Anne's chest. "I have done exactly as you asked. Camila was very accommodating. She is expecting you and will make sure everything is handled with the utmost discretion. But, Alice, please, this is very risky. You need to be extremely careful." Anne traces Alice's footsteps around the bedroom, trying to force eye contact, needing to be sure Alice is paying attention.

"No buts today, Anne. I don't want to hear it. It's been weeks. We've waited long enough. If it's not safe now, I'm not sure it ever will be, and as wonderful as Antoine's letters are, I cannot survive on those alone." She disappears into the dressing room.

Alice raises her arms and stands on her very tiptoes, pushing aside a pile of cashmere scarves from the top shelf, feeling her fingers connect with the smoothness of the small black lacquered box she has hidden there. Her most precious possession.

"Alice! Really, not now. *Please.* What if Albert comes in?" Anne moves across the room, weighting herself against the bedroom door. She knows she won't stop him, but she may just delay Albert long enough, should he decide to make a surprise appearance.

"I just want to read the last one again, that's all. We have time." Alice sits on the edge of the bed and takes out the most recent of Antoine's beautiful love letters, those ferried across Paris by Anne. Alice's own fountain pen has never been so productive. The second she finishes one of his, she pens her own, filling it with all her hopes and dreams for the future they will soon be planning together, sealing it with a kiss, and insisting Anne leave the residence to post it that very moment. She reads the words aloud, causing Anne to pin herself even tighter to the doorframe.

> *What are these few weeks when we know we will have forever together? That's what I keep telling myself. But being apart from you, Alice, is a pain I have never known before. I can't even sustain myself with the memory of our last kiss because I believed it was our very last. How do you kiss goodbye someone you know you will love for a lifetime? Even longer? Every day I think of you in that prison with him and it physically hurts me. Come to me, Alice, let's build a future together that is full of love and happiness. One where he doesn't exist. One where you wake every morning smiling and your every day is filled with laughter. I so desperately want to do that for you.*
>
> *I want to be that man.*

Antoine's letter only serves to remind Alice quite what is at stake today, and, reading the fear on her face, Anne takes the box from her and places it back in its hiding place.

"I know I have asked you this a million times, but are you absolutely sure he never had you followed to Antoine's apartment that day?"

"As sure as I can be." Anne, like Alice, is doubting herself now that the moment they will know the answer to that question is almost upon them. Because Alice is *almost* confident she has been patient and clever enough. *Almost* sure her acting skills have been convincing enough. *Almost* sure of what she wants.

But she also knows Albert is not a man she can afford to underestimate. If he had Anne followed after Antoine passionately kissed Alice in the embassy gardens, he'll know that within hours of staging their goodbye, Alice risked everything, writing with details of this meeting. If he has somehow seen the note Anne was instructed to deliver, he will know where to find them today—in one of the small private rooms on the upper levels of Dior on avenue Montaigne. Somewhere she feels safe. Somewhere they won't be disturbed—if all goes according to plan.

But has she done enough? She thinks back to breakfast this morning with Albert and how it followed the same pattern as every breakfast since he delivered his ultimatum. She shudders as she thinks about how she bolted her eggs and bacon, nearly gagging on the rind, barely tasting a mouthful, keen to be away from him as soon as possible, yet somehow trying to look relaxed and guilt-free. How every morning his slow, deliberate, calculated movements have made her stomach churn with an acidic hatred. Seeing in the lightness of his face how much he enjoys keeping her seated under his gaze and the scrutiny of his questioning. Watching him raise a fork to his mouth, keeping it held aloft, unhurried, while he finishes reading a sentence in his newspaper. How he relentlessly chews his food, every strong rotation of his jaw making her stiffen with resentment.

"Today's plans?" he asked this morning, without lowering his newspaper.

"An appointment at Dior." She vacuums all hatred from her voice. This is the one place she feels Albert is guaranteed not to venture.

"With?"

"Anne. We should be back by early evening."

"Ah, yes. You mentioned it last week. I confirmed it with . . . Camila, isn't it?"

There is the slightest pause while Alice registers the inquiry he has made to confirm her plans are genuine. While she processes how Camila must have interpreted that intrusion.

"Yes. I'm seeing Camila." Her humiliation stings, but she chooses to look serious and contrite, like a woman who has learned her lesson and is grateful to be given another chance. "And you? What are your plans today?" Is it possible to sound cheerful when your heart is full of hate? She hopes so.

Albert folds his newspaper precisely, slowly, until it is almost the size of a pocket diary.

"Very busy, as usual." Deliberately vague. He can question her. It doesn't work the other way.

But for the first time in weeks, that's where his questioning stops. Is it a trap? Or is he as bored of the relentless accounting for her every movement as she is of being monitored? He didn't drill down on precise timings, her planned journey, who else she might encounter, as he usually does. Will he question her again on her return later, to check that her account remains consistent? Will he arrive unexpectedly early, hoping to catch her out?

She must not get complacent. Not until there is a plan in place. She does not want her memories of Antoine to be all she is left with. Because in the weeks of their forced separation, Alice's addiction has become all-consuming. In the safe darkness of her dreams, his body is as familiar to her as her own. The only thing keeping her going is the knowledge they will be in each other's arms again today and her patience will be rewarded, and there isn't a damned thing Albert can do about it. Of that she is almost sure.

"We need to get going, Alice. This will only work if we stick to the timings." Anne looks frightened. Perhaps she is right to.

THEY ARE ALMOST AT THE BOTTOM OF THE STAIRCASE WHEN AL-ice hears Albert's voice booming out across the hallway.

"Why?!" he demands of someone.

As Alice descends the final few steps, she can see it is Patrice that Albert is shouting at.

"I'm afraid she didn't say, sir." His voice is calm, monotone.

"No message at all?" Albert's is getting louder with every second. She can hear the questions hoarse in the back of his throat as he tries to contain his anger.

"I'm afraid not."

"And you didn't think it appropriate to seek some reasoning?" Alice notes how unattractively flushed his face is, how his chin is thrust forward in annoyance.

"I didn't feel it was quite my place to, no, sir."

"Fucking useless!" With that, Albert stamps toward his study, leaving Alice and Anne standing in silence, waiting for the right moment to question Patrice.

"The plans he had for later have been canceled." Patrice mouths the words as quietly as possible.

"Oh, I see." Alice guesses immediately whom those plans might have involved. "She's canceled him for the second time this week, and now it's everyone's fault but his own?"

"That is about the size of it, yes, madame." Hats off to Patrice, who is as composed as ever, not easy with a brute like Albert spitting expletives at you.

"Okay, well, not much any of us can do about that," says Alice, but she feels the unease low in her stomach. An angry, rejected Albert is not the one she wants to contend with today. He will be looking for someone to blame, and she will be top of his list.

ANNE STAYS IN THE CAR WITH THE DRIVER AND WITH STRICT instructions to remain alert, while Alice rings the polished black doorbell of Dior. Once inside, she feels her nerves gently dissipate, the irritation and frustration beautifully morph to excited anticipation. The reassuringly calm and muted color palette of dove grays and caramels, the luxuriant depth of the spotless cream carpets beneath her heels, the light that bounces off every mirrored surface, and the gentle floral scent that hangs in the air briefly lift her up above the unbearable sadness that haloes around her.

Dior's world is polished and refined, and everything has an exquisite simplicity—something wholly missing from her own life—a simplicity that reveals nothing of the elaborate industry behind the scenes. The "thousand hands" that transform Dior's early sketches into elaborately detailed gowns. Just like the plotting and planning, as well as the sustained and studied performance that has brought her here today.

"Madame Ainsley, my darling! What a pleasure to have you with us this afternoon." Madame Beaufort glides forward, taking both of Alice's hands in hers before whispering two of the softest kisses, which just fail to land on each of Alice's cheeks.

"Look at you, Camila, as chic as ever, naturally. How do you do it, when I know you have been working around the clock these past few months?" The pretense of normality has become easy, second nature.

Alice stands back to admire her friend and fleetingly longs for the days when she would simply have enjoyed the way her black wool pencil skirt pours like liquid down over her slim contours, its matching suit jacket buttoned tightly enough to ensure it rests perfectly at the point her hips subtly curve outward, its sleeves cut just below the bend of her elbow to reveal her delicately proportioned wrists, where neat rows of pearls lie. How her friend is elegant without effort. But now she is also wondering if Camila has fully understood Alice's position—what will happen shortly in one of the rooms above where they are both now standing, engaged in polite conversation.

"You flatter me, Alice. I am very lucky. Monsieur Dior is very generous with his gifts." She pauses and casts a quick look back toward the front door, over Alice's shoulder. "You are the first to arrive. But everything is ready for you. Please, can I take you through?"

Alice nods. Her needs have been understood.

THE TWO OF THEM MAKE THEIR WAY UP THE NARROW CENTRAL staircase that winds through the town house, past a series of closed doors that conceal the making of Dior's magic and the occasional woman in white overalls, a tape measure draped around her neck. A couple of floors farther up, they enter a room dominated by a huge gilt-edged mirror with an armchair set back a few meters from it.

"Our studio," announces Camila. "And the very seat Monsieur Dior will view the early collection from."

Perhaps on any other day, Alice may have cared about this priceless insight. There's a large blackboard with the names of the mannequins chalked on it and a wall filled with fabric rolls. Alice is distracted by a small roll that has been partially pulled out from the others.

"You have a very good eye, Alice," says Camila, noticing her interest. "And very similar taste to Monsieur Dior. He decorated some elements of the salon with the toile de Jouy pattern. He adores it."

Alice traces a finger lightly along it, wondering what the beautifully repetitive detail of the fabric might feel like next to her skin. Wondering if Antoine would love it as much as she does. Before Alice has a chance to say another thing, the two are silenced by the door creaking open again. Alice's heart is in her mouth, knowing who she longs to see, fearing who it could be.

His face is rosy from the wind, his hands stuffed deep into the pockets of his long wool coat, his lips gently parted, ready to greet her but lacking the words. He doesn't need to say a thing. Alice can see the wanting in the narrowing of his eyes, the way they flick to Camila, willing her from the room. Alice feels the sting behind her own eyes, three weeks' worth of tears trying to force their way out. She pinches her lips together through fear her emotions will overwhelm her.

"I'll leave you," says Camila. "Take as much time as you need. No one will disturb you in here."

Alice is vaguely aware that she leaves the room, but she can't drag her eyes from Antoine's face. It's so familiar, and yet she feels she is discovering it all over again. The smooth arch of his brows, partially hidden beneath the casual foppishness of his hair; the pink fleshiness of his lips, a look that hovers between deep distress and desire, with no clue which will triumph. The hollows of his cheeks are more pronounced than she remembers. She can't recall who moves—it might have been her—but the next thing she feels is the tight crush of her ribs against his chest, the heat between her thighs, lips that start on her mouth but are quickly down her neck, every drop of breath sucked from her lungs, hands that sit on her lower back, pulling her in with such force she feels she might snap. One—or is it both?—of them is gently moaning. They drop to their knees, collapsing into a messy heap of clothes and shoes and limbs, their physical connection unbroken. Then he is quietly sobbing in her ear, and it is the most heartbreaking thing she has ever heard.

"Please, never ever do that to me again. I thought I had lost you, Alice." She can feel his breath on the soft patch of skin behind her ear, how he is sucking in the scent of her.

"You couldn't."

He pulls back to face her, their hands clasped between each other. "In the hours between kissing you goodbye and when I received your first note, I had. That's how it felt."

"It needed to be that way. You do know that? I had no choice. He was watching us. It had to look real. He would have known immediately if I had explained it to you." She searches his face for some understanding.

"And now what? We spend the rest of our lives going through convoluted and protracted measures so that we can meet like this?"

They both seem to realize the strangeness of sitting on the floor of a small workroom in Dior, and both manage a small smile at the desperateness of it all.

"You are worth so much more than this, Alice. Please tell me the fact we are meeting today means you know that, and we are going to find a way to be together, properly. That this is not how it is going to be from now on."

"I don't have all the answers. All I know is that I love you and I can't bear to be anywhere near him." She runs her hand over his cheek and smiles again as he takes her fingers and kisses every one of them.

"Then leave him. You can move into my apartment today. What's stopping you?"

"He is." She hangs her head, knowing how weak that sounds—but also knowing it's true.

"Only if you let him." She can hear the undiluted exasperation in the force of Antoine's words.

"He is in a position to make life very difficult for both of us, Antoine, and trust me, he will. If we humiliate him, he will not stop until he has done everything he can to ruin both of us. I hope we can find a way to be together and avoid that. Otherwise, what was the point in staying apart for these few weeks? We need to be clever about this. He's expecting us to fail. Please, let's not give him that satisfaction."

Antoine pauses, breaking their eye contact. Alice watches the slow rise and fall of his chest, the acceptance, she hopes, that she is right, and he must listen to her.

"Whatever it takes, I'll do it. But I have to be able to see you."

"He has only just started to relax a little. This was the very first morning he didn't grill me as hard on my whereabouts for the day. And, who knows, that could be because he knows, Antoine. Maybe he is downstairs speaking to Anne at this very moment."

"I don't care."

"You should." Alice cups his face with both her hands and draws it a little closer to hers. "Please, I know him much better than you do. Trust me on this. I don't want to spend a second longer with him than I need to, but we need to get this right."

Alice is overwhelmed with a feeling of such utter exhaustion. All those days tiptoeing around Albert, second-guessing his next move, carefully considering and editing every word she says to him, playing the part of the woman he wants to see and all the while so desperately feeling the absence of the man she wants to be with. Is it any wonder she is physically and mentally shattered? Her eyes slowly close, her head dipping from the sudden weight of it all, the difficulty of what they need to achieve to be together. And how? How can it be done in a way that Albert will feel less threatened or mocked by? She has none of those answers yet, and it's obvious Antoine doesn't either.

Antoine scoops her up into his arms and carries her to Dior's chair, cradling her across his lap, his own head falling back against the headrest. She feels the weight of her body melt into him. As he smooths her hair back from her face, she senses his purpose, his determination to protect her, even if he has little idea how to, now that she is finally back in his arms.

Before her lids close, she notices how his eyes have fallen onto the roll of fabric that caught her attention when she entered the room with Camila.

"Do you like it?"

"It's beautiful. Like nothing I've ever seen before."

She nods. "I agree." Then she snakes her arms around his shoulders and buries her face in his neck, finally feeling held and loved.

19

Lucille
FRIDAY
LONDON

It's past nine p.m. by the time I get back to my flat in Putney after seeing Veronique safely into a black cab to her hotel.

I run the shower as hot as my parched skin can possibly bear. I stand there and let it power down over me, burning my flesh bright pink, making my whole body swell with the heat, but brilliantly cleansing myself of the journey home. Then I dry off and smother my face in moisturizer, watching as my skin greedily drinks it in, before I throw on a robe and give Mum a quick call.

"Are you back?" is how she answers the phone.

"Hello, Mum, yes, I'm fine, thank you. How are you?"

"Don't be so sarcastic. Are you back or not?"

"I'm back."

"Are you coming over now?"

"No, I'm not. I've just walked through the door from Paris."

"What else have you got to do?" The idea that I may have a life beyond her needs has obviously not occurred to her.

"Well, you know, eat, sleep, catch up with work. There's the small matter of seeing my boss on Monday morning, and I need to prepare . . ."

"Well, at least you have a job to go to."

"Not for much longer, I don't."

"Have you been sacked?" It's classic Mum to assume the decision has been made for me. Not the other way around.

"Nope. I'm resigning."

"To do what? Have you got a new job?"

"No, I haven't. I just can't keep working somewhere I'm not appreciated, for a man I don't respect, being constantly passed over for the best opportunities."

She laughs. It starts small at the back of her throat, where she tries to muffle it with a cough, and then when she realizes she can't, she stops trying and lets go until it's so loud I have to move the phone away from my ear.

"Oh, Lucille, sorry, I know I shouldn't laugh," she says, continuing to laugh. "But honestly! Welcome to the working world and the plight of every woman before you." Her gut reaction is so wildly different from Veronique's, it makes me want to slam the phone down on her. Instead I grit my teeth and plow on.

"I appreciate I'm not alone in this, Mum, but I am going to do something about it and take some control of my career while I still have the time to influence what my future looks like." I wait for the softest hint of a *good for you* or to register even the vaguest pang of self-awareness from her. But there is nothing.

"You're not going to resign, Lucille." She mollifies her tone, like she's patronizing a teenager. "You're going to go in there Monday morning and play the game, like the rest of us have to. Show him you're grateful for what you do have and then work ten times harder than you have been. Put in the hours, be better than everyone else. It's the only way."

"Is it?" I try again, hoping it will make her think.

"Yes, hard work will always pay off. It will always get you noticed."

"Will it, though, Mum?"

"Yes, of course it will." She's starting to sound exasperated. "You can't just walk away from something the second it gets difficult. That's the time to dig deep and battle through."

"How will it pay off?"

"If you want choices in life, if you never want to rely on anyone else for support, then you need to be fully financially independent. Only then can you truly own your own life."

It sounds so mercenary to me. Maybe I like the idea of someone else's support—not for *battling* life, but navigating it, by my side. Lifting each other up, supporting one another when needed. I don't want to be in competition with the world. I don't want it to feel that hard.

I'm happy to accept there will be mistakes and wrong turns and bad decisions, but isn't it supposed to be how you react to those things that makes all the difference? Wasn't it in the days Veronique spent working her way around Europe *without* a master plan that she became the woman she is today? Open, trusting, and confident, and perceptive to people and places that don't mimic her own experience of life?

It sounds like there has been little self-analysis since the company Mum devoted herself to decided to drop her from the payroll. I wonder if she'll ever work it out. The balance of the rich rewards versus what it cost her to get them. I think of the gated estate she calls home just off Fulham Road, and its completely gratuitous number of security barriers to navigate before you gain entry. The big, wide-open empty roads because so few people can actually afford to live there.

I can see why it is appealing. How clear a mark of success it is. She has every conceivable choice of bar, restaurant, shop, yoga studio, hairdresser all within easy reach. She blasts hundreds of pounds in each of them every week, but it never occurs to her to pay the small taxi fare the few miles to Wimbledon to see her own mother.

"How's Granny?"

"Fine. Why?"

"You've seen her?"

"No. I don't need to."

"You don't *need* to see your elderly mother?"

"Natasha calls me every day, Lucille. Trust me, not one day goes by when I don't get a very detailed voicemail updating me on every minute facet of your grandmother's day. How many Weetabix she ate for breakfast. How her bunions are doing. How much shouting she's done at the TV, which seems to be as accurate a gauge as any for her general well-being." I imagine Mum has Natasha's number plugged into her phone purely for the purpose of avoiding her calls. Never making the mistake of answering and having to hear for herself what kind of day Granny has had. "And actually, I was thinking about going over there tomorrow. If I have time."

"I was hoping to see you then." I say it quickly before I change my mind.

"Even better." That's how effortlessly Granny is mentally struck off Mum's to-do list. "Come over at one, I'll have lunch ready for us, and we can talk some more about your career strategy then."

We're going to talk about a lot more than that, not that she knows it yet.

I go to bed and lie there feeling lighter, more energized, and more optimistic than I have in ages. I can't sleep, but it's for the right reasons.

I'm excited. The world suddenly feels full of possibilities again—like I just created the first space in my life for them to swim in.

20

Alice
DECEMBER 1953, PARIS

What a blissful hour with you that was. Sixty whole minutes that felt lived, when I could relax enough to be myself. To be reminded of the long-forgotten me, the kind of woman she can be. After everything you have been through, Antoine, it amazes me that you have the courage you do. To challenge yourself to live honestly and encourage me to do the same. It may have taken great individual sadness to bring us together, but I hope to only see happiness in our future. You breathe so much life into me, Antoine, I wonder how I ever lived without you. Now I know I didn't live at all. They were meaningless days, my every simple act designed to keep others happy. I will always think of myself now as the woman I was before you, and after you—because of you.

The note is one of her more recent to Antoine, written in the heady aftermath of their first secret meeting at Dior two weeks ago. There is something so intoxicating about reading it again now, as her naked body lies warm and satisfied under his twisted bedsheets. She slips it back into the envelope on the bedside table and allows her eyes to cast around the room. His apartment is covered in sketches of her, from memories still hotly imprinted in his mind. Her tears have gone, replaced by rushed depictions of Alice with her back arched beautifully above him or lying almost broken on the bed after they have finally fallen away from each other. Dangerous, snatched hours have been lost in his bed as their need for each other grows stronger, her fear pushed foolishly aside under Antoine's influence.

The only bit she hates is rehearsing her story with him, qualifying every detail before she heads back to the residence to be questioned. Thank goodness for Anne and her endless alibis. Her charade is just that little bit easier, more practiced—or have they simply become more careless? Because the mere thought of being caught out, the idea that she will trip over herself on a minor detail that Albert seizes upon, is still enough to make her blood run cold.

Their plan to be together is rudimentary and loosely formed. Their time together is so short, neither of them is willing to sacrifice any to Albert, to allow his name to dominate their discussions.

"Can you stay a little longer today? *Please?*" Antoine whispers into her ear, his breath mimicking the soft trace of his fingers down over her hip and onto her thigh. As her consciousness slowly unfolds back into the present, she stretches before curling back into him.

"I can't. I'm due in a meeting today about the Queen's birthday celebrations. I can't miss it. It's been in everyone's diary for weeks."

"It's months away. *Please.*"

"I know it is, but there's so much to do. Albert wants all the fanfare, obviously. And he's expecting me, Antoine. I need to be there." She immediately regrets mentioning his name as Antoine flashes his eyes skyward, clearly frustrated that Albert is still commanding her time, getting what he wants, when he wants it.

"There is something I want us to do together." He climbs out of bed and crosses the room to the window, gently easing the curtains open and casting a thin veil of watery winter light across himself. Alice allows her eyes to slowly travel over him, to appreciate the muscular curve of his legs, the tautness of his chest and torso, the manly rounding of his arms as they flex to pull the curtain. Even all these weeks on, she still can't look at him without feeling the swell of pleasure ripple up inside her. She only has to close her eyes, plunge herself into a private darkness, to remember how he feels, how he makes *her* feel, knowing she never wants to let either sensation go.

"What is it? Maybe I have time before I go. But I can't be late, Antoine."

"Wait here." She watches as he heads for the door. "I won't be long."

Alice props herself up on her elbows and winces at the headache spreading out across her forehead. She has been drinking too much recently. At home, to numb herself against the daily ordeal of Albert's moods. And here, rolling around with Antoine, always one eye on the clock, one part of her brain rehearsing the story she'll tell Albert later. She makes a mental note to cut down, which won't be easy so close to Christmas, and with it the grim prospect of her and Albert being forced to spend more time together. She hasn't dared to raise the subject with him. She has fantasized he'll spend Christmas in London with family, leaving her and Antoine free to enjoy it together. But with no mention of any such plans, she's accepted the chances of that happening are slim. The only thing worse will be if he insists that she travel with him.

Should she simply have left Albert as soon as the reality of her situation dawned? If she had acted sooner, might she be happier now, more settled? But left him for where? With no source of income, she would have had to rely on her parents to facilitate her return to England; would they have financed her escape? She's not confident the answer to that question is yes. And what of the life she would be returning to, where everything would fall back under their control and where, unimaginably, there would be no Antoine? To expose herself without an airtight solution would have been reckless. If she had moved in with Antoine, his parents would have severed all support. How would they have lived? No, she's used to coping; she can cope with this a little longer.

Her thoughts are interrupted by the sound of Antoine dragging something heavy up the stairs, and when he lunges back into the room, she sees it is a Christmas tree, its fresh, piney scent immediately filling the room, Antoine laughing. And before she can work out why, Alice feels a wave of emotion collapse on her, and she's inexplicably on the verge of tears.

Is it because this should be a perfectly romantic landmark moment in their relationship? A young couple in the passionate grip of new love, about to spend their first Christmas together. If only it were that simple. Is it because she has no memory of ever decorating a Christmas tree as a child? It was something that magically appeared overnight when she was in bed. A job the housekeeper took care of, it never occurring to her parents that she might like to share the joyful task with them like other children got to with their families.

Or is it because she knows that however blissful the next hour might be, that's all it will be today, and she will have to return to the residence and Albert? While Antoine wrestles the tree into position, she buries her face in the bedsheet, not wanting to ruin the moment for him with her tears.

"I got it yesterday." He beams. "I wouldn't normally bother, but I wanted us to decorate it together." He balances it against the wall and offers her a paper bag that she knows will contain their usual patisserie and coffee.

Alice smiles, but there is a horrible uneasiness taking root inside her this morning. She loves what Antoine is doing, trying to make this look and feel as normal as possible for them. But as hard as he may try, she can't shake the fact that this is make-believe, that they won't open presents together on Christmas Eve like thousands of other couples across Paris. That they may not even get to see each other at all if Albert stays put.

"It's such a lovely thought" is all she can manage. The smell of the freshly brewed coffee is making her stomach turn, and she knows she won't drink it. Even the warmth of the buttery pastry spreading through the bag is unappealing. "Will you spend Christmas with your parents?"

"No! I want to spend it with you, Alice." He's moved back over to the bed now, his face belatedly concerned that this might not be possible.

Alice tries to divert the subject away from herself. "Surely your mother will be expecting you there. How has she been since, well, you know? You haven't mentioned her much since the night of the Monet exhibition."

"Oh, who knows what she thinks. I suspect she will have told herself either that we are no longer seeing each other or that some sort of understanding has been reached with your husband. I certainly haven't bothered to provide the details for her."

Alice's throat tightens, like a small stone has lodged itself there. Surely Madame du Parcq is not that easily diverted? She hasn't presented herself as the kind of woman who would simply move on and let her son make his own decisions. He must know that.

"You think she doesn't know about us, what's really going on?" Alice asks tentatively. "She's accepted it was just one kiss on that one evening?" Alice can't keep the panic from rising in her voice. That all seems so unlikely to her. But now doesn't feel like the right time to raise all this. Not when she knows she will have to dress and leave soon with no idea when she'll be able to see Antoine again.

"Can we please not waste our time together talking about what she may or may not know? I really don't care, Alice." Antoine takes a small box from the wardrobe and hands it to her, his face glowing with happiness. "Do you like them?"

She opens the lid and discovers a selection of beautiful wooden tree decorations. Ballet dancers, candles, wreaths, stars, and drums, all carefully wrapped in old, discolored tissue paper.

"They belonged to my grandmother. Apparently I was obsessed with them as a child, so they came to me when she passed away. I've never felt the need to get them out before, but this year I want to."

"They are precious." Alice lifts one of the ballet dancers from the box. Her arms and legs are gracefully extended like she is about to land an impressive jump. Her flared tutu is painted gold, and she still has the gossamer ribbons of her ballet slippers snaking up her slender legs. Alice holds it in her hand, and a thousand thoughts about her childhood, her marriage, the kind of woman she has become all collide at once, and she starts to quietly sob.

"None of it is real, Antoine. None of this can last, and I can't bear it."

He grabs hold of both her arms and firmly shakes her. "Yes, it can! Don't even think it. Of course we can be together. I'm ready, Alice. I've told you, you can move in here today as far as I'm concerned."

They have been over and over this. But she will say it again, hoping this time Antoine will listen.

"We must wait for Albert's anger to burn itself out, to at least subside beyond its current fever. Please." She wipes her tears on the back of her hand, keeping Antoine from losing patience now her priority.

"Why must he dictate *everything*?"

"He isn't dictating this, is he?" She strokes a hand along Antoine's face, reminding him that she is here now, with him, exactly where she wants to be.

"We need a sign, Antoine, something that tells me we're no longer his priority, that we've been replaced by another one of his late-night distractions or a crisis at work. It won't be long. One will come. In the meantime, I will do as we planned. I will start to look for some work, perhaps something at the Sorbonne. And I'll begin to bring some of my things here. Small things that are important to me but that he won't notice are missing."

"It's not enough, Alice. I want to be with you properly, I want to marry you!"

They both pause. Antoine looks just as shocked by what he's said as she is. Why? Because he doesn't know how she'll react? Or he wasn't expecting to hear himself say it? Alice stays silent, but her emotions are exploding inside of her. She wants to scream yes, a thousand times over. She wants to rail at the unfairness of her life never colliding with Antoine's before Albert's. She wants to forget every responsibility she ever signed up to and run off with this beautiful man to somewhere they'll never be found. To distill her life down to the simple love story she wants it to be. But her lips stay clamped shut. She needs to hear more from him. Is that a proposal? Or an exaggeration of the pleasure their bodies create together? A hint of what he sees in his dreams, in their future beyond Albert, if such a thing is even possible.

"If two people are meant to be together, then they will be. Do you really think Albert can stand in the way of that?" He shakes his head vehemently, and she watches as he delves back into the box and pulls out a favorite decoration.

Alice's gaze drops to her wedding ring, and she thinks how much happier she would be if Antoine were the man who had put it there. Maybe she has been overthinking this. Maybe Albert is just a man on borrowed time, one who is soon to realize that despite all his plotting and dictating, his wife has disobeyed him every step of the way. And maybe she can face up to that reality, too, with Antoine firmly by her side.

By the time Alice steps back into the residence an hour or so later, she feels like heading straight back to bed. But rest will have to wait. She is due in the library in fifteen minutes with Albert, Anne,

Eloise, Patrice, and their head chef to advance discussions about the Queen's birthday celebrations they will host.

As planned, the residence has been transformed overnight with a thousand glittering Christmas decorations. Their appearance is late, but Alice just couldn't muster the enthusiasm to direct the job. Everywhere she turns, there is a reminder in the branches of the Christmas trees and the glowing lanterns that line the staircase of how joyful this month should be—and how impossible it is for her to feel that way while she is splitting herself in two.

She is the last one to take her seat in the library, and she tries to ignore the barely disguised look of disgust brewing across Albert's face as she sits down, pen and paper at the ready in front of her.

"Where have you been?" he demands, much louder than necessary.

Alice swallows hard. Please, not now, not in front of everyone, she thinks, and not when she feels so incapable of a retaliation.

"With the florist." She aims for light and assured, but her tone sounds fearful inside her own mouth.

"Which one?" He's onto her. The confident stillness of his face and the tightness of his grip on his pen give away his looming anger.

"Le Joli Bouquet, I think I mentioned it?" The staff gathered around the table are starting to shift in their seats, unsure, like her, where this is going to end. She decides to push the meeting forward.

"Eloise, would you like to start us off with the guest list, please?"

Eloise opens her mouth to speak but is immediately drowned out by Albert.

"I thought they were closed on Thursday."

Albert is not interested in the fripperies of entertaining enough to know whether a particular florist is open on a Thursday or not. He is merely trying to unsettle Alice. To remind her that every story she tells can—and will—be checked. She has no choice in the circumstances but to stick to her story.

"No, very much open. And selling some of the finest snowberries and eucalyptus. I've asked for some to be delivered next week." She immediately sees Anne scribble on her notepad, knowing she will be writing a cryptic reminder to herself to place the order with the florist. "Eloise, do go on." Alice pours herself a large glass of water and drains it in one go, immediately refilling the glass, prompting Anne to ask if she is okay.

"Yes, fine, thank you. Just a little tired," she whispers back, noticing how the corners of Albert's mouth have subtly shifted upward.

"We closed the guest list last week after everyone's feedback, and we now have our final call of names," Eloise informs everyone.

"And how many do we stand at?" asks Alice.

"Two hundred and fifteen. That's one hundred and fifty for the formal drinks reception and an additional sixty-five joining us for the banqueting dinner. It's going to be extremely tight, but if there really is no one we feel we can exclude at this point, then that's the final call."

"When will the invitations go out?" Alice can feel beads of sweat starting to gently tickle her forehead and reaches for the water again, noticing that her hand is shaking a little, the kind of depleted tremors she gets when she's too busy and skips a meal. It takes both her hands to steady the glass enough to raise it to her lips, and she can feel Anne's concerned eyes on her. She leans in closer to Alice.

"Would you like me to cancel your appointments this afternoon, Madame Ainsley? You really don't seem too well."

"No, no. I'll be fine. Once we're done here, I'll take a nap. Sorry, Eloise, please go on."

"The proof is with the private secretary at Downing Street now, more as a courtesy than anything else. So, assuming that is signed off before the Christmas break, we will post the invitations the second week of January, when everyone is very much back in the swing of it."

"And let's please try to plan some additional events at the Athénée. It's my favorite hotel in the whole of Paris, and I know Olivier, the general manager there, would hugely appreciate the publicity. We've got such a great relationship with him now, let's make sure it stays that way."

"A lovely idea, I will liaise with them. We'll be asking for these RSVPs by the beginning of February so Chef can start planning and get the necessary orders in well ahead of schedule."

"Okay, which leads us nicely on to the menus. Have you given much thought to the canapés for the drinks reception, Chef?" Alice's mouth is parched, and she can feel her throat cracking as she speaks. Albert shifts forward in his chair, keeping his eyes trained on her.

"I thought a wonderful mix of all her British and French favorites. We should serve champagne as well as her favorite cocktail, gin and Dubonnet. Then some bite-size roast beef and Yorkshire puddings, some game, of course, probably venison cooked in a Scottish whiskey sauce, before we move on to something sweet, perhaps chocolate, Earl Grey scented and served with strawberries, which will be in season by then. Maybe an orange-blossom crème brûlée?"

"That sounds like more than enough," interjects Albert. "Don't you think, Alice?" He's directing the question at her because he can see full well that all the color has drained from her cheeks. She is holding her head in her hands and attempting to push her chair back to leave the room.

"Sorry, everyone, will you excuse me for a moment?" Anne helps her to her feet, and Alice is enormously grateful for her guiding hand. Less so for the glare Albert is now rewarding her with, knowing he'll have to take the lead while she is away from the meeting.

"I'm not sure I have time to be bored senseless with this sort of thing," Albert announces to the sound of his chair scraping backward. "Just make the best-informed decisions, which is what all of you are here to do," he barks as he shoves past Alice and Anne on his way out of the room.

Anne negotiates the stairs at a snail's pace, stopping frequently for Alice to breathe and control the seesawing feeling of dizziness. They make it as far as her bedroom door before Alice feels the room darken around her and her body collapses into Anne.

"I think I need to call you a doctor," says Anne. "You're not well enough to make it to the surgery yourself."

Alice doesn't argue. She allows Anne to lift and move her rag doll arms and legs out of her dress and to help recline her back onto the bed. Moments later she is sound asleep.

WHEN SHE COMES TO, ANNE AND HER REGULAR DOCTOR ARE standing by her bedside, Anne's hand on her cold, clammy arm.

"Madame Ainsley, I have Dr. Bertrand with me. He's going to check a few of your vitals to reassure us all it's nothing serious. Is that okay?"

"Yes, of course. You'll have had a wasted journey, I'm sure, but please do what you feel is necessary." Anne helps to sit her up, stacking two large pillows behind her. She feels a little weak, almost like the sleep never happened.

"I am very happy to have my time wasted if it means you are well, Madame Ainsley. Now, let me have your arm and we'll start with your pulse and blood pressure." He takes a firm hold of her arm with one hand and pops a thermometer under her tongue with the other.

"Are you taking any medications I should be aware of?"

She shakes her head.

"Your pulse is fine, but your blood pressure is a little low. Aside from the fainting, have you had any other symptoms?"

"Not at all, I am in perfect health."

"Okay. Well, I am happy that you seem fine for now. But I want to be called if there are any further symptoms, please."

"Of course, but honestly I think we can consider this a one-off." Alice shuffles up higher in the bed, keen to demonstrate she doesn't intend to be in it for much longer.

"And I would like you to do a urine test, please." He hands Anne a small tubular container. "It's the best way to highlight an infection that we may otherwise miss. It will give us a good overview of your protein, sugar, and hormone levels so we can rule out anything serious. Perhaps you will be good enough to bring the sample downstairs to me when Madame Ainsley is done?" he asks Anne.

"Of course. We'll just be a couple of minutes." She guides the doctor back toward the bedroom door.

"The results will take a few days, and who knows, we may be looking for bad news where there is only good," he adds, allowing his face to soften slightly into the whisper of a smile.

"Oh, what an almighty fuss," moans Alice the second he is out of earshot. "But while you are down there, please will you grab a tape measure, Anne? I need you to take my latest measurements and phone them through to Dior. I don't have time to go back into the boutique."

"Of course. I won't be long."

WHILE ANNE IS GONE, ALICE'S THOUGHTS TURN TO THE TOILE DE Jouy fabric from her last visit to Dior. She thinks about Antoine's words this morning, his determination for them to be together, his blind insistence that they will be. But before she can fully lose herself in the fantasy, the bedroom door flies open and Anne flails into the room, her face ashen.

"What on earth?" Alice sits bolt upright.

"Albert." One single word capable of striking a cold shard of fear through Alice.

"My God, now what? What has he said to you?"

"Nothing. He never said a word. I walked into the cloakroom to find my handbag, I always keep a tape measure in there."

"Yes, and?"

"And Albert was in there. Alice, he was searching through my handbag."

"*What?* What a total invasion. What can he possibly be thinking?" But even as the words are leaving Alice's lips, her brain has jumped ahead of her. "Oh my God. Did he see it?" The room seems to drain of all its warmth, the air thinning around them. "My letter to Antoine. Please tell me it wasn't in there. Please, Anne!"

"It was." Her hands are pulling at her hair, her mouth slashed open in a panicked grimace. "But it's not now. I'm so sorry, Alice, I think he has it."

21

Lucille
SATURDAY
LONDON

Stepping into Mum's vast apartment is like entering an air vacuum. It's hard to believe any human or plant life-form can exist in it. If she had Do Not Touch signs strategically positioned, it wouldn't be any more of a deterrent than the freakish tidiness of the place already is.

Seriously, who lives like this? Everything is so precisely considered and angled. Nothing is accidental. Symmetry reigns supreme. But it does provide a wonderful window into the mind of someone for whom control, accuracy, and single-mindedness are *everything*. The effort to achieve it must swallow hours of her time, every single day.

Color is common, apparently, so everything is a shade that ranges from white through beige to gray. Cream hydrangeas look crisp enough to have been picked this morning; cushions, like they have been lined up with a ruler. To most people, I imagine this is the high-shine dream. To me it's clinical and frigid. It makes me want to shout something vulgar or violently swing my handbag at something expensive. Give me the cake-crumb comfort of Granny's cottage any day.

I enter through her double-height, blond wooden door and onto a gleaming marble floor that's more like the intimidating lobby of a city bank than someone's actual home. Then the space opens out into a cavernous living area, bigger than my local library and with ceilings so high they practically disappear from view. To one side of three central stone pillars, she has a dining table that can comfortably seat twenty, and I wonder, who are all these people she's entertaining? She doesn't have a boyfriend—the mere idea is weird to me. She was never going to make space in her diary for a date over a business debrief. I've never once heard her talk of dinners or parties or late nights that have taken place here. Certainly none that I've ever been invited to.

I follow her into the kitchen, a space that looks nothing like one until she starts gently stroking doors and they slide or bounce open to reveal the fridge or a wine chiller. She has already laid lunch out for us in the center of her comically long dining table, and I can physically feel myself stiffen, like I might at a job interview. I toss my bag casually to the floor, making it the single piece of clutter in the place, and she notices as a hair-filled brush tumbles out. She opens her mouth to complain, then obviously thinks better of it despite the *mess* making her uncomfortable. Her eyes continually flick back to it.

"I'm so glad you could come over, Lucille. I've been feeling rotten while you've been away." She pours me a glass of white wine, and I can't be bothered to tell her I much prefer red.

"Have you been unwell too?"

"Unwell? Try abandoned and forgotten." We both take a seat on wide polished wooden benches to either side of the table.

"Oh, come on, Mum, you've lost your job. I know it seems unfair, but you haven't just been diagnosed with something terrifying." I smile to indicate that while I might be making light of the situation, I am still on her side—to the degree that being related to her demands.

"It might feel that way to you, but it doesn't to me. I know career has never been terribly important to you, Lucille—you are, after all, contemplating walking away from a perfectly good role without another one to go to—but I've spent my entire life building that business up. I've wiped out whole weekends, when everyone else was out in the sun, to work on pitches. I said no to countless social invitations to work on new protocols, so many that the invites just stopped coming after a while. If I added up the hours I have spent at the office versus in my own home, it would be shocking, frankly." I fear this little speech is going to run and run, but then she pauses and gulps back a huge glug of wine, sighing loudly as she gently replaces the long-stemmed glass on a coaster, perfectly aligning the two.

"None of this is news to me, Mum. I lived through it with you. Or rather, I didn't." She's starting to spoon some of the three large salads onto her plate, and all I can see on her face is excitement. She's thinking only of the pricey asparagus covered in Parmesan shavings, the gnocchi with pesto that isn't out of a jar, and the caramelized bulbs of fennel that are scattered with wild rice and pine nuts. Looking at it, I'm guessing she's spent one hundred pounds in one of her favorite organic delis this morning. What is completely absent is any sense of regret, and I can't let her get away with it.

"Do you feel bad looking back, Mum, like you missed out?" I say it gently. I don't want to attack her, but I do want her to think about it for once.

"What do you mean?" she asks as she's forking the food into her mouth.

"Now you can see that despite all your devotion and hard work, in the end you are dispensable. Just like the rest of us. That perhaps they didn't value you as highly as the sacrifices you made. Was it all worth it?"

She drops her fork to her plate, pleased at the abrupt clatter it makes as it lands. "I had to earn a living, Lucille. Who else was going to? If I had stopped to ask myself these questions, what good would it have done me? Or you? I might have come to the same conclusions you seem to have reached, but then what? At least I can say you never wanted for anything." And I want to tell her, Yes, I did, I wanted you, my mum. That she might have been far from perfect, but no one is perfect, and besides, she was mine and I needed her. But the words stick in my throat, because it will make me the bad person, the ungrateful one, if I voice them.

"Is that what you think? I did all right?" I try again, but I can see the irritation building in the color of her cheeks. Her defense mechanism is about to kick in. She's not embarrassed; she's getting cross because she doesn't want to face what we have both avoided for years. In the past this would have been enough to silence me, or at least force a change of subject. I help myself to a large swig of wine too. If I'm going to do this, I'll need some fortification, I realize. The three feet she's sitting across the table from me suddenly doesn't feel like far enough.

"Didn't you?" Her tone is challenging, and she's moving toward the fight, trying to scare me off the subject because it's too painful to confront. I can hear it building in her deep inhalations. It's my warning not to take this any further. This is supposed to be the lunch where she ticks *Lucille time* off her to-do list, dispenses some unwanted career advice that will make her feel motherly, has a moan about how unfairly she's been treated, and then sends me on my way.

But I'm in the mood for more honesty than that.

"No. I missed you." Saying the words aloud sends a giant flood of sadness through me that I didn't realize was coming, and I tighten my stomach muscles to stop it from spilling into the space between us. "Every single day, I missed you. I felt alone."

She won't know how to handle my tears, so I try to stick to the facts, despite the awful flashbacks that are starting to appear behind my eyelids. The crying into my pillow night after night, being the only one whose mum never attended school events, the pitying looks from my teachers.

She isn't in the mood to be conciliatory—is she ever? "Oh, for goodness' sake, Lucille, can we not just have a nice lunch together? This was all a very long time ago. I always tried to get the best child-care I could. I thought you loved Amy."

Poor Amy, my long-suffering nanny, who was always glued to the phone, apologizing to someone for being late because her boss *still* wasn't home yet. How it made me feel like a massive inconvenience who had to be passed from person to person, no one really wanting to be responsible for me.

"Of course I didn't *love* Amy. Is that what you told yourself? It was okay to come home late every night because I had Amy? A girl who couldn't wait for you to arrive so she could get out of the house and on with whatever she really wanted to be doing." I can feel the emotion trying to hammer its way out of me now, and my mouth is contorting as I struggle to keep it in.

"I put you to bed some nights." The outrage in my mum's voice is only making me more determined to finish this conversation and make her understand that a few hours tossed my way occasionally did not constitute parenting.

"Yes, I remember those nights. How you used to skip pages from my bedtime storybooks to speed it up."

"I had *work* to do, Lucille, don't you understand that? I was under so much pressure at the office."

"I was *six*, Mum! I knew what you were doing."

Something shifts in her then. Her eyes empty of anger, and I see a profound sadness shining there. "But what you don't know, because you were always sleeping by then, is the apology I whispered into your ear most nights, when I finally closed the laptop and could head to bed myself." The first tentative signs of emotion creep into her voice. "There were never enough hours in the day or night. However hard I worked, I never had time to just be with you. I had to be tough. I was scared of what might happen if I wasn't." She looks like someone has let the air out of her. Her shoulders sag; her eyelids soften.

I take a moment to calm myself, to spoon some of the food I know I won't eat onto my plate, and look around, noting some of the newer pieces that have appeared since my last visit months ago. The selection of these pieces will have taken considerably more of her time than it took to deposit the £150 into my bank account for this year's belated birthday present. An enormous crystal vase that sits empty, an exhibit all on its own. A new sprawling light fixture that's suspended above us, casting a clinically bright light into all corners of the dining space. Mum has furnished her apartment with items you will never see anywhere else. They have been collected during her travels for work. While most working mums might be dashing around the airport shops looking for thoughtful presents for the children they left behind at the beginning of the working week, Mum would be negotiating the safe return of a new armchair or an oversize rug through customs. As a child I envied her those trips. They held an almost magical allure. I'd lie in bed thinking of her flying through the sky above me, her evening lit by the same bright moon as mine. But she would wake in a foreign land so enticing it took her away from me time and time again. What was there that she wanted so much more than me?

The air between us cools a degree, enough for me to ask her the question I have wanted to for years. I'm not sure what's giving me the courage now when it was so lacking before. Maybe it's because she might not make time for another lunch anytime soon. Maybe because I feel the safety net of not expecting an honest answer, or perhaps I've just heard enough about family secrets for one week. It feels like at least some of them should be set free.

"Why was I so unlovable, Mum?" I let her feel the shock of those taboo words weighted in the air around us. I feel her absorb them; then, when there is nowhere else for them to go, swallow them. I register the flicker of panic in her hard blue eyes. She has to say something, and it has to be enough to satisfy all those years of hurt and loneliness.

I watch her slowly, deliberately place her cutlery back onto her plate. The expensive culinary experience ruined. Slowly she lifts her head, pushes her plate to one side, and laces her fingers together in front of her on the table. The management consultant braced to out-maneuver a belligerent client. Or is she about to face up to something she's avoided for as long as I have? She looks directly at me and speaks.

"I didn't know how to love you."

Her voice is heavy with emotion now. The words are whispered, not dictated. She drops her head a little as if ever so slightly ashamed of her confession.

"Go on." I'm in no hurry. I came here with one purpose today, and I'm not leaving until I've got answers to the questions that have troubled me for years.

"Granny Sylvie was very distant when I was growing up. I know you'll find that hard to believe." She raises a hand and cuts me off when she can see I am about to protest the likelihood of it. "But it's true, she was. She must have hugged me, but I don't remember it happening very often. She was around, she never worked after she married Granddad and had me, but I don't ever remember feeling loved. She was an incredibly sad person."

Mum's recollections of Granny are so hard to equate with the woman who has never shown me anything but love—or the recklessly romantic one who opened her heart in Paris, seemingly unafraid of the consequences. But I can't share any of it, not until I know the ending.

"I grew up feeling almost that she didn't want me. I would struggle to recall one special moment we shared. She was always very preoc-cupied."

"With what?" I lean in across the table, closing the physical distance between the two of us, completely opening myself up to the possibility of answers.

"I don't know"—she shakes her head sadly—"but I do remember her moods shifting dramatically with the arrival of letters she used to receive from a friend in Paris. Daddy always warned me never to interrupt her when she was reading or writing one of her letters. He said it was her special alone time. They seemed more important to her than anything else. They could alter the entire mood of the day. Sometimes one would arrive, and she would disappear to her room to read it. For a couple of hours afterward she would be so happy."

Her face breaks into a half smile and I can tell she is back there, seeing it as if the scene is unfolding in front of us both. "Suddenly we'd be baking together, or she'd want to take me for a walk or to the park. I'd feel as though I had my mummy back."

Then just as quickly it's gone. "But the joy never lasted, and by teatime she would be sad again, disappearing to her bedroom, locking the door, and ignoring all my pleas to be let in."

"Oh, Mum. Why haven't you shared any of this with me before?" I instinctively reach a hand across the table to her, and she clings to it like it's her only lifeline.

"These things are best forgotten. They weren't happy times. I didn't see the point in resurfacing it all." I understand her wanting to avoid the subject and leave painful memories in the past. But to ignore it for all these years also seems so cowardly. Didn't she ever feel like she deserved some answers too?

"And you've never asked her about it?"

"We don't have that sort of relationship. We weren't close then and we aren't close now. She's very old, Lucille. Despite how distant she was as a mother, I don't hate her for it. I've learned to live with it, and I certainly don't want to make the final years of her life any more painful than they might already be."

"And there were no other clues as to what was causing her so much upset?"

"Your grandfather told me once that there was a great sadness to my mother that she would never lose and that I shouldn't try to understand it. I grew up thinking she was ill, terrified that I would wake up one morning and find her gone. I used to picture myself standing at her graveside, unable to cry because she would never let me love her. I thought everyone would look at me and see what a terrible daughter I was, incapable of shedding tears at her own mother's funeral. Can you even begin to imagine what that felt like, Lucille?"

"I can't, no. I'm so sorry, Mum. But didn't Granddad ever tell you anything more as you got older?"

"Never. Whatever it was, Lucille, she never wanted it known. She obviously wasn't ill, so in later years I assumed it was in some way connected to the fact that her parents were never part of her life or mine."

"What about Paris? Did she ever talk about the city or anything that might have happened there? If it was where she met Granddad, then it must have been important to her." There is so much more I could say, but now is not the time.

She thinks for a minute.

"Yes, actually, there was one trip I remember her taking to Paris when I was about three or four years old. I think it must be one of my earliest memories of her."

"You went with her?"

"No, she went alone. It wasn't the trip itself that I remember, she never spoke about it. But after she returned home, it was like a huge dark cloud settled above the house and nothing could shift it. She would spend day after day in bed crying, curtains closed, refusing to see me. She got painfully thin. Daddy called the doctor out to her, and I remember after that how a row of little brown pill bottles appeared on her bedside table. So many pills. I thought they were to help her love me. But they never worked."

"She does love you, I know she does! She always asks after you when I'm with her." It sounds like a horribly weak defense, I know.

"Like you ask the postman if he had a nice weekend or the woman at the corner shop if her sick dog is better. Polite inquiries don't constitute love, Lucille. I bet you've never heard her speak about me fondly. Or heard her express genuine love or affection for me. Have you ever felt that she misses me? Or is proud of me and everything I've achieved?" Despite the confidence with which she says all this, I can see there is a glimmer of hope in my mother's face. She studies my features across the table; she wants me to contradict her.

And my mouth opens to tell her how wrong she is, and the words should be tumbling out of me, but they're not, and the pause sits sadly between us. I watch as she drops her head, knowing for sure now that she is right.

"She can be very vague some days," I offer. "Some days she struggles to tell me what she ate two hours earlier." But I know that the following day she might be incredibly lucid, recalling details and times with such clarity it's like they happened that morning. I always put it down to selective memory. But Mum is right. None of Granny's stories have ever made Mum the focus. Whenever we've spoken of Mum, it's been largely me doing the talking and, more usually, moaning, Granny shaking her head and looking disappointed. I hope the guilt isn't showing on my face.

"It's an awful thing to admit, Lucille, but seeing how devoted she is to you only makes it worse. The fact she sent you to Paris—a city that obviously means something to her—and never me hurts. From the moment you were born, she wanted to see you all the time. No matter how often we had her over or took you to visit her, it was never enough. She showered you with an affection that was completely alien to me. It got to the point where your father and I had to invent reasons why she couldn't pop round—you'd had a bad night's sleep, or you were running a temperature—just to give us some breathing space."

"Why do you think that was?"

"I've no idea, but I suspect Granddad knew. He caught the irritation on my face one afternoon on another of her impromptu visits and took me to the side. I can't remember his exact words now, but he asked me to be patient with her. Said that if I knew why she was behaving the way she was, I would understand. That was as much as he would say on the subject. He was devoted to her, and I knew he would never betray any confidences she'd trusted him with. They were never more than friends when they first met and spent time together in Paris. It wasn't until later, when she walked into one of the smart hotels in Wimbledon to collect some cakes for an afternoon tea, that he emerged from the kitchen to hand them to her. I remember him telling me how he never did that. A member of the waiting staff should have given them to Mum. But he said he had an overwhelming feeling that forced him from behind the scenes that day."

"Oh, wow, really?"

"Yes, when he saw her, stood there with no idea their paths were about to cross again, his heart nearly exploded in his chest, he said. They were reunited after more than five years apart and fairly inseparable from then on—until she finally lost him."

Mum's recollections fit perfectly with the man I remember making fresh shortbread for Granny every weekend, filling their home with a warm, buttery smell that will forever remind me of him.

"Anyway, I expected that her interest in you would wane in your first few months, but it never did. She's as fascinated by you now as she ever was." I can see the hurt is still there, as fresh for Mum today as it might have been thirty-two years ago.

"And you grew to resent me?" It's a hard question to ask her, so I do it softly, letting my voice tell her that I understand if the answer is yes, I just need to know. She's being more open and honest with me this afternoon than she's ever been and might ever be again.

"I didn't think of it that way at the time, but maybe just a little, yes. You have to understand my own mother had been so distant from me, I just couldn't grasp what this tiny baby in my arms possessed that I never did myself. Eventually, of course, I put it down to her simply making amends with her granddaughter. That she was determined to set right with her actions what she was never able to voice to me. Does that make sense?"

"It does, Mum, but can't you see how the cycle has repeated itself?" I reach both hands across the table and she takes them. "How you have kept me away? How if the two of you had resolved all this years ago, *our* relationship might have been better?"

"I'm so sorry, Lucille. I want you to know that I do love you and I always have. I am going to do everything I can to make things better between us. If you will let me? If I'm not too late?" She starts to quietly cry, something I have never seen my own mother do. Her bottom lip is quivering, and I know she won't take her eyes off me until she has my answer.

"Of course it's not too late, Mum. But it's not just about you and me. I think you need to make your peace with Granny, too—and she does with you. Before it's too late."

She nods and I know she means it. There's no smart comment or caveat or even a raise of her lashes to the sky. I find my thoughts turn to Veronique and how right she was when we shared the plate of charcuterie and a bottle of wine, just after Mum lost her job and pleaded with me to return home. She said there would be a reason behind Mum's behavior and how careless it was for me to judge her until I knew it.

"Good old Veronique," I mutter under my breath, but Mum catches it.

"Who is Veronique?" she asks.

"Someone a lot wiser than I am," I say through a half smile.

22

Alice
DECEMBER 1953, PARIS

"Congratulations, Madame Ainsley, you're going to be a mother."

Alice immediately feels her legs weaken, her center of gravity swim away from her. The backs of her knees make contact with the bed behind her, and she takes a seat there.

"Really? Are you sure? I mean, absolutely sure?" In the days she's had to ponder the outcome of her doctor's first visit, not once has she allowed her mind to wander to this conclusion. She was expecting to hear words like *anemia*, *exhaustion*, *stress*, and *alcohol intake* pass his lips this morning.

Not this.

She glances at Anne, but judging by the downcast look of acceptance on her face, this is not as big a surprise for her. She watches as Anne takes a long, deep breath to keep her emotions in check. This is difficult news for her to hear.

It's true, Alice and Antoine have been far from careful—careless, in fact—at protecting themselves. They've been so lost in each other, never pausing to consider how a moment together today might affect everyone for a lifetime. But her body wanted this. In the dark emptiness of her belly and the deep recesses of her heart that Albert has never wanted to touch, she truly wanted this.

"Your urine test shows a surprisingly high level of pregnancy hormones for this early stage. Consider it confirmed," he adds definitively.

Alice's ears seem to pop and fill with water. She can see the doctor's mouth moving through a huge congratulatory smile, but she can't hear a word he's saying.

It's Antoine's beautiful face Alice can see imprinted on her eyelids, where the fantasy of delivering this sweet news to him is already taking shape. They're both laughing, he's starting to cry, throwing his arms around her, lifting her, spinning her round and round until she has to tell him to stop, both of them euphoric, like this is everything they ever wanted. A gift that will unite them conclusively. No one in this world will be able to stand between them now.

"I wanted to personally deliver the news myself to ensure there are no leaks." The doctor's words pull Alice back into the room. "There will obviously be a press announcement in due course, and I didn't want to risk anything getting out before you and Monsieur Ainsley are absolutely ready to talk about it. You'll naturally want to get beyond the first twelve weeks, of course, but you are slight, Madame Ainsley, and you will start to show much sooner than you think. As I say, it's very early days, but by my estimation, your due date is early August."

Alice's hands move protectively to her belly. "Thank you, Doctor. I appreciate your taking the time to come here today." Her words feel robotic, delivered automatically without thought. She's thinking only of the magic being created inside of her. How she must protect it. She watches the back of the doctor's head as Anne escorts him from her bedroom, glancing back over her shoulder to check that it's okay to leave Alice alone for a few minutes.

As the door closes behind them, Alice can feel her breath quicken. The mention of Albert's name has released a toxic cloud of worry into the room. He can have no part of this. It's not his baby, at least of that she can be absolutely certain. But his silence over the past few days since her letter to Antoine went missing has been menacing. She's been too afraid to risk contacting Antoine, fearful any warning she might attempt would simply provide the final piece of evidence Albert needs.

Is she right? Has Albert deliberately distanced himself, removed himself from the residence more? Is he avoiding her? Giving her no chance to gauge his next move? She looks at her belly, lacing her fingers across it. Does she seem swollen? The last measurements Anne took certainly suggest so. Did she realize? Are people already looking at her and guessing there will be an announcement soon? Why hadn't she noticed the differences herself? It suddenly seems so obvious.

Anne returns and takes a seat next to Alice on the bed. "Are you okay, Alice? My goodness. I know this is a lot to take in, but what on earth are you going to do?"

Alice looks at her quizzically. "What do you mean?"

"What will you say to Albert?"

"The baby isn't his." Alice doesn't want to talk about Albert. This moment should not be about him.

"Do you know that for sure?" A flicker of embarrassment crosses Anne's face as she perhaps realizes what an impertinent question this is, even between two women whose relationship has deepened well beyond a professional one.

"For a very long time, Albert hasn't been interested in me. That part of our relationship, like many others, died when we arrived in Paris. It is simply not possible for this to be his baby."

"Okay. If you are sure the baby is Antoine's, how do you feel about that? What will you do? Albert will have to be told something, won't he? He'll know as well as you that it can't be his." Alice can forgive Anne's focus on the immediate practicalities because her thoughts and feelings aren't clouded by the same soaring emotion that is exploding inside of her.

"I don't have any of those answers." The incontrovertible bluntness of the situation lands. "This is not what I had planned. There will be no way of explaining this to Albert that will end well. But, Anne . . . next summer I will be holding Antoine's baby in my arms. I have a new life growing within me—the most unexpected and beautiful gift I could have been given. I have to nurture it and protect it at all costs." Alice stops abruptly when she sees that Anne's eyes have silently filled with tears and her chin has dropped toward her chest. She rises from the bed looking for a distraction, but Alice pulls her back down again.

"I am so sorry, Anne, please forgive me. I wasn't thinking at all. Oh, Anne, that was so insensitive. Upsetting you is the very last thing I want to do." Alice lifts her hand to Anne's face and gently brushes a fresh tear away.

"It's okay, really. I thought it would get easier, that's all. But it never does. Every time a friend or relative tells me she is pregnant, as hard as I try, I just can't keep the tears in. I am happy for you, Alice, please don't think I'm not. But I'm also worried, about how Albert will react and whether Antoine has any idea of what you'll soon be telling him."

Alice drops her voice. "I'll arrange to see him as soon as possible." She walks purposefully across the room and lifts the handset on the small desk in her bedroom. She lets it ring several times before accepting defeat and pulling a small notepad from the desk drawer. She hurriedly scrawls a few lines and then seals the note in an envelope.

"Please will you ask someone to drive this over to his apartment immediately? It says I need him to contact me as soon as possible. Then please let Patrice know that when he calls, he needs to be put through to me straightaway, whatever I'm doing. If I am asleep, please wake me."

"Yes, I'll do it immediately." But there is little pleasure on Anne's face, just a grim concern for what the day will hold.

While Anne busies herself, Alice starts to lightly sketch the outline of a dress, with a full skirt and ruffled neckline, next to the words *toile de Jouy.* Her drawing is basic and crude, and she'll be relying on the masters at Dior to turn her fantasy into something truly special, something worthy of the day she intends it for. She shows it to Anne.

"What do you think?"

She takes a moment to appreciate the gravitas of the gown she is looking at.

"I think it might just be the most beautiful dress yet." She smiles as she takes it from Alice. "I'll keep it safe for you."

ALICE BARELY TOUCHES HER LUNCH. HOW CAN SHE, WHEN SHE has still yet to share the news with Antoine?

There has been no word from him all morning, despite her near constant reminders to Anne that his call must be put straight through to her. She remains in her bedroom, pacing the same patch of floor, back and forth for hours, alone and ready, just as she needs to be for this conversation. But nothing.

By four o'clock, she can tolerate her own company no longer and ventures from her bedroom. As she approaches the small anteroom on her right, she notices a soft throw of light under the door and slows her pace. It can only be Albert; no one else uses this room. She lightens her footsteps, hoping to make it past unheard, but he suddenly steps out onto the landing, causing her to reel backward.

"A minute of your time, if you don't mind." He's standing in front of her, blocking her route along the corridor, and she has little choice but to step toward the doorway he came from.

"I'm really not feeling great, Albert. Can this wait, please?"

"No, it can't." He herds her into the room, so close behind her they're practically touching, and she can smell the tang of alcohol on his breath. She sees the open bottle of whiskey on the desk, and a cold tingle of nerves passes down her spine. Then he closes the solid oak door behind him, sealing them both into the confined space.

Being alone with him is a mistake, she knows it. She wants so desperately to turn and leave the room but fears how he will respond, how it might escalate into a situation she may not be able to talk herself out of. She knows she'll never be able to heave the door back open quickly enough. The room is lined with dense wood paneling, an effective soundproofing, and as she feels the space constrict around her, she realizes he has chosen his location deliberately. Whatever he wants to say to her, he has planned to do it away from the eyes and ears of the staff this time.

He moves toward the desk that sits under an imposing portrait of the Duke of Wellington, chest puffed, comfortable with his own authority. The painting is flanked by a run of small oil sketches, the solemn men of the war council, and just as she is wondering if they have inspired Albert to whatever confrontation he is building to, the silence is shattered by a sound, almost roar-like, of his deep-felt frustration, rocketing out of his lungs toward Alice. Then she hears the splintering of his whiskey glass against the wall behind her, so close to Alice's face she feels the ends of her hair lift as it travels through the air past her.

"My God, Albert, please!" She starts to cry and cradles her arms protectively around herself. He can't possibly know today's news. It is only she and Anne who are privy to it, and there is absolutely no way on earth her friend would have shared it. Surely this can't be about the letter, days after its discovery?

"Do you know what your father told me before we were married, Alice? Do you?" He bellows the words, as if she were standing at the opposite end of the corridor, not two meters from him, sending hate-fueled spit into the air between them.

"No." Her voice is barely audible, and she knows this will only anger him further, but she can't force the words out of her mouth with any conviction.

"Speak up!"

"No, Albert." She's anchored to the spot and can feel the quiver through her knees, strong enough to make the hem of her skirt flutter.

"He said I had made a good choice, because you would never cause me any trouble. He said you only ever wanted to please." He's tripping over his words, so angry he can't correctly pace what he wants to say. Alice knows she must choose her words very carefully. That he needs to feel in charge and in control of her. She understands that he wants to see her fear.

"I'm so sorry. I never wanted to hurt you, Albert. You deserve better." She lowers her eyes and hangs her head, trying to demonstrate submissiveness.

"Now you're contrite! Well, your father was right to a degree, wasn't he? You have been so *very* keen to please. When you've been running across the city with the scent of your lover still fresh on your skin, the pair of you couldn't be *more* pleased. But it was never your husband, never *me*, who you thought worth pleasing. It's not *me* you save yourself for." He's perched on the edge of his desk, arms folded across his chest, legs wide, facing Alice, keeping her standing in front of him, knowing she'll be too scared to move.

More than anything, she wants to tell him she tried, so very hard, in the beginning. How she married him with every intention of loving him and letting him love her, but he wasn't there, physically or emotionally. He wanted a business partner, not a wife. A representative, not a confidant. Another member of staff, never an equal. *He* never truly loved *her*. But she can't. He doesn't want to be contradicted. He won't accept any blame. Her best hope of ending this is to try to establish what has fueled his latest outburst and reassure him that she can fix it, whatever it is.

"I've tried to give him up, I've tried to be discreet . . ." She barely has time to draw breath before Albert flies from the desk, across the small space between them, and shouts directly into her face, his nose clashing with hers, causing her to stumble backward.

"I'd hardly call getting pregnant being fucking discreet, would you!? How do you intend to conceal *that*!" He's so close she can see the cracked dryness of his lips, the pockmarked skin across his nose and chin, and it's repulsive. She lowers her arms across her belly, trying her best to force some distance between them, sobbing loudly now. If he wants to see he has broken her, he can. She shakes her head from side to side, trying to make sense of what he's saying, how he can possibly know. She refuses to believe Anne has spoken to him. She was careful to give nothing away in the letter to Antoine, knowing there was a good chance it would be intercepted.

"Let me put you out of your misery. I can see you're struggling to keep up with this. How do you think I felt this morning, when your doctor was putting on his coat to leave, then shook my hand and congratulated me on becoming a father? I haven't been anywhere near you for months, so it didn't take long to work that out."

Alice's mind races back to this morning. Recalling the pleasure on her doctor's face, how keen he was to help keep their news under wraps until she and Albert were ready to go public. Why didn't she think to caution him about any word to her husband until she had spoken to Albert first?

"Oh my God. I'm sorry. I didn't think he'd . . ."

"Well, he did. Because he has quite wrongly assumed we have a solid marriage. You're so far out of your depth, Alice. You haven't got the first fucking clue how to manage yourself, let alone a baby. So, what happens next will have to fall to me."

"What do you mean?" Whatever comes out of Albert's mouth next will not be up for discussion.

"You're going to listen to me from now on. I've had all day to think about how I can salvage the mess you've created, how I can come out of this as unscathed as possible, and there is only one option. Because, believe me, I am not about to let the stupidity of others affect *every-thing* I have worked for. Not again. Not this time." He steps back a little from her, and she can see the red stain of anger that's bloomed from underneath his shirt collar, all the way up his neck and into his cheeks. But his demeanor is calmer. He's not expecting any resistance from her now.

"If Madame du Parcq and I are right, your relationship with Antoine is all but over, so . . ."

Alice feels her breath shudder to a halt inside her, and she bites down hard on her bottom lip. If only she had spoken to Antoine this morning, he would be here with her now, drawing a line through whatever futile plan Albert thinks she will go along with.

"Let me guess, you haven't heard from him today, correct?"

"What have you done?" Alice feels the strength returning to her voice, but she can't hide the fear in her eyes, knowing Albert is right.

"It was very easy, once I found your silly little love letter. I called Madame du Parcq and played on her worst fears—that unless he walks away from you, her darling son will never have a respectable career in this city or any other, and the family will be ostracized. It helped of course that I was clever enough to have your goodbye kiss photographed. Well, if she was determined to cut between the two of you before, my goodness, she was indomitable during our call this morning, after your doctor unwittingly dropped his little bombshell. I suppose I should be thanking him, really. Antoine may be young and stupid, but he does at least know how indebted he is to his parents, financially and morally. Madame du Parcq knows her son better than anyone, and she has taken care of him because he is so incapable of doing it himself. Now, here's what *we* are going to do."

Alice can't take it all in. Her mind is such a scramble of emotions and facts and panic, it's impossible to separate one from the others. How much of this is bluster? How much of it is true? She knows Albert will say whatever is necessary to get the result he wants.

"Your relationship with him is over, and as long as you can accept that, then have the baby. You will raise it as our own. It will give you something to do with all the spare time you'll now have. I will support you financially, but that's as far as it goes. I want nothing to do with the child."

"I . . . I need to speak to Antoine, I can't just . . ." There is a building pain inside her head from trying to cut through everything he is throwing at her.

"Let me be very clear. I'm not offering you a choice, Alice. This is it. I can't think there are many husbands who would be so generous. Now get out of my sight. I can't bear to look at you for another minute."

ALICE LIES ON THE BED, ALONE IN HER ROOM, LOOKING AT THE ceiling, waiting for a sleep she knows won't come. Willing herself not to do the one thing Albert wants, to question Antoine's love for her. Hours pass as she goes over and over what Albert claims has happened in the course of a day that started with such promise and is ending with her feeling more isolated than ever. Can Antoine really already know about the baby? Why hasn't he responded to her letter? Why hasn't he come straight to her and forced his way into the residence if necessary?

Eventually, the morning light starts to inch back into the room, bringing with it the cold chill of realization.

Antoine isn't coming—and she can't stay with Albert.

23

※

Lucille
SUNDAY
LONDON

"No pens, just pencils. No food or drink, obviously, and all your bags and coats need to go into the locker, please. Nothing is allowed to go in with you." The security guard at the front desk of the V&A is leaving nothing to chance, and his brusque efficiency is only escalating the nervousness pumping through me as Veronique and I prepare to be taken up to the study room.

"I need to see photo ID from both of you, then you can sign in here"—he flips open a black leather notebook—"and I'll issue you both a wristband." Veronique and I exchange a look. This is it. The day we will see dress number eight, the final one in Granny's collection. The one with the beautiful toile de Jouy fabric and the metaphorical full stop at the end of Granny's story.

I am about to discover, I hope, why she sent me to Paris.

"You're very lucky to get a Sunday appointment, they're like gold dust," he adds with a smile, becoming a little more human, a little less official. Perhaps he senses our apprehension. "You've got two hours, no longer, so make the most of it."

"Are you ready for this?" asks Veronique.

I am so pleased she is with me today. I don't want to be alone when I see whatever is waiting for me in there. And, let's face it, she has been much better at unraveling this story than I have. I might well need her to make sense of this final clue too. It feels right that it should be Veronique, given how close her own mother was to Granny back in their Paris days. It's like we're closing the circle together, and that both Granny and Veronique's mother would love the idea of us joining forces, helping each other reach the final twist of this mystery.

"I guess so."

A cheerful older lady checks in with the security guard and then turns to face us.

"Hello, I'm Margaret. I'll be helping you today. Have you signed in yet?"

"Just finishing up now," answers the security guy while he directs our faces to the small camera on top of his computer screen. While Veronique has her picture taken, I wonder if the knot of tension that is tightening in my stomach will still be there when we leave. What will we find?

Margaret leads us through a series of wide, tiled, hospital-like corridors that are completely deserted. The stark strip lighting flickers above us like it might give up at any moment. It reminds me of one of those chilling movies that ends with someone being wrongly institutionalized for a crime they didn't commit. I get the feeling Margaret has walked these lonely corridors many times before. She doesn't look spooked like we do. Her eyes are darting ahead of her. There is a keenness to her pace that I'd like to slow. I'm not sure I am ready for this after all.

We take the lift to the third floor and finally emerge into the silence of the study room. It's a relief to see other people. There are several large, high wooden tables grouped together that mark different visitors' research areas. Each is covered with a stretch of protective white paper, the items placed carefully on top. As we walk past some students, I steal a look at what they are viewing; there's a regal fur-lined medieval robe, something more modern that's made from black leather and punctured with hundreds of metal studs, and an incredible feathered tutu that I imagine might have danced across the stage at the Royal Opera House. A girl is slumped over one of the tables, looking thoroughly bored, like she's been here for days making notes she'll never bother to read again.

"You mustn't touch anything yourself," says Margaret. "If you need something adjusted or moved, then just call for one of the archive experts, please, and they will do it for you. We're easy to spot, we're all wearing the protective purple gloves."

Our table is on the far side of the room, the only one set with just a single item beneath a layer of thin white cloth. As we approach it, I see there is a sheet of paper giving us the bare minimum of the dress details.

OBJECT: Dress
PLACE OF ORIGIN: Paris, France
ARTIST/MAKER: Dior, Christian, born 1905, died 1957
   (designer)
MUSEUM ITEM NUMBER: T.45-1954
OBJECT NOTES: Donated by anonymous
GALLERY LOCATION: Storage
PUBLIC ACCESS DESCRIPTION: Toile de Jouy pattern, silk
DESCRIPTIVE LINE: From no known collection of designer

"It looks like everyone is busy, so I'll just pop some gloves on my-self and remove the cloth for you." As Margaret disappears, my eyes pause over the word *anonymous*, wondering again what might have driven Granny to such levels of secrecy. I hand the sheet to Veronique, who seems to study it more closely. I'm not sure what either of us is expecting to see under this cloth. It's been ten days since Granny handed me the Eurostar ticket that took me to Paris, and so much has happened. Meeting Veronique, kissing Leon, peeling back the layers of Granny's life, and taking a few small steps closer to Mum. And what else? What more is to come in the next hour or two? I'm not sure how much of this Granny ever intended to happen, but I hope I'll always be grateful I went.

"Okay, let me take this off so you can get cracking. This is quite a treat for me, you know. Despite this being one of the rarest pieces we have in the archive by Dior, it has barely been viewed in all the time it has been with us—perhaps because so little is known about it. I've worked here for more than thirty years, and I can only remember one lady ever coming to see it."

"Who was she?" I blurt it out before realizing that of course Margaret can't tell me that, even if she knew.

She smiles kindly rather than pointing this out. "It was so sad. She sat and looked at it for the whole two hours she had booked. She had some sort of paper in her hands the whole time, too—it looked like a letter? She never moved, she never asked for it to be lifted or had any questions. I was planning to chat to her afterward to see if she needed anything. But she slipped out when none of us were looking, so I never got the chance."

"When was that?" asks Veronique more sensibly.

"Not that long ago. A year perhaps. She was very elderly. I was surprised that she came alone, to be honest. I did wonder if the dress might have belonged to her once, but it felt too rude to ask, considering the type of dress it is."

Veronique's eyes slide toward mine, just as mine do to hers. We're both thinking the same thing. There *is* something undeniably different or unusual about this dress: it is of a *type*.

"She certainly struck me as the sort of woman who appreciated fashion. She was wearing the most beautiful midnight-blue wool coat with a bateau collar and gloves in the exact same shade that fitted her perfectly. And she had the most exquisite dragonfly brooch pinned to the coat. I expect most people thought it was costume jewelry, but I knew it was the real thing. We all said how elegant she looked."

Of course, I know it's Granny. Who else could it be? Natasha must have helped her organize the trip. Veronique shakes her head and chuckles under her breath. She knows it too. Then, with no further warning, Margaret quickly lifts the protective fabric up and off the dress with the sort of flourish that sends every pair of eyes in the room our way.

And there it is.

The most incredibly delicate dress in Granny's collection. The one that, despite its fragility, carries a heavier secret than any other she has shown us so far. I take a step closer to the table, dropping my arms to my sides, my shoulders suddenly slack, knowing immediately that we will not be needing our two-hour time slot today.

"Oh, Lucille, my goodness, I really was not expecting to see *this*." Veronique clasps her hand to her mouth. She looks pale, genuinely shocked, and she's staring directly at me, checking I understand what I'm seeing, what it means.

"This isn't Granny's dress," I say, rather obviously and to no one in particular. "It's tiny. Is it a . . ." I leave the sentence hanging in the air, and it's up to Margaret to finish it.

"A christening dress, yes. One that was, from what we can tell, never worn."

The way she whispers it makes my eyes glass over, the dress suddenly out of focus, swimming in front of me, having lost all its defined edges. I blink hard and wipe both eyes with the heel of my hand, keen not to miss any of its detail.

It's scattered with tiny threads of metallic embroidery that are barely visible but that give it the faintest rose-gold glow. There is the faded toile de Jouy pattern we have heard so much about, the softest repetition of painterly florals that seem perfectly pure and angelic. The small, rounded neck is trimmed with a pleated frill, repeated at the bottom of two puffed sleeves. Then the fabric gathers across the chest before falling away into the lightest translucent silk skirt, the most precious canvas for the ornate painting that is unfurling across it. It has a femininity that speaks to an entirely different era. More than anything, I can see my grandmother would love it. That it is refined, fitting of the occasion it was made for while still being impossibly pretty.

"Are you sure it's never been worn?" asks Veronique. A strength has returned to her face now that she has recovered from the initial surprise.

"As sure as we can be," offers Margaret. "I always think of our exhibits as the ghosts of distant families. They may be gone, forgotten even, but they always leave traces of themselves behind, their shadows, we say. Think of it like a plaster cast that has been used to set a broken bone. When it is eventually cracked and removed, it is thrown away, considered useless now its job is done. But if you took a moment to look inside, you would see the imprint of the skin's unique markings, the way the tiny baby hairs lay, any imperfections or indentations on the skin. It would all be there for you to see, to build a picture from. And even a dress this delicate has a story to tell. An infant so young wouldn't have left the dress in such perfect condition. There is no evidence of a life within it. Maybe that is a story in itself?"

I watch Veronique swallow hard, and I wonder, is this dress confirmation there was true heartbreak in Granny's past? She had a christening dress made that was never worn.

A dress so full of shame or regret or loss, she couldn't even attach her own name to it when it was donated to the museum.

❧

24

Alice
DECEMBER 1953, PARIS

Alice opens the metal gate that leads into Antoine's small private garden.

She knocks lightly on the door and waits, picturing him placing his pencil and sketch pad down, picking up speed on the stairs, predicting it might be her. She can barely breathe, praying her version of events is the one about to unfold—not something unimaginable, more aligned to Albert's vision of her future.

She waits, then knocks again, rewarded only by a tense silence. She bends down and pushes the small letter box open, peering inside, straining to see any sign of the letter she had delivered to him yesterday. It's not there on the floor, which must mean he has seen it and read it. Could he be on his way to the residence to see her? How can it possibly be just twenty-four hours ago that she placed her hands on the small swell of her belly and wondered if their baby will have Antoine's shot of glossy dark hair or his full lips? Now all she feels is the tension knotting up every ridge of her spine.

She steps back from the door, returns to the courtyard, and rests against the large central tree anchored there. Think. What should she do? She lets her gaze travel up to his bedroom window, *their* bedroom window, hoping to see him waving down at her. Then something catches her eye, forcing her to focus more keenly on the glass. She sees the faintest change in the light behind his windowpane, a subtle shift in the shadows, like something or someone disturbed the air there.

Is it him? Maybe it's the reflection of the tree branches making her think she saw more than she did. She wonders how long she can stand and wait before someone will come and question her. With every second she watches the door, she feels hope slowly ebb away from her. When it does eventually move, she doesn't dare to believe it—she's surely wishing it open when it's not. Then the pointed face of Madame du Parcq appears, flushed with anger, determined to have her say. She's marching toward Alice with not a shred of compassion or understanding to soften her.

"Go home, Madame Ainsley. You will achieve nothing by standing here, humiliating yourself further. Antoine does not want to speak to you." Her eyes flame with anger.

"I don't believe you." It's more of a croak than a statement, but Alice will not allow herself to be brushed off so easily.

"I don't think that matters at this point, do you?"

"For goodness' sake, Madame du Parcq, I'm carrying his baby. He can't just ignore me." She's not sure how she manages the laugh, standing here begging to be seen when a couple of days ago they were decorating a Christmas tree and planning their future together.

Madame du Parcq's voice slows and cools. "I did try to warn you. He's not capable of handling something like this. He completely underestimated the severity of what you were both doing—and the repercussions of it—just as I knew he would. After everything Antoine has put us through, he will never go against my wishes, not in the end. Surely if you know him at all, you know *that*. But I am surprised at you, Madame Ainsley. You know your own husband and what he is capable of. What on earth were you thinking?"

"I love Antoine." Alice can feel the fire light behind her eyelids at the mention of his name.

"You are a married woman. However exciting my son may be to you, you should have walked away. He's still a boy, and a highly privileged one at that. One with personal issues that he isn't even *close* to resolving. Don't you think my family has suffered enough without you adding to it? I hope *this time* you understand my meaning?"

Alice pictures Antoine's body, his strength, the way he lifted her into his arms at Dior like she weighed nothing at all. His determination to make this work. She refuses to believe that their separation is Antoine's choice, that the version of him created by Albert and his mother is the accurate one. She knows him, and this is not him.

"Please, may I just have five minutes with him? It's all I need."

"I'm not his jailer. Don't you think I gave him that option before I came down here? What more evidence do you need? You have made the most awful error in judgment, Madame Ainsley. Now take the only option that remains open to you. Go home, get on your knees, and beg for your husband's forgiveness. Take whatever olive branch he is prepared to offer you. My son is no longer yours to ruin." She sighs, shakes her head, and for a fleeting moment Alice registers a glimmer of sympathy—and it stings, more than her anger.

"Please . . . please just tell him: It will never be too late. I'm ready to listen and understand whenever he wants to talk to me."

What little compassion Madame du Parcq may have felt is snatched away with one swift snap of her head as she glides back into the apartment, no longer happy to have her day dirtied by such an undignified conversation.

Alice's mind loops. He can't possibly be in the apartment, she reasons. He has no idea his mother has just rejected her so brutally, claiming to speak on his behalf. She and Albert must have kept the news of the baby from him.

Why else would any of this be happening?

Should she stay?

Shout his name?

Cause an almighty scene until she can be heard?

Then she sees him, set back from the window, sipping coffee from a small white espresso cup, staring into the glass like his eyes don't move beyond the study of his own reflection projected back at him. He's naked from the waist up, casual, comfortable. He looks like a man whose life is uncluttered by problems, a man with nothing to distract him from the inconveniences of the day.

Alice stumbles back against the tree, and the movement catches his eye. For the briefest moment, they see each other, before his head dips, his expression hardens, and he reaches up to pull the curtain across the windowpane, shutting her out.

Alice places a hand over her mouth to muffle her sobs. All the blood rushes from her head until she feels outside herself, weightless, like a balloon that's carelessly slipped through the fingers of a child, floating upward.

"HAVE A SEAT, PLEASE."

Albert has asked Alice to meet him in the Salon Jaune drawing room on the first floor. It's flooded with late-afternoon sunshine, spotlighted against the yellow silk wall coverings and bouncing off the imposing two-tier crystal chandelier that hangs heavy above them.

He knows it is one of her favorite rooms in which to sit, read, and enjoy a moment of calm reflection, and his demeanor this afternoon seems to match. He is noticeably more restrained, even relaxed. There is no pronounced tension in the veins across his forehead. His tie is loosened, and as she looks around the room, Alice can see the effort he has had someone go to. There are fresh flowers, her preferred pale old English roses, on the glass-topped wooden table in front of them, more, she notices, on two console tables dotted around the room. Afternoon tea is laid out. Perfectly cut, crust-free cucumber sandwiches, warm madeleines, scones generously layered with cream and jam, and a whole Victoria sponge that has yet to be cut. A tea service has been placed on a tray that Albert now offers to pour for her.

"Thank you, yes, please." She watches him struggle with the tea strainer, unpracticed in this everyday ritual. But she stays seated until he places the teacup in front of her, a perfect pour of Earl Grey made undrinkable by the leaves swimming in it.

"How are you feeling?" His eyes flick to the space beneath her waistband. Alice knows he doesn't care; the fact he's asking the question merely means there is an agenda to this meeting, something she needs to agree to, which is unnerving.

"I'm well, thank you." Alice eases her way into the conversation, unsure yet of its destination.

"Good. What can I get you to eat?"

"Nothing, thank you. I may have something later." The smell of the sugar is making her head throb and her insides cartwheel with nausea.

She watches as he cuts a generous slice of cake, then forks a wedge of it into his mouth. She diverts her eyes from the jam that lingers on his upper lip, collected by his tongue, the crumbs that he clumsily brushes off his lap and onto the carpet, knowing someone will clean up after him.

"I have lots to tell you." He's smiling, presenting a completely different version of himself than the man she's seen these last few weeks. The one who shattered heavy cut crystal inches from her face just yesterday. What is it he thinks? she wonders. That if he acts the part of the considerate husband, he'll get what he wants from her? Has she always been that pliable?

"A press release will go out tomorrow announcing your first pregnancy. I have a copy of the draft here so you can see what information will be shared. I have added a quote from you." He hands her a piece of embassy embossed paper and reaches for a madeleine. Her eyes travel swiftly down the words, registering key facts: her name, their wedding date, that the baby is expected in August, a request for the press to respect their privacy at this *wonderful family time*. Then Alice, declaring she has *never been happier* and how it has always been her *dearly held wish* to have a *large family*, ending with how *blessed* they are.

She can feel the bile start to climb up the back of her throat and is forced to take a sip of her tea to refresh her mouth. Her hand is shaking, and the teacup rocks loudly back and forth on its saucer as she raises it from the table.

"You'll need to call your parents this afternoon and tell them the news before it breaks tomorrow."

She nods silently before handing the paper back to him.

"And the other development, which will be announced a couple of weeks later, is that we are moving to America." He doesn't pause for her reaction before he launches straight into the details. "I have been offered an incredible role there, and naturally I have accepted. The team are working on all the relocation details now, but we don't have long. They want us out there soon. One of the social secretaries will be contacting you tomorrow to run through some key events, you know, welcome dinners and drinks receptions mostly," he adds with a casual wave of his hand. "They'll need your input and thoughts on guest lists et cetera, and a bit of a steer on personal needs, arrangements they can put in place before we arrive." He looks up from his cake plate and stares blankly at her.

"Why are you crying?" A note of irritation has returned to his voice.

Alice wasn't aware of her tears until this very moment, but now the room is shifting out of focus, her eyes flooded by the fear and sadness that is overwhelming her.

"How can we just . . ." She's clamoring to think of the words to sum up the seismic shift in their relationship over the past few months, but every time she tries to speak, the words shatter in the back of her throat.

"I've spoken to most of the staff, and they are fully briefed on the timings . . ."

"Albert . . ."

"None of them will be coming with us, so they will all need to find alternative positions, and quick. Marianne has already been sacked for the horribly disloyal and duplicitous role she has played in all of this. She can consider herself incredibly fortunate that I have honored her severance pay, but there will be no reference. Not from me."

Alice feels the shock ricochet through her.

"Please, Albert, I'm begging you, don't do this to Anne. None of this is her fault, and she needs this job." She tries to keep the emotion from her voice but hears it cracking with every word.

"Anne? Is that your little nickname for her?" he scoffs. "I warned you not to get close to the staff. If you have and she has acted on your behalf, believing you to be friends, then that is your fault."

It *is* Alice's fault. She never should have placed Anne in the path of Albert's anger, knowing he has no capacity for forgiveness. Her poor Anne. She does not deserve this. It's simply another way for Albert to punish Alice, to hammer home just how far he will go to keep her in line.

"Albert, please . . ." Fear turns to panic as she realizes he's not listening, his ears are deaf to anything other than a resounding acceptance from her about what their future must now hold, the facts as he lays them out.

"There will be lots of requests for references, so perhaps I can leave you to handle that side of things." Albert returns his plate on the table and swiftly brushes his hands down both legs, readying himself to stand and leave. "That's everything you need to know."

"I need more time." Alice's eyes stay in her lap, watching her tears dot the fabric of her skirt, her words barely audible.

"Alice . . ." Albert's hands are gripped tightly around a white napkin as if he is squeezing the life out of it. "It's over. The sooner you accept that, the better."

"I can't live a lie, it won't work." She pictures herself then, unpacking her life on the other side of the Atlantic. Not just her possessions but every crack and unspoken truth in her marriage, all neatly unwrapped under a big new sky, as perfectly damaged as the day they left Paris. The baby she has yearned for, waking every morning in a bright white nursery to a mother aching with sadness.

Nothing will have changed, beyond their location. Albert will still be Albert. If she believed there might be one shred of forgiveness or culpability within him, maybe she could sit with the idea for a few hours, allow herself to be talked into believing it might just work. But she knows it won't.

Not when her heart will always belong to someone else.

Not when the baby growing inside of her will be a beautifully painful reminder of what was so nearly hers. If only she could speak to Antoine.

"It's a clean break, Alice. A chance to start again. To forget the past and look forward to a successful future with none of the nonsense that you have allowed to distract you here. You *owe* me that much."

"I'm sorry, I just can't . . ."

"And who knows, perhaps this won't be the only baby." His eyes flicker toward her, trying to gauge if the lie he told her once will work again now, only this time the suggestion is repulsive and unthinkable, a mark of his desperation to convince her. Does he really believe her to be that malleable?

Alice simply shakes her head and watches as Albert's expression shifts to pity and confusion.

"He's not coming, Alice, if that's what you're waiting for. You must know that. Are you really prepared to throw everything away for someone who was so easily dissuaded? And did you really think I would be beaten?" His raises his eyebrows, mocking her; then his eyes brighten, as if another idea has landed.

"You know, there is something else I want to share with you." He sits back slowly in his chair, attempting to create a sense of anticipation. "I think you have probably worked out by now that my father never died of tuberculosis, as I had you all believe. My sister all but confirmed it for you on our wedding day."

She studies his face, looking for any clue of what is to come.

"Why are you telling me this now?"

"Because it's your last chance to understand what you are up against. He committed suicide when I was fourteen."

"What? But why did you . . . ?" She shakes her head, at a loss to understand what could have prompted such a rewriting of history.

"A string of bad investments, mounting debts that he knew he'd never clear." Albert's voice is purely factual; he could be reading the day's weather report in the newspaper. "We were left with practically nothing. It was the day I determined I would never be defined by my father's incompetence. My only lifeline was an uncle who, with no sons of his own to promote, financed my education and, when the time came, made some introductions in London. But that was it. The rest was up to me. I had to take control of my own success."

"What happened to your mother? How did she cope without any help?" Alice recalls the many tears Albert's mother shed on their wedding day, the obvious relief that her only son had achieved happiness, despite everything.

"I looked after her. I still do. Without my support, I dread to think where she or my sister might be."

Alice absorbs the facts. She can't help but be warmed by Albert's sustained generosity, but why the deceit? Why invent another persona when the real one was so much more human?

"I think I would have understood. You didn't need to reinvent yourself for my benefit. Why bother?"

"I suppose it's easy to pretend that now, but of course, I did have to. For you, your parents, for every job interview, dinner party, and card game I ever sat through. I didn't want the associated failure to permanently attach itself to me. The point is, Alice, I wasn't about to be beaten by something that was in no way my fault."

The scale of his calculation is chilling. How many versions of this one man might exist in the world? Alice wonders. Does his own mother believe him to be happily married? Does his lover believe him to be rooted in Paris for the long term?

"I've won, Alice. Neither of you stood a chance, I'm sure you can see that now." He throws the napkin at the table and leaves without another look back.

Alice allows the breath she has been holding to escape out of her as she collapses back into her chair. She sees the tautness of the fabric across her belly, how the stitching is already struggling to contain her. She's not sure how long she sits there. Long enough for her heart rate to stabilize and for someone, she doesn't remember who, to come and clear the afternoon tea away and place fresh logs on the fire.

Hours may have passed, but at least Alice now knows what she must do. She will call her mother.

~❧~

25

Lucille
MONDAY
LONDON

Dylan keeps me waiting twenty-five minutes past our arranged meeting time.

The temp, Susie, who has been covering for me, sees me to one of the windowless breakout rooms, and I'm left here to fester. Deliberately long enough for me to feel an uncomfortable prickle of nerves. After the freedom of Paris, being back in an office suddenly feels so formal and alien, like it never should have suited me in the first place. I know now it didn't, and I was fooling myself that sitting at the same meter of gray desk every day, clicking accept to endless meetings I didn't want to be in, was just what I had to do. What everyone has to do before they can make their own choices. I'd got sucked into the very same system my own mother has brilliantly demonstrated is not for me. One lesson that I am grateful for.

Pam from HR arrives, security lanyard proudly swinging across her bosom, armed with all the vital accoutrements of the personnel department: a selection of Biros that she lines up in a neat row on the table in front of her, an unused notepad that she breaks out of the cellophane (I'm honored), and a selection of anecdotes and business observations that I have heard first- and secondhand many times before. Still, she lends an air of seriousness and process that I know Dylan wants.

"I haven't got long." Finally he graces us with his presence. "There's an advertiser lunch in the boardroom that I really can't be late for. A major new travel client, who is shifting its entire media spend our way next year." He never misses an opportunity to toot his own trumpet. He sits at the far end of the oval table from me, despite there being half a dozen empty chairs that are the more natural choice. I resist the urge to theatrically sniff my own armpits.

"So, how are you, Lucille? How are you feeling about your role here?" I know there are protocols, HR ways of doing things to avoid tribunals, et cetera, but poor Pam, this is so tedious. We all know where they want this meeting to end, and I'm tempted to just ask if we can skip to the part of the script that she'd arrive at anyway in about half an hour. "You've been with us for eighteen months now, so it's a good chance for us to check in and see that everything is working." Or to act before the crucial two-year milestone, when it becomes much harder to manage me out of the business. I have seen enough people come and go in my time here to know this is their way.

"Well, it's a very *broad* role, Pam. It might be worth revisiting the job description, actually, it needs some updating." Dylan's head twitches up from the emails he is scanning on his phone.

"Would you say you are managing to achieve everything you need to?" She's warming up. She lifts a pen and braces herself for detailed note taking.

"My copy is always on time. The top three trafficking stories last month were all mine. Not bad for a travel writer who hasn't actually traveled anywhere since she was hired." Pamela lets the pen relax in her hand. I'm not sure this is the positive feedback she's wanting.

"Dylan? Anything to add to Lucille's observations?" I could actually cringe for Pam. How does she keep up the charade when it's blindingly obvious that Dylan's already laid out why he's not happy and wants me gone?

"Lucille does have the occasional good idea, but there have been some significant errors recently that have placed an unfair burden on the rest of the team. Not enough time devoted to my diary management, multiple unapproved days off with no good reason, and a general lack of attention to detail. I think there are core elements of the job that she is really struggling with." He directs all his comments to Pam, refusing to personally acknowledge me at all. Maybe he can't because somewhere deep down inside that obnoxious exterior, he can admit the tiniest sense of injustice. That it's not entirely fair to pay someone the minuscule amount they pay me and then expect me to work 24/7 responding to every whim of the editor, professional *and* personal. But mostly personal.

And this is how we pass the next thirty minutes, me nobly pointing out my achievements; Dylan chipping away, trying to build a case for why I'm the wrong person in the wrong job; Pam diligently noting down everything he says and very little of what I offer. Before finally she gets to look like the good guy and make me the very fair offer I can't refuse.

"Sometimes, through no one's fault, things just don't work out as we had all hoped. And I always think in that scenario, it is far better to deal with it head-on than let it groan on. So, with that in mind, I would like to make you an offer without prejudice, Lucille, so that you have a fair cushion to take some time to think about your next role. Obviously, you would not be expected to work out any notice period in this case." Then she slides a folded piece of paper across the table to me. "This is what we had in mind."

I have an overwhelming urge to laugh out loud, and I have to force my thumbnail into the soft flesh of my palm, using the pain as a distraction. I feel like I'm in some badly dubbed American TV drama, until the faux sympathetic face Dylan has constructed helps me regain composure. I unfold it and stare at the figure. It represents many things—the equivalent of a very cheap, last-minute package holiday to the Canaries or somewhere equally low-budget, a year's annual gym membership at my local council-run leisure center assuming I stay off-peak, maybe a couple of appointments to get my highlights done somewhere half-decent for once.

It does not represent fair.

"Thank you, Pam." I reach into my handbag, pull out my mobile phone, and quickly log in to my emails, hitting send on one that sits ready in my drafts folder. "I wonder if I could ask you to take a look at the email I have just sent to you, please, and then I will be very happy to receive a revised offer from you. You'll see it has two attachments. One contains a good selection of the unprofessional, expletive-filled texts and emails Dylan regularly sends me. The other has my more accurate job description, one that reflects the work I actually do. I've also included copies of his last six months' worth of expenses, high-lighting all of Dylan's lunches and dinners that were *not* business re-lated but that this company paid for nonetheless. I think if you check the names of the people he claimed to be with, you'll find most of them are fictional." Then I calmly pick up my handbag, watching the color of guilt flood Dylan's face, before I shake Pam's hand, thank her for her time, and make for the door.

"Enjoy your lunch, Dylan" are my last words before I exit the room and walk for the very last time across the editorial floor. And it feels good. Very good.

I HAND MY SECURITY PASS BACK TO THE FRONT DESK AND SIGN myself out for the last time. Then I step out onto Soho's Greek Street feeling triumphant, knowing I will miss the place more than the job itself. My lunch breaks spent watching people brazenly meandering in and out of the sex shops, not caring if they're seen. The never-ending arrival of new vegan delis. Sitting in random coffee shops, overhearing creative meetings, watching people who never have to wear a suit to work, envying them their jobs where they're actually trusted to spend their time productively. I decide to reward myself with the coffee I haven't been offered all morning and head to my usual place, just across the road.

As I step off the pavement, I look through the glass frontage, making sure there is a spare seat, and that's when I see him. The unmistakable shot of blond hair, the sexy smile, the casual gorgeousness that immediately transports me back to the pretty streets of Paris. I stop and stare, slack-jawed. He isn't looking my way, and I need him to, to be completely sure my mind isn't playing evil tricks on me. Why would he be here? Right outside my office? It's impossible. Then, as if to answer my questions, he turns, our eyes connect, and his smile deepens— just as the piercing sound of a black cab's horn forces me to shift.

Leon waves me into the café, giving me barely a dozen steps in which to scramble my thoughts together. As I open the door and step inside, he rises from his stool and throws his arms wide open, scorching any awkwardness before I allow it to creep from me to him. Then I'm buried in his arms as he's folding them tight around me, kissing the top of my head.

"Surprise!" I love that he shouts it, not thinking how it will attract the interest of everyone around us. He doesn't care or even notice. All his attention is on me.

"Yes, it is! What are you doing here?" I can't help laughing. Could this morning actually get any better?

"Well, you told me where you work and it's a working day, so I figured . . ."

"*Here*, in London, when you live in Paris."

"Yes, I knew you'd ask me that." We both take a seat on the stools, close enough that our legs are crisscrossing together.

"And?"

"And I spent the entire Eurostar journey here trying to work out what to say. Maybe that work sent me on an unexpected assignment or there's a relative I forgot to mention who lives in London that I suddenly needed to visit. But then I thought, why not just be honest?"

"Honesty is always welcome." I'm not sure I can wait much longer before the urge to kiss him outweighs my strong desire not to embarrass myself in a café that's rammed full, a queue—an audience—now forming at the door.

"And the truth is, I missed you." He has the confidence not to elaborate, but lets the words settle on me as his face gets a little more serious.

Bloody hell, this man.

"It's only been a few days." That sounds a lot less romantic than I want it to be.

"Three in fact, no time at all. But long enough for me to start to worry. What if she gets so entangled in life back in London that she forgets to think about me? Or even worse, that she starts to believe I'm not thinking about her."

I can feel my cheeks warm, partly from the attention this beautiful man is lavishing on me and partly because I am struggling to think of something equally tender to say back to him. He deserves something special. Now is definitely the time to brilliantly convey quite how happy I am to see him, but the words are deserting me. He registers the pause and kindly fills it.

"And then I realized, I don't want *us* to be something that exists in an email inbox. Not when the way I feel about you is so real. I think we should give it a try. Slowly. That's if you want to?" The corners of his mouth gently curl upward, and he looks at me through that mess of hair that hangs sexily over his eyes. "If I am wrong, or you don't want to, or it's too soon, I can just go, and you don't have to feel awkward. It will be my mistake."

Still my brain won't function. It's like the performance back in front of Dylan has sapped me of all intellect, so I throw caution to the wind and use my lips to make the point instead. I kiss him exactly as I have always wanted to be kissed. Tender at first, nervous and unsure, but building so that within seconds my whole body feels like it is blending into his. Our kiss is deep and spontaneous and greedy, and I have to pull back from it because, before I know it, I'm almost on his lap and I'm not sure I want us to be the sort of people who straddle each other in the middle of a busy café in Soho.

"How long are you here?" I laugh, raising a hand to my lips to gauge how far across my face my lipstick is smudged. He reads my concern and runs a thumb just under my lower lip, signaling all is good with another quick kiss.

"Not long. Work can only spare me for a few days." His hands are resting on my thighs, making my entire lower body tense with desire.

"Where are you staying?" I know where I'd like him to be staying.

"Somewhere cheap and cheerful in King's Cross. It's not the Athénée, but it's close to the Eurostar terminal, so it works." He orders us two cappuccinos, and I take the opportunity while he's chatting to the waitress to study his face. Only then does my brain start to get creative again.

I imagine him taking shape in my life, like a Polaroid slowly developing. He's there, waking up in my bed, washing up in my kitchen, curled up with me on a long lazy Sunday afternoon when we are enough for each other, the distractions of the outside world completely superfluous. He's there, every day, kissing me awake in the mornings and burying his face into my neck as we both drift off into sleep late at night.

What I don't want to see is the wide expanse of the sea that separates us and how we will overcome that. For now, it fills my heart with so much happiness to think this man woke in his bed in Paris this morning, decided he had to come and see me, and changed any plans he might have had so he could. Can this actually be happening? Am

I really the sort of woman that these things happen to? Maybe I am, and I just never gave myself the chance to let them happen to me before.

"So, did you make it to the V and A? Did you see the final dress?" His eyes are keen, and I'm touched it's one of the first things he asks me about.

"Yes!" I had emailed him a quick update about Granny's role at the British embassy in case it could help with tracking down any info about Antoine, but he doesn't know the latest developments. "So, we think my grandmother was pregnant. The final dress wasn't exactly for her—it was a christening dress. The question is, if we are right, what happened to the baby?"

"Wow." He pauses for a while and lets the implications of this latest news wash over him. "Have you asked her?"

"No, it doesn't feel like a conversation to have over the phone. I'm due to see her tomorrow, so that will be my chance, but there's no guarantee she will want to tell me."

"Am I being stupid, could this baby not just have been your mother?"

"That was my first thought, but Mum was born in 1958. We know from the dress notes that it was made in 1954, so no, the dates just don't add up. I think we can confidently dismiss that theory."

"Who, then? Does Veronique have any ideas?"

"The options, as we see them, are this: The baby was Albert's. As much as we believe that's not the case, theoretically, it could be. Or the baby was Antoine's, and when my grandmother returned to London, she left him or her there with him. But there was no birth recorded at the time she was still with Albert. Nothing we've read online around the time they were married and both living at the British embassy residence says anything about children—and it would have been news, surely? Veronique checked too. As far as the official birth registrations in Paris are concerned, it was a childless marriage; the family tree comes to an abrupt end. The other option is that the baby was born and adopted, in which case we have no idea of the adoptive parents' names to search for. Or we have to consider the option that the baby didn't survive, for whatever reason."

Leon rubs his chin and looks down toward his feet. "I don't think it's Antoine." He shakes his head. "I mean, I'm not saying he can't be the father, but I don't think he raised the child."

"What makes you think that?"

"I did some research myself, like you asked me to. The only Antoine I can find with any association to the British embassy in Paris around the time your grandmother was there is an Antoine du Parcq. His name appears on some of the published guest lists for official events, and he is captioned on some of the photographs, although it's never clear which one he is in the pictures."

"Okay, go on."

"That wasn't terribly conclusive, but after Alice left Paris in 1954, this Antoine briefly attended the National School of Fine Arts." He reaches into the rucksack that's sitting on the floor, wedged between the legs of his stool, and pulls out his laptop. "Let me show you." He clicks until a map of the Saint-Germain area of Paris loads.

"The school was conveniently right at the end of the road he lived on. He's listed as one of the alumni. Some of his early sketches are archived on the school's website." I watch as his fingers dance across the keyboard, now balanced precariously on his crossed legs, like he knows exactly what he is looking for. He turns the laptop around to face me.

"Does she look familiar?"

The screen is filled with expertly crafted line drawings, brilliantly capturing the contours of the human body with astonishingly few marks. Leon scrolls slowly down the screen as more and more appear. Antoine's subject is shown standing, sitting, fully reclining, socializing, caught off guard, posing, walking through a park—only two things remain consistent throughout: the quality of Antoine's work and his subject.

I've gazed at some of these dresses long enough to know for certain they are from Granny's collection—the Maxim's, the Batignolles, the Debussy, the Cygne Noir—they're all here, and Leon knows it too. But it is the woman wearing them who is truly captivating. I'm not sure, as accomplished as he clearly is, if Antoine could have created such magic without the raw beauty he had to copy. She is divine, no question of that. But it is in the spark in my grandmother's eyes, the energy in her face, the excitement rippling through every sinew of her body. I can see how her happiness explodes from within her. Even in the less studied sketches, the ones of her asleep in bed, or waiting, for him perhaps, leaning against a wall or sitting on a park bench, her quiet happiness shines through.

"I need to print these off. I want to show them to her. Look how much he loved her!"

"I've already done it for you. There is a file in my bag with a print of each. I wasn't sure if you would share them with your grandmother, but I felt sure you would want copies for yourself."

"Oh, I do. I do, thank you, Leon. You are incredible." And I see immediately how much that means to him. He tries, and fails, to hide his smile, more shy this time.

"His work, specifically these sketches, was well received. He was marked out as one to watch at a time when Paris was alive with the thrum of creativity. And for a while he was on the upward trajectory. But then, barely six months later, he drops out of the school and stops sketching altogether. He remained living in the Saint-Germain area for about another year, from what I've been able to trace, but then he moved to the Right Bank, a completely different neighborhood. That was his last known address. I don't know, but perhaps if he wasn't working, he was forced to move back in with his family? The point is, the records show he never had any children. And realistically, he couldn't have been studying at the school and looking after a newborn baby, too, could he?"

"No, he probably couldn't." I can't keep the deflation out of my voice. There are no other theories on the table, and all my hopes are now pinned on Granny filling in the final part of the story—and given that she hasn't said a word about any of this for all these years, how likely is that? "If I do have an aunt or uncle out there somewhere, then I'll have to convince Granny of how much I would desperately love to know about it, however painful it may be for her."

"There is one other thing, Lucille. The records also show that Antoine died in 1971, when he was only forty-three. I'm sorry."

I feel my shoulders drop. I don't know what to be more sorry about. That there won't be any big reconciliation for Granny? That I can't deliver this ghost from her past to her front door—or more likely via a video call—as the script might demand I should? If she has unanswered questions, they may have to stay that way. Would she even have wanted to see him again, had it been possible? I've no idea. Or is it the realization that everything depends on Granny now that the facts will be strictly limited to however much she chooses to share—which may be little more than I already know?

I feel bad that Leon has traveled all this way and now there seems little to celebrate, and that I'm going to have to rally myself into not feeling glum all afternoon. My phone pings, and I glance down at it, hoping it might be Pam's revised offer already. But it's something entirely unexpected. Something I thought I really wanted, but now that I see it illuminated on the small screen in my palm, I'm not so sure.

"What is it?" Leon has heard the *oh Christ* that I thought was only in my head.

"It's about a job."

"I thought you had a job?"

"I did, until I resigned about half an hour ago."

"Okay, you don't waste any time, do you?" He's smiling, for now, but will he still be when I tell him where this job is?

"Veronique thought I should apply for it, so I did, on the train back to London on Friday, and they've already got in touch. It's an editorial position at the Museum of Decorative Arts. In Paris."

Leon pauses mid-sip of his cappuccino, and I watch, holding my breath, as the milky foam settles on his top lip. "Are you serious?"

"They've just messaged me. They want to set up an initial phone chat as soon as possible. As part of the application process, they asked for ideas for future exhibits, personal stories that might translate well into physical installations. I told them a little about Granny's dresses and my journey across Paris and, well, I think it may have helped."

He frowns and looks away from me, and I can feel my face start to crumple, my smile weaken and fade. He said we should take things slowly. Me uprooting and moving my life to Paris is probably not what he had in mind.

"Now I wonder if I shouldn't have come to London. If it was the wrong thing to do."

"Why? I'm glad you're here, I *want* you to be here. It's the best thing that's happened to me in ages." I take both of his hands in mine. I'm so overkeen, but I can't help it. He *did* get on the train, he is here, and I can't bear that he now thinks he shouldn't be. "It doesn't have to mean anything, Leon, we don't suddenly have to move in together or get too serious."

"That's exactly what I thought you might say. Stop holding back, Lucille, because I'm not going to. You coming to Paris is exactly what I hoped for, and I'm not going to hide that. And in the spirit of total disclosure, neither do I want to stay at my horrible hotel tonight. Can I come home with you?"

His smile is back, and the only thing I'm thinking is how quickly I can get this man into a cab.

꧁ ✦ ꧂

26

Alice
DECEMBER 1953, PARIS

The ring echoes in Alice's ear three times before the unyielding, polished tone of her mother's voice sends her straight back to the pine-fringed sand dunes of her childhood. To the loneliness she felt then—that she still feels now. Standing in the near darkness of her bedroom, she sees the beach where she spent so many solitary hours, imagining the faces of longed-for friends in the markings on the pebbles and in the oddities that the sea washed her way. She can almost smell the salty ripeness of the waves, hear the loud honk of the geese that used to scare her so much.

"Hello? Is anyone there?" Impatience laces her mother's voice.

"It's me, Mum, Alice."

"Oh." Alice pictures her mother standing in her orderly sitting room at Broadview, the soft pink brick house in Norfolk where Alice grew up. There will be a to-do list somewhere nearby that she'll be keen to get back to. Alice must get to the point.

"I was hoping to come home, Mum." She feels the emotion hum in her chest.

"When did you have in mind? There is quite a lot in the diary for the next few weeks, obviously."

"As soon as possible." Tears have started to cloud her eyes. She wants to let them go, to sob to her mother, completely reveal herself, tell her how much she needs her and to hear the words *Come, come now, my darling. We're here and we love you.*

"Why do I get the distinct feeling that all is not well, Alice?" It's more an accusation than a concerned inquiry.

There is little point stringing out the pretense; Alice knows she lacks that level of fortitude anyway. "I'm pregnant." A cold wash of anxiety bridges across her shoulders. Whatever disappointment she caused as a child, enough to ensure there was never a sibling, is nothing compared to what's coming.

"Well, I was not expecting to hear that, although you've been married long enough, it shouldn't be surprising news."

How can she explain the next part to her mother in a way she will understand? A woman for whom obedience and service have been the guiding principles that have seen her marriage last well into its third decade. And here is Alice, about to complain she wants an end to hers before the second anniversary.

"Albert and I are . . ." Alice is flailing, aware she is about to shatter her mother's icy calm.

"You're what?"

"I'm not happy."

Her mother laughs. "My goodness, since when did marriage have anything to do with being happy? Having a baby will give you something solid of your own to focus on. What exactly is the problem?" When did this hardness seed in her mother? Alice wonders. Was she created this way, or has a life of continual compromise ironed out any softness within her?

"I don't love Albert. I don't think I have ever loved Albert. I'm in love . . ."

A silence scratches between them while Alice fumbles for the words.

"I am in love with someone else." She aims for authority, but she sounds weak and apologetic.

"Don't be ridiculous! You're about to have a baby, for goodness' sake. Do you have any idea how juvenile that sounds?"

Alice closes her eyes and waits for the moment of realization to arrive. It doesn't take long. There is a sharp intake of breath down the line, and then her mother's voice is harder, more urgent, but whispered.

"My God, Alice. Are you trying to tell me this is not Albert's baby? That you have been stupid enough to jeopardize everything you have? Does Albert know?"

"Yes, he knows." Alice refuses to feel ashamed. Her mum has yet to understand the true nature of her husband, and when she does, she will be more sympathetic.

"Is that why you are calling? Has he thrown you out? Has he asked for a divorce?" She's allowed a shrillness to creep into her voice, a sure sign she is panicking—as much as her mother ever can.

"No. He wants us to move to America so he can take up a new position there. To start again." Alice is surprisingly calm, laying out the facts for her mother, while accepting it will be virtually impossible for her to understand them yet.

"Then for goodness' sake, go! What better offer could you possibly expect from him?" She's incredulous, entirely missing the point.

"You're not listening. I don't want to be with him. I'm in love with Antoine." Nothing is going to change the fact, no matter the level of her mother's outrage.

"And who is this Antoine? Where is he? What does he have to say about it all?"

"I haven't been able to speak to him." Her mother has taken her onto much less sure ground.

"But he knows you are pregnant with his child?" She hears her mother close a door. Perhaps her father is at home too.

"I think so, yes."

"Alice, do not leave Paris. Stay and do whatever it takes to salvage your marriage and forget that this Antoine ever existed. There is no better advice I can give you."

"Aren't you going to ask me why I *can't* stay married to Albert?"

"No, I'm not."

"He's horrible, Mother. He's mean and threatening and doesn't love me at all."

"And do you think my years of marriage have all been picture-postcard rosy? This is the world in which we live, Alice. Accept it. You can't change it. And you can't stay here, if that's what you're thinking. Your father will never hear of it. And neither will I."

Alice opens her mouth to appeal, to plead for her mother's understanding, but is cut off.

"It is your husband's job to support you, not ours. How on earth do you intend to cope financially if you leave Albert? How will you support a baby? Where will you live? Have you thought any of this through properly?"

"I was hoping you might . . . help me, Mother. At least let me stay there for a while until I have made some other plans." Now the tears are coming, spurred on by the knowledge that at her lowest possible moment, when she needs her help the most, her mother is unwilling.

"Absolutely not. There is nothing to stop you from staying in Paris, in my opinion." Neither of them says a thing while her mother silently seethes, completely unmoved by Alice's tears.

"Do not come here, Alice, I mean it. It's the worst thing you could do. Your father will never recover from the disappointment."

Alice thinks about the man she once called Daddy. A bright afternoon, a couple of years ago when she walked into the same sitting room her mother stands in now, interrupting a meeting between her father and Albert. They both rose from the sofa. She remembers the firm handshake, like they'd just completed the long negotiations of a complicated business deal. Then a shared smirk that felt at her expense. The following day Albert proposed. Her father wasn't immune to Albert's charms, either—but did he have any hint of the deep sadness he was committing his daughter to?

"It's Christmas Eve, Mum." She's not sure why she bothers to point this out; it's hardly likely to make any difference.

"Even more reason to pull yourself together. When you have spoken to Albert and ironed all this out, call me back and reassure me that I didn't completely fail as a mother."

Then the line goes dead.

"I'VE ASKED CHEF TO PREPARE SOMETHING SPECIAL FOR DINNER tonight. Let's call it a little celebration, shall we? I've taken the afternoon off. I thought we'd eat around seven, if that suits you?"

Alice stands in the doorway of the drawing room where Albert is sitting, newspaper open, resting on the roundness of his belly. She places the small holdall at her feet and stares at him, waiting for him to fully register her. This isn't going to be loud and aggressive. It's going to be sad, for her at least. Maybe there will be a moment many years from now when he might look back and wonder how it came to this.

His eyes fall to the holdall.

"Ah. It seems you have other plans."

"I'm leaving, Albert. I'm leaving you." She waits for a reaction, to prove that she actually said it.

He closes the newspaper, placing it beside him, crosses his legs, and folds his hands into his lap.

"Really? And how long do you think it will be until you are back?"

She's not going to give him time to intimidate her. She's not looking for a confrontation, even to get anything off her chest. She just knows she needs to leave, and despite everything, there is still a vein of decency within her that makes her stand here and tell him that, face-to-face.

"I'm not coming back. Ever." She watches the statement settle on him, the faintest twitch of his eyebrows the only unreadable response. And remarkably, there is still a small space in her heart for forgiveness. Is this entirely his fault? She married the wrong man. Could it be that he is the right man for someone? Another woman out there who might enjoy having every decision made for her, to know she only had to wake every morning to respond to someone else's needs, that she could be relieved of the necessity for ambition, opinion, and romance. Are there women who can live like that? Was his crime—where this all began—that he mistook her for one? Maybe he feels every bit as duped as she does.

He snorts. "Is that right?" He's smiling, but she knows his blood will be warming, his heart starting to thump a little harder. She senses the nastiness bubbling just beneath his clean-shaven, moisturized skin.

"You asked me recently why none of this was enough for me, Albert, and I owe you an answer. *You* are not enough for me. I'm not sure you ever were. But then you never showed me the real you, so perhaps that's hardly surprising. I'm still not sure who that man is." She maintains eye contact. He needs to know she means it. She's not saying it to be unkind. It's the truth, and she wants him to hear it.

"It's very easy to be principled when you're cushioned from the hard realities of life, Alice, as, unlike me, you always have been." Even now he can't help but patronize her. "The ones you are about to experience for yourself. You can't cope without me. You know it."

Alice feels no threat from his words. They land on her and slide straight off, having lost all their impact. He's no longer under her skin, like an unreachable itch, scratching away at her.

"Losing Antoine will break my heart, I won't deny it. But walking away from you will be a relief. There are many things I can live without. But I can't spend another day in a house so devoid of love. Anything will be better than that." She reaches for the holdall.

"You've made your position clear." He stands, looking for all the world like he is about to shake her hand and move on with his day, having lost a business deal, not a wife. "You're on your own. I'll start divorce proceedings at the first opportunity." He reaches again for his newspaper. "Perhaps on your way out you'd be kind enough to tell Chef not to bother with dinner."

Eighteen months of marriage, dissolved in less than eighteen minutes.

"OH, ALICE, I HOPED YOU'D COME. LET ME TAKE THAT. GOODness, you haven't lugged it up four floors, have you?" Anne takes Alice's bag and ushers her in through the small faded wooden door of her apartment. Alice smiles as she feels the warmth, from being inside and from Anne's good heart, wrap itself around her.

"Anne, your job. I'm so, so sorry. I hope he wasn't too awful to you. I'll do everything I can to help you find another, you know I will."

"Don't worry about any of that. Please, let me take your coat. I'd like you to meet my husband. Sébastien!"

Alice looks up to see a hand extended toward her. "It's so lovely to meet you, Madame Ainsley." Sébastien looks shy, not quite meeting Alice's gaze, but she is relieved to see from the softness of his face, the way he looks to Anne for what to say next, that he is not displeased to see her here. And he could be, given her husband's treatment of his wife. The invasion of her privacy, the callous sacking she has suffered because of the things Alice has asked her to do.

"Please, call me Alice; I'm not likely to be Madame Ainsley for much longer." She doesn't want him to think of her as that woman.

"I know you and Anne have lots to discuss, so I will leave you to it. I have a few things to do before dinner, but perhaps we can talk more then?"

Alice's eyes flick to the holdall at her feet, suddenly embarrassed by its presence.

"Thank you, Sébastien, that would be lovely."

"I HAVE MADE THE SPARE ROOM UP FOR YOU, ALICE. IT'S YOURS for as long as you would like. I've already discussed it with Sébastien, he's very happy for you to stay too." Anne leads her down a central corridor toward a small bedroom on the left-hand side. "It's not much, I'm afraid, but it's yours. You'll be comfortable here."

Alice angles her head into the room, which is furnished basically, with a neat dresser, an armoire, and a single bed that is piled high with folded quilts. Anne has tucked something into the frame of the mirror that sits on the dresser. Alice smiles as she realizes it's the sketch of the dress Anne promised to keep safe for her. There is a small case-ment window overlooking the rooftops of the city, no shutters, just a thin curtain that she can see will let in the morning light and a radia-tor that is rattling out its own tune. A room she could be sad in, if she weren't so grateful to be here.

"How did you know I would need it?" She thinks of Anne, return-ing for the last time from the residence and preparing the room, checking the bedding was freshly laundered. The great act of kindness that took when she must be so worried about her own future.

Anne smiles, perhaps trying to convey a lack of judgment on her part. "Everything was escalating so fast, Alice, beyond your control. But I'm not sure I realized, until I saw Albert with my handbag, just how far he was prepared to go. Have you heard from Antoine? Does he know about the baby?"

Alice sits on the edge of the bed, suddenly feeling so deflated, exhausted by the day's events, unable yet to share details of the fresh rejection by her own mother.

"I believe he does. I've heard nothing from him directly; there's been no response to my letter, no attempt to talk to me when he could have done. For now, I continue to hope, but . . . I fear I'm on my own."

Anne places Alice's bag at the end of the bed and takes a seat next to her. "You're not alone. I'm here and I will help you for as long as you need it. And leaving Albert was the only thing you could do. He was slowly but surely suffocating you. I'll contact Patrice and arrange for him to have your things sent over. We'll cancel your immediate appointments and make sure everything is taken care of, I promise. But for tonight, please, enjoy dinner with Sébastien and me. Everything will seem better in the morning."

DINNER IS ROAST TURKEY BREAST WITH CHESTNUTS, BOUGHT AND cooked for two and spread too thinly across three plates. Anne has decorated a small Christmas tree that Alice deliberately sits with her back to, not needing the reminder of the last tree she decorated. As they all clear their plates of the final course, three cheeses and a simple salad, Sébastien collects a small gift from under the tree and hands it to Alice.

"A little something for you. I hope you like it."

How completely thoughtless of her not to bring a single contribution, Alice scolds herself. "My goodness, how incredibly kind of you, thank you."

She pulls the gift tag with her name written across it from the parcel and unwraps it. It's a fine-milled soap, bluebell scented, exactly the fragrance Anne loves and always smells of. The gesture makes Alice's throat contract. Anne has sacrificed one of her gifts from Sébastien so that Alice can feel included. She stands from her seat and kisses Sébastien warmly on both cheeks, making him color and look down at his shoes. Then she moves around the small oval table and embraces her friend.

"You are wonderful, Anne, and so precious to me. I will never forget your kindness as long as I live."

As the weeks tumble forward, and Alice's body starts to swell to a size she never thought possible, the three of them develop a neat routine.

Anne is always first up, preparing breakfast. Sébastien kisses his wife's forehead before he disappears for another long day at the bank. Alice helps Anne to clean, shop, and cook, enjoying her instruction, always so sensitively delivered. Everything works. There is a harmony to their little arrangement, the way the three of them—soon to be four—inhabit a space clearly designed for two.

But no one can ignore the fact that Anne has so far failed to secure another role. Ten interviews in as many weeks, and not one of them has resulted in an offer of employment.

"Please will you let me write you a full reference, Anne?" Alice pleads. "Take it with you and force them to read it. Don't wait to be asked."

Anne slumps down at the dining table, all her usual stoicism replaced by a grim acceptance of her fate that is entirely at odds with the woman Alice knows.

"There is no point. Albert, I believe, has seen to that."

27

Lucille
TUESDAY
LONDON

I've never once felt nervous in Granny's company. But today my throat is dry, my head aches with tension, my shoulders feel clenched. As I sit by the fire and wait for her to join me, I can feel the acidic churn of my own stomach. I realize it's more than nerves. I'm scared of everything I am about to hear and my own reaction to it. The significance that has been placed on this moment by the time it took to get here.

I see the same feelings on Granny's face as she joins me, so I do the only thing that feels natural. I hug her. As firmly as I can, registering how little of her there is to hold these days, before I guide her into her usual chair. I take hold of her hand, allowing my thumb to move gently back and forth across the papery creases of her skin, wondering how to ease her into the conversation we need to have.

Do I ask the question, or do I present it as a statement of fact? Was there a baby? Or, you were pregnant, Granny. I'm watching as her eyes close. She has the ability to drift into the lightest sleep and then come back into the room moments later, still smiling, still the grandmother I love so much.

She's silent, and I realize she is waiting for me to speak. She isn't going to reveal a thing until I tell her what I think I know. Maybe she has no words for this, but then I'm not sure I do either. I ease my way into it.

"I went to the V and A. I saw the final dress, Granny." As soon as I say it, her grip strengthens around my fingers. Her lips seal a little tighter together. This conversation is going to take real courage.

"Then you know, my darling. You know what I have been hiding all these years." She closes her eyes again briefly, and next time she opens them, they are full of tears and a look that pleads for me to do the talking. She nods, as if confirming my understanding.

"I'm not sure I understand everything though, Granny. The baby . . ." The mere mention of the word and all its implied defenselessness sends those tears spilling over, dropping onto my own hand, where I let them sit, knowing there are probably many more to come. I try again.

"It couldn't have been Mum. The timings aren't right, are they?" I feel my lips curl inward. I'm not at all sure how she will cope with me sliding back the doors to her past so presumptively. I register the smallest nod, telling me to go on, and my heart aches with the pain of all that she must have been through. She wants to have this conversation, however hard it will be, and I feel my lungs inflate with the almost unbearable sense of anticipation. The days have all been building to it, not that I understood that at all when I first set off for Paris—but she did.

"It was a different baby."

She opens her mouth and lets some of the pain seep out through a slow, splintered breath.

"Yes, there was another baby. A child that brought a change in my life, one that needed to happen—a change that in many ways saved me. A little girl I hope can help us heal our broken family again before it is too late."

"Antoine's baby?" I say it so quietly, giving her the option to pretend she hasn't heard me if she wants to, but her eyes remain steady at the mention of his name.

"Antoine's baby. *Our* baby. The start of something so beautiful, but the end of us, sadly."

I let the fact sink in. All that romance, all those illicit meetings, so many promises made, secret hours stolen, and after all that, he let her down? I can't believe it.

"So, he never supported you?"

"I'm afraid not. I wanted him to, but . . ." She's searching for the words to summarize what must have been a devastating blow at the time. "He wasn't able to."

I see the confusion dance across her eyes. The shadow of all that hurt and rejection still there, all these years on, diminished but not erased. So much time lapsed, and with it the passing of a lifetime's worth of memories. But still, this one makes no sense, and she is left to wonder and imagine what might have happened to him. Why he made a decision that colored her entire future.

"Why? I don't understand. If you were both so in love, why didn't he help you, Granny?"

"I have spent a lifetime wondering, Lucille, and I'm afraid I don't know. We were young, both scared. There was a lot at stake. Albert, my husband, was determined to keep us apart, and so was Antoine's mother. I'm not sure Antoine was brave enough to take on the two of them. I never doubted my love for him, but I have had to accept that he didn't feel the same. That it was easier for him to walk away."

"Oh, Granny. So, the only support you had was from your parents?"

She looks back toward the fire and slowly shakes her head. "No. It was all too much for them. A newly married daughter, pregnant with another man's child, walking out on her successful husband but abandoned by her lover. I'm not sure I could have brought worse news to them. The day I called my mother asking for her help, she made it clear I wouldn't be welcome back at the family home. I never saw her again."

It is almost unimaginable to me that in the depths of her despair, when she had no one else to turn to, when her parents, unlike her, had a choice, they made the worst possible decision. They turned their backs, leaving her with a sadness I suspect has hovered just at the edge of her consciousness every day since.

She stops talking because I'm sobbing, louder than I can ever remember crying before. And, I realize, I'm angry.

"How could they? How could they abandon you like that? All of them. Albert, Antoine, your own parents? It's beyond cruel."

"Darling, it's okay. Please. You have to understand it was a very different time. My parents did what they thought they had to do, what they believed was best for me, and I am reconciled with that, to some degree." She smiles, and again I marvel at her courage.

"How can you say that?" I can't help feeling someone needs to be held accountable. That it was fundamentally wrong to leave a woman, seven years younger than I am now, all alone to cope. "You should have been at home with your family—or with Antoine."

"The fact was that the father of my child was not my husband. The moralists of the time would never accept that, and my parents knew it. I agree they were protecting themselves first and foremost, but they also thought they were protecting me, from a lifetime of judgment and closed doors and rejection. I think my mother truly believed that without their support, I would stay with Albert. She was adamant it was the right thing to do."

"But you didn't. Where did you go?"

"A wonderful friend and her husband took me in until the baby was born. It wasn't easy. Money was incredibly tight, but the three—and then the four—of us muddled through, for a while."

"The parties, the staff, your wardrobe, your home—it all went?

Didn't you ever doubt that you had made the right decision, that you should have tried to make it work with Albert?"

"Not once. He wanted to. That's what angered my mother the most. She couldn't understand why I would give up that life, but it means nothing if you're forced to share it with someone you have grown to despise. What I chose was more honest than the life I had been living. There was no deceit. I wasn't trying to fool anyone anymore, least of all myself. I had my freedom, Lucille, don't you see? As hard as it was, for probably the first time in my life, I wasn't answerable to anyone. I was truly happy to say goodbye to Alice's life and *almost* everything that she had."

"But still. Couldn't you have appealed to Albert to send you some money, or at least some of your things to sell so you could set up somewhere on your own?" I stroke the back of her hand, hoping my questions don't seem foolish or naive.

"No, Lucille. I'd done the difficult thing in leaving him, preventing him from telling the world it was our baby, which was his plan. I couldn't reverse it all by asking for his help or his money. He wouldn't have given them anyway. Besides, none of the things at the embassy were mine. They were either owned by the British government or on loan from other countries, or they were his. I never earned my own money, so I had no honest claim to any of it. Albert moved to America, we divorced, and I got nothing apart from some of my beautiful dresses. But I have never been bitter about that. I had already allowed him to take too much of me. I wasn't going to hand him my future too."

"So that was it? Your marriage was dissolved, and then what? Did your parents ever get in touch?"

She forces a small, brave smile to hide the emotion this heartlessness still provokes in her. "I wrote to my mother when the baby was born, hoping she might feel differently by then. I received one letter back from her. She didn't mention the baby at all. She wrote to tell me that a parcel had arrived in Norfolk for me, all the way from Dior in

Paris. It was the christening dress, not that I knew that then. The last time I had seen it, it was just a sketch on paper. I had no idea it had even been ordered. With everything else that was going on, it was the last thing on my mind. So I wrote back and told her to donate whatever was inside the package. Obviously, when she opened it and saw what it was, she decided it had to be donated anonymously. It was just one more way of erasing a link between my actions and the family name, I suppose."

I take her hand again and lower my face to it, planting a kiss, wishing there could have been so many more. That I could somehow have sent my love and kisses through the universe, racing back through time to when she needed them most, so she knew she was loved, so deeply loved. I allow my head to rest there for a minute, turning my cheek so I can feel the coolness of the back of her hand on my skin. I feel her fingers lovingly smooth my hair, and I look back up at her face.

Perhaps for the first time, it is not the tired features of an elderly lady looking back at me. All I can see is Granny's strength and fortitude, the fire in her belly. I see a life fully lived, one where her determination to survive, to reclaim herself, was so much stronger than the hurdles placed in front of her. I see the burden of secrets carried close to her heart for an unimaginably long time. I think about all the other women who must have envied her, wrongly apportioning their own desire on the parts of Alice's life that meant the least to my grandmother. I see her grit, her optimism, and her forgiveness.

I see the sort of woman I want to be.

And I also feel the unasked question that threads between the two of us, hot on the edge of my lips. The conclusion that will have to wait. I can't ask her tonight, not when she has unburdened so much already.

"Why did you send me to Paris, Granny? Why did you wait all this time and then make me think it was all about the dresses?"

She shifts forward in her chair, like she needs me to hear every word she is about to say, then fixes me with her full focus. "I needed you to see my life, Lucille, to discover the woman I *was* so you can understand the choices I made and the woman I became. To give you a window into the world Alice lived in. If I had simply told you the story, it would have been as if you were seeing it in black and white. I wanted to open your heart, my darling, to the richness of it. The pain and the elation. For it to be real. My choices back then are your choices now, albeit made in a very different time. You are lucky, Lucille. I was one very small footnote in a much bigger story, where the other characters dictated a lot of the action. My voice was small, but yours can be big. I was dependent until I forced myself not to be, but you can be truly free, if you choose to be. Please promise me you won't waste that privilege. Find true love, even if it shatters your heart. You owe it to yourself to experience it. Chase down your happiness. It wants to be found."

I grip her hand a little tighter. "I promise you, I will. I already am." And I mean it. I have never meant anything more.

"This makes me happier than anything else could. I have made mistakes, Lucille, ones that I must ask you to forgive me for. Ones that altered your life in ways you don't even know about yet. And it is my guilt that has caused you the most pain. I struggled to show your mother the power of love, and so she has been incapable of giving it to you. For that, I will always be truly sorry."

"Please don't apologize, Granny. Mum has had many chances to be a good mother and she never took them. But she will, I can see now that she will, and I will be there when she does. We will get there together, slowly."

"Thank you, Lucille." Her eyelids look heavy, and I know that if I stop asking questions and let a silence creep between us, she will be asleep in a few minutes.

"My goodness, I almost forgot. The dresses. I have them all with me. Would you like to see them?"

Granny raises a hand to her heart and laughs. "I suppose I should, since I sent you such a long way to get them. Do you have the Debussy? I'd love to see that one."

"I do, yes. I have all of them. Why don't I make a quick cuppa and you can have a moment alone with them? I know it's been a very long time."

I lift the Debussy from its stiff cotton hanging case and drape it across her lap, its feathers lifting on the air just as I imagine they might have done the evening she wore it to the Monet exhibition. I step back out of the room but linger in the doorway to the kitchen, where I know she can't see me. She lifts the dress to her face, seems to study the detail across the bodice, then pulls it in closer to her, wrapping her arms tightly around it, holding it to her heart. Then she is searching inside, and I know exactly what she is looking for. The two entwined initials of A&A. The clue that she laid all those years ago when she believed herself on the brink of the greatest love affair of her life. She traces a finger lovingly across every one of her stitches, and then she whispers something that makes me stand up a little straighter.

What did she say? It sounded like *my dearest Antoine*, but I can't be sure.

I want to ask her, but I can't interrupt such sweet reflection. It isn't a sadness or loss I'm witnessing, but a deep, satisfying love I hear in the low gravel of her voice. Whatever memories she has of the past, it feels as if they have been eclipsed in this moment by something more enduring. Any pain has long since receded, shifted into perspective, way back beyond the bigger issues she has had to face. Maybe now she can look back as the woman she *is* to the woman she once was and see there is just as much good as there was bad? I think she might have an admiration and respect for Sylvie that she never had for Alice.

Only once she has allowed the dress to fall slack across her lap again do I step back into the room. There is so much more I want to ask her. I offer her a cup of tea, but she waves her hand, and I know she won't drink it. I place it on the ottoman at her feet in case she changes her mind, return the dress to its hanger, and start to gather my things.

"The story isn't quite finished, darling. I know you have more questions, and there is more to tell. Will you come again tomorrow, and we will finally get there together? Can you do that for me, please? I need to rest now."

"I'll be here, Granny, of course I will."

IT'S GETTING LATE, BUT AS I LEAVE, I CALL VERONIQUE AND TELL her some of what I now know.

She is leaving tomorrow to return to Paris, and I know she'll be wondering how the story ends, what Granny had to say after our discovery at the V&A. We arrange to meet briefly tomorrow in Wimbledon Village for coffee before I return to see Granny and she heads for the Eurostar. Despite the excitement of my impending job interview, which I have yet to thank her for, I know our time together on this journey is coming to a close, and I feel an emptiness in my chest, a sadness that is surprisingly sharp. Not even the thought of Leon, waiting patiently for me back at my place, can soften it.

28

Alice
SEPTEMBER 1954, PARIS

Alice isn't sure when exactly she makes the decision to leave.

Is it in the blur of semiconscious tiredness, the ghostly hinterland, when her mind slips between two worlds? The one where her aching and still-sore body is heavy on the thin mattress, feeling the coiled wires protrude into her flesh every time she moves? Or when she is pacing the floor of Anne's shrinking apartment, the baby bent over her shoulder, flexing her lungs with such vigor that Sébastien removes himself and Anne takes over again, settling her much quicker than Alice seems able to?

Or did the decision come in the early hours, when it feels like the rest of Paris is still sleeping, and her baby is pressed tightly to her breast? When above the sound of the child's satisfied muffle, she can pick out the voices of Anne and Sébastien through the wall, arguing about money, the lack of it. How Sébastien's income alone cannot stretch to support the four of them.

Maybe it was sooner. Right back when Patrice's delivery arrived and she unpacked the remains of her unwanted life into the cramped confines of her new bedroom, forced to revisit the dresses, her notes, memories of a time when her heart was so full of hope, when she felt understood.

It's early morning and Paris is waking up.

She can hear deliveries arriving at the shops on the streets below, loud voices unconcerned about the hour and who they might be disturbing. Far too much normality.

Alice is up, dressed, and sitting at the side of her daughter's small wooden cot, allowing her to furl a strong finger around her own, watching the hands on the bedside clock tick far too quickly. With every minute that passes, she can feel herself harden, building a wall around her own heart. A heart that is slowing, shutting down, switching off, and preparing itself for the break to come.

She said her goodbyes to Sébastien last night, watched as he tried to steady the lump in his throat, knowing the wave of sadness that was crashing onto them was nothing compared to what is coming this morning.

She's been a mother for a precious six short weeks, felt the fury of a love so strong she's not sure how her body contains it. Today she will package her love up. Leave it with instructions. Somehow quiet her heart and allow herself to be led by the glaring, unavoidable practicalities.

She looks down into her baby's busy little face, her eyes wide, darting around the room, soaking in every detail she can. How will those eyes make sense of tomorrow, when they open and it's not her mother they see first? Will she cry? Will she hold her delicate arms aloft, searching for her somewhere she won't be found? Alice rests her head against the cot, forcing the tears back down inside of her. She will let them come tonight when all this is done. When she is settling into another bedroom, alone this time, but determined to map out a future where money won't stop her being the mother she's promised to be.

For now, she won't let her final hours with her baby be sad ones. Alice won't let that be the memory she leaves her with.

She keeps her voice light, knowing how receptive her tiny daughter already is to her tone. She's given herself the time she needs while it is still just the two of them. As sunshine splinters through the curtain, coloring the room with an orange glow, Alice takes her daughter's hand in hers, draws her face closer to the soft white blanket she's swaddled in, and sends her breathy words down toward her pretty, unknowing face.

I'm not leaving you, my darling, I promise you I'm not. I'm making things better, you must remember that. I'm coming back for you, angel. I'm going to build a life for us, one where you will be safe, and I can care for you properly. And I promise you that every day we are apart, I will never stop loving you. I will hold you in my heart, I will dream about you, I will see you every day when I close my eyes, growing stronger and stronger. I will talk to you, I will pray for you, I will make time for you, I will sit with you in my thoughts and imagine the sweet moment when I will hold you again.

How can she do it?

How can she leave this tiny bundle alone in a city full of danger? Will Alice remember her smell, the way it mimics the scent of her own skin; the sharpness of her fingernails against her own flesh; the way her daughter's face, held next to hers, will instinctively search for the protective warmth of her mother's neck? Then she thinks about her daughter's tiny lips, how they arch tentatively upward when she enters the room, how they might dip again when the shape she sees is the wrong one.

This is a love that started deep inside of Alice when she sat, lonely, staring at her own tiny toes on the beach in Norfolk, knowing even then she would never allow her own child to feel abandoned. Is she wrong? Is it better that they suffer together, rather than coping apart? Should she stay?

No, she mustn't let the panic overwhelm her now.

She places a kiss on her now sleeping baby's cheek, feeling the flutter of eyelashes against her own skin, and whispers another *I love you* into her ear, hoping it will linger there, as long as it needs to. She studies her baby's perfect little face one last time, still in awe that she managed to create someone so beautiful. Then she wonders at her capacity for forgiveness, hoping there is a gentleness already seeding inside her daughter.

That one day she will understand.

ANNE IS WAITING FOR HER, PACING THE SITTING ROOM, HER creased face a sign she has been up even longer than Alice this morning. The two women embrace, and Alice's tears are there, balanced on the very rim of her eyes. She will not let them fall. Not now. But this needs to be swift.

"You know it, of course, but I have written down her full routine. It's in the bag next to her cot. Please will you stick to it? It's what's familiar to her. I think it will help."

"I will, of course I will, I promise." Anne is about to break, and Alice is relieved Sébastien left early this morning, that he isn't here to see more pain she has caused his wife.

Alice lets her lungs expand with a huge intake of breath. "She already loves you, Anne, just as I do. Please try to remember all the things that will help her feel safe when she realizes I'm gone."

Anne can only manage a small nod.

"When you are changing her, remember how I place a small towel across her belly. She hates to feel cold and exposed, it will stop her crying. If she is struggling to sleep, put her on your shoulder and hum like you do sometimes, the vibrations always calm her. She sleeps best in the cot, on her front. Her small white bunny is in there, don't lose it. If you run your finger along her jawline, it will make her smile."

Alice can hear the wavering in her voice, the pace of her words tumbling out of her far quicker than she intends.

She plows on.

"When she's upset, I rest a knuckle on her lower lip and she will suck it. Remember to tie your hair back when you are feeding her, or she will pull hard on it and won't let go. And, Anne, I don't ever want her to feel alone, even for a second. Please don't ever leave her crying like some mums do." Alice has to throw the final words from her mouth. Her throat clings to them, trying to drag them back in, holding on to the final part of this speech like it will make some difference to the outcome.

"I understand. I will do everything you say. She will be safe, and she will be loved, and I will make sure you know just how much until you return."

"Thank you. She's sleeping in her cot now, so I will go."

"Are you sure? If you need more time . . ."

"I'm sure. It has to be now."

The tears will overwhelm her soon. She watches as Anne opens the door, unsure that her feet will move to carry her through it, unable to think about how she will cope without her dear Anne by her side each day.

"There is one more thing. Please don't shorten her name. I think it suits her just as it is."

"Of course, I wouldn't dream of—"

"I know. I just needed to say it." She allows her eyes to cast back toward the bedroom door, praying with all her heart that her baby girl stays sleeping just long enough for her to make it down to the street. If she hears her now, everything will be undone.

She walks through the courtyard and out onto the cobbles, feeling the heat already filtering into the day. How cruel that it's sunny, when the day demands a low, rolling thunderstorm or a cataclysmic downpour. That's what she deserves. Not a day that promises happiness and a trip to the park. She looks up and down the street, sees the baker, happy to be serving his first customer of the day, a street sweeper bent heavy over his broom, working with conviction. As she passes him, he raises his head and smiles, wishing her a good morning. She wants to yell at him, Don't show me any kindness. The woman you think you see is not who I am. Don't be fooled by the smartness of my coat, the neatness of my hair. It's all a horrible trick. Can he see in her face what she's done? If he could, would it be sympathy or a cold judgment he'd feel?

Then she moves, as fast as her luggage will allow, to release the energy that will otherwise become a cry, then a scream that will never stop.

29

Lucille
WEDNESDAY
LONDON

"Are you looking forward to getting home?"

Veronique is sitting opposite me in a chic café in Wimbledon Village, the sort of place where unsliced cakes sit under giant glass cloches and are photographed but rarely eaten. It's just around the corner from Granny's place and a short walk downhill for Veronique to the train station.

"Yes, for a decent slice of tart if nothing else!" She turns up her nose at the synthetic creation in front of her, and I have to agree it doesn't come close to what Paris has to offer. "Would you like me to come with you?"

"Thank you, but no. I feel like I should do this alone." I'm picking at the tart with my own fork, despite its disappointment.

"I agree. I just wanted you to know the offer is there, if you need it." She takes my arm across the table and gives it a reassuring rub. "When is your interview? Perhaps we can meet beforehand for a run-through?"

"That would be great. It's next week. I'm arriving in Paris on Wednesday morning, and the interview is Thursday afternoon."

"Well, you must stay with me, then, don't pay for a hotel. Unless . . ."

She knows why I won't accept her offer, even before I start to giggle.

"Of course, silly me. You'll be staying with Leon. That's great! I'm so happy for you, Lucille."

"Well, let's see. It's early days, but I've got a very good feeling about him. He makes me forget myself in the loveliest way." And I deliver a toothy grin across the table to her to prove it.

"And how about this morning? How are you feeling about your chat with your grandmother? This is it, isn't it? The last piece of the story?" Her smile doesn't match mine. She looks nervous on my behalf, her mouth tight, her shoulders raised a little.

"I just want to understand how it all ended and what happened to her baby. Where she might be and whether there is even the slightest chance we might meet one day. Wouldn't that be incredible, if we could?" I drain the last of my coffee, feeling the much-needed surge of caffeine hit my veins.

"It really would. Paris will have delivered so much for you then." She smiles in that self-assured way of hers, like her thoughts are always one step ahead of my own. "I thought you should have this." She reaches into her bag and hands me the letter that is addressed to Alice, the one she found with the others from my granny to her mother, that made less sense to her at the time. "I should have given it to you on the train. I think your grandmother might like to read whatever is in there."

"Of course, I had completely forgotten about it. I'll give it to her today." I wedge it into my own bag. "You know, it's funny, I always thought Paris was a bit predictable before Granny sent me. Somewhere you went when you weren't imaginative enough to think beyond the obvious. For new lovers who want to play it safe, to follow the same path as so many before them, or middle-aged, married couples who can't remember what it is to be adventurous. How wrong I was! Now two of my absolute favorite people in the world live there." I feel my cheeks warm a little and hope she doesn't mind me gushing over her, but I want her to return to Paris knowing the impact she has had on me. "I owe you a huge thank-you, Veronique. The trail across Paris would never have got started without your help."

"You would have worked it out." She's being generous.

"Maybe, maybe not. But it's highly unlikely I would have made it to the V and A, and I certainly wouldn't be considering a job in another country if it weren't for you. You've done so much for me. This has all been so overwhelming, so life changing. Thank you." I stand and hug her, and she reciprocates with a deep, firm embrace that feels wonderful and right, and that she's in no hurry to release me from.

"Well, you better get going, and I have a train to catch. Take care of yourself and say hello to Leon for me." She winks, kisses me on both cheeks, then breezes away, unwittingly dragging the envious gaze of several women up from their phone screens and out the door with her.

GRANNY IS STILL TUCKED UP IN BED WHEN I LET MYSELF IN. I drop my bag and jacket over the arm of a chair in the sitting room and tiptoe in through her bedroom door, pulling a seat up next to her side of the bed. Her eyes ease open.

"Is everything okay, can I get you anything?" I check the time on her bedside clock. It's ten thirty a.m.; Natasha will have been and gone already, so we'll be free from interruptions.

"I'm fine. Just tired, that's all." Natasha has propped her up on two plump pillows, pulled the covers tight across her chest, and tucked them neatly under each arm. Granny's hands are clasped in front of her. She looks ready, but am I?

"Are you sure you're up to this? We can always chat another day if not." It sounds like I'm trying to give her an out, but really it's me who is backtracking, knowing that in about half an hour from now, I will know everything there is to know. I'll have an even deeper under-standing of this wonderful woman and who I really am. If Granny senses my nerves, she's typically having none of it.

"No, no, I promised you an ending today, and that's what you're going to get. You've waited long enough, Lucille."

"Okay, well, in your own time, Granny, there's really no rush. Shall I make you a tea or something to nibble first?" I start to rise from my seat.

"Just sit, please, Lucille, we're going to do this together." She takes a deep breath; I see how she holds the air inside her lungs for a few seconds before she releases it, channeling her confidence, giving her-self the strength to say the words she must have believed might never be aired.

She starts to speak, very slowly, enunciating every word clearly, so sure of the narrative she's taking us on.

"Saying goodbye to my daughter was the hardest thing I've ever had to do. It tore me apart, Lucille, in ways I couldn't possibly imagine until it was all far too late."

The swell of emotion writhes up from somewhere deep inside my belly almost the second she starts to speak. I refuse to let it force itself any higher than my chest, where it sits painfully, slowing my breath, making it sound labored.

"What happened?" I manage to whisper.

"I couldn't stay in Paris. It wasn't fair to place such a burden on my friend. She would never have told me that, but I could see for myself. The money just didn't stretch far enough. We had six weeks, that was all. More than enough time for me to fall completely in love with her. Then I returned to England with just a case full of my more practical belongings, determined to find work. I left my baby in Paris, the city where she started life. The place I felt she belonged if she couldn't be with me." The weight in my chest tightens, something standing to attention deep inside of me, but I keep my focus on Granny.

"Antoine? Did he finally . . ."

"No. We never spoke again. It wouldn't have been hard for him to trace me. There were people who knew where I was, but when I needed him most, he was silent." She allows her head to fall, and I can see the toll that all those years of disappointment have had on her. The deep-rooted rejection that still lives behind every line on her face, every quiver of her lips. Then I think about the letter in my bag, addressed to Alice in a handwriting that was so different from every other in the bundle that Veronique's mother kept.

"I can't be sure, but I think he might have tried, Granny. Hang on." I dash back into the sitting room and delve into my bag for the letter, feeling again the small, hard shape within it. When I hand it to Granny, she confirms my hunch immediately.

"Yes, it's from him. The letters, look." She turns the envelope back to face me. "The strokes of an artist. It's definitely from him." She scans the envelope for a date. "Sent in March 1956, long after I left Paris. She would have been about a year and a half old by then."

"Do you want to read it? I can step back into the other room if you need some time alone?"

I see the flicker of indecision cross her face as she turns the letter over and over in her hand, feeling the contents within it, trying to predict what it might say. "My friend told me about this letter when it arrived. She wanted to send it to me, but I insisted she shouldn't. I was just starting to get myself together, I had been reunited with your grandfather by then, and I was worried whatever Antoine had to say would plunge me backward. I do want to read it, Lucille, but I'm a little scared of what it might say. For years I've told myself Antoine was simply frightened to face the future we created together. It made sense, even if I couldn't possibly agree with it at the time. But what if there was something else? I'm not sure I can bear to hear him say it was all a mistake, that he never loved me. That he regretted us."

I can't believe for a second that's what's contained in this letter, but at the same time anything feels possible. "I could read it to you, if that makes it any easier?" That way I can scan ahead and stop if I need to. "Would that help?"

She jumps at the suggestion. "Yes please, darling. You read it." I ease two sheets of thin blue writing paper out of their envelope and unfold them, catching the smooth pearl earring that drops from within. I hold it up so Granny can see it.

"My goodness. I left it at his apartment the very first night we spent together. He kept it all that time . . ." The tension seems to seep from her face a little. "Read, Lucille, please."

It's my turn to take a deep breath. I start slowly, lingering on every word, making sure nothing is lost, painfully aware that I am opening a door to her past. One that has been locked shut for decades.

March 13, 1956

Darling Alice,

I want you to know that none of it was your fault. You did nothing wrong. I hope if nothing else you know that. You were so irresistible, but more than that, so easy to love. I shouldn't have made you love me. I should have walked away.

That very first night at the residence, when I saw you and the whole room fell silent around me, when I realized in that split second that my life would never be the same again, that was the point at which I should have turned and left. But I didn't. I couldn't. No one since Thomas had understood me the way you did. You bewitched me, and I was greedy, selfish, and spoiled, determined to have what was never mine to take. And now we know the consequences of that boundless arrogance. Like a child, I thought only of satisfying myself.

You were everything to me. However much you gave me, I wanted more. I helped myself to every part of you, and then, when you asked me to simply stand by what I had done, where was I? I failed you.

I was afraid, Alice—of failing you in the same way I failed to achieve so many other things. I was convinced that I couldn't become the man you needed me to be, that I would once again fall short of expectations. That somehow our love would sour, you would hate me for it, and both our lives would be full of regret. It was easier to do nothing, to pretend none of it was happening, to let forces beyond me decide, while you shouldered all the darkness alone.

I have replayed the day you came to my apartment and I refused to speak to you over and over in my mind. I felt your anguish burrow into my heart, where it rightly stayed, tormenting me, reminding me every day of my weakness. You gave me the chance to be better and I wasted it. For months I wondered how you could ever have loved the man I was.

The day you left Paris was the day I lost everything, just as I deserved to. I lost you, our baby, any respect I had for myself, the future we could have had, and my passion for my work. The sketches I did of you were by far my best. Nothing else ever came close. Once you left, there was nothing to inspire me or fill me with confidence, and the limitations of my talent became glaringly apparent. My days are long, empty, and unproductive. All this time to think of you, turning your earring over and over in my fingers, torturing myself with images of you the night you left it here. But still I did nothing. I told myself you would build a better life. You are strong. You won't allow yourself to fail, as I did.

For another year, I stayed in Saint-Germain. I used to sit outside our church and listen to the bells ringing, just to remind me of you. In the beginning I hoped I'd look up and see you there—that you would make it easy by appearing before me, our baby in your arms. My cowardice was breathtaking. When I finally accepted you were never coming back to me, I crawled back to my parents' apartment, which is only a fraction of the punishment I deserve. I'm rotting here. Mother's satisfaction is like a noose around my neck, tightening a little more with every day.

You said once that it would never be too late. I hope you still believe that. I hope this letter, whenever you are reading it, offers some explanation. I wasn't good enough. You painted a picture of a man far better than the one who stood in front of you. It is no more complicated than that.

I know it is worthless and meaningless now, but I never stopped loving you, Alice. You still dance through my dreams at night. It's all I have left, but it's still so much more than I deserve.

Yours, forever,
Antoine

My cheeks are wet, and I wipe the back of my sleeve across my face, sniffing loudly.

"Granny?" Her eyes are closed. She's perfectly still. Just lying there, letting Antoine's words sink deeply into her, with the very faintest smile curling across her lips.

"I feel better." She opens her eyes and I'm relieved to see they are dry. "It has taken far too long, but he has made me feel better, and for that I am grateful. He gave Alice her escape, Lucille, do you see? Despite his failings, Antoine made me see that I was worth more; he helped save me from a lifetime of living a lie, even if he couldn't be mine. He was right. He wasn't good enough for me, and neither was Albert. But Edward? Your wonderful granddad Teddy, he was."

"But the baby, Granny. Didn't you want to get her back?"

"Oh my goodness, more than anything, yes. Everything started well. I found work as a housekeeper in a huge residence, not far from here, a job that eventually pulled Teddy and me back together again. That's when I changed my name too. Sylvie was my mother's middle name. It seems silly now, but despite the rejection, it made me feel that there might be hope, that we might one day be reconciled if I still had that connection to her. I was wrong about that, but if there was one thing I did know, it was how to run a home that size, how to organize the other staff and make sure everything ran like clockwork. But the hours were impossibly long, and the pay only just covered my own living expenses. As hard as I tried, I never managed to save anything. Even if it had paid more, there was no way my hours could accommodate a newborn baby."

"Oh, Granny, did you ever see her again?"

"I did once, yes. It was after Edward and I were married; your mother was still small. I traveled to Paris on my own and watched her in the park with her new mummy. She was so happy. They both were. And I knew that had to be enough. By then I had given up work, but it was all too late, Lucille. How could I possibly have forced my way back into her life then? There was only one person who would have benefited from that, and it wasn't my innocent daughter or the wonderful woman raising her. I couldn't be that selfish. I knew she was well, her mummy made sure I always knew."

"And Mum knows none of this? You've never told her this story?"

"No. But I will. She deserves to hear the truth too. It may seem like the wrong way around, Lucille, but I wanted you to hear it first. You're still so young. You have the most to learn from it. I knew you would unravel it and see the good that is buried in it all."

My lips find her fingers. "I'm so sorry, Granny. It's all so desperately sad. Do you have anything of the baby's? Anything to remind you of her that you kept?"

"I have all my letters."

"Your letters?"

"Yes, from her mummy. They have kept me going over the years, telling me everything. Her first words, first steps, the day she started school. It was all there for me to experience too."

I feel a slow dawning start to spread across my chest, a connection being made. A feeling of space opens up inside my head, my subconsciousness making room for something that I am not quite ready to let in.

"I owe her a debt of gratitude that can never be repaid, God rest her soul. She was the key, in the end, to me forgiving myself."

"What do you mean?"

"I gave her the freedom to raise the baby as she wanted to. I gave her the family she always wanted. And in return she gave me a reason to feel some good about myself. That some happiness could rise from all the sadness." She pauses, looks deep into my eyes like she is searching for a level of understanding there before she continues.

"She confessed much later that she was the one who secretly ordered the christening dress. She knew how much I wanted it for the baby, and I suppose it was also her way of trying to ensure I had a presence the day it was worn. But some wires got crossed, and in all the rush of Albert leaving for America, the box was accidentally shipped back to Norfolk with the last of my belongings, and never worn." She smiles to herself then, like that might have been the best possible outcome.

"I only ever asked one thing of her, that she kept the pretty French name I gave my daughter at birth. I always felt Veronique suited her so well. She was raised by Anne, my dearest friend and confidant from my time in Paris."

My body seems to instantly cool, so that I can feel the warm pulse of my blood moving through me, the beat of my heart in the back of my throat.

"Veronique? The woman I have been in Paris with for a week? The one who came to the V and A with me? The one who is helping me to find a new job? Her? They are the same woman? And you knew all along, from the day you sent me to Paris?" My heart rate rockets, and I am instantly torn in two, veering wildly between sheer joy and frustration.

Joy that it is Veronique, that the closeness I have felt to her is real and genuine—we *are* connected. We are *family*.

And a red-hot frustration that Granny didn't just tell me this while Veronique was here, or I was there in Paris, so we could have sat together and talked it all through. So that I could have been there to help at the moment when Veronique realizes the woman she called her mother for her entire life was not biologically so. That the woman she so recently buried took this enormous secret with her.

Why does everything have to be so late?

"But she's on her way back to Paris as we speak. And she doesn't know? Has she been told any of this?" I'm standing now, knowing that I need to act before it is too late and she gets onto the tube. She'll be underground with no signal and I won't be able to stop her before she boards the Eurostar. I don't want to have this conversation over the phone.

"No. Anne loved her enough for both of us. We agreed there was nothing to be gained from telling her the truth, unless she raised suspicions or started asking questions, but that was so unlikely under the circumstances."

"Hang on. Anne? 'My dearest Anne . . . ' That's the name you said yesterday when you were holding the Debussy dress. But you told me the initials stood for Alice and Antoine."

"It started that way, darling. At a time when I believed Antoine was the one great love of my life, I wanted to record how he made me feel. The dresses were the best way of doing that. The cards and the initials, it was something so personal and intimate I could hide deep within the layers, the perfect place to bury my secrets." She smiles at the memory.

"But of course we know now he wasn't the hero of my story. She was. My wonderful, loyal, brave Anne. We were two women with so little in common, it seemed at first, we might have passed each other on the street without feeling the vaguest hint of a connection. But we came to rely on each other in a way perhaps only two women can. She had everything to lose, but still she stood by my side. Even when there was nothing for her to gain, she never deserted me. I'm not sure you or I would be sitting here now if it wasn't for her."

"That's incredible," I manage through my tears.

"*She* was incredible. My love affair with Antoine was ephemeral by comparison. But my feelings for Anne never diminished. They never will. Alice and Anne. A and A. She was the only person I could have trusted with the precious gift of my daughter."

"She's still in London, Granny. Veronique. I can stop her from going back to Paris. Wouldn't you love to see her again?"

"More than anything, yes, I would. But I have no expectations, Lucille. Veronique has lived her own life, many miles from here. She may not want to see me, and I have to understand that. And so do you."

"At least let me try. Can I just try to call her, please?" I look at my watch. She'll have made it to the bottom of the hill by now and, saving any major delays, she'll be on the train, I know it. But the first half dozen stops are overground. Maybe her phone will connect, maybe I can just say enough to get her off the train.

"If you think it is the right thing to do, Lucille, I won't stop you."

I grab my mobile from my bag and head toward the door, knowing Granny's unreliable phone reception will be stronger if I'm in the garden. My heart is hammering against my ribs as I throw the door open with one hand, phone balancing between my ear and left shoulder, simultaneously trying to force my right arm into my jacket.

Then I freeze, and the phone cracks against the path beneath me.

Veronique is leaning against Granny's garden gate, her eyes bright with tears. She shifts abruptly upright at the sight of me.

"What are you . . ?" She's looking at me with such level calmness that I can't finish my own sentence. She says nothing, and her silence is the biggest clue of all.

"You knew! My God, you knew, and you didn't tell me!" I'm not angry, exactly, but neither am I relaxed. I feel deceived. I feel stupid. How could we have just shared a casual coffee together—not to mention a week in Paris—her knowing full well the conversation I was about to have?

She takes four deliberately slow steps toward me, like she thinks I might bolt, her eyes fixed to mine, her mouth softening to a smile as she gets closer.

"No, I didn't know. I couldn't possibly have known."

Her arms are on my shoulders now, weighted there, anchoring me. "Not until you opened the door just then and I saw it in your face. But I felt it, Lucille. That day in the V and A. For the first time, I wondered. Why, when my maman loved children so much, were there never any siblings? You saw it yourself, I look nothing like her. How could that be right? Not to share even a hint, however subtle, of what made us both? And I felt it in my connection to you. I felt instantly happier every time we were together, a different happiness, more special."

I open my mouth to whine that I'm always the last one to put the pieces together, then thankfully think better of it.

"There was always someone pointing out our differences, and every time they did, I felt her wince next to me," continues Veronique. "She was never comfortable with the observation, always forcing the conversation on just a little too quickly. Then so many letters. Have you ever known two women to write to each other that much? I stopped reading the ones from your grandmother in the end. I felt if there was something to discover, I wanted to discover it with you, not alone in my maman's old apartment. It just didn't seem right."

The fact she wanted to be with me at the precise moment her family history was unraveling around her makes my eyes sting, and I bury them in the palms of my hands.

"So, I allowed myself to imagine it, and it really wasn't so difficult. Your grandmother, my . . ." She can't bring herself to say it. Veronique may have had more time than me to think all this through, but still, it's quite some leap on the family tree. "She is a very clever lady, Lucille. She had the good grace to wait until my maman had passed away so none of this could hurt her. Then she placed you in my path and waited for us to find each other. It was the kindest way to let it happen, don't you think?"

We're both interrupted by the sound of Granny calling my name.

"She wants to see you. Will you come in? Do you feel like you can?" Please let her say yes. I couldn't deliver Antoine to Granny's doorstep, and now I know she wouldn't have wanted me to, but I can do this. I can give her another chance, however brief it might have to be, to rebuild a relationship far more precious.

There is the briefest hesitation while Veronique's face clouds with the confusion of all the questions she must have. Then she straightens her shoulders and gives in to the opportunity in front of her, like it's the only, obvious answer she could give.

"Of course I will. I want to meet the woman my maman loved so dearly."

We step back into the cottage together and I lead Veronique through to the bedroom, where Granny is waiting.

I don't need to say a thing.

The second their eyes meet, Granny knows, and then her tears come before Veronique has said a word. Every strain of emotion that has remained caged inside of her comes pouring out of her tired body. I feel my feet move to rush to her, but then a hand on my arm stops me. I have played my part, it is Veronique's turn now, so I simply nod my acceptance that I am happy for her to be the one to comfort Granny. Then I watch as Veronique walks to Granny's side of the bed and drops to her knees, allowing her face to be cupped by my grandmother's thin fingers.

I take a few small, quiet steps backward, giving them the space they both deserve. I'm silently edging out of the room when I see the Debussy, hanging on the door of her wardrobe—the lightness of the midnight-blue feathers, the delicate sparkle that has survived the decades just as well as Granny has, just as Dior intended.

My eyes move between the dress, my grandmother, and Veronique, both still holding each other—and I smile as I think of the precious secret this dress has held and how much richer my life will be now that I know it.

30

Sylvie
1961, LONDON

My dearest Anne,

I'm not sure I can ever thank you enough for allowing me to visit you in Paris last week. You always were very intuitive, and I wonder if you guessed at my deeper reasons for coming. If not, I will confess them here so you understand how much I will always love and respect you.

I have to be honest—because you deserve no less—that my journey was fueled with what I can now appreciate were unkind thoughts. Please understand that despite the luck and good fortune life has shown me since I left Paris, it has also been very hard. To know that there is a precious part of me I can never reach, that I will never be truly whole without, has weighed heavily on my heart every single day. So, as much as I loathe myself for saying it, it is also true that my intention in coming to Paris was to alleviate my own sadness, with less thought for the pain I might cause.

I convinced myself on the journey that you would understand, that Veronique returning to me, even after all this time, was the natural course of events—the rightful ending to a story we started to write together all those years ago. The human mind is a wonderful thing. If you want something desperately, it will allow you to believe that others want it for you too. Fantasy is the great seducer, so much stronger than logic or reason. Thankfully my love for you proved a much tougher opponent, easily defeating my selfishness.

So, as I stood at a safe distance in the park and watched you and Veronique play, it was one of the happiest hours of my life. I saw for myself the deep trust she has in you, how she threw her small arms around your waist, fully committing herself, never doubting you would catch her. I watched as her shoes launched skyward and you swung her through the air. How she buried her face in your skirt. I saw the strength of her grip on you, wanting to protect you as much as you were protecting her.

And my heart broke, Anne. Because it was the moment I realized she will never be mine again.

I scanned your face for the slightest inclination of a retreat from the very great promise you made to me. Was there anything that said you understood? That you might choose to take my pain away once more? How foolish that sounds now. Of course, all I saw was the ferocity of your love for her, exactly as I had hoped I would when I left your apartment for the last time.

She is beautiful, and only someone with no heart at all would seek to cast any doubt on her happiness. I know it will be many years before my heart stops hurting, but I won't ask to see her again. If there is any doubt in your mind, please know that she is yours and that is good and right, and nothing will change that now. Once again you have inspired me, Anne. This time to value the treasures my new life has given me—to be a better wife and mother myself. Dear Edward and Genevieve deserve to be loved just as well.

I will learn to cherish the time Veronique spends in my thoughts. You have given me such a positive image to always remember her by. I hope now I can learn to let go of the innocent baby who has haunted my darkest hours and rejoice in the happy little girl you have raised, who knows nothing of the sadness that circles her story. I won't lie to you and say it will be easy—there will be many tough days ahead, but my greatest hope is that I will find a way to live with the sadness that will forever be a part of me. I will try, Anne, to no longer let it rule me.

I wish we could have spoken, my dear friend. I would have loved to sit on that bench with you both and share a few bites of whatever it was you were enjoying together. I would have loved to feel her head drop onto my shoulder, as it did on yours, or to have hugged you tightly. Isn't that one of the great afflictions of being human, always wanting more? What I have now will have to be enough, and sometimes I can feel my spirits lifting with that sense of acceptance.

I hope you are proud, Anne. Of Veronique, of the incredible gift of peace you have given me, and of the magnificent woman that you are. I'm sure I will not have a better friend as long as I live, or Veronique a better maman.

All my love, forever,
Sylvie x

EPILOGUE

ONE YEAR LATER

The day dawns pink and bright, and I know Granny would have thought it fitting. No black, she said, not even gray, and remarkably the sky has obliged her, despite how the year is drawing to its end.

I was wondering how Veronique might cope with the dress code, given that she lives in black, but she looks immaculate in a slate-blue suit. The collar sits high on her neck, then it drapes across her body, cutting in sharply at the waist, where there are two angled pockets. There isn't a millimeter of slack in the skirt, it has been tailored so tightly to her curves. She's added a pair of chocolate-brown leather gloves, edged with fur, and a small pillbox hat in a matching color with a tiny birdcage veil that grazes her eyebrows.

Granny would have loved this look.

At Veronique's collarbone there is one solitary pearl—granny's earring reimagined as a necklace, and perhaps Veronique's last remaining connection to her biological father. I notice her touching it sometimes, rubbing it between her fingers absentmindedly, just like he did every day while he was forced to think about everything he'd lost.

"The suit is from Bettina," she tells me as we walk together through the church grounds. "It seemed like a fitting choice."

"Tell me you'll take me," Mum adds. "I've heard so much about this place, I desperately want to see it for myself."

"We will!" Veronique and I answer in unison.

"It's one of the highlights of the tour, Mum. You're going to see everything, I promise. Just as I did."

I refuse to feel sad today. It's not what Granny wanted, and how can I, when there is so much to be thankful and grateful for? So much to look forward to, thanks to her. And all because she refused to give up. Because she always had hope and believed that things could be made better.

I picture the different versions of her as I gaze down at the freshly laid headstone, marveling even now at her many reinventions before she finally found her peace. I know how much easier it would have been to quit. But she was so fixed in her ambition to set right what she couldn't control for all those years. She waited and was patient—she knew it would come if she didn't force it.

And in the end, it did.

The cost to her was all the lost years, but she has gifted those back to us, the most incredible goodbye present imaginable. Her family is now united, and it is all because of her. Veronique and Mum would say it's because of me, and I'll admit I played my part, but it was only possible because she showed me how.

So, while it's almost unbearable to stem the flow of my tears today, I will, for her. The three of us stand together, my left hand in Veronique's, my right in Mum's.

SYLVIE ALICE LORD
Loved, admired, strong—until the very end.

Just as she wanted it. Just as we all agreed it should be.

· · ·

WE HEAD TO THE CARS PARKED ON THE EDGE OF THE COMMON, and as we climb in, I see my mum starting to fuss about something. She is rooting around in her handbag and insisting that Veronique sit next to her, that she has something she wants to give her before we arrive back at Mum's place. As we pull away, I look back over my shoulder and see it is a bundle of letters, and I understand.

"I found them in her cottage, afterward," offers Mum. "They were left out on the sideboard in her bedroom. I think she did it deliberately to be sure they would be seen. They're the ones that Anne wrote to her from Paris, after my mum returned to England."

"Oh, that's so wonderful. She kept them all?" Veronique's face lights up at the prospect of another opportunity to hear both women's voices.

"There's quite a few, so yes, I think so. And I hope you don't mind, Veronique, but I did read several of them." Mum frowns, afraid she has done the wrong thing and caused disappointment.

"My goodness, of course not. How could I mind?"

"I'm so thankful that Mum and I got to talk as much as we did before she died, but there is something about the letters that can't be re-created or retold. They are so authentic, so representative of Anne and Mum's relationship at the time. But more than that, they reveal all the questions Mum asked, all the answers she sought. Not just the big things, but every little detail. She wanted to know everything about you. She never stopped asking."

"Thank you, Genevieve. I'd love to read every one of them. Maybe we can sit down and look at them all together one day?"

"I would love that."

"You know, I still have the letters your maman wrote at the time you were born too. You're very welcome to take a look. It's obvious how much love she felt for you too."

Mum bites down hard on her bottom lip and nods. It's all she can manage for now.

We pull up outside Mum's place, and I can't quite believe she has relaxed enough over the past few months to allow the party (as Granny specified it should be) to happen here.

There are going to be crisps down the back of her expensive sofa, shoe smudges on the marble. Someone might actually upend a drink or—heaven forbid—forget to use a coaster. But she doesn't care. Bizarrely, it's the happiest I have seen her in ages. Her sense of purpose has returned, and she is embracing it. She circulates effortlessly with none of her old stress and irritation, making sure champagne flutes are full, nibbles are dispersed, and introductions are made, and then she curls up on one of her giant sofas with Veronique—without even taking her shoes off, I notice—and the two of them are inseparable for the rest of the afternoon. I wish I could stay longer, but Mum is visiting me next weekend. We can chew over everything together then.

"I hate to say it, but we better make a move." Leon appears at my side with our things. "If we miss the Eurostar, we'll be staying the night in London and you'll be late for work the day your exhibition opens."

I see the pleasure he still gets from repeating my achievements. And I'm going to allow myself to feel proud too. All of Granny's dresses and the accompanying cards will go on show tomorrow, with the full story, as told by me, including some of the reportage photographs Leon took of our hunt across Paris together and some of the long-forgotten treasures from Bettina. "Is it okay, today of all days, to be really excited that you are coming home with me, to *our* place?"

"I think so. She would have appreciated you appreciating me, don't you think? I just need to say my goodbyes."

I head to the couch where Mum and Veronique are sharing a joke.

Mum sees the coat draped over my arm and knows that I haven't got time to linger.

She stands and takes my face in her hands, a small act of intimacy that has never existed between us before, then draws her face a little closer to mine.

"She was so incredibly proud of you, you know, and so am I. I'm only sorry it has taken me all this time to tell you that."

"I'm proud of you too, Mum," I tell her—and I mean it. "I'll see you next weekend in Paris!"

ACKNOWLEDGMENTS

The starting point of this novel was back in 2019 as I wandered the halls of the Victoria and Albert Museum in London and its *Christian Dior: Designer of Dreams* exhibition. It was packed with people all keen to catch a glimpse of pieces pulled from both the V&A's national collection of fashion and the House of Dior's own archive. There were more than five hundred objects on display that day, including rare haute couture garments, design drawings, fashion illustrations, and previously unseen photography.

I entered the building without any intention of writing a novel influenced by Dior's fashion legacy, but I left knowing that I would, and with several questions hot on my lips: What kind of woman would wear such a dress? How might it change her life? What secrets might she bury in it?

A few months later I returned to the V&A's Clothworkers' Centre and was able to personally inspect and study most of the dresses you've read about in this book. It was an incredible experience, bringing the gowns to life and helping me form the characters who would come to own them in my story. Thank you to the staff there for their invaluable advice and expertise.

Fast-forward a few more months and I was heading to the South of France with brilliant author Daisy Buchanan for a writer's retreat at Chez Castillon, hosted by the wonderful Mickey and Janie and taught by author Rowan Coleman. It seems fitting that the very first words were penned in France. Then came Paris. Three days, sixty thousand steps, and Lucille's romantic dash across the city was plotted. Thank you to Thea Darricotte for ensuring we had somewhere truly luxurious to lay our heads at the end of each day. Thank you to Celine Kelly for licking the resulting first draft into sparkling shape.

I wrote this story out of contract with no guarantee it would be published when it was finished, so enormous thanks must go to my UK and US agents, Sheila Crowley at Curtis Brown in London and Kristyn Keene Benton at ICM in New York, for ensuring I had not, in fact, wasted a year and a half of my life! Thank you also to Katie McGowan and Callum Mollison at Curtis Brown for taking the story far and wide.

Very special thanks to my brilliantly talented US editors at Penguin Random House/Berkley, Amanda Bergeron and Sareer Khader, who unpicked my manuscript and stitched it back together with a genius level of creativity. Sareer, chapter 23, my favorite one to write, really ought to have your name on it.

Thank you to my wonderful first readers and friends Jenni, Anna, and Caroline, who gave such confidence-boosting feedback, precisely when it was needed most. There is another one coming your way soon!

And to all you readers, it really is the most thrilling thought that someone who lives in your village or on the other side of the world might take the time to read what you have written. I hope with all my heart that you have enjoyed it.

An equally large debt of gratitude to all the authors who graciously gave their time and quotes to support this book's launch. It is hugely appreciated, as is the immensely important role of booksellers, journalists, and book bloggers everywhere. When you have so much exceptional work to choose from, thank you for sometimes choosing mine.

Thank you to Clara for proudly telling anyone who will listen, "My mummy writes books," and to Laila, who I am hoping will mastermind the TikTok marketing campaign. I love you both dearly.

And to Stephen, you're going to have to read it now! We took our first trip to Paris together for our first wedding anniversary in 2002, and our last to research this book. As I write this, we approach our twentieth anniversary. I wonder if you will buy me a little something from Christian Dior? Just a thought! Life with you is the best.

Additional thanks to the following authors and their books for helping to inform and guide this story:

Dior by Dior: The Autobiography of Christian Dior by Christian Dior

Christian Dior by Oriole Cullen and Connie Karol Burks

The Golden Age of Couture: Paris and London 1947-57 by Claire Wilcox

Patch Work: A Life Amongst Clothes by Claire Wilcox

The British Ambassador's Residence in Paris by Tim Knox

The Englishwoman's Wardrobe by Angela Huth

Diana Cooper: The Biography of Lady Diana Cooper by Philip Ziegler

Don't Tell Alfred by Nancy Mitford

The Dud Avocado by Elaine Dundy

Another Me: A Memoir by Ann Montgomery

An Unexpected Guest by Anne Korkeakivi

THE
LAST DRESS
FROM
Paris

JADE BEER

BEHIND THE BOOK

For several years I was fortunate enough to have a day job editing a glossy magazine that occasionally required me to fly from London to New York or to a European city and look at a designer's collection. Whether I was sitting at a fashion show, watching the gowns snake past me, or chatting to the designer during a private viewing, the first questions I asked myself were rarely the ones people assumed I did. It was not *What do I think of this dress?* Or *Is it a successful development on from the designer's previous collection?* Those tended to come later, back in the office, planning the pages.

It was instead always *Who is this dress destined for, and how will it make her feel? In what ways might it change her or the course of her life? What thoughts and feelings might she experience while wearing a dress like this, that she may never share with another living soul?*

All of these questions returned to me one January morning in 2019 when I found myself in the crush of people at London's Victoria and Albert Museum for the *Christian Dior: Designer of Dreams* exhibition. The show had started its life in Paris in 2017 at the Musée des Arts Décoratifs to mark the seventieth anniversary of the House of Dior, and then been reimagined for a London audience. It was hot, it was loud, it was mildly stressful as everyone jostled to see some of the standout items on display—including the monochrome Bar suit with its tiny nineteen-inch waist, a piece that came to define Dior's much-lauded New Look fashion, and that remains, to this day, the most requested item to study in the museum's Clothworkers' Centre.

In among the dresses was fashion footage, cleverly interspersing models from decades past with the drama of the modern runway spectacle. The toile room revealed the test garments, Dior's prototypes that came before the final gowns, exposing the famous dresses, as if they were undressed themselves.

When I left the museum that day, I knew so much more about the work of Christian Dior and how he defined an era of fashion. Much has been written of his legacy. But what of the women he dressed? I wondered. What happened to all of them and their beautiful gowns when they left the boutique for the final time? It was never quiet in the museum that day, there was never a moment for peaceful reflection, but I do remember thinking: What would the women, Dior's clients, whisper from behind the glass cabinets if they could? If they could lean over the rope, what would they tell me about the occasion on which they wore these dresses? As Christian Dior once said himself, "the past lies so vividly around."

The book that accompanied the exhibition referenced "three formidable women" whom Dior hired at the very beginning to oversee the making of his collections. It seemed fitting that there should be strong women in this story too.

With my imagination truly fired up, I started to think about the women I had encountered in my life and career so far. My own mother, who sacrificed everything to raise a happy family, and what I have learned from her example, despite our lives taking very different courses; friends who had unwittingly sacrificed a family to prioritize a career; women who worked round the clock to climb the career ladder, only to discover their dream job existed only in their imaginations; entrepreneurial businesswomen who lived and breathed their brands, whose daily accomplishments made me wince at my own inadequacies. I thought about how I might have been a different woman if I had had a sister as well as two brothers. How some of the strongest moments of friendship I've experienced have been with the very newest of friends. I thought about all the meetings and lunches and drinks I had enjoyed with women whose lives seemed incredibly enviable from the outside, only for the gloss to slide off once we were really chatting. It wasn't that they necessarily hid the truth, just that I had projected an easier, simpler reality onto them, just as those in Alice's world do to her. Rarely was anything what it outwardly appeared. Is it ever?

There were so many dresses I fell in love with that day at the V&A, ones that I had to say goodbye to, that didn't fit the timeline of the story or the lifestyle of the character who would wear them. Take a moment, if you can, to look at two near misses: the Blandine dress from Dior's spring/summer 1957 collection, and the Muguet dress from the same collection, a dress that is covered in delicate rows of lily of the valley, Dior's favorite flower—so much so that he is said to have asked seamstresses to sew a sprig into the hems of dresses for good luck. Did some of that luck rub off on the women who wore them?

Sometimes I think I would like to go back and write this story all over again with an entirely different set of dresses, to see how it would alter the balance, change the course of the narrative, and flick the women's lives in a different direction. Can a dress do that? What if Alice hadn't worn the Debussy to the Musée de l'Orangerie that night? But then, just as with a couture dress, isn't it the strength and construction of what is on the *inside* that shapes and molds what is on the outside? I think that notion is what is truly at the heart of this story.

QUESTIONS FOR DISCUSSION

1. Are Antoine's actions forgivable? What about those of Alice's mother?

2. Who is the bravest woman: Genevieve, Lucille, Alice, Veronique, or Marianne?

3. In what ways does the book challenge traditional ideas of motherhood?

4. Why do you think Alice changes her name to Sylvie after leaving Paris? Would you have done the same?

5. What is the most memorable dress you have ever worn? In what way was it transformative?

6. Do you believe a sense of style can be taught and learned?

7. How did a previous life choice—romantic, platonic, or other—shape your future? Do you think it was for the better?

8. If you could wear one of the Dior dresses featured in this book, which would it be? What life event would you wear it to?

9. In your own experience, which type of love is strongest: familial love, romantic love, love between friends, or self-love?

10. Christian Dior offers to make you a dress. What is your brief to him?

ON MY "TO BE READ" PILE

I'm researching my next book and immersing myself in the deep, messy trenches of familial love, so I'll be reading and in some cases rereading . . .

The Consequences of Love by Gavanndra Hodge
Conversations on Love by Natasha Lunn
Dear Life by Rachel Clarke
Travel Light, Move Fast by Alexandra Fuller
Somebody I Used to Know by Wendy Mitchell
After the End by Clare Mackintosh
Where We Belong by Anstey Harris
Lady in Waiting by Anne Glenconner

JADE BEER is an award-winning editor, journalist, and novelist who has worked across the UK national press for more than twenty years. Most recently, she was the editor in chief of Condé Nast's *Brides*. She also writes for other leading titles, including the *Sunday Times Style*, *Harper's Bazaar*, the *Mail on Sunday's YOU* magazine, The Telegraph, the *Daily Mail*, the *Tatler* wedding guide, *Glamour*, and *Stella* magazine. Jade lives in the Cotswolds with her husband and two daughters.

Ready to find
your next great read?

Let us help.

Visit prh.com/nextread

Penguin
Random
House